PRAISE

"Your books are bound to get banned somewhere."

— ANONYMOUS FRIEND OF AUTHOR

Kedves Hernek család,

Thanks for the pasties!

Jann Thorngot

NOW. THEN. TO COME.

JOURNEY ACROSS GENES SAGA
BOOK 1

FENN THORNBOT

Photography by
CALLIE ARCHBOLD

CC4r (c) 2023 by legal author Fenn Thornbot

Copyleft with a difference: This is a collective work, you are invited to copy, distribute, and modify it under the terms of the CC4r.

This is a work of fiction. Unless otherwise indicated, all the names, characters, businesses, places, events and incidents in this book are either the product of the author's imagination or used in a fictitious manner. Any resemblance to actual persons, living or dead, or actual events is purely coincidental.

❦ Created with Vellum

CONTENTS

Introduction	vi
PART ONE: NOW	
Prologue	3
Chapter One: The Átmeneti	11
Chapter Two: Waterfetchers	29
Chapter Three: Old River	66
Chapter Four: Turning	88
PART TWO: THEN	
Chapter One: The bunker	125
Chapter Two: Hell	135
Chapter Three: The missing ring	141
Chapter Four: Glass Mountain	177
Interlude	197
Chapter Five: Bedap	203
PART THREE: TO COME	
Chapter One: Trell	217
Chapter Two: Old Tátos	258
Chapter Three: Prison letters	279
Chapter Four: The way	292
Epilogue	310
About the Author	321

INTRODUCTION

The worlds that you, dear audience, are about to be thrown into may seem to you, at first, very different from the world that you know, that you shape. Your observations would not be remiss. If you are reading these pages in or around the year 2023 and you live in what many people call the United States of America—I think the US project is a more accurate term, it is something that is actively being created, a construct of sorts, with very real effects on the people within and transcending its imagined borders, sometimes all at once—if you live in the US project, I can confidently assume that you, as I do, experience some of the same effects from our shared lived experiences. We are affected by and, thus, shaped by countless policies, practices, and the nexus of institutions that exist alongside them, and that more often than not help maintain different systems, modes of thinking, and governing practices that we contend with every day. For example, if you are a genderqueer person with a full beard, this may mean that you may worry about getting attacked or ridiculed for wearing a dress, make up, and or manicured nails out in public, especially in an area where trans people aren't as visible as gender conforming ones.

It can be exhausting being involved in creating and shaping communities that are constantly under attack, murdered, and actively marginalized by groups of people (e.g. politicians, religious leaders, etc.) who are backed by the rich donor class who don't want us to have our share in their beloved institutions, whether marriage, family, or having access to healthcare that our physician has deemed to be critical for our wellbeing. I remember how scared I was for myself and many of my friends after Omar Mateen shot and killed or wounded over 100 people at the Pulse nightclub in June of 2016 in Orlando, Florida. Was he influenced by all the anti-LGBTQIA2S+ vitriol spewed on social media and other platforms?

Maybe because of a hashtag that brought you to this book, I can venture a guess that you yourself or someone you know closely identifies somewhere on the LGBTQIA2S+ spectrums, especially #queer[1] and/or #transgender spectrums, and, thus, you likely understand, to some extent, what a day in the life of someone who identifies as such is like—what it's like for us to get misgendered by the cashier at the grocery store, to be called brother or sister when sibling feels better somehow, to choose to hold our partner's or partners' hand(s), fearless, or even fearful, of being verbally harassed by some bigot, to decide to take the dress off because the in-laws are coming over and then to experience self-disappointment for prioritizing the comfort of others over our own, to experience dysphoria when we look in the mirror and don't recognize the person we see in your own heads, to get murdered at a bar that for us is more of a sanctuary than a place to drink and meet people with whom to hookup, to have politicians vehemently deny our existence and then pass laws to keep us from getting healthcare, from participating in certain rites of passage, and from becoming respected members of the institutions that they feel are exclusively for them.

Personally, I'd rather sit by and watch as their institutions and the buildings that house them burn down, figuratively of course, because the US Capitol—forever empty of technocrats—will make a great museum someday, or even better, a village meeting space at the heart of a new society where cooperation is the goal instead of competition, where hierarchies have lost their anachronistic legacy, where there are no longer cages, where public safety is valued over obedience enforcement through the threat of violence or death[2].

Some of the characters in the following pages, especially the Átmeneti, don't have the same institutions or the same ideological state apparatuses[3] to contend with as we do. The metaphorical tentacled sea monster that is often referred to as Empire[4] that plagues us currently is but an echo of the past told rarely in dialogue form but appears in the expository aspects of stories that have been passed down for generations upon generations. Makk, one of the protagonists, for example, grows up not having to contend with capitalism and the effects that are experienced alongside it, and *because* of it, that pervade most aspects of our contemporary 21st-century, US project.

However, a new sea monster with different tentacles has taken its place. Therefore, Makk does have to navigate the issues that plague their own society. How to defend oneself against an attack of vadkutya, or wild dogs that tend to hunt in packs? Where to get water safely if the watermakers can't make any, or the water peddler doesn't have any to sell, or the Old River is dried up? How to fit into a community that ostracizes you for being different? How to (or more obviously why) learn to read in a society where paper books no longer exist and the ones that do are few, and, instead of being written, stories are passed down through oral conventions rather? And, what would it be like to live amongst illiterate people in society and therefore not being able to read, then, finding yourself in a position where you *need* to learn to read. Then, almost prophetically after learning to read, you and your sibling discover the hidden journals of genetic ancestors from long, long ago. And what if the stories in these journals contain keys needed to unlock secrets of the past that become necessary to shape the future? And, if you could manipulate the past, would you? Would you risk changing your present?

These are just a few questions that I explore through the characters and the worlds that they navigate in this series. I invite you to use these first introductory words as a guiding map of sorts, dear audience. Think of this journey as an experiment in language use, ideas of gender and its undoing, family structures aka intim units, hierarchy and the lack of it, navigating differences and opening up to those who are unlike you. In times where, at least to me, mainstream media (one of Althusser's ideological state apparatuses) seems bent on making neighbors afraid of neighbors, what if we got to know our neighbor instead, if it's safe to do so? Nowadays, for many, feeling safe is a luxury that cannot easily be achieved. But we can change that, we can make the world different despite the ever-changing obstacles that come into our paths. It's up to us after all to shape the world around us. It was Octavia E. Butler[5] who taught me that. I miss her and all the wisdom that she was supposed to keep providing us before her life was taken from her way too early.

There are many, many more matters, questions, and concepts that I will elucidate in the following pages. Now, come with me and brace yourself as we embark, together, on this journey across genes!

Glossary and Pronunciation and Grammar Guide

To help you along this journey, I've provided a glossary (Gloss) and a pronunciation guide (PG) on my website: FENN THORNBOT. Some words and expressions that you'll stumble across might not exist in your linguistic repertoire[6], your language toolbox, if you will. I also avoid using named languages[7], and when I do I use the named language as a verb, an action, instead of a noun, a thing. English is something that one does, not something that one has. Although important due to the very real effects they bear upon people in society, (radical re: very cool) linguistic anthropologists argue that named languages like English are social constructions and have no linguistic basis in reality, and have been *invented* by nation-states and colonial powers to wield power over subjected populations[8].

Although the dialogues are written mostly using englishing, the inhabitants of the following pages don't necessarily english the way some of us are familiar with and some don't english at all. Thus, for the reader's convenience, I've written the dialogues mainly using my own 21st-century englishing practices.

The majority of the words or linguistic features in the glossary are names based on foods that are foraged. The Átmeneti (temporary re: nomadic) inhabitants of this new, old world get most of their calories from foraging, thus it's an integral part of their cultural practices, so much so that they name their children after these foods. Other words have been included because of their cultural significance and possibly because they don't exist as concepts in or aren't easily translatable into other named languages.

~

Guide to Pronouns

A they - e - she - per - he - fae
B them - em - her - per - him - faer
C their - eir - her - per - his - faer
D theirs - eirs - hers - pers - his - faers
E themself - eirself - herself - perself - himself - faerself

A - Subject (Nominative):

_A_ lives in a nomadic commune.

Examples: **They** *lives in a nomadic commune. /* **E** *lives in a nomadic commune. /* **She** *lives in a nomadic commune.*

B - Object (Accusative/Dative):

Fenn sees _B_ in the park. (accusative)

Fenn gives _B_ a pocketful of *pogácsa*. (dative)

Examples: Fenn sees **him** *in the park. Fenn gives* **him** *a pocketful of pogácsa. / Fenn sees* **per** *in the park. Fenn gives* **per** *a pocketful of pogácsa.*

C - **Possessive adjective (Genitive):**

_C_ shoes were found in a landfill.

Examples: **Per** *shoes were found in a landfill. /* **Eir** *shoes were found in a landfill.*

D - **Possessive noun (Genitive):**

These old shoes are _D_.

Examples: These old shoes are **his.** */ These old shoes are* **hers.** */ These old shoes are* **faers.**

E - **Reflexive (Ablative):**

When _A_ looks into a mirror, _A_ sees _E_.

Examples: When e looks into a mirror, e sees **eirself.** */ When* **they** *looks into a mirror,* **they** *sees* **themself.**

The pages to come invite you to throw out some basic ideas about grammar that you may or may not take for granted. For example, 'they' is usually conjugated in the 3rd person plural: *they are, they walk, they run, etc.* However, among the Átmeneti, 'they' is conjugated in the 3rd person singular when the person that uses the 'they' pronoun is indeed singular: *they is, they walks, they runs, etc.* 'They are' is reserved for reference to more than one person. The narrator also uses these conventions, but I'll leave it at that. No spoilers necessary. E, per, and fae, as well as their other pronominal counterparts, are an integral part of the Átmeneti grammar.

"Why do I have to mess with sacred grammar conventions?" you may be asking (for a friend).

Simply put, I love to build up my own truncated linguistic repertoire, language tool box, and my mind is always accommodating new forms of conjugation in a new named language that might have never existed *to me* before I learned them. So, I thought: How hard could it be to retrain my own brain to english using new lexical items, as well as what sometimes unimaginative language scientists call closed classes like pronouns and verb conjugations? Basically, if I want people to refer to me using the 'they' pronoun and terms like sibling, person, partner, spouse, offspring, child, etcetera, (instead of the gendered alternatives brother, guy, husband, son, etc.) I need to be able to be linguistically flexible myself. So this was began as an experiment for me. Now, it's an experiment for you.

To be candid, writing certain characters into being and having them use a specific pronoun and to constantly write in that pronoun proved, and continues to be extremely challenging, for some of the characters. Yet, after only weeks of writing, I stopped misgendering particular characters. While bringing this character to life, I kept seeing them with what we in the US project were taught to be masculine features despite the Átmeneti not doing gender in a way that we, US projectors, would recognize. But, then, I went a step further and asked myself part of a question that I'm convinced that all speculative fiction writers ask themselves, "What if...?"

So, what if out of the ashes of this world grew a new world in which binary gender was so unheard of that the grammar of a particular people evolved to accommodate such a phenomenon. In the grammar of the Átmeneti, all seven of the following nominal 3rd-person pronouns are used (she, it, they, per, fae, e, he). As an englisher (someone who does English) who grew up in the US project, I was trained to conjugate so-called 'regular' verbs, change their forms in specific ways. For example, he, she, and it call for the 3rd person, singular, conjugation: *He walks, she walks, it walks.* The subject pronoun 'they' calls for the 3rd person, plural, conjugation: *They walk*. 'They's' verb conjugation corresponds to the other subject pronouns both singular and plural: *I walk, you (singular) walk, we walk, y'all/you (plural) walk*. I don't think I was ever formally taught the 'they' that I like to call the-person-who-can't-easily-be-put-into-a-gender-binary 'they.' This 'they' usually refers to an unnamed, anonymous person who, for example, sent an email and "now I'm about to tell you about what this person, (singular) 'they' wrote in the email." Here's a visual:

Me: Jess, I got this horrible email earlier from someone at the main office.

Jess: Oh no! Who was it from?

Me: I have no idea. But they were obviously upset about the outcome of the event that we put on.

Jess: What!? The event was flawless. What did they say about it?

Etc, etc, etc.

The gender of the person who wrote the email is unknown and thus becomes background noise. Their gender isn't important at that moment in the conversation.

Let me bring your attention back to how I chose to change the grammar of the Átmeneti. While I was proofreading what I had written, anytime I wanted to make a change in person or pronoun, I found myself making a lot of annoying repetitive changes that I eventually convinced myself weren't necessary. So, I decided to embark on an experiment and asked, "What if 'they' could have a singular form and a plural form?" If we add an -s, or its equivalent, to verbs that need to agree with he, she, and it, why not do it for other singular individuals? *They walks, per walks, fae walks, and e walks.*

Conjugating 'they' using 3rd person singular verbs is nothing new. In African American Vernacular English (AAVE) grammar *they is, they has, they was*, etc. are linguistically normative. And, when people denigrate AAVE, what they are really doing is upholding white supremacist ideals that are driven by the linguistic hegemony, or dominance, of Standardized English, which is an essential tool used in the US project —a project that itself is founded on and continues to uphold principles of white supremacy.

Some of you, dear audience, will hate my experiment. Some of you will love it. So, hang in there as your grammatical expectations are taken on a rollercoaster ride. Just remember to have fun, even if you feel like your going to fly out of your seat.

---

1. Read Mary Nardini Gang's manifesto entitled Toward the Queerest Insurrection for their interpretation of the word queer. For them, queer is "not merely another identity that can be tacked onto a list of neat social categories, nor the quantitative sum of our identities. Rather, it is the qualitative position of opposition to presentations of stability — an identity that problematizes the manageable limits of identity."
2. Ursula Kroeber Le Guin showed me this possible world in her 1974 novel, The Dispossessed: An Ambiguous Utopia. Thanks, Red, for introducing me to this book back in 2017 during a solidarity potluck at a pavilion in a park on the West Coast. After your recommendation, I went home and bought it online and finished it within a few days. I've reread it several times since. I've also listened to the audiobook. There's an abridged radio play interpretation of the book on Youtube, as well that I've listened to multiple times. This book is partially dedicated to Ursula K. Le Guin and her memory.
3. Ideological State Apparatuses (e.g. schools, churches, friend groups, family) spread ideologies (e.g. the belief in a gender binary, man or woman) and demand conformity through fear of social rejection (e.g. getting ridiculed for having a full beard and wearing make up). There are sites where you can read about this concept without contending with a paywall. Search for: Louis Althusser 1970 Ideology and Ideological State Apparatuses.
4. Read Joyful Militancy: Building Thriving Resistance in Toxic Times by Carla Bergman and Nick Montgomery and then read it again.
5. I've read and listened to The Parable of the Sower and The Parable of the Talents so many times and I'll keep reading it. In a way, this book is a dedication to OEB and those two books, especially. I recommend reading all of her stuff, and, then, read it all again.

6. Pennycook, A. (2011). [Review of The sociolinguistics of globalization, by J. Blommaert]. Language, 87(4), 884–887. http://www.jstor.org/stable/41348868. Reach out to Fenn Thornbot for questions regarding access to this paywalled document.
7. For more on named languages, skip the reading (at first, then go back to it) and watch Mike Mena break down translanguaging versus code-switching: https://www.youtube.com/watch?v=Xv6cXSna4RY
8. For more on this topic, I recommend reading Sinfree Makoni and Alastair Pennycook's Disinventing and Reconstituting Languages published in 2006 by Multilingual Matters. And if you're an educator reading this book, I recommend Ofelia Garcia and Li Wei's Translanguaging: Language, Bilingualism and Education published in 2014 by Palgrave Pivot, London.

PART ONE: NOW

PROLOGUE

The echo of water droplets plummeting into the mostly hollow metallic receptacle brings her out of a deep slumber for a split second before acoustically lulling her back into unconsciousness.

In her bunker where she is lying on her bed, it is cold, but not freezing. Unawares, she shivers and hugs her short, thick arms tight around her broad torso. Then, like using muscle memory, she reaches down and pulls the covers up to her chin, olive toned, and rosy from the cold.

As she slides back into unconsciousness, she is aware, again, that she is riding on the back of some strange bio-drone; its hum is so loud that she can barely stand it. So, she tells herself, *Tune it out, Self.*

And, she does.

She is a passenger on this flight, so she has no control over where she is going. It's like she is in prehistoric times—not that she would know about that part of Earth's history—like she is flying through a jungle of grass as tall as trees, like enormous corn stalks that scrape the skies, bristles sticking out like soft spines on a cactus. Her drone is adept at aviation, dodging tree-like, towering dandelions and other botanical monstrosities. Then, she begins to hear another noise in the back of her consciousness; it's coming from somewhere deep, and it's becoming more and more intense.

Tink, tink, tink.

What is that sound? Her subconscious echoes to the part of her mind that gives her awareness.

Then, suddenly her drone takes a hard turn to the right. She grabs on tight to her airship, almost losing her grip on the carpet-like patch which she straddles like a mounted horse.

Drip, drip, tink.

She hears it again and a memory comes to her thoughts in her mind's eye. She remembers that there had been a tin can—full of dents but unopened—in the yellow box, and that she'd decided to put it to use a few months before when that new leak had sprung before the ground began to freeze.

The floor of the underground dwelling is littered with other tin cans and myriad receptacles in a variety of shapes and sizes, upright, some empty, some full to the brim with rust-colored water.

The dripping eventually slows to a stop before starting up again.

Drip, drip..., tink.

She keeps the various containers in their respective places to catch the precious drops of water that would eventually come on full force when the ground thaws again. The new tin can made a slightly different noise. She'd been astonished by the fact that the label on the can in question was still intact. Only a few minor abrasions can be seen.

The label reads <Kecskeméti sűrített paradicsom>. Written using linguistic features from an ancient language family, it roughly translates to Kecskemét-style tomato paste. And with no way of looking up Kecskeméti—there being no books or electronic devices to use—she will probably never know what it means, despite the fact that she *can* read: a practice that, too, is mostly extinct among the contemporary peoples in the immediate region. Hundreds of Reawakenings before—her people mark the new year each Reawakening—centuries before Kecskemét was only a thirty-minute ride by maglev—magnetic levitation—train from the capital.

Before the Great Dying, the small city had had a popular Sunday market that folks would flock to from neighboring areas. Food trucks and blue and gray tarpaulins had dotted the dirt two-track that formed a circle enclosing the market which popped up on the outskirts of the town. Because public transportation was readily accessible to most, it was easy and fairly inexpensive to travel to the market from the city center, until it wasn't. Even during the winter months, the smoky smell of grilled sausages made from animal flesh had filled the nostrils of the patrons in search of cheap, used clothing and other goods: vases, ashtrays, World War II memorabilia. Those were the typical items that could be found in the flea markets of the time. Items that, nowadays, have to be scavenged from landfills or homes long abandoned, not by choice. Though, present-day, for some of the other people that frequented the market that her people had operated before her entire village was pillaged and she'd had to run away, few if any of those people who aren't exactly her people are brave enough to cross the thresholds of the ruined dwellings of those who didn't survive the Great Dying.

The label on the can is red and there is a white silhouette of an animal with horns in the shape of sickles rising up on its hind legs. A beard protrudes from its pointed chin. The can must be two- or three-hundred Reawakenings old. The contents had gone rancid despite the lack of dents or openings in the metallic container: gooey reddish green, black, pulpy blobs. Putrid juice. Ghastly smell.

Don't puke! Keep the can. Discard the rest.

The hermetically sealed, slightly pliable, yellow box that is neither metal nor wood must have helped conserve the fibrous material on which the words and images are emblazoned, but not its contents. The mother had told her to keep that tartó box in a safe place where raiders couldn't find it. Hers and the lives of many generations to come depended on its safekeeping. She never really understood the implication of the mother's warning. She *would* understand one day.

Its contents were invaluable, a time capsule, a glimpse into the forgotten past. The interior of the box is lined with charcoal gray foam that has been cut and molded to hold a handful of smaller items. Besides the can of tomato paste which seemed like an afterthought based on the other contents—she was desperately hungry those first few days that she was alone and with no one around to scold her she opened it only to find rot —inside the case there was a pair of metallic tongs designed to grasp minute objects using the forefinger and thumb, a clear glass vial with a rubber stopper that holds a single strand of black, crimped hair, several shiny crystal-like disks the size and thickness of a small coin, a shiny, obsidian clamshell case that is seemingly un-openable, a paperback novel with the front cover torn off that sits in the center of an empty indent in the shape of a large ring. The ring imprint is about the size of one of those tossing disks used for recreation centuries before. The ring is missing.

Drip, drip, tink.

The frozen water that had saturated the ground for the past twenty or so Naps—days—is melting.

Back in the dream vision, she is trying her best to maintain her grip as her legs fly up behind her like a bull rider at a rodeo —a practice that had also been long extinct. As she finally gets back onto her saddle, the drone veers sharply again and crashes into a stalk. She feels in slow motion as her body is thrown, hurdling over the top of the drone, and right as her lower back makes contact with the structure, she opens her eyes and mutters a moaning sound.

She springs forward in her makeshift bed of wooden pallets and old pieces of tattered cloth that she'd gleaned from the burned shelters of her pillaged home what seemed to her like years before. Her short, dark hair lies matted on both sides. Indents from the head padding line her lush face. Sleep crusts around the caruncles of her buckwheat brown, almond-shaped eyes. She rubs it out with the tips of her thick fingers and stretches out her arms. A long yawn flows from deep within.

Pushing the covers off, she twists to put her feet on the chilly ground and stands up. Almost forgetting, she sits back down on the bed and blindly feels for the markings on the wall. The formidable walls of the bunker are heavily corroded from centuries of exposure to the elements. She reaches for her shank that she'd rigged from an old rusted piece of metal rod that she keeps close to her bed, just in case. Then, she scratches a fifth line horizontally through four vertical, adjacent lines.

She feels with her fingers and counts in her head, *Yesternight was six-hundred ninety-nine. Plus one is seven hundred.* But she counts again, no easy task. It takes a few minutes. There are fifteen columns and almost ten complete rows of engraved slashes in groups of five etched on the rusted, steel wall. The tenth row only has five columns.

Nine rows times fifteen columns plus five more groups of five slashes. Seven-hundred sleeps.

Seven-hundred sleeps since she'd started counting. Seven-hundred Holds since she'd happened upon that ancient, damp, pitch-dark bunker that she has come to call home: her new home, her not-so-new home.

In the dark, she reaches for one of her almost empty water containers, grabs it by its smooth, cold neck, feels for the opening, and places it under the dripping faucet that leaks from another tiny crack in the steel ceiling. She is careful not to waste one drop.

She has become accustomed to moving around in the obscurity of her safe haven without knocking everything over.

She doesn't know it, but the bunker once served as a snug, temporary shelter for a cramped family of four, hundreds of Reawakenings before—a widowed mother, her widowed sister, and two young infants. One of which became bone-sick from the cold, dampness of the underground refuge. Bone tuberculosis they'd called it.

And who knows what purpose the bunker had served before that? Before the flying machines threatened to release and then did indeed drop explosives all over the city destroying homes, bridges, and schools, and more, killing so many, if not directly, indirectly from slow starvation and sickness afterward. Slowly the inhabitants began to rebuild, never really fully recovering before the next bombardment, and the next. Then, the Great Dying happened. And only a very few survived that. And from that very few, only a small percentage managed to persevere.

The bunker is chilly, dark, and dank but it is hers. It eventually took on new smells, her smells. And even after almost two Reawakenings, no one has bothered her. She's heard voices nearby before, but she managed to disguise the entrance well enough with old junk and forest debris that no one bothers it, at least no one that she knows of, at least not when she is home.

Although she spends most of the time in the dark while inside the bunker, she does have the means to see by fire that she produces by rubbing dry sticks together over wood shavings that she keeps in a dry-enough box. She has candles that she transfers the fire to.

The mother had taught her how to make candles. That was the main item they traded with. She has to make them herself now. She can't stock up at market like she used to be able to.

There is no longer a market. She reserves the candles for the cold days when she can't be outside for long periods of time when she can't read outside, shaded from the scorching Nap. When the scorching Nap is too high in the sky, she doesn't dare go outside, even in the shade, without risking the danger of skin burns or heat exhaustion. So she often reads inside the shelter of the bunker. She only has the one book. The one book that she re-reads over and over again. The book that shouldn't exist.

Reading is something that her people had been known for. It had been something of a lost art that never fully recovered, except among a few people in her community that dabbled in the cryptic craft. She'd heard stories of how many, many Reawakenings before reading was much more widespread. Until it wasn't. Until books were banned and then burned. Until those few who could read only read on augmented ocular projections that required a special technology that was long out of use. Or even more scarce, the physical books that managed to live on in spite of the eradication of reading material on paper. Electronic words were more easily controlled. Words on paper were dangerous.

She is the only one that she knows who reads. As a matter of fact, she is the only *one* she knows. At least the only person she knows. There are other people, but they aren't her people. Her people are gone and she is alone. She has no one to talk to except for her bird and ant friends and they don't talk back. She'd always had animal and insect friends, though, even before her people were killed or taken away by the marauders.

She goes to the various glass bottles and cans scattered around the bunk, careful not to knock any over. She will need every last drop to make enough potable water before she has to venture down to the river. Even with the thaw, she is running low. No. She will have to get more after all.

Scorching Nap! She thinks in disappointment.

Listening cautiously for any movement up above, she throws on her red cloak, the only one she has, and scurries up the ladder tube with her metallic jug in-tote. She will try to get to the river before the scorching hours begin. Nap is slowly rising from the east. Given that she is to the west, she has some time to spare before the treacherous rays reach her side of the river.

But she doesn't have very long.

CHAPTER ONE: THE ÁTMENETI

A dotted sea of black crows, there must be over two hundred, nestles atop the bare trees surrounding the settlement. Their raucous chatter echoes across the naked canopy. Growing ever darker, the gnarly branches outline the dusky sky as the day's light prepares to take its nightly rest into the western horizon.

Scorch off!

You think as you turn over to face away from the purple and orange hues pouring through the gap in the thatched wall that acts as a window in the carefully constructed chaparral dwelling.

You pull the covers over your honey face, lined with age, struggling with yourself and frustrated to be awake. You don't want the dream to end, even though it's more like a nightmare.

You just need a few more minutes back in the nightmare. If only you can just reach her in time. You can save your child from the snatcher.

Squaaaawwk!

Stupid birds. Stupid, beautiful birds.

Your eyes open slowly, squinting from the narrow ray of light positioned perfectly in your line of sight. You scrunch up your eyebrows.

Is it almost dusk already?

The smell of yeast, pumpkin, and amaranth wafts through the air. The dwelling's outdoor cooking area is just a few paces outside the window. Your nostrils catch a whiff of the grilled dough and instantly your mouth begins salivating.

Is it already time to break the fast?

It feels like you just laid down. But, yes, you are hungry. Your stomach gurgles.

The dimly lit room begins to come into focus as your eyes adjust to the rays of dusk light filtering through the thatch. Two other hammocks hang on either side of you, empty, except for the thin, folded patchwork coverings. Besides for the birds, it's rather quiet. Although, as you become more and more aware and awake you can hear the occasional cries of children playing in the next dwelling over.

As you sit up in the bedswing, you remember that it's your workshop day. You'd better get up and around. You prop your arms on either side of your body, holding the edges of the hammock, then swing your legs gracefully to the side facing the entrance to the sleeproom. It's a rather small room. It's just big enough to accommodate three adult-sized hammocks without making it feel cramped.

The entranceway to the sleeproom has no hinged door, but rather a screen-like cloth drapes across the threshold. The walls of the circular room are made mostly of woven saplings and vines and thus are various colors of browns and grays. The colors of young bark from maples, oaks, beeches, and other hardwood trees and vines.

You slide off the bedswing and land on both feet. The woven, nettle mat makes a scuffing sound as your feet and the mat make contact. The dirt floor underneath doesn't feel as cold as it did this time a few Holds ago. Hibernation—Alvás—must be coming to an end. That means that there is much work to be done.

You quickly focus and decide to grab a quick bite of whatever your partner is making for breakfast. It smells divine. You'd need to hurry though, the children would be arriving soon.

The vécé (water closet) for washing up is outside and to the back of the dwelling. Water is running low at the community level so you will only wash up. Plus, there's no time for a bath. You are thirsty so you'll fetch enough potable water to drink and clean up. Plus, the cool water will force you to wake up.

You pour the jug of fresh water into the basin and lean over it, making sure not to bang your head on a piece of wood that protrudes out from the thatched wall. You close your eyes and splash water on your face. Images flash in your mind. The raid still lies heavily on your mind and it keeps playing itself over and over again in your head. Those screams cause you to squish up your eyes and embrace yourself for the dizziness.

You can remember it so clearly as if it were yesterday. It might as well have been yesterday for there's not a day that goes by that the images and sounds of that horrible day don't come flashing back out of nowhere.

The refectory area near the main entrance of the settlement was in flames. A distraction, it turns out. People woke up in a panic from their deep mid-Nap slumbers, stumbling out of their dwellings. The ones closest to the communal cooking and dining area were coughing from the acrid smoke. They clumsily scattered in all directions looking for whatever they could find to put out the fire. The smoke forced tears from their eyes making everything twice as difficult. It was complete chaos.

The overwatchers sounded the alarms like they practiced in training, clanking metallic pipes together rapidly. Three times for a fire. Five times for a raid.

Clank! Clonk! Clunk! ... wait a few seconds and then repeat. Only three times.

You jumped out of your bedswing in a daze. Without much thought, you hopped off and ran out the back entrance of the dwelling, underclothes still scrunched up your legs from sleeping in a hammock. There was no time to put on your protective cloak. You grabbed the bucket of gray water from the water closet and took off toward the fire and the crowd of people desperately trying to put it out.

You were halfway across the camp to the refectory when, suddenly, screams poured out from near your dwelling. Or were they coming from your own dwelling?

Stop thinking about it. Focus. You have work to do. The children will be here any moment. Focus.

It's been over two Holds since the raid. The attacks seem to be happening more and more frequently nowadays. But, Alvás is just coming to an end. Reawakening is upon you and your fellow Átmeneti. A lot still has to be done before you begin your relocation.

The last thing your people needed was a raid. Who knows when it'll happen again? It will definitely happen again. Those who feel the need to use force and violence haven't disappeared since the Great Dying. There will probably always be someone who will take what they want by force if they can. Unless we find another way of coexisting.

There has to be another way. You think as you dry your face with nettle cloth.

Are you up, Test (sibling)?

You hear your own voice in your head but know that it's

your partner Delores. You note the all too familiar tug of the invisible rope as she mindspeaks to you.

Don't you have workshop with the children? Come eat. I made your favorite.

You walk around the outside of the dwelling to the cooking area and grab a bun from the clay grill that rests on the edge of the fire pit. Its savory pumpkin filling—from last Harvest—leaves your taste buds and belly feeling very satisfied.

You kiss Delores on the salty, cinnamon-colored cheek, smack her behind, and take off in the direction of the main garden, around fifteen paces from your dwelling near the watermaking shed.

You pass the peacemaking house that lies to the left of the path, adjacent to the watershed. It's much the same as the other dwellings in which people sleep except it lacks the usual dividers to segregate sleeping quarters. The oval, tent-like roof consists of layers of woven nettle canvas attached to a large beam, sculpted from a girthy thuja trunk, and chiseled to a point. Two other pointed beams meet toward the pointy end of the main beam creaking a fork-like support structure. The bark on all three beams has been stripped and repurposed for use in other materials.

Inside, there is a circle in session. There was a domestic dispute yesternight, and the victim and offender in question convened the peacemaking council to help resolve their conflict. These sessions are not forced upon the antagonists involved, but rather are the Átmeneti way of navigating disagreements, crime, and other types of transgressions that occur whenever social beings share space. Reconciliation and transformation are the goals, rather than placing blame and enacting punishment. The peacemaking council is a way of gathering the affected people and those close to them to come together in community to address the issue.

Trying not to eavesdrop, you overhear someone saying,

"well, since you've claimed accountability for what you've done, are you ready to make amends?"

You decide to give them their privacy and pick up your pace.

You go to the watermarking shed, watering kanna in hand. The watermakers are busy at work, filtering and distilling the water from the barrels. This Alvás has been the wettest it has been for several years. The rain is a welcome blessing.

Isten must be happy. You think automatically, right before taking it back. You don't believe in any of that superstitious nonsense.

You can see the water level in the blue rain barrel with the broken spout, and it's already half empty, and there are still many seedlings to start before Sowing. But you won't sow them until your people finally move to your new camp. *Uhh,* you think. *What's the point?* You're not looking forward to relocating.

Hopefully, more rain will come before we begin relocating our settlement. You dread the thought of not having enough water to keep the seedlings alive for the move.

You set the make-shift watering kanna down—a 2L plastic bottle with pins holes poked into its lid— and twist open the spout, carefully so as not to let any water escape. Although, if any water does escape, the contraption is designed in such a way that water would not be wasted. The hardy, potted herbs underneath would drink from the renegade drops.

Thankfully, the garden isn't the main source of food for the settlement. Fungi, acorns, greens, insects, and other wild foods provide the main source of calories for the small community of seventy-eight—well, seventy-seven people now, since your Ursula was taken, kidnapped by those scorching marauders who raided your encampment.

But nothing can be done about that now. Nothing could have been done then, even though you tried. You searched for weeks. You never found her. Those scorching thieves are good at hiding their tracks.

There is so much to do. No time to waste thinking about what could have been done differently. Forward is the direction to move. Not backward.

The garden gates open with a creek—more deterrent than decoration. The younguns are starting to arrive, wearing big toothy smiles and full of boisterous laughter.

In the typical non-hierarchical fashion, they greet you, their mester, "Good breakfast, testvérunk (our sibling)!"

It's common and expected to call everyone that is not your parent testvér, even your partner. If you're part of a group, you'll use *our* before sibling and if you're alone, *my*.

"Good breakfast to you all, édes testvérekem (my sweet siblings)." You reply, bringing your hands together and touching your chest as if pulling their invisible energy toward your heart.

Delores comes over into the garden with a basketful of the breakfast buns. Her long, gray hair itself is twisted up into a bun atop her head. She walks carefully as to not step on any jagged pebbles with her bare feet. The little ones go running to her, each one taking turns grabbing a warm bun. Smiling and giggling with excitement, all the younguns, except for the littlest of them, all thank Delores almost in chorus.

"Thank you, édes testverünk (our sweet sibling)!"

You grab another bun and kiss Delores on the cheek again.

Playfully making fun of you, three of the younguns mock kiss each other making the others giggle in raucous laughter as Delores walks away, blowing one last kiss to you and winking at the children. Two other children, siblings, about eight and twelve Reawakenings old respectively, are off to one side no doubt silently singing as they sit cross-legged, breakfast buns clenched between their teeth. They are playing some sort of game, taking turns clapping their own hands together and then clapping the hand of the other one as if giving a high five.

I went 'cross the Old River
to see what I could see see see
They snatched me up and tied me down
Be-fore I could flee flee flee

This goes on for several minutes. They giggle through a mouthful of the buns.

"While we plant the seeds, let's tell the story of how the original seven planted their first garden centuries ago. Who wants to go first?"

You look toward the eldest youngun who is celebrating their Turning Sixteen this upcoming Reawakening.

"Maki, would you like to start?"

You know that Makk is soon going to be transitioning from what your community considers to be a child to an adult. It's a special time for Makk and their fellow sixteens. When Alvás shows signs of being over, they will fetch water for the festivities while considering the pronouns they will use as adults, both having been rites of passage for over two hundred Reawakenings among the Átmeneti.

As adults, Makk and the other waterfetchers will choose an art to pursue and gain further proficiency in. And Makk has shown signs of being rather skillful in the art of storyweaving. Today is a great opportunity for them to practice that skill, while the focus of everyone is on planting seeds and not the storyweaver. This way Makk won't be the center of attention.

"Remember, Huri," you speak in a soft tone, "don't bury the carrot seeds too deeply. They like shallow cradles to mature in. And give them a few fingers' space between each cradle hole."

Planting seeds is one of your favorite activities. The magic of growing something from seed has never ceased to impress you. And, yestermorning before Nap rose high into the sky signaling bedtime, you'd already prepared the containers, filling them with dirt. Just a few nights before that, Makk's eggblood Málna had dropped off a whole bucket load of old transparent containers that he'd scavenged from an old dump heap near the old People's Park. They look like some form of vessel that the Old People drank from before their world went to crap. Some of the flimsy, polymer receptacles still show the remnants of a dark green image of a long-haired person-like creature with two tails encircling them. (Sometimes you are gifted preserved paper cups which are great for planting because you fill them with dirt, grow the seedling, and, then, plant the cups directly into the ground.) These resin cups hold dirt and water very well and are lightweight. But, before filling them with rich earth mixed with some of the dirt from the compost, you line the cups with leaves and leaf mould. It makes it easier to pull them out when transplanting them into the garden at the new site that you'll be moving to after the Turning celebration has ended.

Makk agrees to tell the story by acknowledging you silently with a slight head bow, and, then, promptly begins.

"I believe the Last Ones first planted their garden when they weren't quite the Last Ones yet."

"Very good memory, Maki." You comment.

Makk continues.

"Five of the original seven, Boots, Hack, Scrip, Tele, and Ora had just been rescued for the umteenth time since they all had left their walled city across the vast oceans and months later ended up in SzabadPest..."

Tele looked down at the seedling, a kink preventing its light green and white stalk from standing upright. Per watered it anyway. After all, there was a chance that it might survive.

It was a sunny morning. The wooden tables opposite the

makeshift school entrance were bustling with life: a green menagerie of plants. A few cactuses. Other succulents. And the seedlings that, with a bit of luck and even more love, would grow to be hearty and then transplanted into the new school garden: tomatoes, cucumbers, marigolds, sunflowers, a ton of garlic, lettuce, spinach, the list goes on; there was even a tank with a few small goldfish and tens of tiny orange snails that the students loved to stop and point at.

Per often wondered what the young ones were talking about when they stopped in pairs or small groups and hovered over the tables, admiring the seedlings. Per linguistic proficiency was quite basic, after all; per had only been living in SzabadPest for five weeks. Despite the upheaval outside the barriers of the free zone, those had been the calmest five weeks per had had since per began per journey almost a year earlier.

The lacey, eggshell curtain that rested on the generous windows above the tables acted as a screen, protecting the plants from the more harsh evening sun. There was more sunshine those days. Winter was coming to an end. Smaller birds could be seen eating the seed cakes that the young ones had made back in early January. The weather was finally warming up, too.

Just yesterday, per and the younguns were outside washing down some discarded bus tires to get them ready for painting. The plan was to make a colorful, multi-layered garden bed and fill it with vegetables and flowers; that's what the seedlings were for. Teachers, staff, and students alike walked by and admired the indoor greenhouse. It seemed like they were as excited about the garden project as they were about the uprisings popping up in different districts across the city.

And, although this was the first free zone, there were rumors that more were sprouting up around the city. Parts of neighboring District 9 were planning to join them, too!

As per was typing per name on the watering schedule, the

art teacher, Eni, came over and grabbed per arm, "Gyere, Tele! *Come here!*" She then led per down the narrow hall toward the opposite wing of the school; she had something to show per. Her smile and a twinkle in her eyes told per that she was very proud of herself and was excited to share something that she'd found. As per got closer to the warehouse-storeroom-turned-art-room, the overpowering presence of dust tickled per nose, causing per to sneeze two, three, then a fourth time.

"Egészségedre! Gesundheit!"

Eni handed Tele a corner of the cloth, "take this." As they unfolded it, the black words painted on the white, cloth banner, probably an old bed sheet, became legible. "A SZTRÁJK ALAPJOG," it read. Loosely translated, it meant "STRIKING IS A BASIC RIGHT." That banner was just one of many that had been stored in the dusty, dimly lit closet.

"What a find!" Eni's smile was big and toothy. She'd just stumbled across a bit of history. "I remember learning about the teacher's strikes that started about a hundred years ago here in this city during the dark years of the Ulvám Administration." At that time, banners like that could be seen hung all over schools in the city and around the country. Education workers, students, and parents had risen up in response to a recent court decision that essentially banned teachers from striking. Little did the courts expect that they were opening up a can of worms.

Little had changed in a hundred years.

JANI, a stern-looking but friendly English Teacher from the East shot a sly grimace at Tele. "Did you imagine you'd be in such a place at such a chaotic time?" She took a puff of her cigarette.

"I don't mind being in the middle of the action. It seems like

I'm always in the middle of something." Tele smirked, stepping back a bit from the cigarette smoke as it wafted past per. "But, I didn't expect to witness the beginning of a hot war just a few hundred meters away from me. The civil disobedience I'm all for. Hiding in make-shift bomb shelters is another story."

"You're a natural rebel," she giggled.

Then, out of nowhere, there were loud sounds of humming engines and whirling, *chuff, chuff, chuff*. Jani, Tele, and Virág, a tall, sturdy woman with short, blue-highlighted blonde hair, who was just ending a phone call, her blue eyes as light-hued as her pale skin, looked up toward the clear blue, midday sky. First, one, two, then a string of five military helicopters in total appeared overhead, flying low.

"Those are definitely not medical helicopters." Tele blurted out, barely audible over the loud chuffing.

"Bazzeg!" Virág exclaimed. "It's another show of force. How many is that today?" One after the other, the helicopters disappeared into the horizon behind the roof of the main building of the pop-up school. "They want us to know who really is in charge during this whole uprising." They all laughed uneasily.

"They are after you, Tele!" Jani giggled. "They can spot a refugee when they see one.

"Aren't we all refugees here?" Tele responded, ducking a bit intuitively. "A liberated zone surrounded by military and police sure has the feel of a refugee encampment. I should know. I've seen a few close up over these past months. But at least you all are doing something more here than just surviving, something intentional. I guess that's what makes this place special."

Ever since the bombings that per barely escaped from with the downhillers, Tele was unsurprisingly skittish when aircrafts flew overhead. Per never truly recovered from the post-traumatic stress. It stays with per until per last days. Little did per know that per'd be one of the few survivors during those last days.

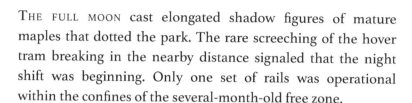

THE FULL MOON cast elongated shadow figures of mature maples that dotted the park. The rare screeching of the hover tram breaking in the nearby distance signaled that the night shift was beginning. Only one set of rails was operational within the confines of the several-month-old free zone.

A warm, dank breeze blew some leftover detritus from the budding bushes and plants. It smelled almost sweet after the nonstop barrage of acrid tear gas all last week that penetrated the periphery of their new home. A face mask would be helpful, but those were reserved for the various provisional medical stations scattered throughout the zone. Oh, but the sweet smells in the air! Spring had finally arrived! The temperatures had ceased to drop below freezing and people were out and about in full force.

An elderly woman with a grave face pulled at their plaid foldable grocery cart, no doubt heading home with their rations. The gravel path made the haul a bit more tricky, but she persisted toward her destination, undoubtedly blissful to be outdoors past six pm without having to wear several layers of clothing and a bulky coat.

Two other neighborhood-patrol volunteers walked past Boots and Scrip, guffawing at something that must have been hilarious. The two newcomers waved and the others waved back, "Szervusztok." "Szervusztok," they greeted in return. Boots had met one of them the week before when fae volunteered to do morning patrol.

Morning patrol, night patrol. There wasn't much difference. Those who volunteered for the patrol committee got to walk the streets of SzabadPest and get some exercise and fresh air while they were at it.

The residents of the worker's occupied zone got trained on de-escalation and other important skills needed for public safety. Originally, Scrip signed up for street cleaning duty that evening, but one of eir roommates in the make-shift living quarters asked Scrip if e would trade with her since she'd recently pulled a muscle in her leg and was a bit less mobile at the moment. Scrip was happy to switch since that would give em time to hang out with Boots.

Street patrol shifts were only three hours long and they provided an opportunity to meet new people in the zone. Also, for the newcomer refugees it gave them the chance to practice their languaging skills—or not. It depended on the linguistic repertoire of the patrol buddy. Since it was just Boots and Scrip together, they wouldn't be practicing the newly acquired features in their truncated linguistic repertoire.

Boots looked at faer watch. 6 pm. "Oh crap! I'm on kitchen clean-up duty tonight. I'd better skedaddle to the refectory. I'm sure they are waiting for me." Boots put out faer cigarette on the sidewalk, tossed the butt in the green metal bin, and began heading up the street.

"Where are you off to next, Scrip?"

"I have the rest of the evening off. It's my downtime since I was on gardening duty this morning with Tele and Ora. I think I'm going to take some time to reflect on the past few weeks and months."

Scrip had gotten eir hands on some antiquated but functioning tech. It's not quite like the projections e'd been used to back home, but it worked for what e needed it for. Home. What a strange word. It seemed like forever since that night that eir and the others' lives drastically changed.

When e got back to the dorm, e turned on eir device and began logging.

∼

FROM THE LOGS OF SCRIP - MARCH 30TH, 2122 - SZABADPEST, FREE ZONE

When people write about it in the future—and they will write about it. I'm sure of it—they'll probably call it a revolution. Since we arrived here five weeks ago, I've been doing a bit of reading from a set of forbidden digital archives, and the uprisings of 1848 were also later called a revolution. They weren't wrong.

It is definitely an uprising, much like the one we serendipitously experienced back in WalKoch the night everything changed. I heard people back there, and here it's no different. People are tired of the same old bullshit. Shitty pay. Crap work conditions. Sociopathic mega rich people living extravagant lives while the workers barely make ends meet. Technocrats profiting off the death of millions from viral pandemic after viral pandemic. Walls built around entire swaths of land to keep out the desperate poor. Yeah, it's the same old story that has echoed throughout the dim corridors of history. Stories kept hidden from us at the indoctrination center. Unnecessary suffering. And for what? So that some megacorp can make a profit. So that the monarchies in other not-too-distant lands can keep their royal, ridiculous lifestyles? Well, enough is enough. Again.

People have already started giving it a name. SzabadPest. SzabadZóna. Anarres II. Le Guin's was the first and original Anarres. The names will change. That's for sure. Change is the only certainty that is everlasting was the wisdom that Octavia E. Butler left us with before she departed this world too early—way too damn early—over a hundred years ago. Thank you, whoever it was that broke the law and risked their lives and that of their family members to save those antique treasures. The Parable of the Sowers, The Parable of the Talents, The Dispossessed.

SzabadPest. Whatever the name it has at the moment

doesn't really matter. It's what it *is* that matters. It's the thing we are creating. Have created. Will continue to create even if the forces of evil decide to bomb us once and for all. You can't destroy an idea; another will always sprout from the compost of its ruins.

Along Orzy tér and Fiumei Cemetery is where the first barriers went up. They were meant to keep out the traffic, especially police cars, armored tanks, and other vehicles of the traitors of the working class.

Drivers in the transportation industry who'd been going about their day, taking passengers around Pest, collectively parked sky-blue, BKK magnetic hover buses bumper to bumper along Orzy út and Fiumei út from Üllői út until Kerepesi út at first. Later, another line of old-school *wheeled* buses doubled up alongside the already parked buses, staggering the gaps much like you'd see done with bricks on the decaying facades of the city.

The numbers 28, 28A, and 62 trackless airtrams that run along Kőbányai út also played an important role in the blockade efforts. A number 62 tram strategically parked itself at the intersection of Fiumei út and Kőbányai út so that no other tram could pass. Not that the unionized mechanics would. Despite being driverless or automated, there was a manual override feature that human mechanics—mostly software hackers—could use to take control of the vehicles.

In fact, it was the striking workers from the transportation union that began the first direct actions in District 8. After weeks of organizing, they'd decided to put a halt to the normal functioning of this part of the city. No bus, tram, train, or metro driver would think of crossing a line established by their fellow workers, except for the scabs. Scabs were outnumbered and didn't dare risk the wrath of the fellow workers.

Soon, education workers and workers from other industries joined the fight.

Keleti Station, one of the city's largest transportation hubs was a strategic point of course, as a main vein of the city that connected it to other parts of the city and other regions of the country. Passenger, as well as freight trains blocked the tracks there. Isolation was the goal. Yet, vital goods like food and supplies could still come in and out of the zone. At least until the military or some other force dismantles the tracks on the periphery. That has yet to come.

Along Üllői út from Orzy tér to Határ út drivers of firetrucks, garbage trucks, and lories copied the bus drivers. But I haven't ventured out that far, yet. There is so much to do here. No one cares that I spent the last twelve months traveling across the world in one shipping container or another. No one cares that I come from a mansion on a hill in a walled city. I think some people are suspicious of me and the others, but I've heard that these people have a history of being suspicious.

Geopolitically, this region of the world has been at the heart of so many conflicts. They are rightfully worried about spy infiltration. But we are not spies. We came here in shipping containers with nothing but the clothes on our backs. We are the dispossessed. Much like the ones Ursula K. Le Guin wrote about a little over one-hundred-fifty years ago. Nothing to give except for our mutual aid. But, actually, I'm not completely dispossessed. I have the books. The actual, physical books. Maybe some of the only bound, paper books to have survived. And I have the journals. Both kinds of relics should be in a museum. No. I take that back. They should be copied and disseminated to everyone. Their very existence is forbidden. Therefore, they *need* to be read. I must do what I can to keep them safe. They were given to me to keep safe. That is what I'll do if my life depends on it.

Anyway. There is so much to document, but I'm tired. I was up early working in the garden. It's going to be beautiful. And, there's nothing like putting your hands in the soil. My anxiety instantly melts away when I'm working with the earth. We didn't have gardens back home. Now that I think of it, I never even knew where the food that I ate came from. I never even wondered for a second! I...*we* were brainwashed so well.

Well, thankfully we're not there anymore. I don't even miss my family. I never really had a good relationship with my parents and I am an only child. I'll document that life some other time. Now, I just want to forget. I just want to focus on what's here. What we're creating here. This. Here. Now is paramount. I'll document more about how we got here at a later time. I'm exhausted and ready for bed. Good night.

CHAPTER TWO: WATERFETCHERS

Heat rises off the cracked, eroded asphalt so high that the distant hills in the old, western half of the ancient city are almost a blur. If they hadn't known that those hills were there, the group of sixteens might have thought it was seeing a desert mirage. After all, the flowing oasis that they seek out in that urb-gone-forest trickles slowly, outlining those faraway hills and separating west from east as it has done for millennia.

In fact, that ancient watering hole had once been a main artery on which bustling cities were built. Hundreds of millions of peoples had been connected for thousands of kilometers and tens of centuries. But most of that history is lost to the contemporary peoples that now sparsely populate the semi-arid landscape. Presently, the river that inspired famous works of art for hundreds of Reawakenings is but a much narrower stream in a mostly dusty, scrub tree-covered, shallow gorge. Flora and fauna that thrive in extreme temperatures with infrequent rainfall have taken over much of the once-vibrant city. After all, for many, many Reawakenings, lack of human intervention has allowed the landscape to become its old anarchistic self. Free. Untamed. Wild. Without systemic, anthropogenic intervention.

From the gray-cloaked crow's view, the former urban centers are mostly covered in various shades of greens and browns for as far as the eye can see. Centuries-old vehiculars, rusted and overgrown with kudzu vines, dot the desolate landscape. Dilapidated buildings line the street corridors, also unable to escape the inevitability of being consumed by trailing plant life. Once vibrantly colored green trashcans line the old Long Road at various stops where hundreds of years before people waited for the hover tram or maglev buses to commute around the metropolis. Nowadays, there are no people to be seen anywhere along the vast interconnected streets, just the relics from their past, a past that was determined to end badly.

The Long Road is still mostly exposed to direct sunlight: browns, grays, some greens, the colors of late Alvás. Centuries of deforestation, before, had stolen the little natural shade that used to line the once longest avenue of the great city in patches. Even the old park is nothing but a collection of centuries-old mounds of trash and crumbling buildings. The old planetarium is just a heaping pile of bricks and scrap metal and of course, plastic. Who creates a material that takes tens if not hundreds of years to decompose? And, who creates that material for single use? Pockets of old oak groves still exist. But, almost no natural, living shelter can be found protecting the rare brave soul—human or non-human—who ventures out in this post-urban wasteland.

∼

FROM THEIR CURRENT ENCAMPMENT, it is a two-day—or rather two-night—foot to the Old River and back, with necessary stops for resting and refueling. No one dares to attempt travel during scorching hours. Centuries before, the same hike could be done in six hours. But, those were different times. Though only the street poor, and the occasional adventurous newcomer, had ever traveled it on foot.

Because of the sporadic droughts that can last months at a time, water is fairly scarce.

The everyday water that the Átmeneti consume mainly comes from their own watermakers. However, some is acquired from the water hustlers that roam the area, trading the liquid gold for clothes, tools, or even food. There are also makeshift water holding stations that pop up between disparate settlements across the old city and its outskirts. However, once a year water is collected in a unique way.

The Turning-Sixteen Celebration, or just Turning as they call it, is coming up, and the Átmeneti are in full preparation mode. It is a special opportunity for those commemorating their sixteenth Reawakening to gather the water for the festivities. No experienced adult will join them. It is a kind of ritual tradition to mark the moving on from childhood into maturation.

It is not too often that younguns get to venture that far from the commune. And for good reason. If someone doesn't pass out from overexposure to the sun, or Nap as they called it, some marauder or thief may take off with one of the smaller travelers or at least their water and the clothes off their backs. Dog attacks aren't that uncommon either.

Just before the Átmeneti settle in for a long Alvás, Old Mester recounts to the younguns of how on her Turning, at least fifty Reawakenings before, the waterfetchers were surrounded and attacked by a pack of seven or more fairly large and vicious vadkutya, or wild dogs.

"It was different times then," Old Mester narrates.

The Old River had only been a night foot round trip from the camp. Alvás season was coming to an end, and Old Mester and the other Átmeneti had just started planning the move to their new camp as they normally did right after Reawakening.

There were fewer people in the commune then. About twenty-five Átmeneti in total, after several units split off because of ideological division.

"I don't need to repeat *that* story," she reminds the group.

About half of the Átmeneti were under sixteen Reawakenings. Only five of them were preparing to celebrate their sixteenth Rewawakening, thus only five of them went water-fetching that cycle.

"And, we didn't have any házikutya to take with us for protection," she emphasized.

The children looked all around to each other, eyes wide and mouths gaped. It was unheard of to travel with no house dogs.

Just as they began to work their way down the gorge, they heard the growls and yipes.

"We caught them unawares!" She raises her raspy voice for dramatic effect. "And it ain't a good idea to surprise a vadkutya. Especially when they're feeding."

The Old Mester takes a moment to let that sink in. She makes eye contact with each of the children, one by one.

Then, she is interrupted with a barrage of questions.

"No, no one died, Szilv.... Yes, Gombi, it was very scary. No, we didn't scream for help. Now, hold your questions, and let me tell the story!"

Old Mester continues.

They'd decided to stray from the old, crumbling cement footpath just enough to get some shade in one of the few groves that still lined the gorge at the time. They had strayed too far. And before they knew it, one of the vadkutyas had its teeth on the tail of little Alma's robe and was hauling them backward across the grove.

"Little Eper, the youngest of the group, yelled to the two

biggest of us, me and Egres, to stand up big and wave our arms around while screaming and jumping up and down."

Despite the real fear that the terrifying tale provokes, it is comical to see Old Mester making herself big, flailing her staff around as she spreads her arms and legs wide apart to reenact the scene. The children chuckle in spite of being a little scared. For some of them, their waterfetching journey was coming up after things started to melt and turn green again.

"The rest of the group quickly got to the trees and climbed up as far as they could. Even little Alma who was smart enough to shake off their robe managed to escape and climb up a smaller oak." She wipes imaginary sweat off her wrinkled, gray brow.

"Luckily, we must have caught them off guard when their bellies were full. Once they realized that we weren't trying to steal their food or hurt them, they ran off and left us alone. Yes, Tea, we were very lucky."

At this point, the few almost-sixteens that are taking part in that particular storytelling workshop are shifting on their cushions and glancing at each other from side to side. Their journey is going to be twice as long. Fortunately, they have the numbers to be intimidating enough: there are nine of them and three young and agile házikutya. Despite the lingering unease about the possible dangers that awaited them, they are mostly excited about their journey. They still have time to prepare.

Makk is particularly excited about the journey because they often feels somehow estranged from the larger community, and especially from their fellow sixteens, given their impediment. Waterfetching will give them a chance to get away from the larger commune and prove themself in other ways.

Later that night, Makk, alone, decides to forage for their own meal and takes a walk to the edge of the camp near a thicket of trees.

It is a shame that the commune will be moving camp after the festivities are done, they thinks to themself.

They really likes this camp. There is a lot of space to seek solitude. They often goes off on their own and practices mindspeaking in hopes that someone may mindhear them.

A very slim chance.

Here goes nothing. Makk speaks inward toward their mind hoping that someone, anyone can mindhear them. Maybe a stranger passing nearby the camp. But the stranger would have to be genetically related for the sharing to work.

I really hope someone is receiving this. Our camp is about a two-night foot from the Old River or Life as we call it. It's almost Turning, and I am still not able to mindspeak with my bloodfolk.

They is a bit worried since the waterfetching rite is coming up and their sibling, or bodyblood, Gomba, or Gombi for short, will be there, too. They won't be able to send and receive to and from each other if there is any danger or if they are separated somehow. Makk and Gomba are twins, despite looking nothing alike. And, Makk is the only one in the commune over fifteen that can't communicate that way with at least someone from the same bloodline. It has been extremely frustrating for them, to say the least. Mindspeaking is one of the arts that all Átmeneti are supposed to be able to learn and perfect. Most people will have fully developed the art by the time they are eight Reawakenings old, and only a handful that Makk knows of have had to wait until after they began getting armpit hair to be completely proficient.

Makk is the only one who can't mindspeak, except for Dió, who was adopted into the commune at the age of three from a different community about a three-night foot from their current encampment. Gomba, Makk, and the others who won't have any bloodfolk with them on that trek will have to stick together and find other ways of silently communicating without calling attention to themselves in the case that danger appears.

Makk has been told that the way mindspeaking works is that two or more people can share thoughts. The younguns, like Makk and Gomba, call it sharing. One's thoughts show up as images, a voice, emotions, symbols, or letters for those that can read. Makk can't read, nor can most of the other Átmeneti. Not all that is thought is shared, so goes the understanding. Makk imagines that the person sending gets to pick and choose what is shared and with whom.

Makk has been training since they can remember being able to talk. But, they's never received sharing. They's sent out countless attempts, like the current one, but no one that Makk knows of has been able to receive from them.

In the mind-art workshop, one of the learning techniques Old Mester uses involves filling in the gaps.

Bloodfolk are paired up, testvér (bodybloods or siblings), cousins, etc. Each person in the pair is given an image sketched onto a leaf or fibrous leaflets when they have them in supply. Makk usually gets paired up with bodyblood, Gomba. The two siblings, fraternal twins, supposedly share the same parents, so they should be able to mindspeak. Gomba and Makk haven't always gotten along, but they try to put aside their differences during training. It is normal that Gomba gets frustrated with Makk. After all, Gomba can share with the other bodyblood in their intim unit or immediate family, as well as with the eggblood. The spermblood lives in a different community and they are not in contact with each other for reasons that are completely normative to the Átmeneti.

At that point, after so many Reawakenings, Gomba doesn't even try very hard. Reawakening after Reawakening they have done these exercises and still there has been no progress with Makk.

With little hope and even less enthusiasm, Gomba stares at

the image on the leaf, and Makk closes their eyes and tries to receive the image. Nothing. Time after time. Nothing. Old Mester is beginning to think that Makk has some impediment. Makk has been thinking that forever. But, Makk refuses to give up.

Who knows? Maybe Makk is just a late bloomer. Old Mester even said that she had a student, Hegedűfej—Hegi for short—who hadn't been able to share until they was seventeen. Unfortunately, Hegi is no longer in the commune. They had left before Makk was born to move to another community over a seven-night foot away.

Maybe after Reawakening, I can make the trek to meet them and get some mentoring, Makk wonders. But a seven-night foot is a long and dangerous journey. And Makk is not brave enough to go alone. On top of it all, the commune council would never support Makk's going alone. And even if Makk was to go with someone else, how could two people be away from the commune that long? Fourteen nights round trek plus however long mentoring takes?! There is always too much to be done around here to prepare for Hiding.

Makk ponders, *I'm beginning to think that maybe I didn't get the gift of sharing. Or, maybe the bloodfolk that I call eggblood and bodybloods aren't really bloodfolk after all. Maybe I was adopted, like Dió. Wouldn't my eggblood have told me?*

NAP IS JUST STARTING to settle down for its nightly rest. Its golden hue spreads across the ruins of dwellings and trees that dot the eastern horizon. The thin, upper canopy of the distant oaks and beeches shines, gilded like a golden cloth being draped across a sea of browns with hints of greens from the nascent, budding leaves. The duff along the outskirts of the new-growth forest is no longer covered in frost.

Reawakening is knocking at the door.

Reawakening isn't the most important of the seven seasons but it is one of the most eventful.

The word 'seasons' must be understood from a cultural point of view in addition to a climatological one, although the climate does indeed influence the practices of the Átmeneti. Reawakening is named after just that. For a month or so prior to Reawakening, during Alvás, a time of rest and outdoor inactivity, the Átmeneti do very little more than sleep. Alvás is the time of year when food is the most scarce and coincides with winter in the northern hemisphere, though much shorter than centuries past. So it is that during Alvás the Átmeneti have adopted the practice of reducing their caloric intake and exerting very little energy besides what the body requires daily.

Reawakening is also the time when the Átmeneti relocate their entire camp.

The Átmeneti are a nomadic people, but they only move once every year. And because they move on foot, it can take them several nights to move their camp. When they have finally moved into their new, temporary home, they begin sowing the seeds: pumpkins, squash, beans, corn, and other food items that cannot be foraged. This of course happens when the threat of frost is no longer an issue. And, this is also why Átmeneti also refer to Reawakening as Sowing.

After, and inevitably overlapping the end of Reawakening, comes First Forage.

Foraging is a core practice for the Átmeneti since the majority of their calories come from foraged foods. Dandelions, dead nettles, mushrooms of all kinds, and other plants that sprout right after the thawing of the ground and when the daylight stays longer and longer.

Hiding is when the Átmeneti do what the name of the season implies. It consists of the days, weeks, and months when the temperature is the most brutal. It could be argued that

Hiding takes place all year long since exposure to Nap is unbearable to most. But, during Hiding, the Átmeneti rarely venture out looking for food or water even when Nap falls below the horizon.

Nap is the name that the Átmeneti have given to the sun. Its name is an expletive and is used in many insults along with its correlative verb 'scorch.' Go scorch yourself! Kiss Nap and scorch off! to list two of the favorite impertinences.

Given the disdain for Nap, while also understanding the paradox of its importance for processes like photosynthesis and the continuation of life in general, the Átmeneti are a nocturnal people. They do the majority of their activities during the nightfall or when Nap begins its descent into and ascent out of the horizon.

During Hiding, almost no activity is done outdoors when Nap is at full scorch.

When the worst of the heat has come to an end, the Átmeneti call that period of time Second Forage. At that time, many berries and other small bush fruits and flowers are at their peak. Also, much of the food that had been sown during Reawakening can be harvested, except for the squash and other gourd plants. They are cultivated during Harvesting.

Harvesting comes before the Third, and last, Forage, several weeks before the onslaught of Alvás.

THIS EVENING, Old Mester, or Delores as she is also known by, and her four-legged, furry companion, Bobi, are out foraging for breakfast. Her long, colorful jute skirt creates a crunchy wake as she glides barefoot along a timeworn, narrow animal trail, stepping on brown leaves and twigs. Her long, gray-white hair is pinned up in a bun. A sumac-red stained grapevine basket dangles from her left arm.

Suddenly, she starts. Out of the corner of her eye, she sees Bobi dart out in front of her, growing diminutive the further away from her they runs.

It must be a rabbit, she thinks to herself, being careful to control her mindspeak so that she doesn't unintentionally alert any of her bloodfolk to false danger. It is easy to get startled and accidentally send out a red hue to the bloodfolk in closest proximity.

Looks like Bobi found their meal. What are we going to fill our bellies with this post-scorching, Old Mester?

Just then, she looks down next to her right, tawny, ashed foot and sees the lime-green fronds of sprouting fiddleheads, barely visible given Nap's impending exodus. Six fronds to be precise. She looks a little further and sees several more patches of fiddleheads. All of them are about the same size.

It is time.

She raises her pointer finger, gently pressing it to her right temple. There is a give to the elastic, aged skin that reminds her that she is no longer a spring chicken. She finds that doing this helps her concentrate. Then, picturing her bloodchild, she mindspeaks.

Octavia.

No answer.

She tries again, putting a little more emphasis on the name the second time around.

Octavia. Octavia.

After a few seconds, Octavia responds with a bit of distorted imagery of shut eyes. She is still deep in slumber. The scorching hours are only coming to an end. Then, Octavia sends an audible groan. Long and raspy. At least it is audible to Old Mester inside her thoughts.

Octavia replies with a sense of annoyance at being woken up.

What is it, Anya? Is everything okay?

Old Mester sends the image of the various patches of fiddleheads followed by a picture of the river, Life. And then, she speaks these words into her bloodchild's mind.

Please go round up the sixteens. It's time. The first fiddleheads have sprouted. There is no time to waste.

SIXTEEN IS a special age in the community. At the onset of Reawakening, all the younguns for whom it is their sixteenth Reawakening take part in a collective commemoration. The entire commune takes part in the celebration. For the Átmeneti, the sixteens are at an important turning point in their developmental stage. And because of that, they take part in two very significant rites—the ceremonial waterfetching and the pronouning. The former symbolizes independence and the importance of collective action and mutual aid. Hence, gathering water for the festivities for everyone to use. The latter usually takes place publicly upon the return of the waterfetchers and may culminate in the choosing of a new name and pronoun, a name and pronoun more suitable to a different identity.

Of course, festivities abound. It's the first big celebration after Alvás and it takes place right before the Átmeneti seek out a new space to relocate their encampment. It's the perfect time to use up any of the food that they have in abundance that would could possibly slow down the move to the new encampment.

Makk is packing their bag—a faded burgundy backpack with functioning zippers, a rarity that they found a few Reawakenings back in one of the landfills near the Old River—when their netherblood, Bodza, sneaks up and embraces them from behind. Bodza is the youngest partner of Makk's eggblood and is not biologically related to Makk, hence *nether* in netherblood.

Families, or intim units as the Átmeneti refer to them, take a variety of different shapes. Makk's intim unit consists of three maturated adults and three unmaturated younguns. Makk's spermblood does not form part of their intim unit although she does live in a nearby commune that their people trade with frequently.

Among the Átmeneti, the eggblood is the parent whose eggs are provided for one's procreation. Each individual has an eggblood as well as a spermblood.

It is common for an intim unit to have more than two maturated adults if there are more than two unmaturated younguns. Sometimes, an additional adult will be added if there is space and the need arises, for example, the birth of another child. Procreative arrangements are made to conceive offspring but rarely last longer than the procreation sessions themselves.

Most intim units are a mix-match of biologically and non-biologically related people.

In Makk's case, the three maturated adults are: netherblood, Bodza who uses the they pronoun; eggblood, Málna who uses the he pronoun; and another spermblood, Szeder who uses the she pronoun.

Bodza's long, dark chestnut hair braid and long, thick braided beard tickle the nape of Makk's neck. Makk scrunches up their shoulders and lets out a giggle. Bodza smiles.

"Did you pack the pumpkin seeds I wrapped for you?"

Their deep voice vibrates, causing goosebumps to form on the tickled nape. Makk giggles again and squirms out of the hug playfully.

"Do you remember when you went waterfetching? Were you scared, Nether?" Makk nervously inquires as they packs the last of the rations and zips up the bag with finality.

"My waterfetching was rather uneventful, Dear One. That year was much cooler than what we'd been used to, and our camp, at the time, was only a five-hour foot from the Old River. So, we were there and back before we knew it. We didn't even have to set up a make-shift camp to rest during the scorching hours. There were few scorching hours that particular Reawakening."

Bodza takes Makk by the shoulders, turns them to face them, and kisses them on the forehead. And then speaks the customary departing salutation, "I won't breakfast with you this evening, but we'll sup together on the morrow."

Which, technically, isn't accurate. Makk won't be back from waterfetching for at least three more sups, that is if there are no storms or unexpected encounters with marauders or hostile members of neighboring communities.

As the eldest member of the commune, Old Mester leads the departing ceremony. Nap threatens to disappear as most intim units are finishing up with breakfast. The sixteens are with Old Mester under the patchwork canopy that covers the communal refectory area of the camp. They don full traveling gear: canopy rolls, knapsacks with tools that will help them set up their refuges from Nap and which can be used as weapons of self-defense if it becomes necessary. And of course, collapsable salvaged jugs which they will fill with Life and bring back to the celebration.

Festivity is in the air. Laughter and music can be heard, mainly coming from around the refectory. Intim units slowly gather forming a big circle around the outer perimeter of the five bonfires. The sixteens sit in the middle, center stage. The fires flicker and make it seem like they are swaying side to side. Yet, they are as still as stones. Házikutya and youngun toddlers chase each other playfully around the seating areas of cushions and woven mats laid out for the ceremony. Bodza is leading a small group of younguns in a chant-like song. As they undulate and giggle they sing. One of the little ones gets up and dances to the beat of Bodza's drum.

FETCHING LIFE, fetching water
 Water is Life, Life is water
 Go now and fetch water
 Discovery yourself at the water
 Life will guide you, Life is water
 Come back as your new self from fetching water

WHEN THE MUSIC STOPS, Bodza goes and sits down with their intim unit. Old Mester comes out from the refectory, crosses the sea of bodies, and stands in the epicenter. Upon seeing her, the raucous chatter quiets down to only a few whispers and occasional bursts of laughter.

"There was, where there was not, across seven seas, through the high glass mountains, and over the pits of poison left to us by the ones who came before and destroyed the Old World, under the tent sky with its celestial holes, a giant tree. That giant tree stood in the center of everything."

All attention is focused on Old Mester. Even the youngest of the younguns don't make peep.

Old Mester continues.

"From the bottom of its leaf-covered branches to its tippy top lived the gods. Most important of the gods was Isten."

"Hála Istennek!" the liturgical words slips from the mouths of the onlookers, echoing across the encampment, "Thank God for that!"

Old Mester continues after her pause at the mention of Isten.

"In its roots, deep into the ground lived the devil. Together with the devil, Isten created our realm in the trunk of the tree.

And, together, they schemed and wove the trials and tribulations that the humans would experience in the mortal dimension of the great tree trunk."

Makk glances over at Gomba who just happens to be glancing in their direction. They make eye contact with each other and shivers reverberate throughout their stone-stiff bodies. It is finally happening. It is their turn to make the journey. A slew of emotions come and go: excitement, fear, intrigue, fear, and more excitement. Maybe a bit of pride?

Old Mester waves her staff through the flames of the nearest bonfire. If it had been completely dark the effect would have been more dramatic but alas.

"The waterfetching ritual is but one of those crucibles that must be overcome. It is a dangerous journey. It can be a cruel journey. Not everyone is guaranteed to return. But those who return will move beyond mere childhood to enjoy the tribulations and joys of adulthood. They will know themselves better. They may come back as different people. They may choose a different name for themselves. A different pronoun. But those who make it back will be welcomed with honor."

Silence.

"Thank you for gathering with us on this early pre-dusk of Reawakening. Tonight our sixteens embark upon their journey of discovery as they fetch the water that brings us all life. May Isten give them guidance as they complete their journey."

"Hála Istennek!"

"Now, let the vows begin," Old Mester finishes.

It is tradition in that commune for each of the sixteens to recite a short vow and mindspeak it to their bloodfolk, who look upon them from the crowd. But given their impediment, Makk can't mindspeak and, instead, has to physically go to their intim unit and speak the vow aloud. That disrupts the otherwise silence and causes a stir among the people who don't have bloodfolk celebrating the sixteens. Makk's pale, parsnip skin turns rosy from embarrassment. Vows are very intimate and personal, and they don't like the onlookers dropping eaves.

"I shall spend this journey with you in my thoughts," they whispers quietly enough so that only a few nearby eavesdroppers can catch a few words of the vow. "You have been an important influence in my rearing, and as I consider my pronoun, I will ask the river, Life, to guide me. When I return, I may be a different person with a different name but I will always be me."

Málna, Szeder, and Bodza wipe the tears from their eyes and take turns hugging Makk, backpack and all. Then, Bodza takes something from a pocket and places it in Makk's hand. Taking Makk's chin between their index finger and thumb and looking intently into their eyes, they speaks to Makk.

"I hope this protects you from anyone or anything who wishes you harm. Remember to drink lots of water. And, stay close to fellow fetchers. Listen to the strong mindspeakers. They might be able to pick up any signs of danger that may be lurking. Most of all, have fun and be safe!"

Next, Gomba takes their turn and mindspeaks to their eggblood, Málna and their other bodyblood sibling. Málna then turns to Bodza and Szeder to repeat to them aloud what Gomba shared with him, as is the custom in mixed-blood families.

And, just like that, twelve of them set off on their first-ever adventure together: nine waterfetchers with empty jugs and three house dogs with empty paws. If all goes well, they will have a solid eight hours of walking before they'll have to find shelter from the onslaught of scorching hours.

As Nap takes its place in the early morning sky, the heat radiating off the old road makes it unbearable, even deadly to traverse. Despite centuries of overgrowth from the short lull in human activity in the late Anthropocene, the petroleum by-product that makes up most of the material out of which the road was constructed has managed to win out over nature.

Crawling vines and small plants that under normal circumstances overtake sidewalks, creating micro-ecosystems in the cracks stand no chance in this poisonous, Frankensteinian dinosaur muck that humans once called bitumen or asphalt. And during scorching hours, the road becomes malleable underfoot, creating a noxious adhesive that will trap even the quickest of sprinters. The group, even the dogs, knows better than to even attempt to cross it. The off gasses alone can make the nearby wanderer nauseous for hours after only a few minutes of exposure. The best option is to find shelter far enough away from the road to protect them from the heat and the toxic fumes that radiate from it.

Among the ruins of what seems to be old dwellings made of seemingly less toxic materials than the old road and some of the narrower side streets, Gomba spots a dilapidated structure that still has an intact roof with an abundance of shade albeit mostly of thorny chaparral. It will do in a pinch. And they are cutting it close. Nap is creeping higher in the sky.

The long cloaks they wear cover them from head to toe. Underneath, their nettle fabric tunics are breathable, but also help trap moisture, regulating the body temperature. The length of the tunic doesn't pose a problem as long as they are on the gravel or heavily trekked paths parallel to it. But, hacking through tall grass, vines, and thorny shrubs can make it tricky.

Luckily, the tunics are designed to be hiked up to the waste or up the leg with ease. So, each of the nine fetchers ties up their underdress and hacks their way to the derelict house. Old filed-down chunks of tin and iron that were scavenged make good makeshift machetes.

When these now hovels were built, it was customary at the time to fence them in—there must have been little trust amongst the humans, even those living just a few steps away from one another. —What a way to live. How did they manage to exchange things easily?—And after centuries of inattention, the fences are reinforced by an entire network of vines and other greenery. Finding a way over will be tricky given the thorns and possible poisonous foliage. Makk sees the opening first.

"Hey! Over here. Someone has already cut through this part."

"Shhh!!!" Gomba puts a swarthy finger to their lips, making a shushing sound. Then, they whispers to the rest of the group.

"We need a brave and also stealthy volunteer to go in there and scope it out before we all rush in. It could already be occupied. We need to know what we're walking into. Plus, they needs to be able to share with someone else in the group. That means either Raki, Csipi, or Gesti."

Rákalma, or Raki as most refer to them, speaks up first.

"I'll go. Csipi and Gesti, focus on my thoughts. Everyone else will hear my screams if I'm in immediate danger."

Raki, a small, brown-faced youngun with big round, buckwheat honey eyes, is the youngest of seven in their intim unit. They comes from a long line of bloodfolk who trained the rest of the Átmeneti in the arts of defense and community safety. It is no surprise to the rest of the group that they volunteers. Gesztenye and Csipkebogyó—Geszti and Csipi is how most people refer to them in the third person—the two bodybloods of the group, are Raki's bloodcousins. They will relay what Raki shares to the rest of the group.

Despite being as quiet as possible, they all can hear as Raki hacks their way through to the shelter. After a few minutes of Raki sharing nonstop, Csipi motions to the group that it is all clear. One after one they duck down and squeeze through the opening.

While they wait out the scorching hours, they do their best to forage for lunch. Dandelions are out in abundance and so are dead nettles and grasshoppers. They will be having a crunchy salad for lunch.

Now, all of them have been foraging for meals their whole lives, but plant identification is still a bit tricky. Some of the less common foods have lookalikes that, if not kill you, will make even the healthiest person sick for days. Luckily, both Szilvi and Afi's intim units train in the foraging arts. Their nuanced knowledge will help keep them safe from misidentification. Szilvi is even an excellent cook back at camp, so their knowledge of food preparation is indispensable.

Szilvi's favorite Reawakening recipes requires a small fire which Cseri, the youngest of the group, is able to start using some dry leaves, twigs, and other crumbled bark from a dead branch of a birch tree. Its paper-like thickness and texture make it easy to ignite.

HERE IS what is on the menu:

Reawakening Salad with Roasted Grasshoppers
2 PARTS:
Dandelion greens (picked before the flower grows tall and opens)
Dead nettles
White clover flowers
Young plantain leaves

1 PART:
Roasted pumpkin seeds
Dried apples

roasted grasshoppers (remove legs and wings and fry until reddish in color)

DRESSING:
Foraged fruit scrap vinegar (Szilvi's grandma's recipe, packed for the journey)

Wild Carrot Mash
Boil roots of Queen Anne's Lace.
Mash with a bit of oil.
Season with salt to taste.

Dandelion Root Coffee
Roast the dandelion root until dark brown.
Seep in hot water until desired taste is reached.

After spending most of the scorching hours securing shelter, foraging, prepping food, eating, and resting, the group is sitting around in their usual cliques. Szilvi and Afi are holding hands under a clump of thuja trees, whispering to each other between kisses. Gyermekláncfű, Gyeri for short, is the last one to dispose of their makeshift food dish. They watches as the leaves-turned-bowl burns, creating a thick smoke that rises above the fence line.

Given that it is still scorching hours, the group isn't too concerned about fire smoke alerting possible dangerous foes to their whereabouts. Not many people venture out at this time of Nap. They still have five hours or so before it would be comfortable enough to continue their journey. Normally, they would sleep during scorching, but they are too excited. So they rest with filled bellies. Then, they will do what became commonplace among their people for at least a hundred years and take advantage of the night to continue the trek.

The contemporary peoples manage to continue their gene

pool because at some point along the way they adapted to their conditions. Some who survived the Great Dying died shortly after due to the ever-increasing hostility of Nap.

Becoming active at night, nocturnal, is what saved the people who came before them, and thus nocturnal activity became the cultural norm. Traveling at night was no different.

That Hold would shine, illuminating the night sky, isn't a guarantee, but they learned other ways of moving around when visibility was limited. Maps were created in a way that utilized landmarks that were easily seen or felt in the dark.

Although it is the group's first time going out on their own to that specific destination, they are familiar with the way because of the songs. However, despite their map and song rhyme, they aren't immune to getting lost. And the level of generalization of the map/rhyme excludes enough nuance that the majority of the group lacks the confidence to take the lead. In addition to avoiding getting lost, they have to worry about marauders making their raids.

"How does the rhyme go again, Maki?" Geszti is staring at Makk, and then shoves an elbow into their bloodfolk's side, the smirk on their face cutting like a knife. Raki and Csipi are smiling at the teasing game. "Aren't you the story weaver in the making? You're supposed to know."

Makk, turning the smooth, oblong stone that Bodza gave them around in their hands, looks up. "We all are responsible for learning it. Sing it to me and I'll tell if you're missing something." They says coldly, used to being picked on my Geszti and their bloodfolk.

"Ugh, whatever!" Geszti utters in disgust, rolling their dark eyes.

A few minutes pass, and, now, Gyeri is putting out the fire with the surrounding dirt that they had moved around to build the ephemeral fire pit. Raki, Csipi, and Geszti are giggling purposefully at this point. The seemingly sinister cachinnation goes on intermittently for several minutes. No audible conversation accompanies the snickering though. Finally, fed up, Afi speaks up.

"Do you three feel like sharing with the rest of the group?"

Afi is the eldest of the group and, despite a general lack of age hierarchy in the commune, feels somehow entitled to question the others' asocial behavior.

Sharing in secret is generally an accepted form of comportment among the Átmeneti as a whole. However, something about the current situation makes it feel a bit strange for Afi, as well as for some of the others. Raki, Csipi, and Geszti are the only bloodfolk in the group, besides Gyeri and Cseri, and so the others feel a bit left out because they have no one to share with in this way. Plus, giggling while looking at people around you who aren't in on the joke is seen as anti-communal, not conforming to social expectations. A bit rude. Off Putting.

Raki speaks up, an obvious sneer in their voice.

"Oh, what? Because Old Mester isn't here, you think you're our teacher?"

Szilvi speaks up this time.

"So, then, certainly you don't mind sharing aloud. I for one would love to know what's so funny."

Makk, who is the moving target that the three seemed to glance at most frequently, chimes in.

"Yeah. Why not let us in on your inside joke? I caught you all looking my way between guffaws. I'd love to know what's so funny."

Gomba, who spends a lot of time with Csipi and Geszti outside of trainings, looks down at their hands a bit awkwardly as they adjust in their seated position. They is well aware of the long-running inside joke in the commune about Makk's sharing impediment and think they know the source of the snickering and giggling.

Gomba interjects, hoping to draw attention away from the rising tensions.

"Why don't we just let it go and start packing up? The sleeping hour is upon us. And I'm ready to rest and then hurry up and get out of this place. It gives me the creeps. It's eerily quiet."

Geszti retorts sarcastically, "Just tell them, Gombi. Tell Makk how you feel. I mean, isn't this journey of self-discovery about trying to figure out who we are?"

"And who we aren't." Csipi finishes Geszti's sentence. "It's no secret that Makk can't share with any of their bloodfolk. Doesn't anyone else find that weird? Anti-communal even?!"

Then, Makk looks at their bodyblood, a bit of disdain rising along with their blood pressure.

They hates being the center of attention.

"Say it, Gombi. You obviously have no problems talking about me with your friends. Just spit it out!" Makk spits.

Fed up with the anti-communal bickering, Szilvi directs their words to the entire group.

"Is this how it's going to be over the next few Naps? Because if this is what it's going to be like, I'd rather risk heat exposure and capture by murderous marauders than put up with this anti-communal horsedong. Why don't you all shut up or go scorch yourselves?! I'm outta here! I'll find another spot to rest away from *you* bunch. You fight amongst yourselves like the selfish, non-Átmeneti that loot our camp each year. Filth!"

Szilvi spits on the ground. A sign of utter disgust and annoyance.

And, just like that, they grabs their pack, pulls the hood over their head, and disappears through the opening in the fence through which everyone entered.

That gets everyone's attention.

Not only is it dangerous to go out while the temperature is as high as it is, but going off alone is just plain stupid.

Afi, obviously annoyed with the group and concerned for Szilvi, begins gathering their things to follow Szilvi out.

"Wait for me, Szilvi." They yells. "Thanks a lot, you scorching jerks!"

Now, Afi has ducked through the opening.

Cseri follows suit, gathering their things. "You all are a bunch of scorching scorchers! You need to get over your pride, Jerks!" Then, Cseri is crouching through the fence.

Gyeri, Cseri's bodyblood, is about to do the same. They ties up their bag and, suddenly, freezes. Wide-eyed and with a look of terror on their face, they quickly motions to the group to be quiet.

Something is wrong.

The commotion from packing up and the residual tension instantly vanishes from the provisionary resting area. The look on Gyeri's face alerts the group that they is sharing with their bodyblood, and it isn't good.

Cseri, Szilvi, and Afi are in trouble.

Then, like someone had turned off a switch, the sharing stops. Gyeri, scrunches up their face as if concentrating, and then a look of devastation sweeps across their face.

Indeed, Cseri is no longer sending or receiving. Gyeri looks to the group of anxious fetchers and then shakes their head indicating that they is no longer sharing with Cseri.

Raki quickly moves to Gyeri, begins comforting them, and then whispers as best as they can to the whole group.

"One of us needs to go out there and see what is going on and share with the rest of the group. Csipi and Geszti, mindlisten for my sharing. I'm going out. Meanwhile, grab something to throw or hit with if someone or something tries to come in here."

The group nods in unison indicating their understanding and approval. Despite never having trained for this exact situation, they work really well together as a cohort. After all, they have been training in the different arts together since they could walk, talk, and mindspeak: mindspeaking, foraging, storytelling, combating, and making. They know each other very well, even if they don't always get along.

Raki grabs a rock about the size of the entire palm of their hand and pokes their head out of the opening in the fence. Then, the group watches as they disappears through the gap.

∼

ALTHOUGH, Csipi, Geszti, and Raki didn't grow up in the same intim unit, they do share a bloodline. This allows them to mindspeak, or share as the younguns prefer to call it.

In spite of their age differences, all three acquired the ability to manipulate the art of sharing around the same time they started learning to make coherent talk. Probably before becoming toddlers, Átmeneti share uncontrollably with their bloodfolk, especially when they are in need of something like food, attention, sleep, or something else. Chaotic, cacophonous sounds and images telepathically fling about abruptly at unexpecting bodybloods or bloodgenitors.

All of this is to say that the present bloodfolk trio has been sharing for many years. This means that they have had ample experience figuring out the unique nuances involved in sharing with each other. They know one another inside and out. So, when Raki shared the sudden red hue, the two bodybloods knew instantly that something was amiss.

Besides Csipi and Geszti, the only ones behind the superficially protective fence barrier are Makk, Gomba, Gyeri, and the three háziku...

Where are the three dogs? Among all the unforeseen chaos, the group had lost track of their furry companions.

∼

DURING SCORCHING HOURS, while the humans were foraging and preparing their food and refuging from the heat as best as they could, the three dogs went off hunting for their own lunch.

In any case, the fact that they are house dogs, Koocha, Fur, and Scruff are well accustomed to finding their own meals.

Being a house dog doesn't take on the same meaning that it had centuries before. At the level of lexicon, the word házikutya roughly translates to house dog. Yet, from a semantics point of view, the meaning underwent a change. House dog just means *not* wild. The dogs live in the camps with the humans but rarely do they stay in the dwellings, unless they prefer that way of life. Some did. Most did not.

These particular three dogs prefer outdoor life. They hunt and eat when they are hungry and they help keep the humans aware of any intruders.

This latter aspect hasn't changed much over the centuries.

That means that the dogs know all the humans at the camp. Over seventy people. Their smells. What they have eaten and even when they have excreted. When they are on their menstrual cycle.

Their olfactory glands allow them to smell far beyond the confines of the camp. And when the Átmeneti change camp after the Turning-sixteen celebration—always being sure to stay within a Hold's hike or so from the Old River—the dogs are essential in helping them settle far enough from other human communities, as well as non-human dangers.

At the peak of scorching hours, the three dogs are hanging out under some thorny shrubs near but not too close to the fenced-in shelter where the humans are resting. Their bellies are full as they digest their lunch of squirrels and grouse.

Koocha is about to rest their head on their front paws to go in for some quick shut-eye when they catch a whiff of something unfamiliar. Their head shoots up and their ears perk alerting Fur and Scruff to possible danger.

Koocha mindspeaks to their two companions.

Do you smell that?

The other two perk up and begin sniffing the air taking in long and then short intermittent sniffs.

Fur mindspeaks in reply.

It smells hooman. But not one of ours. Whoever it is, they are too close. I'm going to go check it out.

Fur is off and Scruff follows.

I'm right behind you. I'll get a bit closer to the black, poisonous trail.

Now, it's important to know that dogs have always had the ability to communicate telepathically. Much longer than humans who only began using the art regularly—and openly —for four or five generations, after the Great Dying.

Along with their strong olfactory sense, mindspeaking, as the humans called it, allows the dogs to share images, sensations like pain and sorrow, as well as encoded smells with each other regardless of bloodline.

In other words, dogs don't need to be connected through DNA to be able to share, unlike humans. But they do, however, need to be within close proximity with whomever they are sharing.

In this way, their ability to smell for very long distances is much more powerful. They cannot, however, share with non-dogs.

Scruff takes off toward the Old Road, but is smart enough not to get in the wake of the toxic fumes that off-gas from the centuries-old asphalt. As they gets closer to the well-beaten path that paralleled old Üllői Út, Scruff detects the scent of three humans. They are strangers. And there is something aggressive about the way they smell.

They are looking for trouble.

Koocha and Fur get the images and the olfactory code that Scruff sends to them just in time to circle around them without being seen.

The plan is to watch in which direction the humans are going. If they get close to the fetchers, they will try and chase them away. But, if they are just passing by, the dogs will keep themselves concealed until the humans' scent is at a safe distance from the fetchers.

The three humans are fully grown. From under their time-frayed Nap-rotted hoods, long, unkempt beards can be seen protruding. One of them wears some sort of device that lies atop the head like a thick ring. Scruff had never seen anything like it before.

The dogs can smell that the three humans had eaten just an hour or so ago. They had eaten meat. It had been cooked so they can't tell what animal it came from. But, the simple fact that they ate meat seemed to make them a little anxious.

They aren't accustomed to humans eating animal meat. At least not the humans in their camp. That fact makes them even more uneasy about the whole situation.

These humans are predators.

The other fact that has the three dogs concerned is that the humans are out during scorching hours. In their several Reawakenings of experience living with humans, vulnerable peoples like humans only risk Nap exposure if there is an emergency or they are defending themselves from an attack or raid, or raiding and attacking camps.

What can these strangers possibly be up to?

Suddenly, stern voices and shouts are coming from behind the overgrown wall. Then, just as Scruff sees one of the strangers pointing towards the thin cloud of smoke that trails up into the trees above where the waterfetchers are supposed to be resting but are instead causing a raucous, Szilvi comes crouching out of the opening in the fence.

The strangers see Szilvi, but Szilvi doesn't seem to see them until it's too late. Szilvi grabs at their head as if they hears a piercing noise and needs to cover their ears. And one of the strangers, who is almost twice as big as Szilvi, grabs them from behind and covers their mouth so the screams can't be heard. But the screams aren't audible anyway despite the agonizing look that Szilvi makes as they scrunches up their face in obvious pain.

The device seems to disable the unexpecting person to the point of immobility and even makes them aphonic, inaudible. The little that the dogs can see through Szilvi's hood, it seems as though they is in distress.

Scruff is about to give away their position and go after Szilvi, when Koocha quickly sends a message of urgency.

Don't give away our advantage. Let's see what they are up to before we attack. We need more information. We won't let them take the hooman.

Of course, that communication is expressed in a combination of images, sensations, and smells rather than words.

Whatever seems to be affecting Szilvi doesn't have an effect on the dogs. However, Fur and Scruff aren't as close to the strangers as Szilvi is. Koocha is even further away.

It is obvious now that the marauders aren't just simple strangers. Their intentions aren't good. Scruff can barely stand the suspense of waiting to form a plan of attack.

Just as Scruff is about to share with Koocha and Fur a sense of urgency to act like right now, Afi comes ducking out of the opening.

The same thing.

Afi immediately grasps at their ears and stumbles around in what looks like a confused state. Another marauder just a little bigger than Afi, cuffs a hand around Afi's mouth and holds them tight from behind, pack and all.

Scruff is getting extremely impatient, and it takes Koocha

sending sensations of reassurance to get them to stay put. After all, as Koocha shares, the marauders are using some sort of weapon and they can be of no use if the weapons are used on them, too. And, plus, the fetchers outnumber the marauders so they still have an advantage. They need more time to see how best to proceed and to do it with caution.

Just then, Cseri appears from out of the crevice.

Cseri immediately grabs at their ears, but not before they is able to share with Gyeri that there is trouble.

All three of the marauders now have their hands full. They have some kind of rope and are tying the fetchers' hands together as they sit on the ground in a stupor. Whatever is affecting the fetchers is also inhibiting them from screaming or running away.

The hoods that protect their heads and faces from Nap make it difficult for the dogs to read any facial expressions. But, based on visual communication alone, they are either in too much pain to run or they are somehow drugged into compliance. Maybe the device gives off pheromones that only affect humans.

Fur is closest to the opening and is the one to send the image to the other two dogs. Raki comes out of the opening of the fence. Fur assumes that Raki sees what is going on, because before the marauders can see Raki, they immediately goes back through the crevice into the makeshift shelter. Unseen.

This is finally their chance.

Now that someone on the inside knows what is happening, the dogs can act.

Koocha is the first to share a plan.

First, we need to figure out if that device affects us as it does the hoomans. I'm the smallest, so I'll go. I'll get as close to the hooman with the device as I can without getting snatched up. If I'm disabled, you two run through the opening into the shelter and get the attention of the fetchers. If I'm not affected, I'll distract while one of you gets that device. Once we all start barking or yipping the fetchers will come out and the fighting can begin. No doubt the tall, menstruating one—the dogs don't know the fetchers by name but rather by distinguishing scents and shapes—*will have told the others to prepare to defend or attack.*

The other two share that they agreed with the plan.

Scruff being the largest of the three—a mix of what used to be known as German shepherd and who knows what else—will go after the largest human. Fur, a bit smaller but just as agile, will grab the device while Koocha makes the human crouch down to try and grab at them. Koocha is about the size of a beagle, but of course, is a mixture of all sorts of old breeds. Their agility and speed make them difficult to catch, but the humans don't know that. They will try.

And just like that, Koocha jumps out from their hiding spot and slowly creeps up to the human with the device wrapped around their hooded head.

That particular human is already crouched down finishing a knot on the rope that keeps the three fetchers restrained and connected. Within biting distance, Koocha hunches down and begins to whimper loudly, tail between their legs.

Scruff and Fur know that nothing is wrong because their companion is still sharing with them. This is an act. The human will be thrown off guard thinking that Koocha is hurt or just lost and hungry.

The plan is working. Once Koocha gets the human's attention, they continue to crouch in a squatting position motioning Koocha to come closer.

"Come here little one. I won't hurt you," the marauder speaks softly using linguistic features that the fetchers probably can't understand. They aren't from around these parts.

The whisper of the human gets the attention of the other two who look up from their knots to see what the commotion is all about. And like a furry gust of wind, Fur jumps from their hiding spot and darts toward the unexpecting humans.

At the same time, Scruff leaps out and lands just a stone's throw from the largest human who is just standing up and reaching for something in their waistline.

Koocha begins to bark and then yipe, alerting the other two to do the same. Fur lets out a growl and lurches on the head of the human knocking the device onto the ground. Koocha latches onto the device, which fits between their teeth as long as they hold their mouth open wide enough, and takes off running in the opposite direction. With the device inactive the three fetchers quickly come out of their stupor and, in a matter of seconds realizing that they can, begin to scream and yell for help.

This all transpires over the course of a minute or two, although as I tell this story I see how it could seem like it had gone on for much longer.

Well, when the fetchers behind the fenced-in shelter hear the dogs barking, yipping, and growling, as well as the audible commotion, they are already armed and ready.

The three biggest fetchers come scurrying out of the opening as fast as they can while the smaller ones stay behind the fence forming a human tower.

Gyeri, who is the smallest, is at the top of the tower and is also the wielder of rocks and thick sticks. The largest marauder who is kicking at Scruff takes a chunk of a branch to the side of the head. Geszti keeps handing Gyeri different projectile weapons as fast as Gyeri can throw them.

While the three humans are busy fending off the dog attacks, Makk and Gomba take turns swinging their makeshift clubs at the outnumbered marauders. Meanwhile, Raki works quickly to cut the bondages from around the hands of the captive fetchers.

Suddenly, all three of them are free and picking up what

they can from the ground around them to use as weapons. Each of them, except for Cseri who could easily be trampled and as such steps out of the way of the excitement, joins in on the attack.

Now with three dogs and five almost full grown fetchers—not to mention the human catapult launching pain-inducing solid objects from behind the fence—defending each other, the marauders must see that they are losing their cause because they begin to stop fighting back and instead run away. They scatter in three different directions.

The fight is over.

But the struggle has just begun for the fetchers. Would the marauders come back? Should they turn back? No. They must keep on going. The Old River isn't too far off now.

The metallic, circular object that had caused the waterfetchers so much pain and anguish lies on the ground where Koocha had dropped it.

Koocha and the other dogs spend a few minutes barking and pulling at the robes of the fetchers to bring their attention to it. The dogs feel that the waterfetchers need to know what had caused them their debilitation. All twelve of the travelers stand around the shiny halo-like ring staring at it.

No one speaks a word or whimpers a sound.

Koocha nudges their nose at it. Afi reaches down and touches it lightly. Instantly, it begins to glow and hum. Everyone, save Makk and the dogs, quickly cringes in pain. Afi jerks their finger back.

Instant relief.

The fetchers don't realize that Makk isn't affected by the object. And, given that Makk already feels marginalized from their waterfetching peers and the larger community in general, they hesitate to say anything. But, then decides that maybe their disability can do them some good.

"I didn't feel anything just now."

All eyes are suddenly on Makk.

Szilvi is the first to break the awkward silence, "You mean to tell us that whatever the hell that thing is didn't just make your head feel like it was going to explode? How is that even possible?"

No one needs to say the obvious. Raki, Csipi, and Geszti exchange a quick set of thoughts. Just one more piece of evidence that proves to them that Makk is broken and somehow doesn't belong.

Cseri and Gyeri also share something similar with each other. But all of them keep silent.

Szilvi speaks up again, "Well, whatever is going on, we can't just leave it here. Those horsedongs might come back here for it."

Afi agrees, nods their head, and then chimes in.

"Whatever we do with it, we need to hurry up and get out of here. Those human traffickers could be on their way back with even more thugs this time. We need to be long gone before that happens."

The fetchers look all around at each other as if searching for consensus.

Afi continues, "I vote that we try traveling at least for a few hours and then we can stop and rest. We'll need to keep a watch. And when night falls again, maybe Hold's shine will brighten our way. Regardless, we must travel by night as usual."

Everyone in the group, except for the three saviors of the day, the dogs who don't understand the linguistic features of humans, agrees to this plan. Nobody seems to want a repeat of what had just happened.

Then, Makk speaks up.

"We don't even know how that thing works. Maybe we should try to destroy it."

Cseri has another idea. They hesitates to say anything at first and then just blurts it out.

"It might be a good idea to keep it. We can take it back to the camp and study it. Maybe there are more of them out there. We should know what it's capable of." Then, after a pause, "Since Makk isn't affected by it, they could carry it in their pack."

Makk shoots Cseri a glare, eyes squinting, nostrils flared. Cseri makes eye contact with Makk, scrunching up their pursed lips to one side of their face and then looks down to the ground at their feet. It's a coy look but there is no malice in their intentions.

Although Nap was slowly moving down from its peak position in the sky, it is still scorching hours and the group is visibly getting exhausted since the waterfetchers are out in the open, unshaded. The group is eager to get on the move. They exchange glances and whispers and look at Makk. Then, Szilvi poses the question.

"Would you be okay with that, Maki? If not, we could strap it to Koocha. They doesn't seem to be bothered by it either, but I think it would limit their mobility. It'd be easier to keep it in a pack that is on someone who doesn't go into agonizing pain."

Cseri jumps in.

"Plus, it only seems to work when someone touches it. You won't be holding it."

Heads nod like ripples in a rare puddle of rainwater, as the rest of the groups seems to agree.

Moments later they are off.

The offensive, ring-like mindsplitter adds little weight to Makk's pack. Despite being metallic, when Makk picks it up, it feels more like the artificial material from which most of the items they scavenged from the landfills is composed. It is hard and unmalleable, but as light as a small carrot. It must have been forged by someone with very bad intentions.

What good can this object do if it causes so much pain?

Makk, for the first time in a long time or maybe ever, is glad that no one can share their thoughts and feelings. At this moment, they feels dread and helplessness. They feels more alone than they'd ever had before.

CHAPTER THREE: OLD RIVER

The golden rays of the dawning Nap illuminate the very tops of the now omnipresent hills of the old city, creating a gilded backdrop to the much-awaited stage which was the destination of the waterfetching journey. The budding leaves of the trees yawn and stretch their tiny sprouting arms letting the world know that they are slowly waking up.

From the concrete precipice, the waterfetchers look down into the sparsely wooded, semi-arid canyon toward the narrow stream that is all that is left of the once great waterway. Up and down the trickling conduit, green shrubs, vines, and the occasional grove of trees sprout alongside the oasis.

Numerous well-beaten paths lead down to the watering hole carving what looks like smaller veins connected to a larger artery. In spite of its semi-aridity, patches of greens, whites, yellows, and purples dot the veiny landscape. Crocuses, dandelions, and other lush vegetation are clear signs of Reawakening and the welcome, albeit sparse rainfalls that help keep Life flowing. Collapsed bridges and vine-covered ruins of once grandiose buildings along the bygone bank remind the waterfetchers that humans once dominated that territory. No more. It now and once again belongs to Nature.

The waterfetchers sit perched along the cracked, overgrown cement where hundreds of years before tourists and residents alike strolled to take in the views of the old city. Old palaces, museums, bath houses had once mingled with modern shopping centers, cafes, and metro stations. Only ruins are left. Remnants of a vibrant, human-centric past.

The moment has finally arrived. From that point on, once they fill their collapsable jugs with Life from the Old River and bathe in its cooling, fresh wetness, they are to start anew. They will choose their pronoun and even a new name if that is their calling. First, they will rest.

They are quite hungry. They haven't had a proper meal since the incident with the marauders. They hadn't dared to stop and rest—let alone start a fire—for as long as they had during the beginning of their journey. Instead, they rested for an hour or two at a time at most. Each of them took turns in pairs acting as the eyes and ears of the group while the rest of them slept if they could. They snacked on dried nuts and whatever fresh greens and flowers they could forage in the light of Hold.

Hold had shone brightly and lit the route enough that they could continue their trek throughout the night with little difficulty. That meant they reached their destination just in time for the break of day.

The timing is ideal because they will be able to start the return journey and walk an hour or two before having to find shelter during scorching hours. Their plan is to take a somewhat longer route back to their home camp. The last thing they want is to run into the marauders again who might be expecting them to take the same route back.

Gyeri and Cseri have already descended a path toward the stream, empty jugs in hand. Szilvi and Afi are sitting on a patch of vegetation, violets, grass, clover, and other living beings that make up that microcosm. They laugh as they take turns feeding eachother white clover flowers that are within reach and dried pumpkin seeds from their satchels. Raki, Csipi, and Geszti sit apart from Makk and Gomba, who get up and begin making their way down the same path that Gyeri and Cseri had gone down, collapsed jugs in hand.

Makk looks back and sees the three staring the two bodybloods down.

Gomba breaks the silence, "You shouldn't let them bother you so much. They just feel superior because they are part of the original bloodline. All of their bloodfolk have that air of supremacy to them. I just try to ignore them."

"That's easy for you to say. You can actually share with our bloodfolk. The fact that I can't makes me a target. So much that we do as a people is based on our ability to share. You'll never understand."

Both bodybloods are quiet for the rest of the hike down to the stream. As they get closer, the air around them becomes a bit cooler. The brush grows taller and thicker and the path narrows. In the distance, both can hear a trickle of what must be running water. Both have only ever heard that noise when it rained hard enough to overflow the collection tanks. The smell of Life rushes through their nostrils. A wave of euphoria floods over the two siblings. Smiling, they begin running toward the flowing water.

Gyeri and Cseri are already buck naked and splashing around flinging water at each other, laughing so hard that they fall over again and again. Standing in the middle of the stream, the water only comes up to Gyeri's flat chest. Gyeri is the shortest of the group, and that means that the water would most likely come up just above Makk's waist line. Makk doesn't wait long to find out. They strips off their cloak and the light underclothes underneath and jumps in. Gomba follows suit.

Despite Nap already illuminating the tippy tops of the hills on the other side of the Old River, the water is still very refreshing. Indeed, it is cold enough to form goose pimples on their bodies. What a delight! Communal bathing water back at the camp is never this invigorating, except for during Alvás. However, baths are few and far between during that colder season. To save water, the Átmeneti use a different bucket-like receptacle that they've scavenged over the years and just wash up their musty bits. The Átmeneti, and especially watermakers, aren't fond of water waste. Once one sees what goes into making potable water for tens of people, one can't blame them.

Makk and the rest of the fetchers sit in the cool, refreshing water on the edge near the bank. The periphery of the stream is a bit cloudier since the mucky sediment is more dense than in the middle. The three dogs are splashing and playing in the water, fighting over the occasional branch or stick that floats by. Are they panting or smiling? Or both?

Gomba breaks the silence.

"I've been doing a lot of thinking and I'm convinced that I'd like to keep my name. I've always been called Gomba. But I think I want to be a he."

Gyeri knows the reasons but wants the others to know. That, after all, is part of what waterfetching is all about: sharing the new self with one's fellow Átmeneti, "Go ahead and tell them why, Gomba. "

Gomba continues.

"Well, I know that I don't need to choose a different pronoun. But, I'm close to my eggblood and some of my other bloodfolk who are hes. I feel a special connection to them. Plus, since in our commune hes are the main scavengers and tinkerers, I'd really like to do that as my main contribution to the community. Repurposing found treasures from the trash heaps of old is my strongest skill."

He would have made an excellent academic archeologist if

that type of scientific trade still existed. But alas. Much of what had been done before the Great Dying has now become obsolete. Maybe one day again.

Makk interjects, "You know that that is just a coincidence. Our spermblood in the next community over is a scavenger and is a she. You know that, Gombi."

Gomba glares at Makk. It's a little playful but also challenging. "Yes, yes. That is what we are taught. But, if you look at the numbers..."

Then, Makk speaks up again, "It sounds like you think being a scavenger requires being a he. What happens when a scavengers decides to change into a fae because the new person they look up to is a fae? It just doesn't make any sense to think that way. Pronouns don't have to be fixed. They've always been fluid, based on our changing influencers."

Just then, the dogs decide they've had enough of the water and came back to the bank shaking off the excess moisture.

Cseri and Gyeri, who are squatting next to one another, squish up their faces as the dogs splatter river water all over their unexpecting bodies. The others laugh so hard that they fall over into the water. Then, everyone jumps back into the middle of the stream and begins splashing each other. Loud laughter accompanies splashes and barking. After a while, things calm down and they return to the grassy bank.

By now, the hills above them are fully illuminated by the morning Nap almost as far down to the point of the bank on the west side of the stream. It is time that they fill their jugs and begin the journey back to the big camp. The rest of the Átmeneti await their return.

The next quarter-Hold, a little over a week in antiquated terms, would be full of festivities. The renaming and pronoun-revealing ceremonies will start them off, as well as the ritual water purification and the liturgical drinking from the cup. The latter symbolizes the collective sharing of Life; a gift from the sixteens, showing that with their new name and pronoun, they can contribute to the larger community in different ways and have proven, by fetching water, that they can begin their own intim unit if they want. They also get to focus on one main art, while still participating in the communal everyday activities that everyone needs to contribute to: foraging, maintaining the encampment, childcare, cleaning out the latrines, all the things that villages do together so that no one has to take on the burden of doing all the hard work.

All the waterfetchers have chosen their new name (or chosen to keep the name they already have) as well as the pronoun they want to be identified by.

Despite identifying strongly with hes, Afi decides to keep they as their pronoun. Their favorite person in the whole community uses the they pronoun. Afi really looks up to them. And although they is capable of menstruation and lactation, the idea of being someone's eggblood doesn't appeal to them. Nine Holds of carrying around a human? No thanks. They will of course participate in the rearing of the children of the community as all Átmeneti do, but sticking to one intim unit doesn't appeal to them, either. They love Szilvi like they love other Átmeneti but they don't see themselves committing to a monogamous relationship with them.

Makk aligns with Afi in this sense. They also like the flexibility that not being tied down to one intim unit lends to them in the community.

As they is closing up their pack, they makes the decision to keep their pronoun. But, will they change their name? They is on the fence. They doesn't feel a strong attachment to the name Makk besides it being the only name they has ever been called, apart from the nicknames that their closest friends and intim unit have coined for them: Test (sibling), Maki. They doesn't know of many names besides those of the fellow Átmeneti and some of the characters from the stories of the past, as well as those that are made up for entertainment and fables.

Makk will do.

Even though the Átmeneti are taught to draw and paint from an early age, the tools required for such an art aren't used for writing. In fact, in general the Átmeneti are illiterate. Neither reading nor writing are arts that the Átmeneti train in. There isn't much to read anyway. At times, fibrous leaflet, notebook-ish things are discovered during scavenging. These are often damaged by water or partly scorched.

To my knowledge, there has never been a book discovered that was complete or in decent condition, besides the original Three Books. But, as the stories that are passed down through storytellers of the community go, these types of physical books have been a rarity for many, many Reawakenings even before the Great Dying. Most things that could have been read were found on what was called the interwebs, or something like that.

The Old Peoples had devices that they hovered above their head or that were somehow attached to the eyeball that connected themselves to other people. They would use these devices to read. And, according to the stories, what they could read was controlled. Unless they had a lot of currency to exchange and break through what was called a paywall.

Afi's netherblood, non-biological parent, for instance, was trained in the art of storytelling. They weaves tales of how at one point in time, long, long ago, laws were created that outlawed books. All books made of fibrous leaflets were scorched. Entire communities of the Old Peoples had to relinquish their books for systematic burning. If they didn't, or if books were found, the people hoarding the books were put in cages. Cages! Like the marauders do to younguns that they kidnap. And, new books weren't made. I guess fibrous leaflets were as hard to come by then as they are now.

Needless to say, because the community that they grew up

in was illiterate, stories are stored in the minds of the storytellers and their audiences. Thus, there are a limited number of stories. Names are passed down from family members and relatives from other communities. Therefore, few names are at the disposal of the Átmeneti. And, no name really calls to Makk. They will keep their given name for now. These are the thoughts running through their head as they puts the last remnants of lunch back in their pack.

That is when Makk hears singing.

THE SONG IS UNFAMILIAR. Yet, the voice singing it is somehow familiar. Makk can't quite put their finger on how it's familiar. But it is definitely very familiar. The cadence. The pitch. Too familiar.

Makk looks around at their fellow waterfetchers to see if they show any indication of hearing the singing. And, then they turns to Gomba who is packing up his satchel only a few steps away.

"Gombi, do you hear that?"

"Hear what, Test?"

The singing continues.

There are no instruments. Just singing. It's a struggle to block it out. It overpowers their thoughts.

A children's song forgotten since I am no longer a child? They ponders trying hard to hear their own thoughts over the din.

It is one person from the sounds of it. It is loud and clear as if the person were standing right next to them.

"Nevermind. I think it might have been a bird or something."

Makk has a moment of vertigo. Their head spins and they tips forward and catches themself by putting out their right foot.

The singing continues. Their thoughts are whirling alongside the song.

If Gombi can't hear it, then no one else can. What the scorching Nap is happening to me?

The singing suddenly stops and then continues. The linguistic features are definitely familiar to Makk, but some of the words seem a bit strange. After getting a grip on the tornado of thoughts and sounds in their head, Makk realizes that the voice singing the song is very familiar because it is their own voice.

There is an old crone who lives near the stream, oh Hold!
There is an old crone who lives near the stream, oh Hold come shine on me!
There is an old crone who lives near the stream
They has black cats, one, two, three
And they'll spare you your precious life, if you give them the key!

The whole experience is very disorienting for Makk. They looks around at their fellow fetchers as they are all packing up and chatting amongst themselves, all of them except for Raki, Csipi, and Geszti who are silent but probably in full on sharing mode. Nobody seems to be as confused as Makk is about the singing. They turns to Gomba.

"I think I dropped something. I'm going to go back down towards the water. I won't be long."

Gomba nods and looks up at Nap as if warning Makk that they'd better hurry up. Time is working against them. They need to be on their way.

"We'll get a head start. Catch up with us."

Makk is barely able to nod their head in agreement and shuffles off clumsily down toward the trail disappearing into the dense thicket, leaving their pack and supplies behind.

Makk hopes to be able to separate themself from the group

to see if the singing will diminish by putting some distance from where they'd been gathered. Before they jumps to conclusions about whether they is hallucinating, they needs some privacy.

The singing is still as loud and clear as it was back up near the others.

The biggest cat has a stubby tail, oh Hold!
The biggest cat has a stubby tail, oh Hold come shine on me!
The biggest cat has a stubby tail
Cause the other two cut it off with a nail
And they'll spare you your precious life, if you give them the key!

Makk covers their ears with both hands and yells silently but loudly in their mind.
STOP!
And just like that, the singing stops. A bright red hue flashes in Makk's mind. And then Makk's own voice.
Hello? Is someone there? Hello?!
Confused and even more dizzy, Makk pushes even harder on their ears. Then, thinks to themself.
Why is this happening?! What is wrong?! Who is in my head?!
Goose pimples form on almost all the surfaces of their body. The hair bun on their head seems to tighten as their scalp becomes taught. Their vision begins to blur slightly as the adrenaline rushes throughout their system. Then, Makk's voice plays again inside their own head.
Hello?! Why is what *happening? Who is this?*
Suddenly, it hits Makk. Another rush of adrenaline rushes at them as they steadies themself on the slippery, rocky path.
They is sharing with someone.
The realization slams into them like a fallen facade from a building in ruins tumbling to the ground.
Am I hallucinating?

They *is* able to share, after all.

But how is it possible? They'd always been taught that sharing only happens with bloodfolk.

They takes a deep breath and exhales. The sensation of sharing with someone for the first time is completely overwhelming, especially since they has no idea with whom or how it is happening. The voice is heard again and then an image of the Old River appears in their mind's eye.

Hello?! Are you there? My name is Takver. Did you get the image I sent you? Tell me who you are. Where you are? Have you finally come looking for me?

For a split second, Makk thinks about how strange the name Takver sounds. *Vér* means blood, but *Ták* doesn't really have a meaning, although the sounds make sense. Then, concentrating really hard, remembering all the years that they'd trained in the art of mindspeaking to no avail, Makk sends out a message.

Umm...Hello. I'm Makk. Did you send me an image of Life?

After a short pause that felt like an eternity, Makk mind-hears their own voice again.

Wow! I don't believe it. Okay. Umm...I don't know what Life is, but if you mean the stream, yes. I hope I can trust you. I...I am going to trust you. I'm down by the stream. Can you come here? You must be close enough to me if we are merging. Look for this rock.

A large, shiny rock that protrudes from the middle stream, the only one of its kind around, flashes in Makk's mind. They isn't sure what merging is but assumes it means something like sharing. Overwhelmed by all that is happening unexpectedly and forgetting about the other waterfetchers preparing to set off on the return trek home, Makk continues down the path that leads to the Old River.

Once they connected, Makk felt the sudden appearance of something like a rope that their entire being was holding onto. The rope doesn't pull hard, but it is noticeably present. It happened very quickly. It was like nothing they had ever experienced before. They had played with pieces of rope before. It felt different than that.

In the games, you hold onto the rope with your hand or hands while someone on the other end does the same. The rope is spun in a way that a third or fourth person can jump in and hop over the rope as it goes from up high back down to the ground in a circular fashion. It is one of their favorite games. No. This is a different feeling, although similar. It is like the rope is wrapped around their rib cage and they can feel the other person holding the rope at the other end. Slack but not too much. Taught but not too much.

As they gets closer to the water, Makk feels as if their heart is going to beat out of their chest. Their endorphins and other bodily chemicals are at peak levels even more so than when they had to help fight off the marauders.

Their whole life they'd been taught that strangers are dangerous and, thus, not to be trusted. The Átmeneti are the only safe people; distrust of others is so central to them that trade with non-Átmeneti communities is forbidden, unless it is for water and only if the watermakers in their own community are struggling to make it. It has been that way since as long as Makk can remember.

No wonder they is feeling uneasy and at the same time excited. They has just shared for the first time in their life. But with someone they doesn't know.

Is they not broken, after all?

Makk's mind voice interrupts their thoughts abruptly.

I don't see you, yet. Are you close?

Makk scans their surroundings, looking up and down stream.

I just reached the Old River, but I don't see anyone. I don't know if I should go up or down river.

Again, their own voice echoes through their mind.

Send me an image of your surroundings. I know this stream pretty well.

Makk hesitates.

I don't know how. I don't have a lot of practice with sharing.

Makk squints their eyes struggling to see far away. They has always had poor vision looking at a distance. It is frustrating not being able to see clearly, especially since it is worse at night and they does most things when it's dark. All Átmeneti are nocturnal. It is especially frustrating at this moment. And then, something red appears, waving in the distance downstream. But on the other side of the stream. Their first instinct is to duck down, but then realization kicks in.

They stands up and starts walking, no it is more of a jog, toward the human waving what seems to be a large, red, patchwork cloak in the air.

Do you see me? I'm waving my cloak.

I see you. I'm coming. But I'm on this side. One of us has to cross.

Then, Makk receives an image. Two bodies in the buff, one brown and one pinkish peach, standing in the middle of the stream.

Now, Makk is certain that their heart is going to jump right out of their chest. The naked aspect of the encounter is the least of their concerns. After all, nudity around other Átmeneti, especially in the intim unit, is an everyday practice. But, the vulnerability of meeting a stranger for the first time and doing so in the buff is overwhelming. As they removes their cloak and underclothes, their hands shake. The cool water imbibing their feet and then their thighs makes them tremble even more.

The water is just as cool as it was when the fetchers first played in it. Makk's breath shortens and goose pimples immediately form all over their body. They clenches their jaw and wraps both hands around their groin and covers it, embracing themself for the shock.

The refreshing water makes the radiating heat from the

ever-rising morning Nap bearable, as the two strangers stand in front of one another. The sediment filled, mud-tinted water barely covers the navels on the two exposed figures. As they stare at each other, it is like they are seeing a reflection of themselves. The main difference is that Makk is pink and pale and wears a twisted, ash-blonde hair bun that sits on the crown of their head while their just-as-full-bodied mirror image has short, hacked dark-brown hair. Takver has a salient golden brown chest that is slightly more protruding than Makk's pale rose pink one. Takver's hair is about three fingers wide in length all over and looks like it was cut with a dull piece of scrap metal, choppy and straight.

How can it be that they look so much like each other? And they can share?!

Makk opens their mouth to break the silence, but Takver raises her finger to her mouth in a shushing gesture. She scrunches up her shoulders a bit and looks from left to right. Then, she mindspeaks.

I don't know if it's safe here. Let's just merge for now. And we should crouch down so we're not so visible.

Takver knows the stream very well. She's been going there for water for as long as she can remember. She'd learned how to swim there. She ran there when her community was attacked. The mother told her to run away to the stream. Those were her last words to her daughter. "Run, my sweet Tak. Go to the stream. Hide. Don't look back." Even now, after three Reawakenings of living on her own, she continues to go there. The stream is the main source of water for many people, and so, too, she is familiar with the dangers. Marauders need water just as much as she does.

Makk nods in agreement and then squats so that the water comes up just below their peach-fuzzed chin. They can barely hold back the urge to squeal from the coolness of the water on their sensitive nipples. Takver does the same while continuing her thought transfer. She had already gotten used to the temperature change since she'd had to swim over to get to where Makk was.

The mother told me that you existed, but I never thought I'd actually get to meet you. The second I laid eyes on you, I knew it had to be you.

Makk furrows their eyebrows and squints their eyes in a look of confusion.

What do you mean? The mother? Meet me?!

Makk doesn't have a chance to think about the fact that they is actually sharing. The fact that it comes so natural as if they'd been doing it their whole life is bewildering yet comfortable.

Just then a hue of red flashes in Makk's thoughts and Takver dunks underwater. Makk turns their head around in time to see two large humans approaching the Old River upstream a ways. Then, they hears the unfriendly barking of dogs in the not-too-far distance.

They quickly takes in a deep breath and joins their sharer underwater. Takver sends an image of a hiding spot where they can go to be unseen, yet observe the two humans. She'd constructed it from branches, duff, and other detritus from the surrounding area a few months back. It is well camouflaged. She'd had needed to use it before on several occasions.

On the west side of the stream not far away from the new acquaintances, the refuge blends in seamlessly with a part of the bank that collects and traps stray debris. Crouching underwater like a snorkeler in a shallow, muddy reef, Makk follows Takver as they quietly make their way to the aquatic covering.

From underneath the beaver dwelling-like structure, they watch as the two, large cloaked figures fill their containers with water. One is taller than the other by at least a head. Both have beard-like facial hair that is matted and dreaded, light colored and gray. The cloaks they wear look like patchwork. Chunks of animal hide and pieces of cloth that were probably scavenged from the landfills of old mingle in a hodgepodge pattern from the hood to the bottom that drags across the ground as they squat down along the bank. Their skin is mostly covered except for at the hands. Makk notices that their eyes are a brilliant green color. He'd only met one other person with that color of eyes and she'd died years before in a raid on their camp.

Makk hears a familiar bark, and, then spots Koocha running downstream with their tail between their legs, ears tucked back. Then, the other two dogs follow behind. They are being chased by a cloaked human with a long, slender rusty metallic object in hand. Makk has to resist the urge to jump out of the river shelter and run to the dogs' aid.

Bazzeg! The fetchers! RUN, dogs! RUN!

Makk screams to themselves suddenly remembering that their people had been packing up and waiting for them. They were preparing to leave the river stream for safer shelter to wait out the scorching hours. Makk had completely forgotten.

The previous ten minutes had been so physically and emotionally overwhelming that the rest of the world vanished from their thoughts.

They *can* share. They met a seemingly friendly outsider. This outsider must be genetically related if they can share with her. How is that even possible?

Suddenly that other world comes wooshing back and fear for their fellow waterfetchers sinks in squeezing the pit of their stomach like a vice. They begins sharing with Takver.

My friends, my community are out there. My bloodfolk! I need to find out if they are in danger. And, I can't share with any of them, so I need to sneak my way up there in body.

Takver shares a flash of red hue indicating how dangerous she feels the idea is. She knows just how murderous marauders are. And, these people are definitely marauders.

From her experience, marauders never travel alone. And,

they always brandish a weapon. The two people at the river prominently display machete-looking objects strapped at the waist. Then, one of the marauders spots Makk's cloak and underclothes and picks them up, saying something inaudible to the marauder who is busy filling their container. There is a pause and the two look around suspiciously. Their demeanor changes drastically. They are now on high alert. Then, the marauder with Makk's cloak stuffs the stolen belongings into a pack hung from their back and both take off in the direction of their companion and the three dogs.

This time Makk sends a red flash to Takver, but it indicates much more than danger. Hints of anger, frustration, and a feeling of stupidity meld together. And Takver needs no nuanced explanation to understand all of the shared emotions. Then, Takver warns, *We can't go there right now. It's too dangerous. Those humans are full-grown. We don't stand a chance against them.*

Takver keeps sharing the red hue as a constant stream while she shares her thought-sounds. She looks over to her new companion and takes both of their hands in hers. They lock eyes. The soft, river pruned fingers feel soothing to Makk.

Pay close attention. Those people or at least people like them ravaged my whole compound years ago. They are killers. I'm the sole survivor that I know of. We can't risk being seen by them. We must wait until we can be sure to remain unseen.

Makk's already river-wet eyes well with tears. Takver squeezes their hands in acknowledgment and solace.

It seems like an eternity before the three humans eventually are out of sight along the streamside. When they both are certain that it is safe, the two shaken tuckaways creep out of their marine refuge. Takver walks upstream a few paces and grabs her clothes and cloak. Then, the two cross the stream.

The scorching hours are mostly upon them and Makk won't last long unclothed and exposed to the radiating rays of heat.

They can already feel the water evaporating off their drenched body. Takver quickly dresses and tells Makk to find some shade. Her plan is to go stealthily up the path and take a look around. She will share everything that she observes. There is no reason for Makk to risk exposure. It would be almost as if Makk were there with her by her side, she explains.

Convinced, Makk spots a covering of vines and branches that stands low within a thicket that is far enough off the beaten path that they feels unexposed to the elements as well as possible unexpecting human passersby.

While Makk scours the shelter for any possible dangers or present inhabitants, Takver disappears up the path. As soon as she disappears, Makk begins receiving images from Takver. Their heart feels like it skips a beat when Takver sends them an image of several youthful humans coming out of various hiding spots up on top of the ridge where there used to be a riverside park where kids would play and couples would stroll centuries before. A wave of relief rushes from Makk to Takver.

As Takver hides herself from the group, Makk quickly makes their way back to where their fellow fetchers await them. They shares with Takver that she should stay hidden until Makk is able to explain to their peers what has happened. The fetchers will be wondering where in the scorching Nap Makk has been.

THE SIXTEENS ARE RESTING IMPATIENTLY in various shady spots that they could find along the concrete precipice. Nap is taking its place in the late morning sky, just beginning to release its fury. No wild animal can be heard—No birds. No small creatures are scurrying to and fro. The scorching hours are upon them in full swing.

What were the old people thinking when they built cities

out of concrete and asphalt? Materials that conducted heat in this way couldn't have been used with much forethought. The designers were either careless or motivated by something other than the hope that the living would thrive.

A few paces away from the rest of the group, Makk and Gomba sit in a covered thicket. Makk is wrapped in a sheet from their pack. Takver tries to eavesdrop to no avail as the two bodybloods exchange heated words. Gomba can't believe what he is hearing. He stares at his bodyblood flabbergasted. His big brown eyes squint as if focusing his vision would change what he is hearing. He whispers.

"Have you scorched your brain? Do you really think they'll let a stranger come into our community after what happened just before Alvás ended? Explain to me how it is that you've lost your good sense, Test!"

Makk stares at their bodyblood. The dark, thin bedding cloth that they had packed and used to cover up with during the day while they slept is draped over their naked body, soft and well woven.

"We can't just leave her here, Test. She lost her whole community. She has no one!"

Makk's patience is running thin.

"And she and I can share, Test! Do you understand what that means?!"

Makk pauses and waits for Gomba to let what they is saying sink in. Then, they continues.

"She's my family, Test. My blood! I can finally share with someone. I'm not broken after all, Test! I need your support more than ever right now. You have to be on my side about this. The others will never accept this if you don't."

Takver remains hidden from the others in a shady thicket several paces down a path from the group. She can hear murmurs from the intense conversation between Makk and their bodyblood. A knot sits heavy in the pit of her stomach.

Does she really want to go with Makk? Is their community really that hostile to outsiders? Should she sneak back to her bunker now? Can she leave Makk behind now that she'd finally found her long-lost sibling?

While the two serendipitously acquainted kindred made their way to find Makk's fellow waterfetchers, Makk had insisted that Takver go with them back to their community. And having spent the last year and some alone, Takver was eager to be with friendly humans again. Hiding from marauders was exhausting despite her talent for it.

And, Makk isn't just any friendly human, they is her kinfolk. They can merge. The bond is already strong. It will only grow stronger.

The two bodybloods continue to argue.

"If she doesn't come with us, Test, I'm staying back with her. I've already made up my mind."

Gomba hadn't considered Makk not returning as a possibility. This changes his tone from defiance to pleading.

"But you know how our community is. I don't have to repeat myself. Come on, Test, think of what you're asking!"

"Test, I've made up my mind. She comes with us or I stay."

Makk takes Gomba's hand and holds it, giving him a half smile full of assurance.

"The scorching hours are upon us already. You all have several hours to decide what to do. Meanwhile, if you want to meet her follow me."

Gomba follows Makk down the narrow path toward where Takver is sitting cross legged under the shade of three large black poplar saplings. Despite being fully aware that they are both coming and having consented to meet Gomba, she startles when they come into view. After all, she isn't used to the company of other people. Over the last two complete Reawakenings, almost three, she's learned to make companions out of wildlife—hedgehogs, birds, turtles, insects.

As they approach her, she is helping a small, shiny green beetle that had climbed up her cloak to safety on a thin limb of the closest sapling.

Makk speaks first as the two join Takver under the refuge from Nap.

"Takver, this is my bodyblood Gomba."

Takver doesn't say anything and then timidly darts her eyes away from Makk's gaze, blushing and looking down to the ground.

"Can you not understand me when I talk aloud?"

And then again, through sharing.

Can you not understand me?

I can't speak. You'll have to do the speaking for me. Some of your words are a bit different for me. So when you speak aloud, speak slowly. Sometimes your pronunciation is a bit tricky, too.

Makk squints their eyes and furrows their brow out of confusion. They have so many questions for her. But in due time. Then, they turns to Gomba.

"She can't talk. And she says we should speak slowly."

Gomba cocks his head to the side, a little confused. Then he looks at Takver.

Takver stares into Gomba's eyes. The look on her face can't be interpreted as anything but shock. She can't believe what she's seeing. Her brother Palat is standing in front of her. But, it can't be him. He's dead. He died, was murdered three Reawakenings ago. She saw his scorched body, held his limpness in her arms, her tears making streak marks down his soot covered face as they fell and rolled to the earth.

Gomba, avoids her gaze at first then returns his gaze, now directed at her. He silently curses himself as he feels his face go from umber to rouge. She is beautiful.

"She's saying that she knows you don't trust her. She doesn't blame you. You two can't merge, so therefore you can't bond."

Gomba directs his utterance to Makk, unable to take his

eyes off the enchantress. Like a moth to a flame, he can't resist the attraction that could end in his or his community's demise. The distrust of outsiders is deeply ingrained in his psyche.

"She can come."

Makk, shocked, steps back a little away from their bodyblood, recoiling out of surprise.

Then, Gomba turns to face Makk.

"She can come. But we still have to get her there. The other fetchers won't have it, but... And, then, comes the issue of the encampment...we either sneak her in or..."

Makk interrupts.

"We'll figure out the rest when we get there. For now, we hide her from the others. I'll think of something. And then, by the time we get back, the festivities should be going strong. It shouldn't be hard to sneak her past the overwatchers if they've had a bit of fermented honey water in celebration."

Makk winks at their bodyblood and then manages a smirk followed by a giggle. Gomba giggles a bit, too. The idea of sneaking someone into the camp is so exciting. Neither have ever attempted something so forbidden. Would they get away with it?

CHAPTER FOUR: TURNING

The sound of neighbors greeting your partner from across the path leading to your dwelling wakes you up. Nap is starting to take its descent into the horizon and neighbors are slowly getting up to cook breakfast. The smell of boiled root vegetables and grilled doughs fill the dusk air.

"Happy Turning!" Delores greets a neighbor, smiling a big toothy grin, one of her two very front teeth chipped and jagged.

"Good breakfast, Mester! Happy Turning to you! Looking forward to tonight's ceremony."

The neighbor to the left of your dwelling tips their woven hat in her direction, ubiquitous Átmeneti gear worn by day workers, mostly. Some activities like roof repair and other maintenance require the light of day and are usually started when Nap is at a lower point in the sky before beginning its daily ascent toward mid sky or in this case its nightly descent into the horizon. Few venture out during the scorching hours: overwatchers and foragers who have the cover of tree canopy, at least when the leaves are in full bloom.

You watch the interaction through the gaps in the thatched

wall from your hammock. You can hear other conversations happening in the general vicinity of your dwelling. There's a lot of excitement in the air already and Nap is only just now penetrating the sparsely leafed, upper canopy of the tree line that encloses the eastern side of the encampment.

You're due at the refectory to help gather kindling and firewood for the bonfires. If all goes as planned, the waterfetchers will be arriving within several hours. The festivities, however, begin in full swing as soon as Nap disappears completely. That's how it has always been since you can remember.

Year after year when the waterfetchers come back from the Old River with their offering of Life along with an identity of their choosing, the community comes together to throw them a big welcome back party.

Come, Test. I've made pumpkin porridge. It's still warm. The invisible string tugs at your chest and you hear your own voice inside your thoughts. It's Delores.

You know unmistakably that it's her. Her tug is unique, subtly distinct from Tejúti's but different enough. Tejúti's tug at the moment is more taught, distant. They are still on overwatch duty. They'll be home in time for the festivities. That's when their shift ends.

Both of your partners are your distant cousins and so you share some genetic make up, more or less fifty centimorgans or fifty million chromosomal base pairs. But you don't know that. All you know is that you can connect with them telepathically. So, you must be related somehow. Delores and you are fairly close cousins, however, you're probably Tejúti's fourth cousin or so, which means you'd share a fourth great-grand parent with them.

Normally, elders like yourself, Delores, and Tejúti are exempt from overwatch duty, but with preparations for Turning in full swing, the younger, stronger, more agile community members are needed for hauling wood, carrying heavy baskets of pumpkins, butternut, and other squashes used as the main source of protein in the extravagant dishes. Turning-Sixteen is the most lavish of the festivities and is when the Harvest stores are used up so they don't have to be hauled to the new settlement.

You're reminded that you're not particularly looking forward to this upcoming move. You've never quite agreed with the tradition of moving camp every year at the onset of Reawakening. It's a lot of work. Not to mention its origin is apocryphal, engendered in superstition that for your scientific mind has no basis in reality. A topic that you and one of your partners in particular, Delores, disagree on. She's always been a bit too superstitious for your liking.

You bring your focus back to the festivities. This is a time for celebration. And the festivities will do your people some good.

Some time has passed since those scorching marauders stole away someone very special to you. Tejúti still wakes up in the middle of the scorching hours, calling out for her. The link between them and Ursula has been severed. Ursula is your eldest child—an adult in her fortieth Reawakening—that was snatched away a few Holds back. That doesn't mean she is dead. She could be just out of range. You pray to Isten, more out ÷÷÷÷.≥≥≥of habit than actual belief, that she is only just outside of your telepathic field and that she isn't suffering.

Octavia, your second child—also an adult tens of Reawakenings old—Delores' egg progeny, has also lost the connection with Ursula. It's been really hard for her. All of this is to say that these festivities are going to be a welcome distraction. Ever since the waterfetchers set off on their journey, you've been preparing.

Out of all the celebrations, this might be your favorite. You know that it's Delores' favorite one. She loves weaving stories, and the ones about your community's inception she is especially good at telling them. They are very exciting after all, full of action and conflict: The story of the Last Ones. The story of the genesis of your community.

Delores is so damned good at telling them, too. Out of all the arts that she practices and mentors in, she excels the most as at storytelling. She practices for hours on end as soon as the waterfetchers leave the camp. After decades of telling the tales, one would think that she'd have a script memorized, but she likes to tell it differently each time. She really has a brilliant imagination.

I'm getting up, I'm getting up... You excited about your big day, Test? Your body aches as you slide out of the bedswing. Your body is telling you that you've been busy at work in preparation for the Turning. Your hands are particularly sore from all the peeling, slicing, chopping, and mixing.

The festivities begin tonight and last for several nights, usually four or five. The weather usually has an impact on the activities. You can only remember a hand handful of years when the rain and wind storms put a damper on the revelry.

What a disappointment those celebrations were, you think.

You look up at the sky. It's rather clear. There's no sign of rain. A little bit of rain would be welcome, however. Not too much. Just a bit is always welcome.

After you finish your squash porridge, you walk to the communal gardens to check on the seedlings. You notice how the peppers and tomatoes are sprouting nicely. You chose to start the Nap-revolvers (sunflowers) in the compostable pots this year as well, since the unexpected frost from last Sowing killed most of them off. You did manage to save a few, but not enough to fill the stores.

Málna, Makk and Gombi's eggblood, is filling the watering kanna from the Nap-faded blue rain barrel.

"Good breakfast, Test!" He pulls invisible energy toward his heart with his free hand. "We're going to have to beg the watermakers to use the reserves. I just used the last of the barrel water."

"Good luck getting a drop from them. I tried yesternight and your partner denied me. Maybe you can use your partnerly charm. My cousinly charmed seemed to have no effect on them." You close both of your eyes quickly, intermittently, indicating your playfulness. A slight grimace unfolds on your freckled, brown face.

"I think you'd have better luck. Bodza has been in a mood since Makk has been gone." He tips the barrel to get the last few drops from the spigot. "It really bothers them that we have no way of sensing them like we can Gombi."

"I'm sure they'll figure out how to connect eventually." You try to give some words of encouragement despite your own doubt about Makk's telepathic ability. "Remember, that one youngun who left the community a few decades back? What was their name?" You pause, digging deep into your long-term memory files. You're definitely feeling your age this morning. Accessing memories from that long ago is no easy task these days. You're well into your sixth decade after all. "Hegi, was it? They didn't get their ability until long after puberty. There's still hope."

Málna shrugs his shoulders, back still turned to you. "I'll finish watering the garden. Go on ahead and do whatever is left for preparations."

You thank him and head out past the watermakers' shelter. The sky grows ever darker. You notice the orange and purple hues in the eastern horizon. There's so much beauty in this world, even among the ugliness.

Where on this scorched earth can you be, Ursula?!

Your thoughts flash back to the day she was taken. You hear the echoes of her screams. The memory still fresh in your mind. If only you were younger, you'd still be out there looking for her.

The severed cord that lost its tug that day feels like a void in your chest. Will you ever connect with her again?

Those scorching marauders will pay someday. I'll get you back my Ursula. Just hold on. We'll come for you.

You mindspeak into the ether, wandering slowly toward the refectory. You haven't given up hope. Hope is the one thing those scorching bastards can't take away from you. Hope is your only weapon against despair. So, you continue to hope.

THE DIN from the festivities can be heard well before the overwatcher stops them and asks for the code—a necessary precaution for a truly xenophobic people. The dimly moonlit jugs of water confirm the identity of the approaching group. The three dogs running toward camp had been the first indication that the waterfetchers had made it back. But aren't there twelve travelers? Three dogs and nine humans. Where are the other two humans?

Makk and Gombi fell behind to make sure no one was following us.

Szilvi shares with the overwatcher who just happens to be their older bodyblood.

"Welcome back, Test! Welcome back to all of you sixteens! Happy Reawakening! Drink some honey pálinka for me!"

From the looks of it, you've already been helping yourself to it in abundance, Test! Szilvi giggles in silence as they gives their bodyblood a tight squeeze, exchanging thoughts. They kiss them on the cheek.

Do we ever have some stories for you! Szilvi shares.

Their bodyblood kisses them back on the right cheek and signals the others to open the gate.

"All is good. Open up!"

The gatekeeper unhinges the metal rod from the iron gate

—a leftover from the Old World. It's one of the few scavenged items from the forbidden dwellings left vacant after the Great Dying. It takes two of them to wield the heft of the cold, rusted, steel bars.

Several of the waterfetcher drop their heavy jugs on the ground and sit while the aperture to the community is opened.

Hold is in full shine and the night is truly beautiful. The sky is clear and the stars that other worlds orbit around peer down upon this once bustling Earth. There's a peacefulness despite the raucous clamor of music, laughter, and conversation reverberating from within the commune.

On the other side of the encampment, jugs in hand, two other cloaked travelers are being stopped while a third, draped in a blanket of sorts, sneaks past the lesser-used gate and stealthily darts toward the opening that they've been using for the past year to weasel in and out of camp unseen.

Makk has always been a loner and frequently sneaks out of the walled community to seek solitude in the nearby thicket. Not wanting to alert the overwatchers each time they scurries off, they created a hole in the fence-like wall near their unit's dwelling just small enough for their body to squeeze through. They sheds their blanket and pushes through the diminutive opening.

As Makk creeps toward the shelter of their intim unit, the smell of lángos fills their nostrils—savory, yeasty acorn flour dough deep fried in Nap-revolver oil. They can almost feel the texture of the chewy inside and the slightly crunchy outer crust. Their mouth waters for the juicy toppings—thinly sliced purple onions, nut quark cream, and garlic. Lots of garlic. A remnant of centuries past eaten at farmers' markets and during vacations at Lake Balaton before it dried up, lángos is something of an indulgence during special celebrations—during the Turning, Harvesting, and right before Alvás.

Makk's stomach begins to growl uncontrollably. Has it been

that long since they'd last eaten? With all the excitement, the trek back to camp from the Old River flew by like a hooded crow seeking refuge from the scorching hours, caught unawares by Nap's deadly rays as it lost track of time while feasting on its carrion lunch. All of the waterfetchers, and their new companion, will be feasting soon, too. That is if the Átmeneti aren't alerted to the presence of the unexpected—and probably at first unwelcome—guest.

Just as planned, and as Makk is putting on some clothes after having spent the trek naked and covered only by bed clothing, Gomba and Takver sneak into the dwelling. Makk stays merged with Takver the whole time and knew things were fine, as far as getting past the overwatcher gatekeepers, but is still relieved when the two cloaked figures appear. Makk takes Takver by the shoulders and hugs her. Then, they focus on Gomba.

"Do you think anyone suspects anything?"

Gomba shakes his head while removing his cloak, walks over to a hanging basket, and grabs a fresh change of clothes.

"I'm going to go wash up before joining the buli. I'm hungry and you both must be, too."

If it hadn't been for the buli—party or celebration—they most likely wouldn't have managed to sneak a stranger into the community so easily.

Takver admires her torch lit surroundings—tent-like, nettle cloth patchwork roof, vine-woven walls, and basket-like containers positioned all around the dwelling. Half-hung hammocks swing from a thick beam that is attached to an even wider tree from under which the hut-like structure was constructed. A different opening from the one from which they entered leads to the other half of the structure.

What's through this opening? Takver thinks to Makk.

The three had decided that it was best to keep her presence a secret from the other waterfetchers. Hence, she traveled in silence. That wasn't difficult because she can't talk. And, they kept conversation between the three of them—Makk interpreting Takver's thoughts aloud for Gomba—to a minimum.

The dogs would know she was around, of course, and hopefully wouldn't blow their cover. But the dogs hadn't seemed to be too concerned about the friendly human whose scent was all over Makk and Gomba. Also, it had been decided that Takver would follow the group while giving them a distant berth and staying off the trail and on the periphery of the Old Road. Makk and Gomba explained that they would fall behind the group to help keep watch of dangers that might approach from behind. Csipi and Raki would go ahead a bit and alert Geszti of any possible dangers. Geszti would then tell the larger group. The dogs, per usual, would also constantly go ahead and behind the group since that is what they did almost instinctively.

"Wouldn't it make more sense to have Cseri or Gyeri fall behind with one of you? Then, they could actually share the approaching danger with their bodyblood in the bigger group," Raki interjected, suspicious of the suggestion from the two bodybloods.

After several minutes, the group reached a consensus. Gomba and Makk fell behind the larger group. That way they were able to discuss how in the scorching Nap they were going to sneak a stranger into camp, in whispers of course. And what were they going to do with her once they snuck her in?

Takver enters the opening that is the threshold to a smaller thatched shelter. More woven hammocks hang from another beam. Fewer baskets line the vine walls. The raised floors are covered in more woven fabrics, thicker than the hammocks. Makk follows her into the room with the torch.

This is where our adults sleep. Now that Gombi and I have turned sixteen, after we move camp, we can choose to stay with our intim unit in their new dwelling or build our own shelter. We can start an intim unit as well if that's what we want to do.

Gomba, undressing and gathering water to wash up before changing clothes, speaks to the two from the other side of the divide.

"We need to figure out what to do with her. She can't just stay here out in the open. Oh, horsedong!"

"What's wrong, Test?"

Gomba, examining the crotch of his underwear, discovers blood spots. He's started his period, menstruation cycle. No wonder he had been feeling a bit hormonally off kilter during the trek back.

"I'm fine. Let's just figure out what we're going to do. We need to hurry. Our people are going to be wondering where we are."

As the night draws on, the festivities continue. Gomba goes off toward the bonfires to sit with his intim unit while Makk grabs a lángos fresh out of the frying pot and appropriates several pogácsa, biscuit-like savory pastries, in the deep pockets of their robe. Takver needs to eat, too. The lángos is a massive, circular doughy disk and can easily be shared by two people. The nut quark topping oozes down their arm, coating the sleeve of their nettle knit, long-sleeve frock. The spinach-dyed greenish ochre hue of the frock glows as they hurry past the flames toward the beech tree where Takver is hiding.

It's chilly outside, but not too chilly that a second layer is needed, especially for those sitting around the fire pits.

Takver is hiding in the perfect spot, halfway up a beech tree on the periphery, the edge of the camp. That way she is out of sight of the passersby and can get a clear view of the pop-up stage amidst the glowing embers of the bonfires. She won't want to miss the storytelling. Makk assures her that it is worth watching. But of course, she is anxious, and yet strangely relieved to be around so many people again. For far too long, she had been hiding and running. Alone. Always alone. Would the perpetual solitude ever end?

The beating of the drums comes to a sudden halt and then starts again but more slowly. This is the signal that the stories are about to begin.

Makk climbs down from the tree, crosses to the refectory, and joins their intim unit that is sitting near one of the fires. The invisible rope between Makk and Takver stretches and becomes a bit more taught than it had done since the two siblings met and shared at the Old River. Takver watches as several big and small people jump to their feet out of excitement and embrace Makk. Simultaneously, Makk lets her share the feelings of warmth and love that penetrate their body from the genuine welcome. Yet, Makk is giving off an vibe of distrust that Takver perceives as a negative sensation but no more nuanced than that.

Makk's netherblood starts to ask how the trip was, but there is no time for questions or any chit-chat at all. Just then, Old Mester enters the stage and stands in the center of the five bonfire pits. Her face flickers in the incandescent lighting from the roaring flames.

Silence all around. Everyone stares at the stage.

"There was, where there was not, across seven seas, over the high glass mountain, above the pits of poison that were left to us by the ones who came before and destroyed the world... there was...a Great Dying."

A tinge of blues and purples begins to overcome Takver's inward eye. They are very soothing and she knows they must be coming from Makk, shared intentionally or not.

There must be tens of stories that Makk has heard over and over again for as long as they can remember. This is one of the stories that they cherish the most, the story of how their community began hundreds of Reawakenings before.

Takver silently shifts on her branch perch. From the monumental beech tree, she stares down at the fire-illuminated community. She counts fifteen or so groups of three to five people gathered in the shape of a crescent moon with the five firepits at the belly. Whether the dogs understand the spoken words, they, too, rest among the humans. Takver must have counted a handful.

The old woman at the center of it all takes turns approaching the different fires. Barefoot, she carries a staff-like walking stick whose end from time to time she uses to stir red-orange coals from the various firepits. That sends up sparks, adding a dramatic flare to the tale she weaves. Even the youngest of children sit still and watch as the story weaver seemingly dances on her stage.

Although the old woman is the main narrator of the story, there are others who join her on stage. Some even dress in costumes that the ancient peoples wore before the Great Dying: long, thick, finely knitted bottoms dyed a dark blue, faded at the knees, tops with writing and images, a cloth head ornament with a piece that protrudes over the brow providing protection from Nap, items that are found in the trash heaps of old, buried under open areas used for human recreation long ago.

Takver herself had grown up hearing stories of how some of the centuries-old crumbling ruins were once vibrant, multistoried markets filled with room after room with variations of the same clothing. These buildings were massive edifices. Mechanical stairs and metallic and glass boxes that rose and fell moved hoards of stationary people from level to level. Massive corridors had been lined with shops and dotted with kiosks as far as the eye could see. Nowadays, most people didn't dare to go into these buildings in ruins. Entering or exploring the old buildings was strictly forbidden—bad luck. Curses of old would follow the families of those who broke the rules. But that didn't stop Takver's people. They were some of the few people who used the ruins. And look where it got them.

As the theatrics continue, Takver can sense an uneasiness coming from her long-lost sibling. She brings her focus back to the live reenactment. She will stop letting her mind wander so easily. After constantly being alone for years, she's come accustomed to living in her memories and thoughts.

Makk listens as Old Mester tells the trying tale of the original seven ancestors who survived the last massive wave of diseases and destruction. This, of course, isn't the first time they's heard the story of the Last Ones and the crucibles of their continuity in hell on Earth. In fact, this story has always been a part of their memory since they could remember comprehending the spoken word. Reawakening after Reawakening, Old Mester recounts the story when the waterfetchers return from their journey.

"The Last Ones hadn't always known true hunger or thirst, a thirst that burned in the throat worse than a skinburn from Nap's scorching touch. No. They hadn't always known those horrors. They had come from families of excess."

According to the tales, five of the original seven had lived rather comfortable lives compared to most humans that lived during their time. They were the children of the most prominent people in their walled city, one of those megacorp towns from the Old World where everyone who lived outside the innermost wall was somehow beholden to, or rather enslaved by the small group of wealthy proprietors and their lackeys inside.

The parents of the five teenagers worked for the megacorp as heads of the private security body that eventually replaced the publicly funded police force— peace force as they had rebranded themselves.—They worked alongside CEOs, managers, politicians, and others who worked behind the scenes to create media content that saturated the devices that almost everyone wore on their eye like a contact lens, just covering the cornea.

<Buy this! Buy that! Buy now!>, constantly popped up like the ads on the smartphones of the 21st Century, a hundred years before the Great Dying.

Messages like, <Almost out of stock! WalKoch credits only!> or, <Don't trust anyone! Your neighbor or your co-worker isn't your friend! If you need help, call a peace officer!>

And there was an abundance of peace officers. It was during the mid-21st century when the salary of peace officers, or rather obedience enforcers rose above that of anyone in the medical field, including anesthesiologists and even brain and heart surgeons, despite heart disease being on the rise.

It was a time of great wealth disparities, but even greater ideological cohesion, at least among the elite families. Members of those families held prestigious positions in the megacorp and its many institutions and lived in mansions on hills surrounded by impenetrable walls.

On the other hand, the workers who were paid in WalKoch credits only lived in makeshift shelters or run down warehouses below. And the workers were few, the unemployed were many, having been mostly replaced by automated equivalents. The WalKoch credits didn't get them through the month. Necessities like running water and access to other important infrastructure were a luxury that most couldn't afford. So, most workers, if not all, ended up borrowing credits from the megacorp bank. Credit debt was nearly impossible to pay back. The debt became perpetual. Two and three generations of workers inherited their family's debt.

Outside the walled city, the dominating forces used violence and the threat of imprisonment or even death to coerce the poor on a daily basis. Many of the working poor died during the construction of the walls that towered around the megacorp towns to keep out the hoards of unwanted transients who roamed from place to place looking for shelter, food, and work, anything that could provide them a little comfort. Yet, while most of the desperate people on the outside were trying to break through the outermost walls to get in, those five young sixteen-year-olds were desperate to run away from it all.

They'd decided to run away, once they were old enough to understand, truly understand how things worked in WalKoch.

How the machinist that maintained the robotic machines at the manufacturing plant that assembled the armored cars they rode in had to walk over an hour to get to work one-way, rain or shine. And how every weekend that same armored vehicular operated by ACE—the automated car engineer—collected the students from the indoctrination center and took them up through the winding underground tunnels to their palace-like homes. How the ANNs—automated nannies and nurses—had a hot meal ready for them in the dining room upon arrival. How they had never met anyone their own age that didn't live in a mansion on a hill. How was that even possible?

The monotonous subjects taught in the indoctrination centers trained them to be good little soldiers for the megacorp town: Managing the Undeserving, War and Profit, Generational Wealth and Debt, among others. Peace Keeping was the least favorite subject of Scrip, the youngest and most fervently vocal of the five friends. The idea that peace is something that you have to beat into people seemed riddled with paradox.

Among the inseparable five, each of them secretly had a name that they'd given themself. A name that reflected their skills and interests. Also, none of them identified with the sex that they had been assigned at birth. And, none of them dared to perform their true gender identity for fear of being burned alive like the people in the projections they saw in Peace Keeping class.

There was one particular projection from the year 2045

during what they called the Great Gender Cleansing. Transgendered women and men and gender non-conforming individuals were stripped naked, tied to poles, genitally mutilated, covered in some combustible viscous liquid, and then set afire, burned alive while hundreds, thousands of spectators stood around and watched, applauding while drinking their iced coffees and smoothies. Rows of children on a field trip sat in the front row, eating confections sold in the concession stands. That happened all over the world, as the history was told.

It was because of that projection in particular that the five friends discovered each other. They were the only five in the class that weren't laughing and sneering during the projection. And, after that lesson, they began to hang out. Each one realized that they were finally not alone. And, none of them could bear another school year of indoctrination, another day of being misgendered, another day of sitting next to classmates who thrived in school, who thrived under a hierarchical system that permitted them certain privileges so that they too could walk all over someone else, to have someone to compare themselves to, to make themselves feel superior, who talked about nothing more than their killing projection games, the promotions of their parents, and the new things they bought on the intrawebs. No. Not another day. Especially, not since Scrip introduced them to a short story that had been written over a hundred years prior.

They'd been lounging in the common area with about fifteen other boarders where the different dormitories intersected. The glossy white walls gave the room a sterile feel, a bright feel, despite the charcoal clouds in the sky and the cold, sharp rain tapping against the pane of the glass wall. White chairs with high, erect backs dotted the room, filled with studious bodies looking outward as if staring at nothing. Other students were sprawled out along the floor on white, styrofoam mats also gazing off into the distance.

But they weren't staring at nothing. No. They were all very much engaged with the device that cradled their cornea. Some were reading through their notes. There was a big test the next day and they were busy memorizing dates and names of events and people from long ago that they could care less about. Others were playing some shooting game or another. Those ones were obviously not reading given the ever-changing facial expressions that they wore, as well as the sudden jerk of the body as if they'd been hit by a projectile of some sort.

The ones studying sat still, not speaking a word. Although, some were listening to music while they worked on their memorization, occasionally bobbing their head to the beat. From time to time, people would get up to use the facilities, stretch, or just move around a bit. The place had the feel of a 21st-century university library, except for the pocket-less uniforms and lack of books or the absence of paper of any kind.

No notebooks. No bags. Why do you need a bag? Everything you need is on your eyeball and linked into your cerebral cortex. Hence, the lack of desks or tables.

Consumption was digital. The avatar wore the diamond necklace that someone's aunt Jessica bought them for Christmas last year. <Only 5,000 credits! Buy now!> Absurd! 5,000 credits could feed a downhiller family of four for at least a month.

The five friends, although they were in the same room, weren't sitting next to one another. They didn't like others to notice their closeness. They'd preferred to remain anonymous and not call attention to each other or themselves. But connected through their devices, they were constantly merged, messaging back and forth.

Hack, the eldest of the five, had a talent for coding and creating or breaking into virtual private environments where the five could communicate and feel mostly safe behind highly encrypted firewalls filled with booby traps for the unfortunate bot or person who tried to follow them.

So, even though the five friends didn't spend much time together physically, they made up for it virtually. But they never spent too much time in one virtual place. And, sometimes they met up in person. It was exciting, after all, to illegally congregate in non-designated areas.

Suddenly the devices zwoop, swish, and ping. Four of the five friends received a pop-up message on their eye projection. Scrip had sent them an encrypted message.

<Meet me n special place where the surveillance bots r blind. 5 min.>

Using the thought keyboard software that allowed the user to think of a word and select it with a quick eye movement, Ora sent the first text in response.

<What r u ↑ 2 now? Ur gonna get us in trouble>

Then, Tele chimed in, <This better b good about 2 beat this level>

Just like they had always done when they wanted to sneak away without getting caught, the five took staggered turns getting up from their spots and slowly walked toward the secret meeting place, making sure not to be too obvious.

Hack would configure a virus that would temporarily upset the system by scattering the location tracking and scanning of everyone for fifteen minutes or so. It affected everyone in the building, making it hard to identify the perpetrators. But the system did have a fail safe.

LiDar surveillance constantly produced a 3D scan of all rooms and all movement was tracked. This was standard practice at all indoctrination centers and most public spaces, such as the mega commercial centers. If someone was gone for too long from their designated space, they'd get a pop-up notification in their eye device warning them of their violation.

The five would have to hurry.

It wasn't the first time they'd held such an artifact, but definitely one of the few. The story itself was printed—in real ink!—on a sheet of fibrous material that they learned in school had been called paper. It was forbidden. It was exciting! Where on Earth had Scrip procured it? How did e smuggle it in? The uniforms had no pockets.

The five conspirators could remember stories their grandparents told about the stuff and how you could find it everywhere. Almost everyone who was anyone had had an ink printer at home with several reams of paper on standby. Newsstands sold folded-up stacks of it and had done so for centuries. Paper was used for everything from correspondence, advertisement, school work to grocery store receipts and for cleaning yourself after using the toilet. If you ran out, you'd just pop on down to the local grocery store and buy more.

That particular specimen was in the shape of one of those old fan zines that they'd seen in the WalKoch Museum of Antiquities. But it was about a quarter of the size and had only two sheets of paper. It smelled like the courtyard did in the Spring. Earthy. Ripe. Damp.

The title took up most of the front cover and competed with the realistic drawing of a medieval city on a body of water. It was colorful although very faded. There were some tears and folds. It was definitely old. It was definitely forbidden, therefore exciting. Scrip would be in a lot of trouble of it were discovered in eir possession. Every single one of them would be in big trouble. But they read it to each other anyway.

The Ones Who Walk Away From Omelas. Omelas. What a funny name. It might as well have been WalKoch City for all its similarities. Except that there was no sea in that megacorp town. And the people who lived on the hills didn't spend time together in the streets playing music and singing. And the filthy, puss-filled, sore-ridden child that was kept in a cellar in the story, could be multiplied by thousands. But those thousands lived downhill, on the other side of the wall. And the five friends wouldn't know to compare the child to the downhillers. They didn't know much about them or of the world outside their wall besides what they could see with their own eyes and, of course, what they were shown in the projections.

One of the main differences between the allegorical story and the reality of the five friends, as well as the other moneyed people who lived uphill, was the simple fact that children at the indoctrination center didn't learn about the reality of the people who suffered down below.

In the story, the children of Omelas learned about the miserable existence that the small child was forced to endure so that the rest of the people in the city could have happiness and prosperity. Those were the conditions of the magic spell. Children and adults alike would go down to the dank, dreary cellar and peek in on the terrified, lonely, sickly child. Some would even throw things at it. Kick it even. It! The very humanity was stripped away from the pathetically pitiable life of the poor, little one.

The worst part about the story, for the five friends, was that the truth about the child's suffering wasn't hidden. Everyone in that city knew that their full bellies and joyful lives depended on the misery of that lone child.

But why that child? Certainly, it must have *deserved* its lot in life. It must have done horrific things to be punished so. How else could it merit its dreaded existence? Was it so different from those workers that lived downhill in their own megacorp town, outside the wall? After all, that is exactly what they learned in their classes. The downhillers deserved their destitution.

There were the people, like them, the rich, the elite who had things because they deserved to have them. They came from proper stock and that status quo needed to be maintained. If the downhillers only chose to work harder instead of relying on the rich to give them handouts, they could live uphill, too. Right?

Every child learned that from the first day they stepped foot in the indoctrination centers. And how would they know any different? There was no interaction allowed between those that lived above and those that lived below. It was illegal. Forbidden.

Wealthy children had no business going downhill. The automated mega commercial centers uphill had everything they needed: digi-shops, foodcourts, 5D projection cinemas, and more digi-shops. There were no human workers to run those operations. Everything was automated.

If you wanted a bit of outdoor recreation, the parks and forests up above were more spectacular than those down below, outside the wall. At least, that is what they learned in the centers. Did they even have parks downhill?

Of course, kids were kids. And, the curiosity of the elite kids would get them close to the edge of the hills. But, the wall that separated uphill from downhill was only ever traversed virtually. 5D projection games allowed computer-generated exploration of the squalor and dangers of down below. No child needed to risk their life to venture down below to see for themselves.

Yet, after reading the story—the forbidden story in its forbidden format with its forbidden media—the five friends made a pact. They would find out the truth for themselves.

After weeks of planning, the five friends, Scrip, Hack, Boots, Tele, and Ora, decided to disguise themselves as downhillers and uncover the truth.

But what did downhillers look like? What did they wear? How did they interact? What did they sound like? Were they that different from the uphillers?

The fivesome didn't believe the images and stories of the downhillers that were curated for them in the projections.

Augmented reality was commonplace uphill, after all. It would have been easy to fake the reality of the downhillers.

With the lens in place, everyone's environment was augmented, superimposed upon with advertisements, flashing arrows that appeared to flow from your feet providing you with the latest update on the quickest path to your destination. If you veered from the path, the dotted line arrow turned from green to red and redirected you. If you strayed off course too often, the automated peace officer bot popped up in the middle of your view inquiring if you needed assistance and stopping you in your tracks. That is unless you were someone like Hack who always had a command at hand, or rather on thought, that minimized the interference and threw it off to the periphery. No longer obstructing vision.

But hacking into the system and making those around you see an augmented version of you only worked if they wore their lens. Someone without the lens in place wouldn't see your purple hair or the flashy outfit that you projected onto yourself virtually. They would see your white uniform if your a student and whatever the natural state your hair was in. Virtually augmented disguises would only work on the downhillers if the downhillers also wore the lenses.

Either way, the five wayfarers were not safe from the so-called peace officers that patrolled down hill. They would have their lenses in place, but they could easily deactivate a wardrobe and see what uniform awaited underneath. And, was wearing the lens or keeping a drone activated while out in public mandated there, in Downhill, like it was in Uphill? And how would the downhillers treat an uphiller if they came across one on a dim lit street? Not well if they were to believe the projections that they were shown in class and also in the games they played. Not if they could be identified as a possible rich brat whose recovery would be worth whatever amount of credits they demanded for their ransom.

Since Hack was the great purveyor of information procured through digital means, he was able to break through the firewalls that kept the uphill populace ignorant of the reality outside the wall. For a fairly hefty price, one of Hack's contacts among the downhillers provided him with intel on a transport vehicular that carried supplies and goods in and out of the walled hills through the vast subterranean interwebbed rail system.

Hack was excellent at tinkering with electronics and would have to disable the sensors in a specific food transport vehicular that was suspended in a loading bay under the indoctrination center. There would be a change of clothes for each of the five as well as a drone for each. Uphillers had had drones—antiquated technology—years before back when the five friends were just toddlers. But they would remember them well. They would know how to use them albeit clumsily.

Since it was during a week day and they'd only been gone for a few hours. No one missed them in the dormitories after hours. Before climbing out of their beds, Hack had disabled each of their tracking devices that had been implanted during the early days of their infancy.

One by one the five escapees snuck through maintenance corridors of the center and crawled into the maintenance shaft of the vehicular. The hatch clicked shut with an unsettling finality. An awful stench wafted into their nostrils and when they gathered their clothes they realized where it was coming from. Not only did they need to look the part, but they also needed to smell the part. Then, they waited for what seemed like forever until suddenly they felt the forces around them shift suddenly as if they had gone from being static to being in motion.

After exactly twenty-minutes, the hydraulic brakes huffed and puffed as the vehicular came to a resting halt. Was Downhill really within such a close reach? How could something so near seem so far away? When the maintenance hatch opened again, the five truth-seekers stumbled out of the vehicular. Once they got to the outside of the building, they activated their drones.

The things were no larger than a brick, but as light as a pair of glasses, and hovered right in front of their faces. The vertical blade spun so fast that it disappeared and in its place a series of graphics that augmented their reality appeared, much like the contact lenses but more analog and less hardwired to the brain.

"Noxious! This totally brings back memories." Ora was ecstatic about the retro device.

Tele playfully yet seriously jabbed an elbow into an elated Ora's side, "Shhh! Don't call attention to us!"

The night air was thick and damp. But not as damp as the street's surface. The potholes were dark, dank puddles with residue of petrochemicals-turned-rainbow glistening on the surface. Dim, flickering lights lined the outer street.

That particular street was narrow and was more of an alley than a street. And it was not something they were used to navigating Uphill. Up above, streets were designed for driving or being driven on. If you wanted to go for a walk or to go people watching, you went to the mega commercial centers. The streets were for the automated machines, the ACEs, ANNs, and other automated humanoid androids of the world. Those who were pedestrians relied heavily on algorithms to help them get around, mostly from one commercial center to the next.

Hack projected a digital map of the surrounding area onto the alley wall. As part of the package—exploring Downhill as a downhiller had obviously been a secret pastime for certain uphillers since there seemed to be an established market for it —Hack got them a list of suggested public places to which to go and observe without having to worry about standing out.

The alley led to a much busier street. They stepped out from the alley onto a sidewalk turning left to follow the overhang and wall. Somehow it was less disorienting to have a wall to lean on if need be.

There were few other humans in the street besides themselves. Pigeons were underfoot and cats could be seen sheltering under rusted, metallic garbage dumpsters and other rubbish tossed to the curb. The aural contamination was disorienting. Large, hovering buses that transported people en masse huffed and squeaked by, their wake splashing puddles of grey water onto the curb. Apart from the general traffic din of the nocturnal life of the workers and city dwellers, the street was rather mundane and uneventful. That was until they reached the commercial district.

For every tenth or so downhiller they passed in the street there was a peace officer a few paces behind. Their shiny, black uniforms reflected the dim lights that hung over the streets. Hack had been warned not to make eye contact with anyone, especially the uniformed thugs. Having been raised in homes of the heads of the institutions, all five of them knew all too well just how stern and abusive those officer thugs could be. *A strict hierarchy must be maintained,* after all. How else better to maintain one than with the threat of violence and other religiosocial coercive measures. *Honor thy mother and father.* A common household phrase. Even if they beat you and make you drink your own urine?

As the five approached the commercial district they noticed that there were shouts and chants coming from up ahead. More officer thugs were coming out of the woodwork, so to speak, and heading toward the crowds from where the noise generated.

Boots was the first to suggest that they duck into another alley. They needed to regroup. They had obviously stumbled upon a dangerously familiar scenario. They'd seen projections of the protests and manifestations and had even taken part in a few historical ones playing the part of peace officers. It was one of the favorite games in the indoctrination center. Plugged into the server via the lenses, the player, from the perspective of an obedience enforcer, got to wear the disguise of a civilian and wreak havoc upon the protestors. Any weapon was fair game. The sharp, broken end of a placard pole was a favorite weapon to bludgeon with.

Needless to say, the five, shaken friends knew how this would end. It wouldn't be good.

The chants seemed to be getting closer and they could hear the foreboding voice of the sergeant on loudspeakers from up ahead. As they ducked into the alley, their drone screens began to scramble and a picture of the sergeant, the top thug, appeared. It was a transmission on the emergency channel.

"This is an illegal congregation. Leave the area at once or risk detention and/or possible death. I repeat. This is Sergeant Vargas. You are participating in an illegal demonstration. This is an illegal congregation. Leave the area at once or risk detention and/or possible death. This is your last warning."

The sergeant wore a black, glossy uniform. Her helmet covered most of her face except for the area below her dark brown, broad nose. Her voice was harsh and unapologetic. She meant business and she knew that she and her entire force could get away with any kind of punishment they decided to enact on the crowd.

Suddenly, the general atmosphere in the distance changed. The so-called peace force began an offensive attack on the demonstrators. Canisters could be heard launching into the crowds, the sound of tin hitting the asphalt and then a hiss as the acrid gas spewed its poison toward the people who immediately began scattering.

After only moments, the area was transformed into a foggy battlefield. Piercing screams and the thudding sounds of solid material smacking against bodies could be heard echoing through the streets.

To further scatter the crowds, the police unleashed a spread of flash-bang grenades, an oldy but a goody. Those weapons were particularly sinister. First, a whooshing sound filled the air, then as the sound of a small metal box crashing into the pavement in the middle of a crowd, a bright light flashed, temporarily blinding the onlooker before a piercing bang rumbled their eardrums, causing permanent hearing loss if close enough to the source.

That was nothing like the simulated projections that the uphillers played as entertainment. Although the sight, smell, touch, taste and hearing senses were activated during the game, the simulation didn't even come close to the real thing. The poisonous gas made it difficult to breathe and burned the eyes of the unfortunate person who didn't have any personal protection equipment like goggles or a gas mask. Those items were difficult to come by Downhill, but those who had connections with the upper-ups in the second and third economies could procure whatever they needed for a hefty cost. A kidney, or maybe even an eye. The organ trade was still in full swing back then.

"Crap! What do we do now?" Scrip spoke up, eir voice trembling.

Excited to get mixed up in the chaos Boots interjected, "I say we go in there. Those people need help! It doesn't look like the protestors are being violent at all. It's nothing like the games portray it."

"Yeah. These people don't even have weapons" agrees Tele. Boots and Tele tended to be the more feisty ones of the group. But, again, their experience was solely based on projection games where you walk away in one piece and still breathing. That situation was much different. It was analog real, not virtually real. Someone could actually get hurt, could die.

Suddenly a group of fifteen or so downhillers ran past the alley. Five or six officer thugs followed close behind holding raised batons and yelling after the ones they were chasing. The officer at the tail end looked down the alley where the five disguised downhillers sought refuge as he passed by. He slowed his pace, passing the alley. And then suddenly he was there again, blocking the alley and raising his voice toward them.

"Hey! What are you doing out past curfew!"

Ora, who was always quicker on her feet when it came to making excuses for spending too much time out of designated areas, spoke up loudly but with a gentle, timid tone.

"We're sorry, officer. Our shift ended just a few minutes ago and we got caught in this mess on our way back to the...the...."

"...tenement!" Interjected Boots. Boots had been studying some of the linguistic features that the downhillers used for everyday things like where people lived, the foods they ate, and such.

It was dark and the alley was barely lit by the lights coming from the main street. The officer thug extended an arm straight out toward the cowering friends. A beam of bluish-white light shone from the top of the glove, blinding the five of them for a moment. The group flinched in unison.

"Identify yourselves immediately! What are your numbers?"

Just as their stomachs began to sink in terror, another officer came trotting by and stopped to talk with the officer that was interrogating them.

"Come with me! We need all the troops we can get at Pioneer Park. There's a full on riot there. This is going to be fun!"

The officer lowered the blinding spotlight and told them to get home or else. Then, the two officer thugs took off toward their new destination. You could hear the excitement in their voices.

They were indeed having a good time.

As the terrified five's dumbfoundedness slowly began

wearing off, someone cracked open a door a few strides behind them up the alley and called out.

"Quick! In here!" A hand waved them toward the opened door in a hurried motion.

"They were right to doubt what they had learned about the downhillers," Old Mester continued.

Old Mester and the other thespians on the makeshift stage continued to narrate and reenact the tale of how five of the original seven came to inhabit what is now the greater area they call home.

After that eventful, horrifying night, the five sixteen-year-olds never returned to their walled enclave Uphill.

In fact, they had gotten trapped with a slightly larger group of downhillers, surrounded by the violence and chaos they had witnessed outside the walls of the hideout.

And over the next few days they got to know that hideout very well.

Unfortunately, the majority of the demonstrations were quashed. The injustice enforcers and the wanna-be uphillers that stood beside them were eager to crush skulls, puncture flesh, and maim in any way possible. It brought them utter joy to cause such physical pain and psychological torment. And, as proverbial icing on the cake, their actions went unpunished.

If there were emergency medical services available to the downhillers, none came to the rescue. Injured and fatally wounded protestors could be seen seemingly flung about all along the west bank of the river and in sections all over the old financial center of the city and in places like Pioneer Park. Those among the demonstrators with emergency medical knowledge and experience were too overwhelmed to help all of the injured in need of attention. There were just too many people injured, especially after the bombings.

Days turned into weeks, and the danger in the city grew worse. It was almost impossible to escape the smoke from the smoldering ruins of the city. It was when the law enforcement along with the private military began bombarding the city with projectile explosives that the group decided to flee.

The downhillers and the people that lived in that particular city before the walls were erected had had a long history of providing mutual aid to each other in times of social upheaval. That unique moment in its history was no different. The bombs, however, were new for them. And old ways of doing grass roots community support and organizing weren't viable when buildings were being razed all around the city. People were forced to make a choice. Stay and live in a warzone, or flee to wherever they could find safety.

Most people left on foot. But the group of solidarity unionists, the labor organizers who took in the five uphillers in disguise, had connections with the dock workers. The dock workers were, after all, some of the most powerful workers when it came to industrial union organizing. When you cut off the movement of goods, you could easily get the attention of the megacorp executives.

And that city had always been an important commercial port. Since before the European marauders initially ravished, displaced, and murdered the local indigenous populations centuries earlier, the local people of the first nations had used the interconnected rivers for travel and trade. And, the city continued to be a major port up until the Great Dying. At least, that is what the stories told.

The five refugees and their new refugee companions found safety on a container dirigible that was headed halfway around the globe. That specific dirigible would sail against the western coastal current heading south until it veered east, crossing the lock canal before reaching the longest leg of the journey.

For those who had the funds to acquire the necessary credentials to travel by air, the same trip would only take a matter of several hours. But by sea, the trip was several days.

Few port calls were made, and even then, the stowaways were advised against leaving the dirigible. Several people did, though, of course. Some had connections in some of the southernmost sinking cities.

The five friends would follow their new companions to the journey's end where they would stay with other syndicalists who helped found a free zone. SzabadPest was one of its names. All they had to do was get there. But that wouldn't be easy.

"And so five of the seven founders set off. No credits. No pack full of provisions. They were completely at the mercy of those who gave them help with no questions asked. They did offer skills though. Each of the five went by names that they had come up with based on their most proficient skill set.

Ora was good at tale weaving and had quite the imagination. Ora's otherwise timorous demeanor would dissolve as soon as the storytelling began. And if Ora wasn't deeply submerged into an adventure projection through the ubiquitous ocular device, she was deep into making her own stories. Of course, that was forbidden and exciting.

Boots was heavy into fighting projections and spent no less than five hours a day submerged. Boots' love for combat probably stemmed from the fact that faer father was a combat trainer and headed the wing of the peace force that specialized in using sadistic weapons and extremely violent and unethical tactics for the goal of enforcing peace, or rather enforcing obedience. So, since Boots was able to walk, fae trained with the Automated Master that faer father kept in the home gym. The gym itself was about the size of six of the containers that they traveled in on the dirigible. One container fit about ten adults comfortably, arms stretched out above the head. About fifteen people were sardined into that container.

"Tele, on the other hand, was a..."

"AHHHHHH!!!"

Old Mester stops in mid-sentence, a loud scream coming from near the lesser used gate, the one that Gomba and Takver-pretending-to-be-Makk were greeted at when they arrived at the camp only moments, tens of minutes earlier.

There is trouble.

The screaming comes to a sudden halt, almost muffled. The people are first frozen from the abrupt pause. Then, from the tree, Takver watches as several people scurry to stand up from their cross-legged seated positions. Five or so adults take off in the direction that the scream came from.

Stay there, Tak. Makk is now looking in her direction. Enough chaos ensues around the bonfires that they disappears from their family unit unseen. *I'm coming to you.*

The dogs get to the gate first. As Makk grabs a hold of the lowest branch and pulls themself up, they gets a glimpse of the tail end of the pack running in the direction of their dwelling.

Just as the adults get around the corner past the garden, a motorized vehicular of sorts crashes through the iron gates. Three, four, no six more follow. The screeching sound of metal dragging against metal can be heard clearly across the encampment all the way to the refectory.

Upon hearing the shrill sound of metal, the roaring engines, and the barking and yelling, Takver freezes and ceases her inward conversation with Makk for an instance. It's all too familiar. She's immediately taken back to her compound, watching as the scenes of terror unfold. *Makk, we have to get out of here!* The look of horror on her face makes all the hair on Makk's body stand at attention.

What in the scorching earth is happening? What do you know, Tak?!

We have to get out of here! NOW!

I can't leave my people behind. I have to fight!

As the two scramble down the side of the beech tree closest

to the wooded edge, people are frantically running past them in all directions.

Makk looks back toward the refectory where the elders and the youngest children are taking refuge inside its great hall. It's part of the drills that the community does every so often during scorching hours. The safety committee has been administering these exercises ever since the raids began to increase a few years back. It's normal Átmeneti protocol. The elderly and the youngest of the younguns are to take shelter in the refectory. Hide. Run. Then, fight if necessary.

Back at the smashed gate, growls and barks turn to screeches and yipes. Several adults are splayed across the ground clutching their hands against their ears. While one marauder is working away at tying their hands behind their backs, another two vehiculars drive into the encampment.

You can't Makk. There are too many of them!

As Makk and Takver sneak into Makk's intim unit's dwelling, Makk catches a glimpse of Fur with their teeth locked on to a marauders cloak. A second later, another marauder is there with a metal pipe of some sort and swings it at Fur. It all happens in slow motion. The pipe connects with Fur's face and they fall backward onto their side, a loud thump as their body hits the ground. Fur doesn't move, while blood pours from their broken snout.

Makk begins to scream and run toward Fur who continues to lie motionless on the moonlit ground. Takver wraps her hand around Makk's mouth and pulls them into the dwelling backward. The two fall from the force, Takver underneath a struggling Makk.

Several other wounded dogs limp toward the various adults who are held in some silent but seemingly painful trance. Five, six, no seven marauders work almost methodically, tying up the helpless adults.

Under the smashed gate, three dogs lay dead. The other dogs are either missing, severely wounded, or dead, too.

Makk is kneeling on the nettle mat flooring near the half-hung hammocks. Tears pour down from their face as muffled wails squeeze through the cracks of Takver's fingers. Her hand is soaking wet from the first warm, then cold saline tears.

We have to get out of here! Takver repeats in silence. Red hues flashing through Makk's mind's eye.

After getting a grip on the reality of the situation, Makk scrambles to stand up. Their gear is in the corner, already packed from the waterfetching journey. Makk grabs it. Takver peers through the cracks in the thatched walls. Fires are being set to various dwellings along the corridor of the camp. Tens of marauders are dragging the helpless people, adults and children all incapacitated, to the vehiculars.

As they creep through the back exit of the dwelling and out through the aperture that Makk had created many Holds back, Makk sees their people being thrown into the vehiculars, stacked on top of one another by two or three of the marauders.

And just as Takver tugs at Makk's cloak to pull them back out of view, Makk catches a glimpse of the shiny, ring-like objects a top the heads of two of the marauders, and blurts a choking whisper.

"Those scorching rings again!"

Then, the two refugees are off, Makk's home in flames growing more and more diminutive as they run deeper into the forest.

PART TWO: THEN

CHAPTER ONE: THE BUNKER

T*he...ther...*
There. Takver pronounces the word as it appears on the page. Makk follows along with their right pointer finger.

There w...ass ey wahl... Makk continues.

That's it! Just practice the sounds we've been studying. You already have most of these words in your repertoire. Just let the sounds trigger the words that you already know. I'll read and you follow along. Takver takes the book from Makk and places it gently on her lap.

Both are sitting on a moss-covered log outside of the bunker. The weather is pleasant enough to be outside with just a long-sleeve frock. Although, it's cool enough that Makk feels their nipples get a bit unyielding and decides to go inside and fetch their cloak.

I'll be right back.

Makk slides off the half-rotted log. It's a bit damp from the midnight rain. It's nice to be outside just sitting for a change, before retiring for the day. And, since the brunt of the scorching hours will soon be upon them, they only have less than an hour before they have to be inside.

It's been almost an entire Hold cycle since that horrible night that Makk lost everyone; well, almost everyone. They still has Takver.

Makk comes back outside, snuggled by their warm cloak. They reaches out their hand up toward their sibling.

Give me a hand will ya, Tak?

Takver marks her current page with a dry, brown leaf and closes the book, reaching her hand out to her sibling. Once Makk is sitting back in their original spot, they pulls out some dried berries wrapped in a piece of nettle cloth from a pocket on their cloak.

Here. Have some dinner. They hands the berries to Tak. Then, nervously, *I think it's time we go looking for them again.*

She puts the little package of berries on top of the book on her lap, looks over to Makk, and grabs their hands and holds them in hers.

Okay. When should we leave?

Takver knows all too well the desperation that Makk is feeling. She too lost her family to some scorching marauders and spent months looking for any traces of them. Alas, after twenty or thirty failed attempts she gave up and accepted that she might never find them. Makk wasn't at that point, yet. It was still too fresh.

Well, first I think we need to finish planting the rest of the seedlings and sow the new seeds now that the threat of frost seems to be behind us. Then, we can venture out.

A few days earlier, on their way back from searching for Makk's stolen people for the third, no, fourth time, they spotted an area perfect for a garden. It's not too close to the bunker—they don't want to call attention to themselves by having a garden plot too nearby—and it gets plenty of sun but not too much. Plus, the river is only a few minutes away. It'll be a lot of work to haul water, but it'll be worth it if they can grow some food to store. Of course, once they plant it, they'll have to watch out for marauders who might lie and wait, watching to see who is tending the garden. They'll have to be clever.

In one of their trips back to the ruins of Makk's former encampment, Makk managed to salvage some of the seedlings that they'd planted back before the waterfetchers set off on their journey. It brought Makk comfort knowing they still had a little piece of their old life. Any comfort is welcome at this point.

It sounds like we have a plan, then. Takver shares, patting Makk on the left leg. She is so patient and doesn't let Makk feel her feeling of hopelessness. After all, she never found her people. *Let's finish up this chapter while we still have some light. We can figure out the details for the search later.*

She opens the book, tucking the leaf bookmark between the last page and the back cover, still intact despite the torn, missing front cover.

She starts up where they left off, at the very beginning. Makk follows along mindlistening as Takver mindreads the words on the pages. The author is describing a wall that is made out of stones that were mortared together.

What's mortared? Makk interrupts.

It's an old technique that the people used to build with before the end of the Old World. It's kinda like the muddy clay that some people use to seal their dwellings with.

Takver continues. The wall from the book that she's describing is not anything unscalable. Rather, it's such a low wall that kids are known to climb on it and play although they know they shouldn't.

Hold on. Makk interrupts again. *What's the point of having a wall if a child can easily climb over it?*

Just let the story tell itself. Takver shoots Makk a playful glare and then smirks. *You'll find out. I promise.*

As the story opens on a physical wall that does little to deter people from literally crossing over it, the protagonist, Shevek, faces the difficulty of un-building walls. Thus, the stories unfold as he endeavors to traverse a more metaphorical wall that most of his xenophobic people figuratively struggle against. Some even literally try to stop him.

In the very first pages, the author introduces a paradox. An anarchistic people, the Anarresti named after the planet Anarras which they inhabit, who don't know coercive force at a systemic, societal level—they have no prisons, no police force, no cages—but some of who at the same time enact the ultimate form of coercive force—death—as a mob of Anarresti throws rocks and kills one of their own while trying to stop Shevek from boarding the cargo ship set to return to the neighboring planet, Urras. The literal wall represents the metaphorical wall that Shevek is trying to unbuild.

Although Ursula Kroeber Le Guin wrote the book in the late, mid-twentieth Century, almost two-hundred years before the Great Dying, people are still building walls. Of course, the people in her book are fictional, but the challenges that they face are very realistic and relatable, even roughly four centuries later on a non-fictional Earth. And, there are still walls. Makk's people had walls. Little help those walls ended up being. Given enough time, no wall is impenetrable against water. The marauders were like water.

Takver continues. As she reads, the words describe the different preparations that Shevek was making as he prepared to leave his world to unbuild the aforementioned walls. He'd just seen off his partner Takver and their children...

Makk almost intuitively grabs the finger that Takver is using to run along the bottom of the words as she silently reads aloud.

Takver? Makk's sudden cognitive dissonance turns into pleasant surprise, *That's you!* Their grin stretches from their left ear to their right one. It's special that something so old and so rare as a physical book can have familiar components like a simple name.

Takver mindgiggles. *The mother loved this book so much that she named me after her favorite character. I really like the name, too. It sounds good in my head.*

This is not surprising to Makk. Some of the names that the Átmeneti give themselves come from the characters in the stories they have been told throughout the centuries: Delores, Hack, Tele, Ora, Scrip, and Boots, just to name a few.

Although Takver and Makk share a lot of the same contemporary practices—mindspeaking, foraging, water collection, mostly nocturnal activity—the people of Takver's community didn't consider themselves Átmeneti. Therefore, the stories of Delores the martyr and those of the Last Ones that were passed down from previous generations in Makk's community weren't popularized in Takver's community and vice versa. So, Takver was a new name for Makk. In fact, the first time they'd heard it was when they first met beside the Old River, not too long before now.

Takver's people aren't, *weren't* Átmeneti because they weren't Nap-nomads like the Átmeneti, changing settlements every completed year. Instead, they lived for generations in a federated village called a falus that traded with other villages on the westside of Duna as they call the Old River. On the other hand, Makk's people have, *had* always established their temporary encampments to the east of the Old River, ever since the frigy (treaty) over twenty Reawakenings before. In fact, the frigy established boundaries that could be and were only ever crossed if there was an immediate need to see Old Tátos—a shaman of sorts, among other titles—who chose to live as an isolated hermit to the east of Duna. Of course, many thought the Tátos to be a witch. But what is a witch but someone who uses uncustomary means of getting what they needs? Takver was a witch, then, sneaking around by herself, living alone in a bunker beneath the ruins of a house from the Old Times, before the end of the Old World. Makk's people had called it the Great Dying.

Both Makk and Takver grew up hearing stories about the forest shaman: Old Tátos could steal your thoughts, ate wandering little children, had thirteen fingers, and on and on. The truth is that not many people knew much about Old Tátos except that they could perform miracles during a breached birth or put the life back in a babe who didn't come out kicking and crying. Legend has it that Old Tátos brought eggbloods who had died in childbirth back to life, more than once.

Takver and Makk gather their things to go back into the bunker. They have means of seeing in the dark and prefer only to use candles inside during the day. The simple glow from a candle at night could attract the attention of a wandering marauder. Takver managed to go unnoticed by avoiding unwanted attention to herself following that principle. So, they decide to go inside and continue their reading. Scorching hours are here and it's time they go inside anyway and prepare supper before bed.

Takver arranges the kindling just like the mother taught her, alternating the direction that the parallel sticks face as she stacks them. Dry leaves and twigs help ignite the kindling which then sets fire to the larger logs. Makk hands Takver just one log.

Do you need more than this, Tak?

It's not safe to use the woodstove during the day. Smoke can be seen from a long ways away for both the watchful and the unexpecting eye. They wouldn't use it for long anyway, just long enough to boil some water for tea and porridge. The warmth of the fire will also heat up the bunker just enough to take the chill off. The scorching Nap will do the rest once they are in a deep slumber.

Makk sits down on their make-shift sleeping pallet and goes through their knapsack looking for the satchel of dandelion root that they had left over from the waterfetching journey. They dig through the interior pockets, pulling out other satchels of herbs, spices, and the like.

So, did your eggblood ever tell you how she lost me? I mean, she must have lost me. I ended up in a completely different community.

Makk has been wanting to ask this question for some time, but the string of events that led them to this new life in the bunker took priority.

She always said you were switched at birth. She swore that old witc...do you know about Old Tátos? Do your people talk about her?

Takver swings around from facing the stove to look Makk directly in the face, holding the jug of water.

Oh, do we ever! But, they are not a she in our stories. They are many. And, whenever we're being naughty, Stop it! Or else I'm going to throw you to Old Tátos! *Typical threat! We grew up terrified of them.* Makk smiles at the memory.

Well, the story goes...

It was an unusually rainy Hiding. Makk's biological eggblood, Shevek—yes, the same name as the protagonist from the book. Fitting since she was an advocate for unbuilding walls, as well—lay in the infirmary with a fever, her long, dark hair matted around her face with sweat. With every sharp contraction, her screams echoed across the compound despite her weakened state. The falu-orvos, a woman from a neighboring compound and the only village doctor nearby, stood over her, holding a bundle of smoking herbs.

"She'll have to go to the shaman." She looked at Shevek's sisters, the closest kin Shevek had and with whom she shared living quarters in the compound, "There's nothing more I can do."

They would have to cross the river, but if they could get some help carrying her, they could get Shevek to Old Tátos within an hour. The two sisters recruited the help of a distant cousin and their eldest child. Between the four of them, they carried Shevek. The spermblood, Shevek's partner of many years, had been one of the latest victims of the disease that was killing off people in the village. Her closest family was small, but that didn't mean she was alone. Her people helped each other out despite biological ties. The village took care of the village. It had been like that for hundreds of Reawakenings.

On the other side of the river—and unknown to Takver and Makk, even to this day—the same disease was ravishing another community. And, it just so happened that another pregnancy was in peril. Makk's eggblood, Málna, was being taken to Old Tátos. His doula lay sick with half of the other Átmeneti. It was a dark time for their people, so much sickness and death, an awful time to give birth, let alone to twins.

No one skilled in the ways of birthing was well enough when he suddenly began to experience excruciating cramps in his pelvic region. They were so bad that he felt like he was going to tear apart and everything inside was going to come gushing out. He'd never experienced such agony. As he stumbled across the refectory in panic and in so much pain, the blood staining the front of his frock alerted his fellow scavengers that something was terribly wrong.

Minutes later, he was put into a pushcart and was on his way to Old Tátos. Luckily for him, and the babies, their camp was only a short distance from the old recluse's shanty, less than an hour's foot.

The mother said she didn't remember it, but when the two groups converged on the gated shanty at the exact same time, Old Tátos was there at the gate, as if expecting them.

The shanty was small and felt even smaller with all the hostility and panic in the air. The Átmeneti group at first refused to go anywhere near the westsiders despite being familiar with the conditions of the treaty. But in the end, the urgency of the moment took priority over the deeply-rooted xenophobia.

Moments later, the cries from the two sets of not-quite-identical twins could be heard all the way to the river.

That's how I knew you were my sibling, Makk. I look nothing like Palat. But you and I are so so alike.

With all the chaos and Old Tátos tending to both birthers simultaneously, something must have happened and Makk and Palat were switched. Makk and Gomba ended up with Málna. Palat and Takver were kept with the sisters while Old Tátos treated the mother, who spent several days at the shanty and eventually recovered.

Delores and Tejúti stayed with Málna all the while in a temporary shelter that they constructed nearby the shanty so that the shaman could tend to him without the three of them having to share space with the westsiders.

Of course, Palat should have gone with Málna and Makk with Shevek. But, alas, that was not their fate.

Since we were young, the mother suspected something had gone wrong that day. You see, she was never able to merge with Palat, nor was I.

I could never share with Gombi either. For so long I thought I was broken. Tears flow down Makk's puffy cheeks. *I thought there was something wrong with me my whole life. I was so lonely.*

Well, the mother knew from very early on that something was wrong. She felt a connection with me, that familiar invisible tugging thread, but not with Palat. She knew her baby had been taken away from her. She always talked about you, her little Bedap.

She named me? Why didn't she ever come for me? Makk feels something like betrayal begin welling up inside them.

She did! But your stubborn people refused her. More than once! She eventually had to give up. At least, that's how the stories go.

Now, Takver is embracing Makk, their tears creating a puddle on the shoulder of her frock.

She always kept you in our memories. 'My three babies,' she would say, 'Takver, Palat, and dear, sweet, lost Bedap.'

And Palat was taken with the rest of your people?

Silence.

Takver's eyes well up, *No*. A few moments pass. It feels like an eternity to Makk who is gobbling this all up. *I found him.* Now, she is sobbing.

Makk embraces her, holding her tightly and rubbing her back gently. Her tears drench the collar of their frock.

After a few moments, *those scorching scorchers killed him, burned him! I hate them!*

Makk lets go of Takver for a moment, reaching for their knapsack. There are some pieces of nettle cloth in there somewhere. They wants to give Takver a soft fabric to dry her tears with. Fumbling through the bag, they reaches into a deep pocket and brushes up against something hard. The ring is wrapped in the nettle cloth. They slowly pulls it out of the knapsack.

Suddenly, something across the bunker begins thumping and banging against the pallet where Takver sleeps.

Takver and Makk start and are quickly on their feet. Takver instinctively puts herself in front of Makk, in a protective stance.

"What in the scorching earth?!" Makk blurts out aloud.

The shaking continues. Takver creeps over to the pallet bed, hesitantly, and grabs a hold of the blanket that is covering the jumping box. She pulls it back, revealing the tartó box.

Tak, what the dry earth is goi...

Now, she's holding the yellow box. It shakes in her hands and she just stands there, mouth dropped, staring at her sibling in confusion and disbelief. Her eyes dart from Makk to the box and back.

The box had never moved before. Until now.

CHAPTER TWO: HELL

As you slowly regain consciousness, the throbbing in your head makes you wish you were still knocked out. It feels like something is trapped inside your skull, pushing up against the bones, the muscles, the skin, trying to get out.

At the same time, the lower fourth of your body is being crushed by something, *someone*. Gasping for air, the smell of urine and feces chokes you as you come out of your forced coma. The pressure on your chest is too much. If only you could push yourself onto your side. But your hands are tied behind your back. And, there is no room on either side of you, just more bodies.

Presently, you become acutely aware of a strange, continuous humming sound. Vibration. It's coming from an engine, but you wouldn't know that. You'd never heard an engine until these recent events. You have no name for such a thing. There are sounds coming from all around you. Moans. Weeping. Dry heaving. These sounds are human. Occasionally, bursts of laughter, also human, can be heard a bit farther away from the cacophonous chorus of pain and suffering.

You try and reach out to share with your partners. Nothing. Both invisible strings connecting you to them are there, taught, very taught. Your partners are alive, but not physically close. Normally, you can sense them as long as they stay within a certain radius of you.

You can feel the emotions begin to well up, tight in your chest. At least, they are alive. But, what happened to Octavia? You can't feel the connection between you and your second child. You call out to her.

"Gyermekem! My child!"

Silence.

Suddenly you become aware of your olfactory senses again. Besides the urine, feces, and sick, there's another smell lingering in the air. It's not smoke, you're familiar with the smell of burning wood. It's some kind of combustible. Not smoke. In fact, the last smell that you can remember as you, the other elders, and the younguns were forced out of the refectory was caustic smoke.

Suffocating smoke and heat were used to flush you and your community's most vulnerable out from your hiding place. Then, the ringing inside your head and the sudden pressure. The pain knocked you unconscious. Your face smashed against the pebbles as you tripped over something, *someone*.

Now you're here.

Where is *here*? You think.

You are in motion, although your body isn't moving. The occasional bump sends you and those around you up in the air, crashing down again. More moans. There is sobbing, too. Lots of sobbing and sniffling.

"Gyermekem!" You pause. "Anyone!? Can anyone hear me? Say your name and skill."

Your voice is muffled through the stacked bodies.

Just as you begin to hear a few people beginning to answer your call, the vehicle comes to a halt. You and your bound companions are jerked around. Someone's knee jams up against your nose and mouth. Instantly, tears well up in your eyes from the sudden, acute pain. You can taste iron. Several of you release guttural groans.

In the near distance, you can hear deep voices, although you can't make out what they are saying. And then, there is more squirming and shifting around you. Then, someone starts screaming. Then, a loud thud sound. The screaming stops. You hear gasps and then crying.

The deep voices penetrate the pile of bodies surrounding you, but this time they are laughing between unintelligible strings of murmurs. Now, more shuffling of bodies. Two bodies that were smooshing you are hauled off you, suddenly.

With the instant relief of pressure, your diaphragm instinctively inhales a profound, painful breath. You feel your lungs fill with air. Through your blurred vision, you can see what looks like continuous, fuzzy, incandescent lights like from a fire pit but up above you shining down.

A large, uncloaked figure grabs you by your bound hands while someone else takes a hold of your legs. They pull you to the edge of the vehicular and you drop to the floor. All of your own weight seems to crush your right arm and shoulder. You yell out in pain. Someone kicks you in the back. It's not a hard kick. More of a warning of sorts. Still cruel.

You can hear the groans, moans, and whimpering of people all around you.

You try to get a better look around, but your vision is still quite blurred. The pain is unbearable and you wish for nothing more than to be in your hammock, convalescing. But you need to assess the situation. Who is here with you? Who brought you here? Where is here?

You take in a deep breath and focus inward. You try to sense the nexus between you and your partners, but the pain is just too much to bear. Instead, you switch your focus into your body. Does anything feel broken? No. Can you see who is around you? Yes. You count five large figures, obviously at work unloading bodies, people, most likely your people from the vehicular. You can't make them out very clearly, but they look tall and broad. You can't tell if they have facial hair, or if they are wearing some sort of adornment around the front of their necks. Your damned eyesight hasn't been the same since the eye clouding began several Reawakenings ago.

You keep looking around. You can make out some of your neighbors, about ten of them. But, there are some bound people near you that you think look familiar, no you're sure you've never seen them before. *Do these scorching marauders just snatch random people from other settlements after burning down entire encampments? Scorching rotters!*

You realize now that you're inside some sort of expansive structure from the Old World.

In fact, the building you are in was a transportation hub for many centuries. You guess that based on the confluence of iron tracks running along side the walls of the once-glass enclosed building. It's still dark out given that the only light is coming from what seem to be mechanized lamps. You realize now that it's not fire but some form of artificial light. You grew up hearing stories of this kind of lighting, but you'd never experienced it until now. Most of the technology of the Old World has rested, out of use since the Great Dying, as far as you know.

Like in all other parts of the old urban center and its once suburban outskirts, vines and other foliage have taken over the structures, most of which are in ruins. This building, however, has seemed to maintain its structural integrity over the centuries.

As you look around, you notice that a group of people are being lined up and their bondages removed. Then, you begin hearing the screams.

At the front of the line, two marauders are busy at work.

One of them is holding a struggling person by the left arm, while another brandishes an iron rod that glows orange on the end that is then stamped onto the right hand of the person from whom the screams are originating.

What the scorching hell!

From seemingly out of nowhere, one of the marauders grabs you from behind and is standing you up. But you are very weak and you almost pull the marauder down with you as you fall back onto your rear end. Then, you hear a whack, too close. Pressure fills your head. As the pain begins to envelop your whole being, you fall unconscious to the hard, cemented ground.

You awake to a throbbing pulse on the right side of your head. The dull reverberating ache makes it difficult for you to open your eyes, but you manage to squint. You seem to be lying down on a somewhat soft surface. A blurred figure is hovering above you. You can't quite make out the image. You keep squinting and blinking, trying to adjust your vision. Then, you notice an excruciating sensation coming from your right hand. You try and raise it to your line of sight, but you're too weak. Then, someone is talking to you.

"Easy, Ondi. Just try and relax." It's your youngest child, you think. "Here, drink some water."

She puts a gourd jug up to your mouth and you drink.

She's alive! You think, swallowing a gulp of tepid liquid that tastes a bit earthy. It's not refreshing at all. Then, you open your mouth. "Octavia?"

You try and sit up. You're still too weak. You relax your core and give in to whatever you're lying on. It's rigid, but there is some give, maybe a blanket of some sorts.

"Gyermekem." You repeat, but softer this time. Your head is

still pulsating, making it hard to really focus on anything but the pain, making it impossible to initiate sharing, but you can receive.

The figure draws close to your face, her beard tickling you as she embraces you in a way that isn't too obvious for onlookers, "Shhhhh, Ondi. Don't draw attention to us."

Then you get a good glimpse of her. Sharp nose. Chubby cheeks. Long eyelashes. Her thyroid protrusion is pronounced.

"Urs..." You begin to shout out and then quickly remember the warning. "Ursula?!" This time a whisper. "My Ursula! You're alive!"

CHAPTER THREE: THE MISSING RING

Takver squats and sets—more like tosses—the vibrating box down onto the hard, porous floor of the bunker between her and Makk, trying very hard not to just throw it. The box clanks and bangs, seemingly jumping about by itself. She looks at Makk pleadingly, as if they has the answers to the mystery behind its movement.

At almost the same time, Makk throws the ring down on the floor, almost instinctively. It makes a muffled ding thud as it makes contact with the hard surface through the nettle cloth. The box suddenly stops moving. Then, the ring is glowing yellowish orange, like the butts of fireflies that hum throughout the forest floor during the nights of Hiding. It's not a steady radiance, but rather it dims and then intensifies and then dims again, repeating this over and over.

Neither had ever seen artificial light before. Naplight, Holdlight, firelight, starlight, and bioluminescent light that some insects emit are the only forms of illumination they are used to —Hold, the ancient satellite that orbits Earth, reflects the light from the dwarf star that they call Nap. So really they are one in the same. Some of the artificial light fixtures that were prominent in the Old World are still present, albeit nonfunctioning. Even inside the bunker, there are broken lightbulbs that Takver was never curious enough to investigate.

It all happens so fast. And when Takver finally is able to gather her thoughts coherently, she sends a red flashing hue to Makk.

What is that thing, Makk? Wh...why is it on fire? And what in the evil scorching Nap is happening with the tartó box?

Makk is just staring at the glowing ring as if it has them mesmerized in some sort of trance. A slew of images are flashing through their head. At the camp raid, some of the marauders had rings on their heads. And before that, the marauders near the Long Road had a ring. The waterfetchers asked Makk to carry the ring since it didn't incapacitate them when they touched it as it did to everyone else save the dogs.

Now, the ring and the tartó box are affecting each other somehow.

Makk's thoughts come back around to the present. They stares at the glowing ring and the now-unstiring, yellow box, faded from centuries of exposure to the elements.

What's in the box, Tak?

Takver kneels to the floor, hovering over the box. Her heart feels like it's going to beat right out of her chest. The pulsating glow from the ring adds to the already flickering lights from the candles around the bunker. The moment feels ominous, almost prophetic. This box has been handed down in her family for generations. She was told to keep it safe and to give it to her children. She's never understood its contents. *Is that all about to change?*

Takver unfastens the clasps that help hold the box's seal and slowly opens it up.

The box is no longer shaking, but the strange little clamshell case, about a quarter the size of a Rubik's cube, is glowing, pulsating blue. The two Old World apparatuses are reverberating in sync like they share a heartbeat.

Makk and Takver are staring at the glowing objects in silence. Even their mind connection is silent. Then, Makk interrupts the silence.

Tak, where...how...what in the scorched earth is this stuff?

This box has been in my family for generations. It's where I keep the book.

She points to the rectangular impression on the charcoal gray foam, inside the empty imprint in the shape of a large ring.

I don't know what the other things are for or where they came from. They've always just been in there.

Makk moves closer to the box and rubs their finger along the hollow crevice that frames around the book's indentation, a perfect circle. Then, they stares intensely at Takver. And, without mindspeaking their intentions, they reaches behind themself and grabs the bare ring, the cloth lying in the same place that it had been dropped.

The ring stops glowing immediately with their touch. Simultaneously, the glow from the small case inside the tartó box changes from an intermittent to a steady photonic emission. The two mechanisms are definitely communicating with one another.

Makk and Takver look at each other, their mouths slightly open in awe of what they are witnessing. Their eyebrows move up toward their hairline. Then, suddenly, the little case begins vibrating and, all at once, the ring follows suit. Makk quickly places the ring in the hollow impression, dropping it as if the ring is hot to the touch. But it isn't. It is cold despite the warm light it emits.

It fits perfectly. And, in an instant, both devices cease to glow.

Takver quickly reaches over and slams the lid of the box. It closes with a snap. She turns to Makk.

Tha...that, that thing, that ring...Where? How? What is going on, Makk?!

Now, the two siblings are facing each other on the floor. As their eyes adjust to the dimness in the room now that the devices have stopped glowing and the box is closed, they sit there and just stare at one another.

After a moment, Makk begins to start processing their thoughts in real-time.

Tak, some of those raiders...those scorching killers had rings just like this one on their heads! I saw them, Tak. The candlelight glistens off the fresh tears as they drop like icicles melting in the scorching hours of late Alvás. Except these drops are filled with rage and regret and what-ifs.

Takver watches as Makk's posture goes from rigid anger to limp resignation. She cups their cherubic face and notices for the first time that the once lighter peach fuzz on their upper lip is darkening in color and is a bit more coarse. They raises their gaze to meet hers. A tear falls on Takver's left breast and is absorbed quickly by the soft, nettle-cloth frock.

My poor Makk. She's now embracing them, gently patting the nape of their neck just above the collar line. *Let it all out, Sib.*

Sib was a cute nickname she'd created for them. Makk felt a bit formal and they is her sibling after all. Sib just sounds right. Makk likes it, too.

We've gotta go and find them, Tak! We just gotta. Makk repeats over and over again in between sobs. *We just gotta, Tak. We just gotta...*

Takver pulls herself away from the embrace and gently takes Makk by the shoulders and stares them in the eyes. Now, her face is filled with determination. The muscles in her jaw flex.

We're going to figure this out, Sib.

She gives them a gentle shake, and her expression changes to a look of epiphany, eyebrows relaxed and lips bunched to one side. Makk looks up, their eyes meeting hers.

Where did you get it? She's looking at them almost distrustfully.

Makk is staring off into the distance, remembering that day, *The marauders that attacked us on our way to the Old River dropped it. My group decided that I would carry it since I didn't seem to be affected by it like they were.*

Silence. Then Takver continues her train of thought, *There is obviously some connection here. It can't be a coincidence that you happen to have that, that ring thing and I have this box full of gadgets that seems to want to communicate with it. Call it luck if you want, but I say we try and figure out what the scorching earth it could mean.*

Just then, she flings open the lid of the tartó box. Makk turns to face the box. The two of them stare at the contents: a pair of metal tweezers, a glass vile with a strand of what looks like black, coiled hair, a small, shiny, obsidian, crystal case in the shape of a clam, shiny coin-sized disks that sparkle in the dim light of the bunker, and a metal ring made to rest on the head like a light-weight crown.

Hesitantly, Makk picks up the clamshell case. Their adrenaline kicks in a bit and their heart begins to race. Goose pimples begin to form all over their body as they feels their skin tighten and the hair on their arms raises toward the sky. The sensation is similar to when they bites into a fresh lángos or when they first dove into the stream that day back when they met Takver for the first time. It seems like forever ago.

The clamshell is cold. Its geometric angles and weight distinguish it from a live clam; the latter is rounded and heavier. As Makk picks it up, it begins to emit a soft glow, blue and pulsating. And, then, the ring starts glowing as if answering the call from the clamshell. Makk sets the clamshell back into its place. Then, they carefully and methodically takes the glowing ring from its molded groove in the foam using both hands, balancing it as if it were a fragile memento, and they were afraid it would shatter into a million pieces if dropped.

Are you certai... Takver begins to interject a thought before Makk cuts her off with a quick glance that says, 'I'm doing this no matter what!'

It's cold to the touch despite the yellowish-orange glow that emanates from it. And it's so very light in weight. Makk nervously places it on their head, their hands visibly shaking. As they lets go, leaving it resting on their crown, the clamshell opens mechanically slow.

Takver watches as all this unfolds. Her eyes are as big and round as those of an owl lurking on a tree branch while scoping out the underbrush for its nighttime breakfast. The hair on the nape of her neck and her arms stand at a point, her skin tight and full of goose pimples.

Inside the clamshell, there is a hexagonal, miniature plinth and a cylindrical one, both about the size of a large, adult human thumb, and protruding upward to the same level as the bottom half of the case. The one toward the tip of the clamshell, the farthest from the hinge that joins the two halves, has a slot opening in it that runs parallel to the hinge in the back. The plinth closest to the hinge is rounded on top and emits a small intermittent blue light. It's almost as if it were trying to communicate with Makk, 'start here,' 'pick me.' Atop the convex plinth lies a transparent, quarter orb that looks like someone took a hollow glass sphere the size of a marble and cut it vertically into fourths, keeping one of the rounded bits and tossing the rest. It shines like a jewel as the light from beneath it penetrates upward.

Instinctively, Makk touches the hollow, quartered marble with the pointer finger on their free hand. And to their surprise, it sticks to the tip of their finger as if it were a magnet and their finger steel. This seems to make Makk feel a bit uneasy because as soon as they realizes that it's attached itself to them, they begins to shake their hand to make it fall off. They is careful not to drop the clamshell that's in their left hand.

What the scorching...?! They sucks air in through their clenched teeth, making an inward hissing sound.

But it doesn't fall off. The hard, glass-like lens has adhered itself to their finger.

Takver gasps and sends a red hue in panic to Makk, *Sib! What the...does it hurt?*

But it's obvious that Makk isn't in pain unless they is just in shock. But then something remarkable happens. Something so out-of-this-world that the two siblings freeze, their mouths agape.

A light source appears to be coming from the rounded plinth on which the lens rested. It's not just light though. No. Rather it's an image of sorts. It's as diaphanous as the thin fog that gets trapped among the trunks of the trees in the dense woods. Wispy. Fluid-like.

The fog image isn't much bigger than a glass bottle from the Old World, used to store refreshments and other shelf-stable liquids. And as the blue, 3D image becomes even more clear with crisp lines, it becomes obvious that it is a facsimile of a person. Well, at least the diminutive figure is humanoid. The face has lines and there is some signs of sagging around the eyes and sunken cheeks. Their button nose is broad with a low bridge and their eyes are oblique, almond-esque. In contrast to the aged visage, their body is erect and toned. Their flat chest moves, bobbing up and down as if functioning lungs and a diaphragm could be found underneath the photonic flesh of this being made of densely packed light particles.

The thing that stands out the most to Takver and Makk is that this person, this little radiant person that appears to be little more than fog, is dressed in a full-length, skin-tight bodysuit. Light from some invisible source reflects off the glossy, scintillating yellow material as the person is standing, back straight, and gaze forward. It doesn't even occur to Makk to even consider gender, because gender is something that only holds meaning in specific contexts.

Hypothetically, if this person—was it a person? If this facsimile was trained to be a storyweaver, then Makk might assume that it, *they* prefers to be a she, per, or they. For those are the pronouns that Makk associates with those skill sets, despite hypocritically arguing with their brother about associating pronouns with skills. Also, with the exception of pers, storyweavers like to keep their hair long mostly for performance reasons. There's a lot you can do with long hair. If you want short hair, just pull it up and wear an old cap like the baseball players of ancient times. It isn't obvious to Makk at this point what skills this person has or whether they celebrate Hold during its full phase. Therefore, it's, *the person's* gender is superfluous. For Makk, the style of clothing and the alabaster skin of the projection are salient.

It is a projection, after all.

Takver's face goes pale and she turns to face her sibling. Makk just stares ahead at the projection. A million thoughts are running through their head, and they is too distracted to merge and share with Takver.

"こんにちは (konnichiha). 你好 (níhǎo). Bonjour. Hallo. Hello...." The projection begins greeting using a series of linguistic features, some of them possibly extinct. But Makk and Takver had never heard such sound combinations before now.

'Hallo' and 'hello' are features that can be selected from a vast linguistic repertoire that the inhabitants of the region use to do languaging with. Languaging is an act, a social practice, so, therefore, it's a verb. Languaging is something people do.

The particular linguistic toolbox, with its collection of linguistic features, is used all along their area of the Old River, or Duna as Takver's people call, *called* it. It's the main means of languaging by Makk's people, besides mindspeaking. It doesn't have an official name among the Átmeneti. They just refer to the act as nyelving, which means languaging. Takver can understand when others do languaging using features from nyelving, but she is used to a selection of other linguistic features that were more common among her own people. And since she has been self-isolated for almost two years, she had been out of practice. Now, spending time with Makk, she's gotten used to the linguistic differences again.

Makk turns to face Takver. Their eyebrows raise and their mouth gapes open. They has completely forgotten about the lens on the tip of their right index finger. They reacts aloud, "What the scorching earth, Tak?!"

"Linguistic features recognized. Thank you. Please continue with integration." The mouth of the image moves slightly out of sync. The voice quality is human, but the intonation and the inflection feel mechanical somehow. And what it muttered is mostly intelligible to Makk and Takver. But it just doesn't look at them directly. Instead, it just looks forward as if seeing something off in the distance past Makk and Takver.

Both of them are now staring at it again. And it's obvious that at some level the thing is interacting with them. Then it continues.

"Please place lens on cornea for full integration."

Makk instinctively talks back to it, surprising even themself, "Cornea? What is a lens?"

It hesitates and then responds, "A lens is a spherical object made of thin material used to interface with the optical nerve." The voice now sounds a bit more like Makk's voice. It's like the image/person/thing is mimicking them. Learning.

"Lens location activated. Standing by."

Suddenly, Makk remembers the lens resting on their pointer finger. It's now glowing, pulsating a light blue. Then, the projection repeats itself but using more colloquial vocabulary, "Please place lens on your eye."

"My *eye*!?" Makk interjects.

They draws their finger that holds the lens closer to their face as if to inspect it more closely. Their heart is racing and feels like it's going to jump out of their chest.

And in an instant, before Makk can realize what's happening, the lens seemingly leaps off Makk's finger and lands smoothly into their right eye.

"WHOA! What the...scorching earth! Wha...What the!!" Makk jumps up from their seated position, cupping at their right eye.

Takver jumps up, too, *Makk!! Are you okay?*

Makk stumbles backward and trips over themself and falls onto the edge of Takver's sleeping platform. They is flailing their feet and grasping at their face.

"Thank you. Interfacing with optical nerve. Please stand by." And, then, a few seconds later the avatar speaks again, "Integration successful."

Makk is sitting on the floor, legs sprawled apart and face staring off into the distance. Their chest heaves up and down, as if they're trying to catch their breath. Their head is cocked slightly to the side. Takver recognizes the look on Makk's face as awe and wonder.

She saw that look before in them when they first entered her bunker. Despite being terrified and in shock after seeing their entire encampment pillaged and then running away, helpless to fend off the marauders, even after all that, Makk refused to enter the dwelling. Even after the long, exhausting trek there, after fleeing for their lives, their superstition had that much power over them. Takver had had to pull them down the ladder through the opening. Occupying ruined buildings from the Old World was a forbidden act that the Átmeneti took very seriously. Of course, Makk had broken the rules before when they were younger, but they had sworn to themself that they'd never do it again. After all, curses would follow the perpetrator as well as their entire community.

Now, Takver is tugging at the sleeve of Makk's frock. Their body moves back and forth as she pulls them. But there is no reaction. Makk seems to be in a trance. Their eyes focus on something distant, as if they is daydreaming or revisiting a memory. Then, without looking at Takver, Makk studders aloud.

"Tak, aszta kurv...aszta..." Their mouth hangs open, drawing out the aw sound of the word. "Tak...this...this is so amazing, Tak!"

Merge with me, Sib! The message reaches Makk. But something seems to be distracting them. They isn't sharing back with her.

At this point, a spike in epinephrine gives Makk an adrenaline rush. Their heart is going to jump out of their chest, yet again.

Superimposed onto their dimly-lit surroundings in the bunker, Makk watches as a high-resolution digital layer of pixels begins to form. It doesn't block out what they sees in the bunker. Rather, it's as if they is seeing the world through a piece of transparent glass that has vibrant markings and 3D icons strategically positioned around the periphery of their line of sight.

Instantly, about a meter from Makk, the same avatar from the projection appears directly in front of them. Although, instead of being a diminutive projection, this version of the facsimile is life sized. It seems to Makk that the avatar is standing in the room with them. And, this time, it, *they*, is making eye contact with Makk. Takver is directly to the left of the avatar, staring at Makk. She obviously doesn't see what Makk is seeing, or else she'd be just as stunned as they is.

The various icons seemingly float, hovering still in various places along the margins of Makk's vision: a copper and tin contoured object with a long, shiny, black stem made for grasping, a blue, fibrous, flat sheath folded in half with the letters *j-o-u-r-n-a-l-s* on it—Makk struggles to read it—a musical note, its meaning also unknown to Makk, and another flat, rectangular covering labeled *b-o-o-k-s* which Makk *can* make out. They unknowingly sounds the words aloud, lips rounded then flattened, "buh-oooooh-ks." The "oo" is a rounded *ooh*.

The salience of the 3D icons is brilliant compared to the muddled, candlelit objects that are physically scattered around the bunker within their frame of view.

Then, the avatar begins speaking inside of Makk's mind.

Welcome. Please stand by while initialization is completing.

A few second later, *Initialization complete. At any time you require assistance, use the visual call icon in the upper right quadrant.*

The avatar points in the direct of the icon. Makk follows the indication. A small bell in the top right corner of their line of sight begins to pulse, and Makk hears—mindhears?—*ding, ding, ding.* They'd never heard or seen a bell before and don't have a name for it. But its function seems obvious enough.

Then almost automatically Makk mindasks, *How do I make it do that?*

Makk starts a bit, surprising themself. They is mindspeaking with the avatar. They'd only ever mindspoken with Takver. This is new. All of what is happening is very new. Another rush of epinephrine spurts through their body.

Please focus on the icon and will it to move.

Makk focuses their gaze on the bell and gives it a command using mindspeech, *Move.*

Ding, ding, ding.

A shot of dopamine rushes through Makk's body, making the hairs stand up on the back of their neck. They is suddenly overcome with a sense of accomplishment, having been chemically rewarded.

Well done. Remember, I'm just a call away if you need assistance. Good bye.

Then, the avatar disappears. The section of the bunker they'd occupied is vacant but unchanged. This all happens in less than a minute's time. Although, to Makk it seems like several minutes have passed.

Makk finally blinks and then their gaze shifts to meet Takver's eyes.

"You have to see this, Tak."

Takver is losing her patience. Makk knows that look all too well. Her furrowed eyebrows and squinted eyes remind Makk of the times they'd sit by themself pretending to mindspeak to the person in the shard of reflective glass they'd found on one of their scavenging trips. They kept the piece of mirror wrapped in nettle cloth. They'd take it out from time to time and make different faces. Frustration was one of them. Also, mirrors weren't ubiquitous among their people. It was a novelty.

Can you merge with me already!

Takver is shooting daggers at Makk with every glare.

"I'm trying and I can't seem to send my thoughts."

Makk is concentrating, a similar look on their face as when they is squatting in the latrine after eating something that didn't sit well in their digestive tract. Wrinkled forehead. Squinted eyes. Clenched jaw.

But, nothing. They can *receive* from Takver, but can't *send* anything to her. At least not right now. That will change. So, Makk spends the next twenty minutes describing to Takver what they has just experienced: the avatar, the icons, how everything they sees looks like it's in the room, but obviously it can't be.

What kind of magic is this? Makk thinks to themself.

Off in a corner of the bunker near the floor, a small patch of green moss covering a clump of fungus begins to glow, a green hue silently pulsating. But the weak light that it emits eludes the attention of the two siblings before fading away completely minutes later.

THE SCORCHING HOURS are coming to an end. The temperature outside is becoming more and more bearable with the setting of Nap. It's been several sleeps since that day Makk and Takver unearthed the long-dormant technology that has changed their life in many ways. The days are getting longer now that Reawakening is in full swing. They are planting the last of the seedlings and the seeds in their garden not too far from the Old River. Any spot far enough away from camp that gets good sunlight is exploited.

While the waning dusk light holds its last breath before exhaling into the night, Makk plants a variety of Nap-revolvers, the ones that tower over the tallest yearling saplings, in some sections in a clearing. Along with them, they plants some beans and squash. The bean vines will eventually climb up the stalk as the flower grows and the squash will help keep the weeds at their foot at bay. The indigenous ancestors of Turtle Island started growing this way with corn, beans, and squash millenia ago: the three sisters, as they called the medley, were all different in personality and in appearance, but together they were strong and helped each other grow. Makk's people also believe, *believed* that, like the three sisters, together their people were a force to be reckoned with and that only in community could they flourish.

A large mammoth wasp buzzes by Makk's face as they is squatting down, covering the seed with soil. They waves it away, then picks up their makeshift watering kanna, dousing the seeds with cool river water.

If Makk were with their people now, they'd be slowly settling into their new encampment and spending lots of time in its garden. But that isn't how things worked out for any of them.

Where are my people? Makk thinks, *it's time to go looking for them again.*

On their way back to the bunker, Takver is walking a few paces in front of Makk along a new path she is creating as they go. The earthy smell of forest debris fills her nostrils. The ring is resting on her head and the lens sits on the cornea of her right eye. She is giddy. As her eyes focus on a specific plant or insect, a bubble with the common name and taxonomic classification pops up, superimposed on an invisible layer, as if hovering above the object. She stops and squats down to get a closer look at a caterpillar inching across a leaf.

<Kingdom: Animalia; Phylum: Arthropoda; Class: Insecta; Order: Lepidoptera; Family: Nymphalidae; Genus: Danaus; Species: D. plexippus; Common name: Monarch butterfly; Life cycle phase: Larva>

This brings her so much joy and awe that Makk sporadically mindhears her *oh*-s and *hehe*-s.

Makk is quieter than usual, she notes. Then, out of nowhere, Makk interrupts the mind silence.

I think we've been going about it all wrong.

A few more moments pass as Makk gathers their thoughts. Takver gives them space to do this at their own pace. She's distracted, admiring her augmented surroundings.

If I were to kidnap an entire community, I wouldn't want them escaping and finding their way back to their old home so easily. I'd want to make it much more difficult. I'd take them far, far away.

Especially, if I had whatever things they had that they used to crash through our gates.

Takver isn't audibly acknowledging what Makk is saying, but they knows she is paying attention. There is this way of tugging at the invisible thread that connects them that is much like when someone nods their head as a visual acknowledgment. So, Makk continues.

We have to go further. There's a long pause. *Or, we could go to Old Tátos.*

This makes Takver stop in her tracks. She quickly jerks around to make eye contact with Makk. Her big, round eyes and pursed lips tell them that she's concerned about something they'd just mindsaid.

Then, Takver breaks the mind silence.

How is that old witch going to help us?! She is good for nothing! She switched you and Palat at birth! I'll never forgive her for taking you away from me!

Old Tátos know things, Makk quickly comes back.

I'm desperate, Tak! What if they could tell us something? Maybe they've heard things. It can't be a coincidence that both our people have been taken from us. Our people are probably not the only ones who...

Takver interrupts.

She will expect payment. What do we have to offer? I'm not giving my first-born child to that witch.

Is that even a thing?!

Makk is almost furious. Their hands are shaking a bit. A look of bewilderment flushes across their face. Then, they relaxes.

Why are you so afraid of them, Tak? Is it fear?

Takver is now looking Makk in the eyes. Her gaze is intense. She scoops up their hands and holds them in hers.

I don't trust her, them, whatever!, Sib. That's all. And...yes, I'm a little afraid of them. Aren't you? You've heard the stories.

I'm not a little youngun anymore, Tak.

Makk's facial expression is stern.

I don't care about the stories. I need to know if they know something. Anything!

Makk pulls their hands out of Takver's grasp and turns away. They kicks at a fallen tree trunk with their right boot that they recently salvaged from a landfill a few hours hike away from the bunker.

I'm so tired of not knowing, Tak.

Now, they is looking at her again.

Please?! Will you please come with me?

Suddenly, Takver grabs at her lower abdomen, feeling a gush of warmth between her legs. She knows that sensation all too well.

We need to get back to the bunker so I can clean up.

Makk, assuming what has happened based on Takver's reaction, nods in agreement.

Okay. We can talk about this later.

Then, as if remembering something exciting.

Can you start reading the journal entries when we get back?

Takver nods, indicating her agreement.

Makk squees as they hops into the air before doing a little skip out of sheer excitement.

The rest of the walk back to the bunker is done in silence.

OUTSIDE THE BUNKER, the last of the evening light disappears through the cracks of the lowest layers of the forest. Inside, Takver is resting on her make-shift bed while Makk is preparing a snack for both of them: some foraged medvehagyma or ramps and steamed hosta shoots make a yummy salad.

Takver is fully immersed in the device. She's admiring the

different icons that seemingly bob in place around the edges of her vision. A few days prior, when Makk was playing with the ring and lens, they'd discovered that the folder that was labeled j-o-u-r-n-a-l-s was empty. But with the help of the automated avatar, they was instructed to insert the crystalline disks into the clamshell case. The small plinth with the slot acted as an optical reader. Once inserted, the previously empty folder is populated with hundreds of journal entries. By now Makk is getting the hang of their recent introduction to written word literacy. However, they still struggles from time to time and needs their sister's help. At this point they hasn't figured out that the device has accessibility features. Makk will eventually activate them and be able to listen to the journals while they are weeding and do other tasks for which they needs their hands. But, for now, Takver has agreed to mindread the journals to Makk.

Because her mindspeaking skills are much more developed than Makk's, she has no trouble merging with them while she's connected to the device. On the other hand, Makk struggles to send to Takver but has no trouble receiving from her when they interfaces with the antiquated, but-for-them-futuristic technology.

As she lies prone on her palette bed, she stares up at the ceiling. The ring rests on the crown of her head. It is so light that once it's in place she quickly forgets it's there. The same goes for the lens that is on her right cornea. In the upper right corner of her vision, a folder icon with the journals is floating alongside a few other folders. She moves her eyes to the journal folder, concentrates, and it opens. Suddenly, a three-dimensional wooden structure with several shelves vertically atop one another appears directly in front of her, replacing the images of the folders. She starts, letting out a yipe, and, then, intuitively stretches out her hands, palms out, to stop it from falling on her and squashing her whole body. Having such a formidable structure seemingly dangle above her precariously brings out some instinctive reflex in her. After a few seconds, she relaxes, remembering that the only physical thing directly above her is a rusty steel ceiling—the bunker is probably half a millenia old; it's surprising that it has managed to maintain its structural integrity this long.

As she examines the virtual bookshelf, she can smell the simulated varnish that was used to polish the wood from which it is made through digital generation.

Do you smell something, Sib? She mindspeaks to Makk who is boiling some water.

"I'm using fire," they says aloud. They's been using their mouth to speak more and more these days, especially when they are both in the bunker. They misses mouth talking with their intim unit. They especially misses Bodza. They has, *had* always had a strong connection with them.

Takver acknowledges them with a tug at the unseeable rope that joins them telepathically. She decides to just go with it. This device, this seemingly magical instrument is capable of activating not only her visual and auditory receptors but it somehow interfaces with her other senses as well.

All of this happens within a matter of tens of seconds. When she brings her focus back to the bookshelf—she doesn't have a name for this type of shelving unit—a series of bound realistic-looking notebooks begins to populate the shelves. They pop up into her vision like kernels of popcorn bursting through their thin shells from the oil and heat combination. Along the binding of the notebooks are words written in a shiny, metallic color, similar to the color of Nap when it's at its highest in the sky.

She focuses on the letters on the binding of a book labeled <A Leky család>, The Leky Family. Then, out of nowhere, an enormous image pops up and blocks out most of her vision. She can still make out the edges of the ceiling in her visual periphery. Once she is able to regain her focus, she realizes that the image is a book, much like the one with which she uses to teach Makk to read. But, this book has both covers intact and it is lying open as if it were resting on a hard surface and she were standing above it looking down upon its pages, which look more white than the pages of her book, the latter being more yellow and dingy. There is a visually perceptible fibrous texture to them and she can smell the all too familiar smell of sweet and earthy pulp mixed with something acidic and adhesive. There is no musty, fungal smell though, unlike the one that seeps from the actual physical book with its missing front cover.

As she stares at the once-blank pages, black words begin to appear at a slant, covering both pages and leaving enough white space to resemble the format of a journal. It's so real looking she could reach out and hold it. Although, at this close up, it's huge and would weigh a ton. Looking at the words, at first, she can't make them out. She squints a little and tries to refocus. Then, as her eyes move across the augmentation, the words change form and she slowly begins to understand them. It's like as if vowels and consonants are shifting order and spacing in real-time, except for there is a bit of a lag. Eventually, she can scan and focus on random words and they have meaning to her. The technology has seemingly adapted to the features in her linguistic toolbox.

She shakes her head as a quiver shivers throughout her body. The hairs on her arms stand up. She can't help but be physically overcome by the sensations that envelope her entire person while she watches magic happen up close. She scans back to the top left margin of the left page and begins to read. Meanwhile, Makk is trying to connect with her and is feeling a little left out. For, it is taking Takver quite some time to get to the point where she can start reading.

"I'm ready when you are." From a prone position in their

palette bed across the bunker, they turns and looks at Takver who seems to be in a bit of a trance.

She starts mindreading the first line: *Leky Katalin 1-8-7-4-.7-.2-7.*

As is typical of Makk, they interrupts her, "What do those numbers even mean?"

I don't know. Just let me read will ya? She loses her patience a bit and, then, quickly repairs. *Sorry. This thing has all of my senses on edge.*

The numbers don't mean anything to her either. So, she just continues to read. She's merging with Makk; they can see what she sees. So, they follows along as she reads.

Monday, July 27th, 1874

It's my birthday today; I just turned sixteen. What a way to wake up on your birthday! I had a vividly frightening dream last night. My dear Erzsike and I were picking berries down by the river. It was sunny like it always is this time of year. All the different kinds of pollinators—birds, bees, butterflies, wasps—were dancing around the berry bushes. We were also dancing and spinning to the sounds of tango harmonicas and fiddles playing our favorite tunes. We both wore new, flashy dresses and bonnets. Baba, my dad's mom, had just finished the embroidery on mine a few days before. It was mostly red; my all time, absolute favorite color. The smell of freshly cut grass, green on the scythe was thick in the air. It was strange. We were all together. The whole family. Even Erzsike was there. We were getting married! It was a celebration to remember. It was impossible! A woman marrying a woman??!! In *my* family??!!

Then, suddenly, we were both whisked away into a new scene. The sky was full of dark clouds and the wind blew ghostly sounds around us. The smell of a swampy bog was thick. I was holding on tight to a piece of clothing, an apron, but my grip was slipping and I knew I couldn't hold on for much longer. As I looked up toward my dear Erzsike who struggled to hold the other end of the apron, I could see her tears streaming down her dark, silky face. "Don't you dare let go!" she screamed with desperation. The pit of muck that was what was left of the great Danube threatened to swallow me whole. My new dress was black and torn. Then, I heard the voice in my head, resonating through my very being. "This isn't how your life ends."

Then, I woke up.

I hadn't had a dream that scary and vivid since we've been gone. In fact, now that I think about it, I've been having lots of dreams lately. I often wonder if I dreamt the whole mushroom thing.

Anyway, it's been exactly three weeks since we were forced to find shelter away from our villages, our families. Mamma must be worried sick. I have no way of contacting my family, and my dear Erzsike is in the same position. But, that doesn't matter. What matters is that we're finally together. I wish the circumstances were different though. This is the first time that I'm writing about what has happened to us. I never before felt compelled to write down my thoughts, document my experiences—It hasn't helped that writing supplies are hard to come by. But, I've—we've—been fortunate to find some. Yet, after I dreamt that fantastically terrifying dream, the voice in the forest told me to write down everything that I can remember.

Start a diary. It said almost desperately. *Write as much as you can. It's important in more ways than you'll ever know.*

The voice. Yeah, let me start there. About a week ago, I was doing some wash out back behind the barn that we've been staying in. I was kind of just staring off into the distance when I saw something glow a few paces in front of me. It was daylight, so the glow wasn't very intense but it was odd. So, I put down the garment I was scrubbing and went a bit closer. I thought maybe it was a piece of metal or something reflecting the sun. When I got closer, I realized it was a mushroom. A glowing mushroom! Then, suddenly, it stopped glowing. But a bit further away, closer to the edge of the woods, another source of dim, green light began pulsating.

I got down on my knees and brought my eyes closer to the mushroom. The smell of the forest detritus was strong and pleasant: dank and earthy. The mushroom's glow began to go from pulsating to steady. Letting curiosity overcome me, I touched the glowing mushroom.

And, then, I heard it speaking to me, but I didn't really hear it. At least, I don't think I did.

Don't be afraid.

At this point, I thought I had lost it. I guess the mushroom sensed my desire to flee.

Don't go. Please. Don't go, Katalin.

I didn't recognize the voice.

How do you know my name? I asked.

You won't understand if I told you. But, please, just listen to me.

What...who...are you?!

At that point, I began looking around me to make sure Old Farmer Pál or Erzsike weren't around to see me falling off the deep end. But, then I realize that no sound comes from my mouth. My lips don't even move. I'm talking inside my own head.

My name is Bedap. I'm from a place far, far...

"Hold on a second." Makk interrupts Takver, again. "*Bedap?!* Isn't that the character from the book who is one of Shevek's best friends?!"

Yes. Takver replies, *And it's the name that the mother gave you. Let me finish reading and maybe there's an explanation.*

Takver continues.

My name is Bedap. I'm from a place far, far away. I need you to do me a favor.

A favor? What could I possibly do for a mushroom?

I'm not a mushroom. The mushroom is just a vehicular of sorts. But...let me finish. I need you to start a diary. Write as much as you can. It's important in more ways than you'll ever know.

Silence.

All I can tell you is that my name is Bedap and whether or not I will come to exist depends on you staying alive and reproducing.

What is that supposed to mean? And how in the demon trickster are you talking to me through a mushroom?

Silence.

I have to go. Our connection is fading. Watch for another glowing mushroom. And, please! Write down everything that you can.

And, then ,the glowing stopped. I released my grip on the mushroom and, then, Bedap was gone.

So, I became determined to find some kind of writing utensil and materials to write on. My sweet Erzsike thinks I'm a bit crazy, but she still helps me with my endeavors.

"A voice?" She mocks. "Does it tell you to kiss me, too?"

She belly laughs so dramatically that she almost falls off the pile of hay she is sitting on.

"Stop it! I'm serious. The voice told me to write about my life, our lives." I retort in defense.

"Well then, let's find you something to write with and on." She stands up and we begin our search.

Where do you find such implements on a farm in an area with an extremely low literacy rate and population for that matter? We couldn't go to the nearest town. That would've taken at least a day anyway. Besides, we would have been stopped by the police patrols. We are under a mandatory stay-at-home order, after all.

We'd have had to travel by night. Good luck! Plus, buying materials costs money that we don't have.

The farmer is nice enough to let us two stray cats camp out in his barn until the orders are lifted. He even gives us food. I mean, we help out around the farm a bit. But, there isn't a lot to do. Plus, I wouldn't want to be anywhere else. This may sound strange, but I kind of like this crisis.

I mean, I don't like that so many people are dying. At least, that's what we're told. But, Erzsike and I are able to be together. Finally, together! We sleep in the same bed. We have privacy. The farmer thinks we are sisters so he doesn't suspect anything. Otherwise, he'd probably send us away. Or even worse. He might lock us up and have the local vicar come and exorcize the demons out of us.

The farmer, Mr. Pál, is a widow. I don't think he minds the company. Not that we are much company. The only time we see him is when he comes into the barn to feed the geese in the morning or when we're helping out in the gardens and orchards. We eat a meal with him on Sundays. We have our own means to prepare meals here outside. There's a small fire pit that we use to heat water and cook. He lets us glean vegetables from the garden and fruit from the trees. Plus, we forage. Most of our time is actually spent scouring the creek and woods for wild, edible plants. We return the favor of his hospitality by collecting the eggs for him and helping out with slopping the pigs. The little creek out back also serves as a spot where we can wash up and scrub the few garments we have. Mr. Pál gave us some of his wife's old clothing. She wouldn't be needing them in the afterlife.

Anyway, since we've gotten so comfortable here, we decided to do a little exploring in search of materials to do the bidding of my newly acquired mushroom friend. Or, that's what I like to call it.

The barn that we stay in is actually much nicer than the shack my extended family squats in. It might even be less drafty. The upper level of the barn is divided into two lofts, one on either side, giving the center of the barn a cathedral-esque ceiling. Erzsike and I sleep on several palettes pushed together padded with straw and hay in one of the lofts. The farmer offered us the extra rooms in his house, but we decided we preferred privacy over comfort.

We help out by cleaning the house, too. The other day, while dusting the room where the farmer's wife slept, we stumbled upon an old dowry chest in the closet. It was unlocked so we opened it up. And, to our surprise we found writing implements. We asked Mr. Pál's permission to use her old stuff. So, now we have paper and ink for my writing and Erzsike's drawing.

She loves to draw. She loves to draw *me*. She says my sun kissed skin, brown eyes, and black hair are a challenge so that's why she is always drawing me. Practicing. I don't mind that she draws me; usually, only the noble people are drawn and painted to be remembered.

What makes me so special?

TAKVER SITS up and takes the ring off her head. She brings her right pointer finger up to her eye and the lens pops out on to her finger with no hesitation. She looks over at Makk who is looking back at her.

It's your turn, Sib. Let's practice. You can read aloud to me.

Makk, a bit distracted, just lies there as Takver walks over to the side of the bunker.

"Who is this Bedap?" Makk asks, now looking her in the eyes.

They takes the lens from Takver and brings it up to their eye. The lens hops off their finger and then on to their cornea. It's as if the translucent crystal had a mind of its own, robot-like. It knows what to do, as if it has muscle memory. At first, the lens' seemingly autonomous attributes left them awe struck. But, they've normalized its fluid, intelligent-like movements to the point that neither bats an eye at it anymore.

Let's keep reading. I bet we'll find out soon who this Bedap character is. Takver passes the ring to them. As Makk grabs it, there's a give. She hasn't let go of it. She uses the force to bring herself closer to Makk's face.

You've got this, Sib! You're making such good progress. Don't give up today, okay?

Makk tilts their head down and darts a glare at Takver. If they'd had glasses, they'd be peering over the top of the frames, looking like a sassy librarian. Then, they forces a half smirk, coyfully raising their shoulder to their cheek.

They puts the ring on their head. Takver watches how the hair stands up on their arms and the nape of the neck as they interfaces. It's like that feeling one got way back before the Great Dying when one would take a swig of an ice cold pop after a long day in the sun, chemicals rushing through their body rewarding them for coating the taste buds with sugar and carbonic acid. But Takver and Makk wouldn't know about—would have *no clue* about—pop or carbonic acid. Sugar they know about and have consumed on special occasions, even though it is as rare as a harmless UV ray.

"I saw you almost jump out of your skin earlier when that wooden book holder thing appeared. I should have warned you about that. The first time it popped up right in front me while I was lying down I almost crapped my frock."

Makk's smile stretches entirely across their face, a big toothy poo-eating grin. They sure is feeling sassy lately. That makes her very happy to see them cheery and playful. It's a big change from the somber, determined-to-find-their-family Makk. Takver is thinking this as she watches the drama unfold as they reenacts the whole moment, Makk flailing their arms out in front of them like a panicked person swatting away an angry hornet.

"Ahh! Don't fall on me!!" Their voice is high pitched and

their pronunciation forced and ridiculous as they mock their sister.

Takver joins in on the laughter. She doesn't take herself that seriously anyway to get offended even in the least bit by this type of playful, teasing banter. She hadn't known that she missed it so much. She'd been alone for so long until Makk came into the picture.

Makk stops playing around and begins to concentrate inward. There's a moment of silence. Then, Makk speaks up.

"I'm just going to pick a random entry."

Makk begins reading aloud.

"Ffff..rrr...oohhhm...th..the...aahrk...ivezz...uhhv..."

FROM THE ARCHIVES of the Genetic Research Institute for Speculative Genealogy (GSSK - Spekulatív Genealógiai Genetikai Kutatóintézet)—Accessed 2122.03.16—SzabadPest

FILE #A6574001908—Makutek Erzsébet, 1908—Mitochondrial Cell Memory Interpretation

DING! Ding! Ding! Ding! Ding! Ding!

The chilling chime of the ubiquitous servant bell echoes through the cold, damp stone halls.

I wake up suddenly in a stupor, feeling completely out of sorts. My head is pounding and my bones ache something awful, probably from the constant cold chill in the servants' quarters.

"Erzsébet! Erzsébet!"

My master beckons me from the next room over in his gruff, groggy voice.

I throw off the too thin covers and move my legs so they hang from the side of the bed, preparing to slowly slide down on the floor below. The beds are high for mainly two reasons: heat rises and rodents have a harder time climbing up into tall beds.

My breath is as visible as the morning fog that gets trapped in the distant snow peaks of the High Tatras. I cough once, twice, and then a third time. It's a throaty cough. I would sneak down into the kitchen later if I can make it and get some honey and ginger when no one is looking.

I plant my feet down on the stone floor and instantly tumble to the ground with a grunt.

Something isn't right at all, I think to myself as I sit up, watching the room spin.

"Erzsébet! Erzsébet! Get your worthless arse in here this instant! The fire is going out!"

I place the back of my hand on my forehead. I'm burning up, despite my skin being cold and clammy.

"Yes, Master! Coming, Master!" I manage a weak, muddled reply.

Then, I grab on to a wooden bedpost and manage to pull myself up, straightening my night gown that got twisted in the fall.

What time is it? I wonder as I glance at the moonlit clock in vain, forgetting that the minute and second hands were removed to remind me and my fellow servants that time doesn't exist for us; we must always be ready to attend our masters at any given moment.

I look out the open window; a draft is pouring in making my breath even more visible. The full moon illuminates the flank of the mountain castle. Off in the far distance, the foothills outline the eastern horizon. The valley below seems so remote. But my family home is even more distant. How long was the voyage here on horse and buggy all those years ago?

Two days? I wonder how my family is doing. Will I see them again?

"Erzsébet! Erzsébet!"

You'd think the lazy bastard could get his large arse out of bed and feed the fire himself. The masonry heater is in his room, after all.

I scoff at the thought.

"Erzsébet! Wench! Get in here."

I'm not in the mood or in a good physical state to be getting out of bed. I'm in less of a mood to be groped by his lord, the rapist. I just might be delirious enough to do something about it. In my fever induced trance, I open the drawer to my night stand. Among the various odds and ends—matches, buttons, needle and thread, a piece of sheeps cheese and hard bread wrapped in tattered cloth—there's a staghorn handled whittling knife. I grab it and slip it into the right, hip pocket of my ragged pajamas.

My dear mother had taught me to whittle when I was around seven years old. I love carving turtles and other animals that I admire for their freedom, a freedom that I could only dream of.

I grab the pack of wooden matches from the drawer and light a candle. Keeping one hand on the bed, it helps guide my weak, shaking legs along the room to the master's quarters. I step up and open the heavy, oak and wrought iron door.

The door creaks open.

I try to compose myself a bit, using the stucco-covered stone castle wall to guide myself to the stove. Picking up the iron rod, I open the fuel door.

"It's about time, you lazy arse! What took you so long?"

He's looking at me with that, that coy, playful, disgusting look that he gets.

"Forgive me, Master. I'm not well."

I kneel down and put a few logs of hardwood into the ornately baroque-tiled stove, trying with all my might not to fall over from weakness. I use the poker to rearrange the logs, kicking up some sparks. The flames roar as the dry wood catches fire.

"Good. All good then. Now, come over here to your master. You let it get cold in here. Now, I need your body heat to warm me back up."

Did he not just hear that I'm not feeling well? Disgusting sociopath!

I pretend to have not heard him over the rustling of the wood and coals and the clanking of the wrought iron fuel door upon closing it. I stand up and almost topple over.

"Come here, Erzsébet. Get into bed with me."

He's now leaning over and reaching for my nightgown. I turn around and take a few paces back, bowing down to an almost crouch.

"Forgive me, Master. I...I'm vvv...very ill. I need to lie down."

"Lie down here. Come. Don't make me wait any longer."

Please don't do this now. I'm thinking as the rage starts to build in me.

A shot of adrenaline from the sudden fear surges through my body, giving me the strength to quickly move toward the door.

Lord József throws off the covers and leaps out of bed just in time to block the door, trapping me inside.

"Don't you dare scream!" He says through his teeth as he grabs me by my arms.

"Ppp....please, don't. No! I...I...I'm not well!

"Shut up, you little wench!"

Now, with his big hands gripped tightly around my small, skinny arms he starts pulling me toward the bed.

"NO! NO! Please! I beg you!"

He wraps a big hand over my mouth, muffling my begging cries, his hands drenched from my tears. A short, petite young woman, child, of only sixteen, he towers over me like a giant. He manages to pick me up and toss me roughly onto the bed.

Struggling, I'm trying to roll off the other side of the bed, but my weakness and his grip on me stops me from getting away.

Thwump!

He's now on the bed, pinning me down. My screams can be heard throughout that floor of the cold, dreary castle.

"I...said...keep...quiet, ...you stupid...wench!"

But no one comes. They know better than to come. This isn't the first time that screams echo in the night in these halls and it probably won't be the last.

He manages to throw himself on me, his protruding gut crushing against my abdomen.

And then, Schlooock!

His body suddenly freezes.

"Aaa...aaa...aaa....uuhhhgh..."

I look wildly into his wide, shocked, jaundiced eyes. Blood drips from his mouth onto my wrinkled, tattered sleeping gown. His last breath, like a puff of dense smoke in the crisp cold.

I will have to run far away. Where will I go?

After a moment, I manage to push him off of me. And, in a matter of seconds I'm making my way into my quarters.

I must change my clothes. I'm still very dizzy. I need to get out of here. First, I must wash up.

THE SUN IS BEGINNING to peak over the distant mountains, and the birds are chirping away. For them it's a normal day. For me, well, I'm running away from a murder scene.

I've managed to get far enough away that I can safely rest. They will be looking for me soon. As soon as they realize what

I've done... They'll have the dogs out after me. If I can get across the river in time... But I'm so exhausted. My fever seems to have subsided a bit. I think the worst of it might be over.

I walk for what seems like hours and finally get to the bridge. It's springtime so most of the snow has melted away, but icy frost still persists in the shadows where the sun can't reach.

There is no sentry on the narrow bridge; I've been rather fortunate. Crossing it in less than a minute—after eating some bread and meat I stole from the kitchen before sneaking out the gate, I'm feeling much better and moving much more quickly—I escape out of view down a deer trail. Near this bank of the Orava, on the other side of a patch of thick woods, there's a small field for farming vegetables and for sheep to graze. Through the morning fog, I can make out several outbuildings of sorts. There's what looks like a rabbit hutch, a separate structure where the surf family probably keeps a hog to be fattened. I stick to the edge of the woods, taking the long way around to the barn. My footsteps crunch as I walk on the frozen dew.

A few sheep baa and bleat at me as I sneak in. The all-too familiar smells that accompany the trade of animal husbandry fill my nostrils. The pungent, acrid odors bring a feeling of nostalgia; before dad died, he had raised sheep; I'd helped.

There's enough light coming through a window and various other cracks that I can make my way around. I spot a dark corner where there is plenty of hay, or is it straw? No. It's definitely hay; the smell is distinct. I lie down and, because the sheep stop bleating and decide to ignore my presence, I fall asleep.

~

I WAKE up to the sound of mice squeaking and nibbling on hay. I start as my eyes adjust to the darkness and see their little bodies only tens of centimeters away from my face. I must have slept the day away. Barely any light is coming in through the window.

I look around this corner of the barn. There are some gardening implements, a pile of what looks like wood scraps for building, and several stacks of hay. And, that's when I notice it.

Off in the near distance, there's a green light of sorts blinking near the floor. I squint my eyes to focus my vision on the light. It seems to be pulsating. My heart begins to flutter as I realize that I'd never before seen such a thing. A *green* light? I've seen white light from the stars, and fire has hues of yellow, red, orange and even blue sometimes. But *green*?

Suddenly, I'm aware that my stomach is gurgling; I'm hungry. But that will have to wait—I still have some bread and meat left from my misappropriated cache from the castle's main kitchen.

I manage to make my way toward the intermittent glowing object without causing the sheep to stir. When I finally touch the mushroom—it is a small toadstool mushroom, after all, that has formed at the base of a wooden stud and it's luminous—that's when I hear the voice. Is it *hearing* if it happens inside my mind? My ears don't hear a thing, but the voice is loud and clear.

Don't be afraid, Erzsébet.

I must still be a little delirious; there's a mushroom talking to me and saying my name. *How in the hell does it know my name?*

And, just as if it could read my thoughts, it responds.

This must be strange for you. I understand. But, please, Erzsébet, just listen to me. I have some important things to tell you.

Wha...wh...who in the evil devil are you? Is someone playing a malicious trick on me?

My name is Bedap. This mush...

Takver interrupts.

You see! I just knew it! Bedap again. There's got to be an explanation.

"Okay. Okay. Let me keep reading."

Makk continues.

My name is Bedap. This mushroom is just a way for us to communicate. It's a long story. I need you to pay attention to what I'm about to tell you. Can you do that?

Silence.

Hello? Erzsébet? Are you there?

Once my head stops spinning and my heart begins to beat at a normal pace I'm able to answer.

Yeh... Yes. I'm here.

Oh, good. I thought I'd lost you for a second.

Bedap. That's a strange name. Where...? How...how are you... how are we doing this? Talking through a mushroom.

My name? It's a long story. It's new for me, too. I used to go by Maw...

Silence.

Then, instantly, Makk is on their feet. Their head is spinning a bit and they feels disoriented.

The sudden, dramatic change of position causes Takver to stand up, too.

What is it?! What's wrong?

Takver's eyebrows are scrunched up, the space between them and her forehead reduced in half. The look on her face is a mixture of panic and confusion.

Silence.

Makk just stands there looking at their sister, jaw partially drooping. Their blank eyes just stare at her. A million thoughts are running through their head. Their heart is racing.

Sib! Say something! You're freaking me out!

And in that instant, Makk's gaze shifts from Takver to the ladder that leads to the bunker's access hatch. They's seeing something glowing green from out of the corner of their eye.

Makk ignores Takver's confusion and panic and walks toward the ladder to get a closer look.

There, on one of the upper rungs, a dense green clump of moss is pulsating light. As Makk focuses on it closely, a bubble augmentation pops up seemingly hovering above the moss, identifying it:

<Kingdom: Plantae; Division: Bryophyta; Class: Bryopsida; Subclass: Bryidae; Order: Hypnales; Family: Hypnaceae; Genus: Hypnum; Common name: Carpet moss>

Makk swipes the bubble from their view with their right hand and watches as it slides off to the periphery of their vision and then disappears with a bloop.

Takver is just staring at Makk, meanwhile the invisible string is tugging at them as they looks up in the direction of the hatch. Just on the underside of the hatch, another piece of fungus laden moss begins to glow.

Makk starts and looks back at Takver and shrugs. Then, they climbs up the ladder and listens for any noises outside, up above, before opening the hatch and climbing out.

CHAPTER FOUR: GLASS MOUNTAIN

It's colder than it should be this far into Reawakening. The ice-cold dampness penetrates your tired, feeble bones to the point that you want to do nothing but just lie down. Right now, thankfully, you *are* prone. After a long night of intensive, back-breaking labor—picking up heavy chunks of solid stone, hauling them several paces to the holding structure, and picking at the solid walls with pointed metallic tools—you basically crashed down on your make-shift bunk. Lying down is not nearly as soothing as when you had your hammock and could be close to your partners, but at least right now you're not stuck in that narrow, dolomite stone passage where visibility is almost nil.

And, even being outside those cramped corridors, your nose burns from the constant acrid odor that saturates the air. This awful stench is not something that you're familiar with. It doesn't smell natural. It's not as noxious as the off gasses from the melting asphalt that sometimes wafts to your encampment during scorching hours, but it's foul enough to make you and most of the other prisoners wear a rag over your nose and mouth. A stinky, sweaty rag is more bearable than the pestilent air on this forsaken mountain.

A mountain. You can't believe that you are actually on a real mountain. A range of mountains. The hills to the west of the Old River have nothing on these towering monstrosities. Could this be the glass mountain that you've heard about in the tales that your people have woven for as long as you can remember? Maybe at one time it looked like it was made of glass, shiny from the frozen crystals. Now, the jagged, tooth-like peaks are a metallic ochre-gray and seemingly as dry as its semi-arid foothills.

Your prison is somehow built into the facade of one of the mammoth bluffs, a complex network of corridors and enclosures. From inside your stifling, mass cage, you and the others are mostly blind to what is on the outside. There are no windows. It seems that you and your fellow captives are in some kind of extensive, rectangular box. It's mostly made of a thick, durable metal. The walls are solid, but there is some give. In a fit of desperation, one of your fellow captives pounded with their fists to be let out. Then, you could hear that the structure isn't as solid as the mountain's flank that you spent the last several hours chipping away at. This is your first time in the mass cage with the bunks. Before arriving at these sleeping quarters a little over an hour ago, you had spent what felt like an entire day on some sort of transport vehicular—as your captors transported you and the other prisoners to the mines, you peered through the cracks of the off-road cargo vehicular. Hold was shining bright enough, so you were able to sort of make out the distant valleys below. It was as if you were a giant peering down on a miniature swale, a divot in the rocky floor. And you were reminded of how small and insignificant you are in the grand scheme of things.

But even being so infinitesimal, your heart aches for your intim unit, your community, your people—all of your people.

You are here with some of them. But there are a lot of strangers, too. And strangers make you uncomfortable. Strangers are not to be trusted.

Is that even true? You think.

You miss your people so much that it physically hurts. You're not alone, though. The collective pain, the pain of losing loved ones or the simple torture of being held prisoner against your will, is enough to move mountains. Yet, the mountain remains still, even as you hack away at it little by little.

What is all this for anyway? What could anyone do with all this rock?

Suddenly, as you lie there, you're reminded of the throbbing in your hand. It is still healing; you don't heal as fast as you used to. Luckily the imposed wound hasn't gotten infected. The pulsating ache makes it even more difficult to relax on top of the strange noises and stank air. The red, crusty mark on your right looks strangely like a uterus or a capitalized 'T' with a ribbon above it that spans the length of the top bar. The symbol is meaningless to you, because, firstly, you can't read and therefore don't know what a 'T' looks like called as such, and, secondly, you can't bring yourself to look at it long enough to find some sort of pattern. You prefer to pretend it isn't there. If it weren't for the deep, dull irritation, you'd have blocked it out by now.

How long has it been since those scorching marauders branded me?

It seems like it's been weeks since the attack on your encampment. You are constantly weak and hungry. You and the others are being fed by your captors, but there's not enough protein; the porridge-like gruel served in concave dishes consists mostly of carbohydrate fillers. You've lost a substantial amount of body mass and your already ungiving skin sags off your tired bones. And you're constantly exhausted.

How much more of this will my body be able to take?

Since that day you woke up in what unknowing to you the marauders call 'the processing center,' you've been segregated from your intim unit. At least your family *did* survive that awful night. You're thankful for that. You can still feel the taught tug of the unseeable ties that connect you to Delores, Tejúti, Octavia, and Ursula.

Oh, my dear Ursula! You'd thought you lost her for good.

At the so-called processing center, Ursula's string was the most slack, the physically most proximal to you; she was with you briefly before you were shipped off to this labor camp just a day or so ago. You've lost her again, but not before she was able to give you some insight into your terrible situation.

When you and the other captives arrived, you were segregated by genitalia; those thugs, those monsters ripped off your clothes and fondled your genitals. You'd never felt so violated before in your life. Not even when you were bashed across the head and woke up hours later.

How dare they touch me like that without my consent! You remember as angry, furious tears leave streaks down your dusty, sunken cheeks. *Those scorching, evil marauders,* Rapists!

They corralled the people with child bearing organs into one group and those with sperm producing once into another. If the marauders had difficulty categorizing someone's genitals, it was up to them to decide how to confine the person. That practice of segregating people by genitalia wasn't anything new to humans, but it was something very unfamiliar to your people. For hundreds of years, since the Great Dying, ideas of masculinity, femininity, androgyny with connection to genitalia have been separate, deconflated notions. In fact, some anthropologists of the future would look at gender, as the people of the Old World knew it, and might argue that it had ceased to exist for your people.

Your people, the Átmeneti, have been scattering themselves up and down the Old River in temporary encampments for centuries, relocating each new year amid Reawakening. You've lost count, but the last you knew there were seven communes of around sixty to ninety people in each community that identified as Átmeneti. With those other groups, you and your immediate people share a common ethnicity. That is to say, you practice popular customs and have a similar cultural background and ancestry: you share most of the same stories, music, linguistic features, dress, gastronomic practices, and the list goes on and on. You are all somehow descendants of the Last Ones. That means some of you have deep, dark almond flesh while others' tones are light rose or medium golden or a number of other shades. Some of you, like your eggprogeny Octavia, have thick, coiled chicory root hair while others' hair, like Makk's from the dwelling next to yours, is fine, straight, and the color of ash-blown leaves as they fall from their stalks after Harvest. When a baby is born with a dark shade of flesh, it is considered auspicious. Because the lucky almond-hued person can better tolerate sun exposure and is less likely to die from the cancer it is likely to cause.

And, because of your people's xenophobia, you tend to only trade with other Átmeneti, whether that be goods or people. In fact, it is not unusual for your kind to find partners from other Átmeneti communities. Tejúti, *your* Tejúti, one of your partners and the eggblood of your eldest child, Ursula, is from a community about a five-night foot from the section of the river your primary people tend to inhabit. You remember how you discovered that Tejúti shared a certain percentage of DNA with you and Delores, and how the two of you, you and Delores, kept your ability to share with Tejúti a secret to avoid being shamed by the community. After all, the point of partnering with other Átmeneti outside of the immediate commune was to reduce the likelihood of inbreeding. To this day, the secret remains. Not even your children know you can share, mostly to protect them from social shaming. Your genetic relationship with Delores, with whom you share a low percentage of DNA, is common knowledge. But, because your lineage is known and can be traced, the two of you are distant enough cousins that there is no cultural cause for ridicule. It is not too uncommon, nor very common either, that partners share a low percentage of DNA. And, no one really knows how much DNA is needed to be able to share. Mindspeaking, as a science, is something that is just done not studied. At least, that is, your people don't study it. It is just something you can do, like breathing. It is natural. What is not natural among your people, though, is conflating sexual organs with societal notions of performativity. Therefore, the pronouns your people tend to use are not reflective of anything that is natural to your people like the anatomy that you're born with.

Within these disparate Átmeneti communities, there are six prominent pronouns commonly exploited to refer to people: they, she, he, per, e, and fae. What makes pronouncing practices unique to your people is that there is only one pronoun assigned at birth and that is 'they.' The other pronouns are chosen individually by each member of the community upon their sixteenth celebration of Reawakening. Pronouns are not signs that your people use to make meaning around an idea of gender.

As you sit and ponder all of this, your wandering mind takes you back on your waterfetching journey, some fifty Reawakenings before.

That year there were only five of you. Besides getting treed by some roving vadkutya, the trip was rather uneventful. You do remember, however, how you had fallen even more profoundly in love with Delores. At the time she went by Pem and was a they. She had always been so sure of herself. Well before she'd begun the waterfetching journey with you and the three others, she had known she wanted to be a she. She had always looked up to one person in particular. That person was also a storyweaver. Delores was her name as well. And Delores used the she pronoun. So, your Delores, Old Mester as the younguns like to call her, renamed herself Delores and appropriated the she pronoun. You'd admired her so much for knowing what she wanted to do in life, how she would contribute to the greater community.

You, on the other hand, had no idea what name you wanted or what pronoun, for that matter. There wasn't anyone exclusively really that influential in your life to emulate. But, you were good at gardening and rather enjoyed the magic of growing something from planting a seed in the soil. So, you'd decided to be a gardener. But you hated your gardening mester with a passion. She was the last person you were going to look up to. So, you would keep your given name, Egres, and the pronoun you were assigned at birth, they. They both suited you at the time and they were all you needed. You grew up loving Tele from the stories of the Last Ones—per loved gardening and was so brave—but there were already several Teles in your commune. However, you were the only Egres. It was unique to you at the time, even though there were probably other Egreses before your time. That didn't matter though. Just like what genitals someone had didn't matter for pronouning practices. Concepts like man, woman, girl, or boy don't form a binary system in your linguistic repertoire. Words like man, woman, and adult are not based on one's reproductive organs and one's endocrine system.

Your genitals had very little to do with you as a person, unless you were being intim with someone or someones. They —your genitals—would, however, come to be of some importance when it became time to start your intim unit. You would provide the sperm that would eventually fertilize an egg. But, time and time again, Delores miscarried. After years of trying, you'd both decided to invite Tejúti into your intim unit. That is when Ursula came into your lives. Eventually, Octavia would follow a few years later when Delores was finally able to stay pregnant. Of course, that only came after her trip to see Old Tátos. But, alas, that's another story for another time.

When Ursula told you how the marauders had separated you two and the other enslaved people based on your genitals it caused a lot of confusion.

Are they afraid we'll procreate while imprisoned? You ask her, outraged. *What an arbitrary way of separating people!*

I know, Ondi. It makes no sense, Ursula agrees.

She could be with you because her XY chromosomes coded for sexual organs that produce sperm, but the marauders caged Delores, Tejúti, and Octavia together because they had the biology necessary for producing eggs?

What are they going to do use us for breeding?! You exclaim, quietly.

I'm not sure why we were separated this way, Ondi. We just need to focus on how in the scorching Nap we can get out of this mess.

Whatever the reason, the marauders would pay. You don't know how, but they *will* pay for what they've done to you and your family and your community. No. Revenge isn't the way. But, you will do whatever you need to to get out of these terrible conditions, to help your family escape, even if that means fighting your way out. If it comes to that, would you be able to kill?

Just as you begin to drift off into a most welcomed slumber, a blaring sound like a mechanical screeching causes you to jolt upright, almost smacking your head on the underside of the top bunk.

Then, a whirring sound like metal scraping against metal pierces your eardrums. Illuminated gaps form at the very top of the walls, closest to the ceiling, as natural light begins to pour into your stuffy space, specks of dust dancing in the horizontal rays.

A loud, disembodied voice begins to reverberate across the complex. It's as if the person is standing next to you shouting, but no one is there. You see the others around you slowly begin to stir and get up from their respective bunks. You can't understand what is being said, because the linguistic features being spoken are not a part of your repertoire. It's unintelligible.

The person who was lying down on the top bunk just above you climbs down the ladder and sees the confused look on your grim face. This is the first time they've spoken to you since you arrived less than a day ago.

"Let me help you." They extends their right hand in your general direction, "you look like you could use a friend."

You hesitate at first, but then you force a smile. Instantly, you feel the neurotransmitters begin to flow through your body. You accept and grab on to their hand and they helps pull you up. You stagger a bit and use your right, injured hand to grab the post, wincing ever-so slightly. It's still very tender.

"I'm Tirin, Elder." They pulls their hands into their chest, placing the palm of their left hand over the back of the right one, both above the heart. "I'm happy." That roughly translates to 'I'm happy to make your acquaintance.'

The fact that Tirin used both hands and the title Elder, instead of the typical Test, short for testvér, was marked to you. So, you speak up.

"Call me Egres, and please I am your test just like you are mine." You look at them intensely but not aggressively. "No need for formalities. We're all Átmeneti here." You bring your wounded hand to your heart in the typical response. "I, too, am happy."

Tirin then replies with a note of defiance in their voice. "Pardon me, respectfully, but our people separated long ago. We Literalists have long rejected the superstitions of the Átmeneti. And despite that, I think we can look past our differences. Who knows how much longer we'll be here amongst each other. By the looks of it you're fairly new."

"How long have you been here?" You ask, putting your hand gently on their arm as a sign of mutual understanding.

"This is the beginning of our third Reawakening. We still celebrate it, sort of. In our own way. Not so ritualistically like your people, but we still have our ways of welcoming the sowing season."

"Two complete cycles of all seven seasons?" You exclaim, letting your intonation rise at the end of your utterance as a sign of disbelief. "How many from your community?"

"All of us. Well, all of us who made it out alive at least." The sudden flashback makes them tremble.

"Well, Test, I have a lot to learn from you, then." You squeeze the hand that rests on their arm into an acknowledging grip and flatten out your smile, pursing your lips in finality.

"What pronoun do you use?" Tirin asks.

You pause, taken aback by the unexpected question.

"I didn't think your people asked for pronouns. That was one of the ideological wedges that divided our peoples so long ago if I remember correctly from the stories." You comment.

"We don't. You're right. But, I know it's an important practice to you and your people. And, we learn that if we are to come into contact with your people, as we inevitably do, we are to be respectful and ask for your pronouns instead of assuming. After all, I will talk to others about our meeting and I want to know how to refer to you."

"I use they." You smile. "You know. Every time I meet someone from outside of our communes, which isn't very often I might add, I'm reminded of how much our distrust for outsiders is one of our weaknesses."

Tirin blushes a bit. "I think I'm going to like you, too."

"What pronouns do you use?" You ask, returning the question as is custom among your people.

"What do you guess?" Tirin replies with a smirk on their face.

"How would I know? I barely know anything about you, let alone those who may have influenced you." You are asking sincerely.

"My beard doesn't give it away? How about my short hair and the fact that I'm not wearing any make up?" Tirin still wears a smirk.

"How would any of those things give it away?" You reply. "My daughter Ursula has a beard, short hair, and no one amongst our people wears make up, unless you weave stories. And I have a beard, too. Ursula uses the she pronoun and I use the they pronoun. None of those things helps us determine our pronouns."

"But do you remember who Tirin was from the First Book?" Tirin inquires with a bit of surprise.

"I remember Tirin, a friend of Shevek and Bedap's. If my old memory serves me correctly, Tirin was ostracized by the Annaresti because of the criticisms found in the satirical story-weaving they wrote and performed. But I don't remember their pronoun, sadly. And, we don't associate pronouns with genitalia or whether the chemicals in our bodies make us prone to grow facial hair. That practice ended with the Great Dying." You recall.

"*Mostly* ended. There are some of us who still think it's a legitimate practice." Tirin adds.

"And, hence your smaller group splitting from our larger one. Of course, you wouldn't have been born yet. I myself was celebrating my sixteenth Reawakening at the time. I remember missing some of my friends who I never was able to see again after they moved away. Wait. If you're here...are my old friends here, too? What a blessing from Isten." You immediately regret your use of the name and the superstition it invokes.

"Let's go and find out." Tirin takes your arm and leads you

away from the bunks. You notice the brand marking on his hand. The scar looks as if it has been healed for quite some time.

The two of you begin walking toward the exit that is at the opposite end of the elongated dormitory cages. Once there, you and the other prisoners form a line and slowly make your way to the dining hall.

The word dining hall isn't the best term for it because it makes the place sound quaint and even majestic in some way. You've heard stories of how humans used to treat penned up animals the same way you're being treated, keeping them in cages—this is your third, no fourth cage since you were captured—cages that weren't very clean and feeding them the minimum amount of calories to give them just enough energy to help them keep working but little else. Why should you expect to be treated any differently? The fact that you were taken from your home without your consent is a clear indication that your captors don't think of you as their equals. How could they? To them, you must be animals, at the very least not human, or not human enough.

There are what seem to be overseers or sentries, strategically stationed along the corridor and in certain areas outside the large pen-like sleeping quarters. They look like people, but there is something not right about them. They are somehow eerily motionless.

They wear some form of hard face and head covering, like an oval shield of sorts, so you can't see their faces.

Do they even have faces?

The automated people from the stories that are told by the weavers were basically humanoid machines powered by artificial means.

Were these people actually machines?

And where are the human marauders that captured you in

the first place? Is their operation somehow work independently from this one?

There must be twenty or thirty people in the slow-moving line. You don't recognize anyone except your new friend who is in front of you in the line. You can't see very well despite the sunlight coming through slats in the walls of the corridor. Everyone seems to be wearing the same, queer style of clothing: different shades of the color Nap when it sets, faded and vibrant orange one-piece overalls.

"Why are we all wearing this color?" You whisper to Tirin, the curiosity getting the better of you.

"Not many of us have escaped, but if one of us does we'll be easy to spot and recaptured."

"Oh." You sigh.

"You're not thinking of leaving us already are you, Elder? You just got here." Tirin attempts a joke.

Silence.

As you walk along the dreary corridor, you notice various openings along the walls that are blocked by movable barriers that are commonly seen in the structures of the Old World.

"What's behind the different blocked off openings?" You ask your new friend.

"More sleeprooms." Tirin responds. "I'm waiting for you to ask the most important question."

Silence.

And, just as you're about to ask it, your olfactory senses pick up on a new smell in the air. A layer of sweet, cooked grain of some sort can be smelled over the acrid stench of industrial mining.

Presently, the corridor opens into a vast room filled with flat, slab-like articles of furniture each supported on four legs. At each supported slab, there are several objects on which people are sitting, four or five people to a slab. It's all very uniform and mechanical. It reminds you instantly of a scene from the stories of the Old World.

The cue that you form a part of seemingly winds its way to what reminds you of the refectory back at your encampment. Four people in the same orange jumpsuits take turns scooping up and filling bowls with some sort of porridge. Your stomach immediately begins to gurgle. And, suddenly, you're acutely aware that you're hungry and very, very thirsty.

Following Tirin's lead, you take your steaming bowl of gruel and the cup of tepid liquid and sit down in front of him at one of the tables.

You examine the eating and drinking receptacles. They are solid and slightly malleable. The bowl with the hot gruel seems to be more flexible than the cup with almost warm water in it. At least the water tastes potable. Besides the normal caustic smell of the prison, there's a funny smell coming from the material that the vessels are made of. The smell is all too familiar to you. The landfills abound with this kind of material. They used to call it plastique or something like that. Poison is what it is. It's nothing like the compostable bowls that your people eat from.

You look around and watch as the other people are silently slurping their meal. The dull sound of plastic on plastic echoes through the chamber. There are conversations taking place, but the people are speaking so quietly that you can't make out what is being said.

As you look around the room, you get a glimpse of someone you think you know from your own encampment. But they looks very different. You're used to them having long, crimped dark chestnut hair that matches the tone of their flesh, reaching down to their lower back. Their beard is much longer and more unkempt than usual, too.

That's Bodza, Makk's nether. My cousin. You think to yourself. They is looking more or less in your direction but doesn't make eye contact with you. It occurs to you that you should be able to connect with them; they *is* your cousin after all. You search deep for your invisible nexus with them, and to your surprise there is barely anything there. That's odd because there should be some sort of sensation even if only a very slack metaphorical thread dangling between the two of you.

You try to mindspeak to them to get their attention but a heaviness in your mind's mind makes doing telepathy feel as if you're trying to walk through a pond of thick mud up to your neck. It's impossible. But, it shouldn't be. You've been mindspeaking with them their whole life. It shouldn't be this hard. Something is wrong.

There are four of the humanoid sentries overseeing the room, one in each of the four corners. When you notice them seemingly staring at you behind their shiny helmets—how can you not notice them? You can almost feel them watching you somehow—you begin to feel the hairs all over your body stand straight up. Your skin crawls like a million ants are moving all over you.

Then, Bodza finally looks over in your direction. It's too dim in the room to see that far away and your eyesight isn't what it used to be. Their body language changes. They squints their eyes as they look in your direction and a half smile forms on their lips. Their eyebrows raise as they seemingly recognize you, waving the fingers on their right hand rather timidly acknowledging your gaze. Then, they starts to get up to come to your table, but as soon as they goes to stand up, a piercing alarm like a high pitched siren begins to go off in the room and everyone, including yourself, starts grabbing at their ears. The sound is so deafening and disabling that your body weakens and you begin sliding down in your seat. Bodza falls immediately back into the chair. Then, in a split second the screeching stops altogether.

You look around and watch as people try to process what

has just happened. Glaring stares shoot in all directions as the seasoned prisoners begin seeking out the culprit, their eyes darting all across the room. Murmurs and whispers echo throughout the various tables. The people sitting with Bodza seem to be gently reproaching them for their actions, teaching the newcomer the expectations.

Tirin, who is sitting across from you, grabs your forearm gently, a very concerned look on his barely-lined face.

"Are you okay, Elder?"

"I'm fine." You reply in a jolt of frustration. Then, you relax a bit, "I...I just don't understand."

"Someone set off the..." Tirin begins saying before you interrupt him.

"No. Not that. I think I know why the painful noise happened." You try to gather your thoughts for a moment and then continue. "Why can't I mindspeak with my genetic kin?"

You indicate toward Bodza by tilting your head back and puckering your lips, pointing them in Bodza's direction.

"My eggblood's cousin's adult child is just right there. I should be able to share with them."

Tirin turns around in his chair, scanning the people at the tables behind him. Then, he looks you straight in the eyes before looking down.

"Look. We can't merge here. I've been here for two years and haven't been able to once."

He looks at the two sentries that are standing to your back.

"We've figured out that they must emit some sort of invisible something that shuts down our ability to connect with our kin."

Then, he looks down at his gruel and shrugs.

"I've almost forgotten what it was like to merge."

He places his rough, calloused hand on your leathery, liver spotted one.

"I know it's a lot to deal with." He pauses, staring into your eyes and frowning a bit out of compassion. "My first few months here were tough. I'd thought I'd lost everything. But, after a few weeks, I figured out that my family and friends are here, too. They were and still are just in another part of the mountain. I guess because I'm young and strong, they can use me in different places. Moving around here and there, I slowly found out that my people are still mostly alive."

He hunches over the table, lowering his voice to a barely audible whisper.

"We've got a whole secret system figured out," He winks and then looks around at the four sentries stationed in each corner, "If you think your family is alive, we'll find them. When we get back to the bunks, you can write a note and we'll get it passed around to the other prison camps. We'll find your people."

A huge weight seemingly melts away as you hear this, and then realization kicks in. You look down at your gruel.

"But, I can't write."

Silence.

"But, you can speak, Elder. I'll write for you. I'd forgotten that your people frown on reading and writing, too."

You put your hands on his and stare into his eyes like you're about to tell him something that's going to change his life.

"You're wrong, Test." You frown. "The spoken word can't be stolen from us so easily. Have your people forgotten about the burning of the books hundreds of years ago? Whole histories lost to us because paper became forbidden then obsolete. Then, the technology that replaced it was lost to us, too. All we had left were stories passed down through oral traditions. So, no, we don't frown on reading and writing. Instead, we put our energies into keeping stories going by passing them on through storytelling using our mouths."

Tirin smiles a half smile.

"And now look at us!"

He lifts up his hands and looks around the room.

"Caged up like animals from the Old World. Forced to work and fed and herded around like cattle, is that what they called the penned up animals?" He picks up the plastic spoon, scoops up some of the now-slightly-cold gruel and then lets the viscous substance spill off the spoon back into the bowl, "just enough slop to keep us going. What good do our stories do us while we're in *here*?"

You change the topic a bit since the last question was obviously rhetorical. Despite your disagreement with him, you let it go.

"So, tell me, Test," You look over at your cousin Bodza and notice they is looking back at you, "why can't we get up from our tables now? I mean, that is what set off the alarm isn't it? My lil' cousin was going to get up from their table and come see me."

Tirin pauses a moment before responding.

"We've figured out the hard way over these past two years, Elder." Tirin pauses again. "It's been a process. We are allowed to move around only when we're in our sleeping cells and only for a few minutes at a time. If we spend too much time out of our bunks, an alarm will go off."

You shake your head, expressing your confusion.

"But, how do they know? I only saw those guard-looking people, the ones in the uniform, when we first left our cage. They..."

Tirin interrupts you, fixing their gaze on yours very intensely.

"They aren't people, Elder. They..." He hunches down again and his speech goes from a hushed talk to a barely audible whisper, "those things aren't human. The only thing that makes sense is that they are some kind of machine, like the automated bots from the Old World."

Upon hearing this, the hairs stand up on the back of your neck as your skin tightens, forming goose pimples.

"Machines?" Your whole body shivers and you swallow, a gulp fills your throat. "I knew something was off about them. They stand so eerily still."

"Yes. And they won't hesitate to send you into excruciating pain without even moving."

Silence.

"I've watched too many people pass out from pain over the years. After a while, some people just crack and will attack the machines. It never ends well."

"So what are we doing here, Test?!" You say a bit too loudly, because people from other tables start looking over to you. You lower your voice again. "Why are we here? Why are we breaking chunks off the mountain? Who is keeping us here?"

Then, the same alarm as back in the bunker goes off.

"Finish up your slop, Elder. That's the warning buzzer. Eating time is about to end." Tirin picks up his bowl and shovels the rest of the gruel into his mouth, the whiskers from his beard catching some of the cold, liquified grains. "I'll tell you about it when we're back at our bunk."

As you stand up to take your dishes to the washing station where several people are busy scrubbing huge pots and other metal cookware, you catch a glimpse of what looks like a moth flying from the artificial light hanging above you toward the exit, its white, powdering wings very large compared to its fuzzy body. It swings back and lands on your shoulder for a split second before taking off back toward the doorway. You watch as it disappears into the dim corridor.

INTERLUDE

There's so much that you don't know.

Luckily for you, we carry the burden of omniscience. There's so much that we cannot *not* know. Oh, how at times we envy you people, with your inevitable ignorance of almost everything.

By now you are probably discovering that you are part of something much, much larger than you could ever have imagined; to speak metaphorically, you are just one of the many bases that make up a much larger strand of DNA. But, if you could only see things from our perspective, you'd understand that as far as metaphors go, we have to think much more grandiose. The strand of DNA itself that you are but one small component of is only one strand in a vast interconnected web of DNA strands that combine with other macromolecular components to form a cell.

To continue with this metaphor, for the sake of extending this literary device, the isolated cell seen from outside its membrane at a distance looks like the planet Earth in outer space. Earth is a floating spheroid made up of various solids, liquids, and gasses and whatever else falls between. Orbiting the Earth as a satellite is a much different spheroid that lacks a natural atmosphere. Now, let's mess everything up and say that the nucleus in this eukaryotic cell is outside of the cell. So, now we can imagine the much larger Earth/cell with a much smaller Moon/nucleus that is orbiting it. Let's extend our imagination to include the possibility that the Moon/nucleus is the control center of the Earth/cell.

Here's where we lose the metaphor and reality kicks in. You don't know it, but there is an actual control center on the moon, on your Hold, the very object that guides your nocturnal people in your nighttime activities.

Let us help you understand. We'll try to start from the beginning, well, at least *a* beginning.

Hundreds of years ago, there was the Great Dying. Yes. Yes. We know you're familiar with it. You've heard the stories. But, what about the stories that you haven't heard? For you there are the Last Ones. But, if you go around the planet in almost every former grand metropolis there are other Last Ones. After the Great Dying, ninety percent of the human population on Earth was wiped out; the Earth's human inhabitants went from a count of roughly eleven billion people to ten million people in less than a month's time. And even more people died from untreated injuries and the other usual illnesses that don't just disappear when disaster strikes at a global scale. Starvation and the lack of clean water to drink killed many more weeks after the virus was finished with its murderous rampage. If contaminated water didn't cause even further death, then the cancers from the scorching sun, your Nap, killed slowly, painfully.

It took decades for people to figure out how to go from solely surviving to actually living. But, unlike your ancestors who chose to pursue the complex simplicity of living off the land, not everyone wanted to give up the luxuries that life had to offer them before everything went to crap.

Let us rephrase that to make our point more precise.

There were some who'd survived the Great Dying by escaping from this planet. You see. The virus that attacked only humans was so good at what it did. Viruses need a host cell to reproduce. And, like most other species, reproduction is how it perpetuates its existence on this glorious terrestrial spheroid where water meets fire, wind, and earth. (Have you ever wondered why we call it Earth? We should call it Water since it is still mostly made up of that essential element. But that's another story for another time.)

Naturally, that particular virus spread from host to host through any means: vapor particles floating through the air, surfaces that one might touch at the airport, etc. What is an airport? That's really inconsequential to the point that I'm trying to make. Just know that people from all around the world could fly in machines to travel from one place to the next over long distances in a relatively short period of time. And, at an airport was an excellent place for the virus to then spread itself and reproduce in many places.

Well, once the owners of the world, the equivalents of Uphillers from the stories you grew up with, once they got whiff that a virus was coming to kill them, they decided to rule from afar. So, the wealthiest of the wealthy went to the Moon. And, that's how many people from the profit hoarding class survived the viral pandemic. They'd been planning for some disaster for more than a century. It started with space tourism for the mega rich where famous people as well as oligarchs and their families from many different megacorp towns and cities would spend a weekend in a space station hotel built just for their kind. That led to them building an entire complex of structures on the Moon's surface. Of course, they didn't build it themselves. That's what the automated workers were for. So, when the virus began killing off whole swathes of cities in a matter of days, the ones who could afford to flee took to their shuttles and went to the Moon, leaving everyone else here to die.

Fast forward a few hundred years and the rich want to return to claim what they see as their rightful place in this paradise. Insert your people into the story. Why would marauders suddenly begin pillaging entire communes of people and forcing some of them to work in a series of dolomite mines hundreds of kilometers from their homes and other communities? And why not just kidnap all of the different encampments at the same time? Why did they wait two years to kidnap your people from the time they took Takver's people?

Who's Takver? Oh, right. We'll tell you about her later.

You're not asking the right questions. You should be asking what you and your people are doing mining dolomite. Eventually, you will learn more about your and your family's situation. The people who were identified with similar reproductive organs have been divided into several different groups. We won't go into detail right now, but you need to know that the oldest and youngest ones are tasked with grinding the stone down into a powder. So the question is: what are the coordinators of this operation (just one of many) going to do with dolomite powder? Well, since it's a good source of magnesium oxide, it has many purposes, one of which is its usefulness as an alloying agent, especially when manufacturing lightweight products. I'll leave it at that. I've already overloaded your information processors.

So, to make a short story even longer, these Uphillers have decided it's time to come back and they need their slave labor back. But, they don't want you people joining forces to fight back. So, they keep a very low profile. And, of course they have people, like those scorching marauders, who will do their bidding for them, for a price. Some people are willing to do terrible things in exchange for currency. In the very, very old times they were called sell swords, because they exchanged their sword-wielding willingness for something valuable like money or property. Later on, they became known as mercenaries hired to be snipers or even freedom fighters, depending on one's positionality and their relationship to the organization that hired them; police officers became peace officers but they still required a bribe for their services, and how to even count the infinitesimal militias that formed organically and sometimes inorganically to respond to what they saw as a threat, whether it be the government or a transgendered person just trying to use the public bathroom at the mall. The latter did it happily for free, sans currency.

Ah, yes. But what is used as currency *these* days? What does one exchange with people for one's loyalty to them? The answer to that requires much more of our time. And, we think it's best if you rest now. We're tired of wearing these heavy wings anyway. Plus, we've got things of our own to worry about. We have an appointment with two of your people, coming up soon. We don't want to be late for that one. They are in trouble and don't know it. Damn it. Why can't we just be everywhere at once? And when do *we* ever get to rest?

Before we come back to visit you, we'll leave you with this tidbit of advice.

Find a way to organize your people, your Átmeneti. Unlike you, most of them are unwilling to interact with others who they consider outsiders. But they need to. It's the only way you'll ever get out of this mess. You can still change your future for the better. We know that for a fact, for we have seen it happen.

Through Tirin, you know that the other prisoners, who have been here for a while, already have already been organizing in secrecy, with the correspondence chain that they have. You all need to join up with them. Remind your people of the stories that you were taught. Remind them of how the Last

Ones learned to live in community with strangers who were afraid of them and of whom they were afraid as well. But they overcame the fear. They built community. Remind them that community is a verb. It's something that you do, not something that you have. Remind them of that.

Now, keep sleeping, my dear Egres. Forget me, but remember my words. Remember.

CHAPTER FIVE: BEDAP

Hold's shine casts a patchwork of towering silhouettes across the dense, forest floor, making the dew on the underbrush sparkle like a sea of silver speckles. Makk is standing on the ladder. One outstretched hand holds the hatch open from underneath, while the fingers on the other are poking at a glowing clump of moss on the hatch's rim.

Then, Makk's gaze moves further out into the woods away from the ruined structure under which the bunker access is hidden. Over the centuries, the forest has extended its viny tentacles up to the ruins, covering everything in thicket creeper and all kinds of bryophytes and lichens. Parts of the forest floor begin to light up in the same throbbing green. It's almost as if someone is leaving a trail of breadcrumbs like they do in the old children's stories that had ceased to be passed down through the generations. But these bread crumbs are green and they glow.

As they climbs out of the bunker, Takver is right behind them. She's quick to brace her hand up against the hatch so it doesn't slam down onto her head. By now she's seen the glowing carpet moss and has interpreted Makk's silence as shock and intrigue. She is also a bit in shock herself and she's definitely intrigued. It's all very surreal: mushrooms that glow green in the journal entries, now fuzzy moss that lights up and blinks green in the here and now!?

Takver watches as Makk squats down in front of the glowing artifacts, examining each one up close. Finally, Makk interrupts the silence.

"Moss. Moss. Moss. Mushroom."

And then, squatting down in front of the next one, they also squee in excitement.

"Istenem!" Makk let's out another squee. "It's so itty bitty and teeny weeny! Tak! Look at this one."

It's almost as if Makk is in a trance, forgetting that the two of them are outside and shouldn't be making a bunch of noise. Instead, Makk needs to avoid drawing any attention to themself or to Takver.

Takver just stands there on the ladder, holding the hatch open and watching the unlikely scene unfold. She merges with Makk, sending them a warm, red hue of warning.

You shouldn't be making so much noise, Sib.

Then, she too sees the bread-crumb-like trail of fluorescent patches that leads off a ways into the near distance.

Realizing that it's up to her to be on the lookout given Makk's complete disregard of her warnings, she climbs out of the bunker. Despite being really aggravated by Makk's complete disregard, she manages to close the hatch behind her with a quiet thump. Makk is a few paces ahead, and the clumps of moss and other fungi that were once glowing behind them have gone back to being their normal obscured selves.

As she gets closer to Makk, Takver notices that they's gone quiet. A few paces from her, Makk is sitting on their folded legs, resting their rear on their heels. The toes of their foot coverings are touching, while the heels are spread, creating a v-shape. Their frock is mostly bunched up at the front around their knees. They is cupping a toadstool mushroom with their right hand, green light pulsating. Their eyes are closed and they is completely silent.

Takver tries merging. *Sib? Are you okay? Can you share with me?*

Silence.

Meanwhile, unperceived by Takver, Makk is in a deep dream-like, almost catatonic state.

Moments back, when Makk first touches the throbbing mushroom, their flesh makes contact with the mushroom's universal veil that makes up its skin. And in an instant, the mycchorizal network, the thread-like filaments that connect plants, trees, and fungi to one another underground, is activated and communication across space-time can take place. After all, the mycelium as well as old growth trees have been around for hundreds of years. The nexus of roots and filaments with more roots and even more filaments is expansive. Thus, time-space as humans understand it makes little sense to them. They are timeless. We, humans, on the other hand are but a sip of breath in the respiratorial life cycle of an eternity.

Makk's eyes are closed at this point. But, because they is still interfaced with the ring device, they can still see. Although it's more like seeing with their mind's eye, except for the images are neither distant nor faint and blurry.

In an instant, Makk no longer senses the familiar forest smells. Instead, what they smells is evocative and comforting, and at the same time acrid and caustic. It's almost like the aroma of deep fried dough that fills the night air during Turning Sixteen, hints of savory mixed with sweet. It kind of reminds them of the rich fragrance of caramelized sugars when they boil down the maple sap for syrup, but also comingled with toxic poisonous off gases from asphalt from the Old Road.

As they focuses on their abruptly new surroundings, a whole different landscape pixelates into existence around them. The sounds are immediately overwhelming: humming motors, huffing hydraulic breaks, and other audible contamination that one can expect to hear at a busy, multi-level transportation hub.

Suddenly, they is standing in a covered complex, much like a parking garage but open to the ground floor on all sides except for where the shopping mall lies. Large angular support columns, stucco on cement, stretch from ground to ceiling, fifteen of them in their line of vision. To their right, a line of three big blue buses opens their doors to let board the cue of anticipative commuters. Directly in front of Makk there's a wooden, shed-like structure with a window under which there's a horizontal protrusion used to eat or drink at while standing, maybe waiting for one's bus to arrive. Above the window in black lettering reads <KÜRTŐSKALÁCS>. They sees the chimney cakes—spiraled strips of dough rotating on their hot irons—and realizes that's where the sweet, yeasty smell is coming from. There are fluorescent lights indicating that the pop-up establishment sells coffee. And, on the other side of the counter/protrusion inside the structure, there's a person staring directly at Makk. Only the bottom half of their bearded face can be seen from where Makk is looking, the rest is cast behind a shadow from the dim lighting. Under their nose, there is a big, tight lipped smile.

All the other people seem to be scurrying along with some destination in mind. There are a few people hanging out smoking cigarettes but most of them are walking quickly like they have some place to be and they are running late. Everyone, including Makk, is dressed so queerly. It feels to Makk as if they were in one of the performances that the storyweavers put on with Old Mester Delores when they recount the times from before the Great Dying. This particular scene, though, must be from an even older story, because these buses use rubber tires to move about instead of maglev, magnetic levitation. Makk knows what a tire is, their people have many uses for them like planters for flowers or potatoes.

Makk moves closer to the vague-faced person whose smile has ceased to waver, not even for a second. Then, without moving their lips, the person speaks to Makk. Their baritone voice is light and almost whimsical, as if they were talking cheerfully to a group of younguns without mouthing a word. Their face doesn't move at all.

Don't be afraid, Bedap. They is trying to be reassuring. *This is only a game.*

Then, they raises their hands as if signaling all around them. There mouth moves this time. "I created all of this for you."

They brings their once extended hands together, finger tips touching, creating triangle shapes. "Your physical body is still in the forest near the bunker." There's a slight pause. "I thought you'd never find my visual signals. It sure took you long enough." They laughs softly. "It seems like I've been trying to get your attention forever."

Makk interrupts the verbose stranger before their little speech turns into a never-ending monologue.

"Bedap? Why did you just call me Bedap? I'm Makk." The confused look on Makk's face sparks something in the stranger, and their smile transforms into a look of surprise and then to a look of recall.

"Oh, that's right. You're still Makk. I...you haven't adopted my...our, I mean, your new name yet. Oops." They playfully covers their mouth with their fingers, obviously embarrassed by the mistake. "Spoiler alert. Sorry about that. I must have the timeline confused. Have you and Takver gone together to see Old Tátos yet?"

You cock your head, squint your eyes, and scrunch up your forehead in confusion. Then, the person interrupts again.

"Oh, basszuskulc! I just need to stop talking." They's much

more animated than when Makk first saw them, their hands moving all over the place. "Okay. So, where to begin. Um, you are Bedap, but you are also Makk. Or, now you are Makk, but you are Bedap. And, I'm Bedap, too. I'm you. I used to be Makk. Oh, dear. I'm really screwing this one up."

Makk hasn't moved one bit. They just stands there frozen, waiting for something to make sense. Now, the person moves out of the shadows and their whole face is revealed.

"I am Bedap. You are Bedap. I am you. You are me. I mean, I'm an older you, and you are a younger me. We are us." With a confused look, they scratch at their head, one eye scrunched up like they is in deep thought. "Oh, dear. I don't remember it happening like this."

Makk stares at the face that is staring back at them. They realizes that everything around them has paused except for the interaction with this new person. And, then, after a moment, Makk speaks up again.

"So, you're trying to tell me that you are me?"

Now, the look on their face is one of defiance.

"Prove it. How do I know that you're not some imposter? I mean, this could be the ring device messing with me. How do I know you're real and that you're telling me the truth?"

The figure moves their gaze upward as if they's looking off into the distance, their lips scrunch left to form a thoughtful pout. Makk recognizes themself in that face. That light, too light, skin is so rare. It was thought to be bred out of existence. But, of course, Makk, strange, out-of-place Makk just had to be born a light shade of peach. They just had to stand out in more than one way among their people. It wasn't enough that they was, *had been* unable to share for the longest time.

Makk, *Bedap*, brings their attention back to the accused imposter. Then, Bedap speaks up again.

"Okay. I can do this." A few more seconds pass as they's considering how to proceed in this game of self trivia.

"Um...when we were only about seven Reawakenings old, you...we cut ourself on a piece of metal." They pulls up the garment covering their pale, once deep pink leg and reveals a white scar, "and the scar is still here along the bone."

Makk does the same, revealing an identical scar and then replies.

"You could just be making me see what I want to see. You're going to have to do better than that."

Bedap—older Makk—huffs and puffs a bit, folding their arms across their chest and slouching, but then accepts the challenge.

"Okay." And their face lights up as if a lightbulb just went off in their head. "I got it! Your favorite person from the stories of the Last Ones is Tele. Per ability to bring out the latent telepathy in per people after decades of training was always admirable. You...we secretly hoped that our sharing ability was also just latent. You...we had suffered so much until we met Takver."

Younger Bedap's defiance is turning into annoyance as they feels that they's being toyed with.

"This is not proof." New Bedap brings their hands that had been cupping their knees up to rest at their waist in a gesture of affront. "You could've figured that out based on Tak's and my usage of the device. I'm not even close to being convinced, and I'm starting to lose my patience with you."

Then, Not-so-new Bedap remembers something that neither of them has ever told anyone, not even Takver who was their closest friend.

"You've never kissed anyone! There! I said it. You've been around for sixteen Reawakenings and no one has ever shown any romantic interest in you. You're treated like an outcast. And, deep down inside, you are relieved that your people aren't with you because that way you don't have to face the daily shame of being so different from everyone else."

Less-experienced Bedap's face changes shade making them look like a beetroot. They never really meant to have those feelings and once they hears how it sounds when it comes from someone else—even if they's them and vice versa—they's instantly embarrassed and ashamed. How could they be glad that their people are gone? How could they be so callus and cruel to think such a thing? They instinctively looks around to make sure no one else could have heard that. The landscape directly behind them is the woods by the bunker. The shift in visual scenery is followed by an abrupt change that triggeresthe other senses as well. The general smell of the forest was immediately familiar: dew covered leaves and decaying duff. Even the air feels a bit more damp and there is no slight wind blowing up against their face like back at the chimney cake stand.

Then they spots Takver standing behind them, staring at them with their head slightly cocked to the side. The light from Hold outlines her from behind, making her silhouette glow silver.

"Hey. Focus." Chimney-cake-vendor Bedap snaps.

Disoriented Bedap jerks back around, the vendor cart now in front of them. They closes their eyes to help catch their balance as a bout of vertigo hits them.

"Pay attention. I have to go soon. But I want to give you this." They pulls out a shiny, disk-like object. "But I need you to trade with me."

There's a pause while Bedap as their younger self processes all that is happening. The look on their face takes older Bedap back to that very moment and they remembers just how disoriented they felt.

"Sorry. I know this is a lot to happen all at once. But our time is short. I need you to get the strange container with the piece of hair in it. I need you to go get it for me. It's in a see-through, hard glass container."

Now. Then. To Come.

Bedap is looking at their older self. They has so many questions but there's no time to ask.

"Go get it, Makk. Go!" Bedap's urgency causes them to start, and they quickly push themself onto their feet.

They turns around and looks at Takver. She is just staring at them, speechless. Then, new Bedap takes off toward the bunker. As they passes Takver, they says aloud, "Sorry. No time to explain. I'll be right back."

Takver watches as her sibling lifts up the hatch and climbs down into the bunker, letting the hatch close behind them with a bit of a loud thud, louder than she'd normally tolerate. She shakes her head and turns back to where Makk was kneeling. She can now see the glowing mushroom.

She walks toward it slowing, thinking to herself, *This is just like in the journals.* She kneels on the ground in more or less the same spot Makk had just been in. She reaches her hand out, carefully extending her fingers out toward the cap. She's been warned her whole life not to touch mushrooms that she didn't recognize; they could be poisonous after all and you might forget to wash your hands and accidentally put your fingers in your mouth.

Needless to say, she's hesitant because she doesn't recognize this variety. It looks like a toadstool: umbrella-esque cap, leathery scales of a different color than the cap, long stem with a volva at the base which used to protect the fruit when it was still immature.

Takver is just about to make contact with the mushroom when Makk, now Bedap—but she doesn't know that yet—when they returns abruptly. Bedap grabs her hand, stopping it from touching the glowing fungus.

"Wait, Tak. I need to do something first."

Bedap is now squatting next to Takver and touching the mushroom.

"I'll explain soon. There's no time right now."

The Bedap from the other end is back in sight. It seems as though they hasn't moved a centimeter. This other Bedap must be around the age of Bodza, their netherblood, who is several Reawakenings older than Málna, who they grew up thinking was their eggblood. They likes how the older version of them looks with a beard. It's different and it looks good on them.

"Set the vial, the glass thingy with the hair, down at the base of the mushroom." Bearded Bedap interrupts peach-fuzz Bedap's wandering thoughts.

Bedap places the cylindrical crystal vessel at the base of the mushroom. Takver watches as they does this. Then, both watch as the mushroom's volva opens at the ground and seemingly swallows the vial.

What in the dry earth?! Sib! What the!? Takver stiffens and pulls back as if she were afraid that the mushroom would ingest her next.

And just as she thinks things couldn't get any stranger, the impossible happens.

A flat, shiny glass disk comes out of the same orifice into which the vial disappeared only moments earlier.

According to Takver, Makk is reacting way too calmly and collected in response to the strangeness that just took place. Makk takes the disk between their thumb and forefinger and holds it up to inspect it more closely.

It's light and cold to the touch.

Younger Bedap closes their eyes and, within another moment, reopens them. At this point, the mushroom has stopped glowing. Whatever had just transpired seems to have come to an end. Bedap is on their feet again and is heading back toward the bunker.

Makk! STOP! Takver mindyells to them, a red hue flashes through Bedap's mindvision. *Will you tell me what the scorching earth is happening already!?*

Bedap stops suddenly, their hand grasping the handle of the hatch access.

"Bedap." There's a pause. "You can call me Bedap, now."

Presently, they's making eye contact with their sister.

"Bedap. I like the sound of it. And, I really like the beard. I wonder when it'll start to grow." They strokes the ghost beard at their chin and a cheeky grin forms on their face.

Takver thinks they's talking to her, but they's talking more to themself. She gives them a look of bewilderment, reducing the space between her shoulders and her earlobes. Her face is scrunched up. Bedap receives the facial clues, interprets them as confusion, then speaks up.

"Sorry, Tak. Come on let's go. I'll tell you all about it. It's just all too exciting. Hurry up!"

They opens the hatch and is down the ladder before Takver can even straighten herself up. Then, Takver thinks she hears a twig snap off in the distance.

Just as she turns her head to glance over her shoulder, she catches a glimpse of a black-ringed, fluffy cat-like tail before it disappears into the moonlit night.

PART THREE: TO COME

CHAPTER ONE: TRELL

From the Journals of Trell

MONDAY, SEPTEMBER 2ND, 2002 - POPLAR HALL

I was today's years old (22!) when I made my first ever journal entry. I'm writing it right now. I have a blue, ballpoint pen that I found in a box in my dorm room, probably from last semester. But I bought this notebook special just for this class. It's green and gold like the colors of this university and thick, about the the size of my math textbook. I bought it right after class today when I found out that we have to keep a journal that the professor's going to check and read over throughout the course. We have a weekly word count. And it's like almost half of our grade! Wild! I'm excited to start a journal. I mean, I just turned twenty-two this summer. Why hadn't I started a diary or something before now?

This is my second semester here at college and I'm taking

Introduction to Women's Studies and three other classes this term. I'm pretty excited about this course so far. Our first assignment is to read Chapter One and then write our first journal entry from one of the prompts at the end.

The chapter is entitled Sex, Gender, and Social Construction and it opens with this quote from an anonymous author:

~our lives are structured around ideas of what is appropriate for a girl, and what is appropriate for a boy.

Isn't that the truth?

I think it's important to write my notes in here so that my teacher (Hi, Professor Gay!) knows what I'm basing my answer to the prompt on and that I'm actually doing the readings.

Chapter One — Several key concepts:

1) nature vs. nurture - biology vs. social forces

2) SEX: characteristics based on anatomy and/or biology used to classify a person as male or female — e.g. sex organs, chromosomes, hormones, brain structure, and traits like breasts or facial hair

3) INTERSEX: they (singular, the person) have sex traits that make them different from predominant notions of biological femaleness and/or maleness — e.g. genitals that seem somewhat like both sexes (larger clitoris that resembles a penis; external organs resembling one, but internal systems that resemble another e.g. one ovary, one testicle); varied secondary characteristics like body shape, body hair, etc.; some intersex people may find out later in life during puberty or adulthood, and some may never know because externally they resemble one sex, but internally is where the mix is; only 1.7% of population is intersex

4) the SOCIAL CONSTRUCT of sex: sex categories get simplified for social reasons and ignore the spectrum (people are used to a gender binary); sex to some degree was constructed by humans

5) social construct: concept or perception of something based on the collective views developed and maintained within a society or social group — varies among people and cultures; comes from social practices, not nature; one's socially constructed sex is not only determined by biology, but also by human activity and human choice, i.e. political, economic, and cultural factors

6) ASSIGNED sex: a term used instead of biological sex to show that sex is more than just biological fact

7) sex IDENTITY: what one understands to be their own sex with a deeply held internal sense

8) Revised definition of SEX: humans and other organisms are not simply female or male; a better definition would describe that sex is related to our chromosomal, chemical, and anatomical organization; would also take into account that it is more than just biology

9) GENDER: attributes regarding appearance and behavior — traditionally gender has been the non-biological aspects of being female or male in a gender binary; cultural expectations

10) gender EXPRESSION: how one expresses how they identify — externally through one's clothing, hairstyle, the way one acts, moves and speaks, whether or how one wears makeup, their pronoun, among other things

11) gender IDENTITY: one's internal sense of one's gender or of belonging to a group or category — western cultures believe often that sex entails gender; femme vs. butch (can be used for gays that act more feminine or masculine or don't conform to one); sex and gender should not be conflated — sex should describe reproductive organs; feminine and masculine for gender — sex is more biological and gender is less biological

12) TRANSGENDER: when one's sex identity, gender identity, and/or gender expression are not in alignment with binary

ideas of one's assigned/designated sex at birth — some trans individuals undergo hormone therapy and/or gender confirmation surgery; only a small number of trans individuals desire so-called sex operations or to medically transition - nor is it necessary; socially some trans individuals may choose a different name and pronoun

13) CISGENDER: people whose gender identity aligns with their assigned sex at birth

14) gender NONCONFORMING: people whose gender is different from perceived societal expectations

15) GENDERQUEER: express gender non-normatively, may wish to stress the idea that one's gender can change over time or is constantly influx.

16) Revised definition of GENDER: gender is not an either/or situation; less biological and more socially constructed; gender as a process; something one does, not something that one has; unstable and open to change, flexible; the categorization of gender is a problem in and of itself...categories are bound to fall short

I HAVE to stop here and reflect. So, I've gotten gender wrong all along. When I am asked my gender on a form, I should put down man not male. But I don't feel like a man. My dad is a man and I would never want to be compared to him in that way. He's a man's man: degrades women; talks vulgarly about them to make his buddies laugh; gets physically violent with them or at least used to. So, NO, I refuse to be a man. I am pretty feminized in the sense that I spend most of my time with women and feel more comfortable around them, and when we're together we do woman things like sit around and talk about dating and eating ice cream (I've seen women do this in the movies, too). I don't have much to contribute when the topic of "that time of the month" comes up because I don't menstruate for the lack of sexual parts. I buy so-called women's jeans because I like how they fit better. Overall, I can relate more to women than I can to certain men. Out of all the men that I can relate to, gay men are at the top. Unless, they are the "masc only" kind of men that are looking for non-girly guys to date. I definitely am not anyone's masculine guy. The entire "masc only" identification on gay.com is gross and exclusionary. Whatever.

17) SEXUAL ORIENTATION: the attraction one has to others based on one's sex and/or gender in relation to another's sex and/or gender — more than gay, bi, or straight and is fluid, non-static - it can change over time

18) ASEXUAL: someone who experiences little to no sexual attraction to other people — also non-static, fluid

IMPORTANT NOTE: sex identity, gender, gender identity, and sexual orientation are all independent of each other; there can be many combinations of the above. Basically, it's messy

PROMPT: Write about a time that you were made aware of your gender. Use some of the key concepts from the chapter to show that you understood them.

I HAVE SO many stories about my gender struggles but one stands out so I'm going to listen to my intuition and write about the time I was called a sissy by people that I loved and so it hurt. I think it'll fit nicely with the fact that one of our goals in this course is to remember the women in our family. Unfortunately, this story doesn't do a good job at honoring my grandma and my aunt, but it is an important memory that I carry with me and it is a part of their legacy.

I had just turned 8 years old the day before my cousin Angela had her birthday celebration. Her mom is my dad's older sister. At that time and age, I only saw my downstate aunts and cousins twice a year or so. They lived closer to the big city and they had nice houses that didn't smell of mold or wood stove. This particular aunt in question, her husband, her daughter Angela, and Angela's brother had driven the two hours up to the country to have a riverside birthday bash for her. Everyone was there: our grandma and grandpa, me and my mom, dad, and three siblings. My dad has three sisters and two brothers and at that time there were ten cousins or so. We were all there. The goal was to float the river on inner tubes from old tractor tires that you could rent from a small store up river. We'd start up stream and then rest on the lower high banks past the island where my dad had built a hunting shack (it was public land so the shack was probably illegal). There we would eat hotdogs and chips and then my cousin would smash open her piñata and we'd all scream and scramble for the candy. Then, there was the cake. My grandma always made us the coolest birthday cakes. She is such a good cook. That year my cousin who was turning seven got a race car cake because her parents had just gotten her and her brother brand new kid's race cars. Their family was big into that Jr. Nascar Car scene as I like to call it now. I have no idea what the races were really called. My immediate family didn't have that kind of money.

So, there we were, tons of cousins, aunts and uncles, parents, and grandparents, floating down the river. I couldn't swim very good yet, so I had to wear a lifejacket, which was fine with me because the rubber from the inner tube always seemed to rub my nipples to the point they would get raw, and that was a nightmare. The lifejacket was a nylon material and thus much less abrasive on my sensitive bits. Plus, the lifejacket made me look like I had huge chest muscles.

When we finally got to our picnic spot, we were all starving. Playing in the water was hard work.

"Are you sure you want to eat now?" The parents would ask.

"You know you can't swim for a half an hour after you eat. Remember how I told you about Gram's little brother who died when he was just a baby in just two, TWO inches of water?!"

My parents at least were very strict about this rule.

"Yes, we're sure!" Our growling stomachs forced words from our mouths.

It was a particularly sunny day that day but there was the occasional straggler cloud that would cover the sun up enough to make it chilly with the right breeze. So, I grabbed by Mr. T, blue cotton t-shirt and pulled it on over my head. I felt the material stretch to the seams as it took the shape of my ripped, bulky, lifejacket chest.

I was so proud of my new figure as I strutted around the sandy bank, showing off. Eventually, I made it to the picnic table where the chips and pop were. The picnic table was burgundy and the paint pealed off in some sections. I have no idea how whoever put the table there got it there because it was big and heavy and how did people get a car on this side of the river? I grabbed a paper plate and began to pour the greasy, salty, ruffled fried potato slices onto it when I caught the glare of my aunt and grandma who were sitting next to each other on the bench of the table.

"Take that t-shirt off, you little sissy." My aunt sneered, speaking in a low voice as so others couldn't hear the words that were just meant for me and my grandma.

"Boys don't wear shirts when they are swimming. Sissy boy. Take that off." The look of disgust on grandma's face must have left a sour taste in her mouth.

Then, they both looked at each other and started laughing, my grandma covering her mouth a bit to hide her missing molars.

I don't remember what I did after that. But I do remember how I felt. I felt shameful, ridiculous, and unsafe. I don't think I ever told anyone about that before now. That was fourteen years ago!

This is where I circle back to the opening quote:

~our lives are structured around ideas of what is appropriate for a girl, and what is appropriate for a boy.

Auntie and Grandma felt the need to correct my behavior which they saw as not conforming to the gender (re: sex) that I was assigned at birth. Since I was born with external organs that could produce sperm, I was assigned male at birth. That means that most likely after I was born everyone that met me or heard about me for the first time would have ask my mom or whoever was holding me in the moment, "Is it a girl or a boy?" I'm sure after I slid out of the birth canal, the doctor announced, "You have a baby boy."

So, because of the organs between my legs I was lead down a path that had been paved for me with the blood, sweat, and tears of all the other boys assigned at birth who came before me.

Here are some rules I was expected to follow as a boy in training:

DO NOT play with dolls
DO NOT wear pink
DO NOT jump rope with the girls
DO NOT wear a t-shirt when you're swimming
DO NOT sit down when you pee
DO NOT cry, EVER, especially in public
DO NOT let other boys see you being weak
DO NOT act like a girl or you will be called a sissy
And the list goes on.

So, were my aunt and grandma trying to steer me in the right path? Were they trying to protect me? Did they have my best interest in mind? Or, where they reinforcing certain behaviors that they saw appropriate because they agreed with them? Were they truly appalled by my behavior?

I may never know. But here's a guess at the framework that my aunt and grandma used to navigate their world:

To them, gender must be equal to sex and therefore binary, either or, two options only. A baby born with a penis must be a boy. Especially in my rural, backwoods context where students get the opening day of deer season off of school, but not Martin Luther King Jr.'s birthday, almost everyone in my neighborhood is a cousin of some sort and everyone who works is a blue-collar worker. So, boys must not wear dresses or makeup unless they are actors or politicians. Boys must keep short hair unless they are actors or musicians. Boys must play with trucks and tools unless they are barbers then they can play with scissors and brushes and perfumes. Boys must learn to hunt unless they are sissies and then they are subject to ridicule by "both" genders. Etcetera.

Here was my eight-year-old take away. Auntie and Grandma are mean. They made me feel bad and I didn't understand what I had done wrong even after they explained it. I never trusted them after that. I always felt different and unliked. I don't miss them even though I'm over four hundred miles away and will probably only see Grandma when I go home for summer break. This particular aunt was never a really big part of my, our, my and my siblings' lives anyway.

Maybe someday I'll forgive them both.

~

MISSING JOURNAL ENTRIES

~

WEDNESDAY, NOVEMBER 20TH, 2002 - POPLAR HALL

Tomorrow is Thanksgiving. We didn't have classes since break starts today, and despite that the dorm sure is empty. I decided to stay here for the long weekend. Home is fourteen hours away and too long of a drive for such a short weekend. I'll be missing out on yummy food and family, but it'll be nice just to chill out around here. Some of my friends who are from other countries are here, too, but they are traveling to NYC and other places. I'm broke so I'll be eating my ramen noodles in a styrofoam cup and going clubbing later.

On another note (and the main reason I'm writing this entry today), I got my acceptance letter! I'm going to Ghaliza to study abroad next term. I can't believe it! I'm more excited than nervous. I don't really have any details yet except for that school starts in February, which means I'll have a longer break. But, it does go into June so I'll lose some of my summer. But I'll be in Ghaliza! In a beach town! It's more of a city. The city of the olive tree is its nickname. I've done a bit of research and there are over 400,000 inhabitants and they are famous for their seafood, especially octopus. What?! Also, the region is co-officially bilingual so I'll get to use some of the Portuguese I've been studying alongside Spanish.

Next month, I have to drive up to another university for an orientation and meet some of my fellow exchange students. The way the exchange works, I pay my tuition and room and board here at my university and the student that I exchange places with pays their costs, and we just swap places. Pretty cool!

∽

MISSING JOURNAL ENTRIES

∽

WEDNESSDAY, JUNE 25TH, 2003 - AV. DE CASTRELOS
Five days are left until I'm officially done with my last

semester of undergraduate school. These four years have flown by, but I feel like I've accomplished, experienced, and adventured more than I ever had within these almost twenty-three years that I bear. There are so many changes in my life at this time and I feel as if I'm being overloaded. The worst part is that the future is more foggy than ever, yet I'm really comfortable with the unknown. I'm trying to start a new life on a different continent, in a country whose unemployment rate is extremely high right now and where I'm currently undocumented. I've been living here on an expired visa for several months because I didn't take the necessary actions to get my residency. It was a stupid mistake. Plus, I've fallen in love. I've fallen in love with a land, a linguistic variety, a people, and most of all a boy. Well, he's a man but in the gay world we say boy to refer to anyone 18+ years of age who is dateable.

There is no way I can leave now. I have all of these plans and future scenarios running through my head and how I will make it possible so that I can stay here. My dad has been a huge financial help but that will not last much longer. All I really need and desire to do is to become a citizen of the larger union of countries here. It would be the easiest thing for me to do, yet at the same time it is going to be extremely difficult. I've got a world of possibilities in front of me as far as employment goes, yet I'm lacking a work permit and legal status, or my English isn't British. Some of my friends think that it would be so great to have my passport, but little do they know that I'd do almost anything to exchange it to stay here. All I can do is sit here and wait and be the optimist that I am, hoping that the last thing that I have to do is get on a plane and fly back. "My country this of thee, sweet land of manufactured liberty." I don't want to go home.

. . .

SUNDAY, JULY 6TH, 2003 - AV. DE CASTRELOS, NORTH OF PARK

School has been over for a few weeks and Summer is in full swing. This city sure feels different now that the rain has stopped. The sun is almost too hot for me. I'm always finding myself looking for shade as I walk up and down the voluptuous streets of this curvaceous city that I've been calling my home for the past six months. This part of the world is so hilly. My buns have never been so tight in my life!

I had to find a new room to rent a few weeks back. When classes ended our lease ended as well. My fellow exchange students have all left to go back across the ocean or to stay around and travel to other places that for me always seem too far away and too expensive. I decided to stay here and look for work. Luckily, I found a place right across the street from where I was staying before. Javi was in my class and just happened to have a spare room. My new roommates seem nice, too. I guess the flat is Javi's and he rents two rooms: one to me and the other to Kveta, a student from Bratislava. She told me her name means flower blossom. She's beautiful and reminds me of a dark-haired version of the little girl character that what's-her-name played in that vampire movie, Interview something. I can't quite remember. She gave me a small picture of herself; it looks like she cut it out of a year book.

Kveta asked me if my name was Eastern European and so I told her about my grandpa's parents and how they'd left that part of the world and started a new life back in the New World. But, I couldn't tell her much more than that. Then she told me that I should try and get citizenship through my great-grandparents. I had had no idea that that was even an option. She went on to explain how her city used to be part of the same Empire before that project ended in the aftermath of World War I. She explained that she was twelve years old when her country split into two separate countries. And how people in her part of the world are used to turmoil and conflict. She's such an interesting person.

After talking to her, I feel like I know nothing about the larger world even after living here for over six months. I don't even know the stories of my great grandparents. How did these stories become lost to me and my generation? I guess I'm going to have to get some more information if I'm going to try and pursue getting citizenship through my family. I really hope this is an option. And how much will this cost? How long will it take?

I guess one thing I can do to start is learn to speak like the locals there. So, I found a book here in one of my favorite bookstores. I wish it came with a tape or a CD, though, because I don't know how anything is pronounced. And the book's pronunciation guide is crap. But I did learn one phrase so far: szeretlek. I love you.

P.S. I just got a phone call. I have a job interview tomorrow at a kindergarten up the hill toward the university! My friend Francisca is taking me. Wish me luck!

SUNDAY, JULY 27TH, 2003 - AV. DE CASTRELOS NORTH OF PARK

I got a letter from one of my sisters today. She did what I asked of her and had my, *our* grandpa and grandma document some of the missing history of grandpa's parents. Here's what grandma wrote for me:

Leky Imre - 37 years old, widowed

Born in the capital on May 15, 1880. Paid own passage of $50 to board ship. He was 17th in line to board to get off ship. He was a peasant. He had $16. He left on December 2, 1905 and arrived at immigration on December 17, 1905.

Makutek Erzsébet - 20 years old, single

Paid own passage of $50 to board ship. She was 16th in line

to board ship and to get off. She was a servant. She was born in a smaller town outside of the capital. She had $20. She left on December 2, 1905 and arrived at immigration on December 17, 1905. They met on the ship. They got married in 1905.

He worked in a coal mine. They moved to Flint and he ran a fruit market. They had seven kids and then they moved to a farm in Lake Station. He raised beans and cucumbers and sold them. He raised chickens and horses.

Wow. How cool to have this family history. When I go back to visit, I'll have to sit down with Grandma and Grandpa and have them tell me some more stories. Just doing the math, there seems to be some holes in the story, but those can be patched later on. This is a great start. There is so, so much that we don't know. And, it would be a shame to lose those stories. We've already lost so much of their heritage.

MISSING JOURNAL ENTRIES

MONDAY, JULY 27TH, 2020 - DMV

You told me to start writing stuff down again, so here I am. Better late than never I guess.

I'm still not sure who *you* are. Since you first contacted me a little over two months ago, you are always in my thoughts. I'm so curious about you and the world that you live in. You only told me your name. Bedap. What a curious name. I want to know so much more about you.

I've boughten the books you asked for. I also started reading them. I've almost finished The Dispossessed. I've already finished Octavia's Parables. I couldn't put those ones down. They are too good. Scary. Informative. Amazing. And, too good.

There's so much in those books about the necessity of having a community. I'm learning, too, that in The Dispossessed as well, having people on whom to rely and with whom to share the tasks of everyday life is essential not only for survival (because just surviving isn't enough) but also for building relationships through which we experience the joys and the pains of life.

All three books are awesome. But I have to admit that it was pretty cool when I came upon a character named Bedap in The Dispossessed. When I first read the name, I put the stress on the first syllable and the [e] became /eh/ as in /BREHD/ (bread), /BE-dap/. But, then, I played with the pronunciation a bit, putting the stress on the [a]. Once, I said /buh-DAP/, it clicked. I'd heard that name before. And, then the memory of how you pronounced your name came to me clearly. Bedap.

And how is it that you can talk to me through a mushroom? Telepathy? Telekinesis?

Through some sort of tele-something that allows you to communicate into the past is the only way that I can make sense of it.

Is it indeed a backward movement, or is your present—my future—happening at the same time as my present—your past? You said, or rather I heard in my mind, that we were somehow related genetically. Who are our mutual connections? How did you manage to connect to *me*? Why *me*?

I can't help thinking that you aren't even real, that I hallucinated you. Am I delusional? I don't know whether to seek help or just keep my mouth shut. If I am schizophrenic I'd rather not be locked up unless the voices are asking me to do atrocious things, like match my socks. A little humor helps me cope with all of this.

Are you going to come back? Will you speak to me again? This waiting is driving me bonkers! I don't know if you'll ever come back.

Meanwhile, I've started collecting the things you asked for.

Besides the books, I'm researching how to make cloth out of stinging nettles (Ouch! How can that be comfortable?) and jute, and how to not die while foraging. I started following my new favorite forager on social media. She has a lot of awesome tips and tricks for finding safe foods to eat, and her recipes are awesome, too. She's this woman who modifies forager with the word Black which refers to a certain diaspora of people from the African continent. The name itself is a history lesson into ways that white supremacist governments created laws that banned newly freed people from black communities from harvesting wild food in public places like parks and state-owned forests. The idea was to create the conditions so that those formerly enslaved people were forced to go back to their former owners (people legally owned people back then!) to beg for work so they could feed themselves and their families. Can you believe that? The thought of those men (they were mostly men who believed the same lie that they themselves fabricated in order to create a privileged group and the expense of others, the lie of whiteness) sitting in their cozy offices creating laws to keep the oppressed populations poor, desperate, and begging, just the thought of it rages inside of me and makes my hands shake. The idea that this trick has been around and used by powerful people since forever is daunting and it makes me want it all to end just so that we can start from scratch. Sorry for being so cynical. Anyway, what I'm trying to say is that I'm doing what you've asked.

I imagine you must have the need to find your own wild food if you're asking an ancestor from hundreds of years before your time to look up information about it and then write it down, being sure it gets passed down to the next generation. That's wild to think about.

You told me to find the relative who has kept the journals. I'm sorry to report that I have not been lucky so far. I will not give up. But who is this relative? How do I know if they are still alive? And if they are dead, who would have gotten the journals? This task you've given me seems impossible. And, yet you couldn't stress its importance enough. But, you're going to have to give me more information. I need names and dates. I need to know which side of the family to focus on.

There are so many questions that I want to ask you.

How is it that someone from the future is asking someone from the past to get them research material? Is the future as bad as I imagine it has to be? Is access to historical documents so limited that someone has to time travel to learn more about where they come from? I mean it must be time travel. What else?

There is so much I want to know about you.

When are you going to contact me again?

It also feels that this is a message-in-a-bottle kind of communique: will you ever get these journal entries? From the vast ocean, will these floating messages make it to land for one particular person to find? At least the intention of the message in a bottle is for some random person to find the bottle and hopefully then send help to the person who wrote the message; anyone with a boat or the means to rescue the writer is a welcome recipient. But, I'm writing to a specific person and I have no idea where, or when, that person is. I'm just supposed to "make sure the journals get passed down through the generations." I'm going to need more to go on.

You emphasized how important it is that I carry out your wishes, and that so much is resting on me being successful.

Ok... No pressure. Does sarcasm exist in the future?

MONDAY, SEPTEMBER 28TH, 2020 - BH

I don't really know why I'm feeling this way. I mean, it's pretty crappy that I have to turn something that is about someone else—a very special someone who is about to come into this world—into something about me. Something just doesn't feel right about it though.

A good friend of mine invited me and the partner to a so-called 'gender reveal' party for their unborn child. I'd heard of them before, but hadn't thought much about them. It was going to be outside and we would wear masks and try to keep our physical distance from one another. The pandemic is still killings thousands of people everyday. What a strange time to be alive.

Basically, before the party the parents don't know the sex of the baby and by the time the party will have ended the parents will have been told the sex, and everyone will scream and clap their hands. The revelation can be done in many ways and this is where the planner's creativity gets to come into play. At this party, there was cake with white frosting. The parents would cut into the cake revealing a pink sponge if it's a girl and blue if it's a boy. I guess this is a fairly new thing that cake and cupcake makers in the bakeries of the world are hired to do.

Now, don't get me wrong. It's exciting to celebrate babies. I get it. I'm not interested in raising children full-time myself, but I get why other people do. What I don't understand is why the baby's sex is so important at such a young age, especially to friends and even strangers.

Before the party, the baby's sex is determined by a scan that is done using ultrasound technology that involves a lot of sticky gel and a device that is rubbed around the naked, protruding stomach. The device must emit sonic waves that penetrate the womb and allow the technician to capture a distorted image of the fetus. This is mostly done to check on the health of the baby. But, people here are obsessed with knowing the sex of their baby so they can plan.

This is where it starts to feel yucky to me.

How does sex determine the plans for the baby? And why is

it a 'gender' reveal party if what is actually being revealed in the baby's sex?

I mean there is an assumption that the baby is going to either have the capability to produce sperm or produce eggs. Having a baby that falls somewhere on the spectrum of intersex is something that I don't even think expecting parents take into consideration.

But, at a basic level, doesn't it seem strange, even wrong to announce the genitalia of your child to the public?

I mean, why do your friends need to know the sex of your baby unless they are going to help you take care of the baby. Different body parts require special attention, especially when diaper changing is involved, but little else.

Before coming to the party they asked us guests to wear either pink or blue: pink if the baby is a girl; blue if the baby is a boy. This is where things get messy and weird for me.

The elephant in the room, the unspoken assumption is that if you are born with a penis you will be a boy and all the gifts that you buy for the baby boy will either be blue, but rarely pink, and there will be little baby shirts that say things like "LITTLE MR. STEAL YOUR GIRL" or "ON SUNDAYS WE WATCH [insert a picture of a football] WITH DADDY" or "MOMMY'S NEW MAN."

And the right-wingers and their vocal politicians say that *we,* from the LGBTQIA2S+ spectrum, are sexualizing their children will drag shows! "Little Mr. steal your girl" not only sexualizes your child but it perpetuates a key tenet of patriarchy in which girls are for the taking by men.

Now that I'm writing about it, I think I've figured out what bothers me so much.

A basic, unspoken, agreed on understanding at these parties is that there are only two genders, a baby is born with one of them. And, this is where the cuteness breaks down into ugliness for me.

When I was born, my parents decided I was going to be a boy because I was born with a penis and testes. Now, I'm sure it wasn't just my parents. I can imagine that all the staff at the hospital also congratulated my mom (dad wasn't there) on "your new baby boy." Binary gender is the socially accepted norm in mainstream institutions like healthcare and family.

Insert me into this binary norm:

Growing up I wanted to play with my sisters (who were also given a gender at birth) while they were playing with their dolls and dollhouses. I mean, the fast food drive-thru toy was the coolest! On special occasions we got to get nuggets or a cheeseburger and we usually went through the drive-thru. How cool to do that with dolls! Then, I'd hear from someone (mostly mom or dad) who didn't like that I played with dolls: "Why is he playing with dolls?" or "Get outside and do boy things!"

I have this one memory where my mom came to school during recess and she and the recess monitors watched us kids play. We must have been in the second or third grade. I was playing jump rope with my friends—all girls at the time—when my mom came up to me and asked why I didn't want to play with the boys. I just remember that jumping and skipping rope was fun and all those songs and senseless rhymes were so cool (until I discovered the underlying racial bigotry in some of them later on in life)!

One time, my mom took my brother and I to the store in town and we got to pick out outfits. It was the late 80s and neon colors were all the fashion. My mom said we could pick out a pair of shorts and a shirt from the rack with the fluorescent blue, pink, green, and yellow matching tops and bottoms. My brother chose the green and I chose the pink. It was super cool. I remember being so excited. All my friends wore pink, after all. Later that day, my dad gave my mom a bunch of crap for letting me pick out a pink outfit. I'm pretty sure he was mortified, but he let me wear the outfit to his buddy's house up the road. The old man had always been really nice to me and to this day I think it was sincere. My dad made some smart-arse comment about my clothes and the friend looked at me and asked, "Can I call you pinky?" Of course he could! I was thrilled!

One of my uncles always called me twink. I never knew what it meant to him or in general. In the gay community, a twink is a young, usually skinny, guy. Nowadays, if the twink has muscles you can call him a twunk: a combination of twink and hunk. This same uncle used to make fun at my expense all the time, especially around my brother and cousins. I used to have this purple bike with a banana seat and a basket in front with ribbons that flowed from the handle bars. Its frame was designed in a way that a skirt could be worn without causing a wedgie. Someone had gotten it for me in a yard sale. A bike was a bike when you were poor. My uncle proudly christened my bike as "the fairy bike." I remember it making me feel really bad at the time. Now, I'm proud of my fairy bike mainly because I'm a proud fairy.

One time, I was outside in the parking lot of the fast-food equivalent of a hair salon: $8 for a boy's cut, $15 for a girl's. I must have been about thirteen or fourteen. I'd recently had my hair permed but it gave me more of a mushroom hairdo than the gorgeous curls that I'd hoped for. By that time, I had grown some boobs and my nipples protruded a bit from my t-shirts. I used to put bandaids over them so they weren't so obvious. It wasn't that weird for me to have little boobies. My dad and brother both had them, the former because he was always chubby. I wasn't very chubby in the stomach so my boobs stuck out a bit. So, there I was standing in the parking lot of a college town when a car drove by and yelled out in my direction, "Is that a guy or a girl!?" Laughter. I looked around and I was the only person outside in my immediate surroundings. I hid and cried.

In high school, I was called 'gay' and 'fag' and other terms that were supposed to be insults. I took them as insults at the time. But how is being gay an insult for me now? It just isn't. It was used as a way for others to bully me. And, it worked. I hated myself. I hated that I was girly. I hated that I had little boobies. I hated that I had to make excuses for why I didn't want to hang out with the guys. And, it wasn't until I discovered the locker room, among my boy peers, that I started getting strange sensations and would day dream. Now, I love being gay. But, am I gay? Could I be something else? The more I think of the term gay, the more it doesn't sit well with me. It describes a sexuality based on an assumption of gender and assigned sex. If I'm not a man, how can I be gay for being sexually attracted to some men? I'm not a woman. I'm not a man. But, I am sexually attracted to masculine men, but also to feminine ones.

At university, I used to buy so-called girl's jeans because they had the fit that I was going for: tight on the legs, fitting around the hips, and boot cut so the legs flared around my shoes. And, at the time, I didn't have a lot of facial hair and if it did grow in I'd shave it off completely, mainly because it was patchy at best. I had an adorable baby face, though. My friends and I would go out clubbing a lot. One night, I wore big hooped earrings and a cream-colored turtleneck with my girly jeans, my boobies protruding and tightening the fabric in that area of my chest. Standing in line to the Wednesday night drag show, I heard several people looking in my direction: "Who's she? I haven't seen her here before." To this day, I never use the she pronoun unless I'm with my friends. It's normal for my gay guy friends to refer to each other as she. It's also normal for them to denigrate women and vaginas, and that has never been okay with me. '

My whole life, I was made to feel somehow bad about the gender that was prescribed to me. Later on, I convinced myself that I was a gay guy, never man. Man is a word that I'd never use to describe myself. Ever. I can check off male on the form, but never man. I've also never identified as a woman. I do identify as girly or sissy. And, if I have a moment of 'manliness' I'll comment on how butch I am. But, it's always jocular, never serious.

So, here lies the problem.

How does someone like me fit into the gender binary? I'm not a man, and I'm also not a woman. Sometimes, I feel like conforming to the gender that was prescribed to me. Since my mid-30s, I sport a beard. I love how my face looks in a beard. But, I also like to get my nails done. I wear dresses from time to time. I love long cardigans that are bought in the so-called 'women's section' at the store.

Growing up and not conforming to the gender relations that were expected of me made life difficult. It still does. I don't feel comfortable wearing my nightgown to the mailbox for fear of being bullied or, worse, murdered.

In 2020 alone, a human right's organization that tracks such things reported over forty violent fatal attacks against transgender and gender non-conforming people. According to the statistics, the perpetrators overwhelming target Black trans people. But, people like me who are racialized as white are also at risk, especially where I live. This number is based on reports filed. How many incidents have gone unreported?

The gender binary isn't an innocent idea. For those of us who don't fit within its strict limits often don't feel safe.

So-called 'gender reveal' parties only perpetuate the idea that gender is binary and based on sex.

Why don't we call it a sex reveal party? That's what it is, after all.

Maybe because "Look! My baby has a penis" seems weird. But, if you think about it, saying that your baby is a girl or a boy in today's society is saying your baby has a vagina or a penis. It is weird either way.

To the untaught parent who doesn't realize that putting

their child in a gender binary based on sex could have some unfortunate consequences for their dear baby someday, are you open to change? Could you celebrate your baby without celebrating their genitalia? Because, from my perspective and from the perspective of many others, your baby's penis or vagina is unimportant, unless you give me the honor of helping you take care of your baby, then I'll be sure that I know how to clean their body properly when changing their diaper.

And for those of you parents who have already thrown your baby into a binary, if your baby decides one day that they no longer fit into the the role you gave them, will you throw them another gender reveal party? A true one? From my perspective, a true gender reveal party will be thrown when the child is old enough to decide.

Just because the tendency is to choose a gender for your baby at birth, thanks to ideas of commonsense and consumerism, doesn't make it right.

I know it's not easy. When you enroll your child into a school, they will ask you to fill out a form that indicates their genitalia. When you go to buy clothes there is only a boy's and a girl's section. When you find out that you're pregnant, everyone around you asks, "Is it a boy or a girl?" When your child goes to use a public restroom on their own they will usually have two options: Men's or Women's. Not every public place has a family restroom where someone can go in a lock the door behind them.

I worry for my little cousin who was raised to be a girl but who looks, talks, and dresses like a boy. I worry for lil' cousin's safety when they get older. Some Karen someone day may just scream at my lil' cousin when they enter the women's restroom because they'll be mistaken for a man. Security may then come in and drag them out with their pants around their ankles like has happened to so many trans people, including genderqueer and non-conforming trans people.

So, here's my wish. I hope that someday gendering babies based on their sex assigned at birth will be abolished, not by force, but through practice and by recognizing its potential harm.

I hope I'm around to see that day come. In some places it has already arrived. I was visiting a university a few years back for a talk. The restrooms outside this one particular auditorium struck me as different. Instead of Men or Women labels on the doors, the signs on each door described what was in the bathroom: on one door a picture of a toilet, and on the other a picture of a toilet and a urinal. There was another restroom labeled 'Family' with a picture of a diaper changing station. My auntie and I both entered the same restroom and occupied different stalls. After finishing our business, we washed our hands at the sink. There was a stranger who presented as a man a few sinks down from her. When we left, I asked her if she felt unsafe and she said no.

"Was it because I was there?" I asked.

"I don't know." She replied. "I think it's because I wasn't in a Women's restroom. It felt like everyone and anyone belonged in there."

Me saying this is not to minimize the real fear that women (cis- or trans-) may experience in the bathroom. That is not my goal. My only goal is to point out the possibilities of what a future looks like when everyone gets to have access to a restroom for their particular needs, not just Men and Women. Why is it that Men and Women get to have special restroom but not other genders?

Back to me. Did my parents intentionally want to cause me social harm by putting me into the wrong gender category based on a binary? I don't think so. I think they were just doing what most everyone else did and still does. I don't think they were thinking at all, just doing, like little social robots, doing what everyone else does without thinking of the possible consequences.

WEDNESDAY, JANUARY 6TH, 2021 - BH

I saw pictures of a confederate flag being waved inside the Capitol today after it was taken over by a mob of supporters of the Mandarin King, that's what I like to call him.

I don't trust politicians, so I'm not concerned about them. What I worry about is that the people who want Mandarin King in place as a dictator might eventually succeed. That will be a sad day for us who fear being caged or murdered for not fitting in with the so-called "norm."

I'm sad for my friends who are a part of the African diaspora, especially those who come from ancestors who were forced to come here and work as chattel slaves and who were bought and sold like cattle in the South and then later the Confederacy.

I'm not sad for this country, this project. This project is a joke. But, I am sad for the Black people that live here and who have to face such virulent hatred from people who think, and who have been told, that they are white and somehow special, even superior.

I don't have the energy to write anymore, today.

MONDAY, MARCH 8TH, 2021 - BH

I've been doing some research on eating insects.

You asked for information on foraging, so I assumed you meant not only for plants but for insects as well.

It's amazing how many people in this world eat insects. According to one source, as of today there are two billion people worldwide that eat insects. That's a little over a quarter of the world's population.

The big question is why don't I eat insects? I have eaten insects: silk worm hotpot in Shandong Province; the wax worm from a bottle of tequila. Sometimes I find little bodies of some beetle-like insect in my rice. I try to rinse them all out, but I doubt I get them all out. I'm sure they come from hatched eggs that end up on the grains before harvesting. But, I don't incorporate insects in my diet. And, after doing some reading, not all insects are edible.

So, what kind of insects are good to eat? I'll give you a recipe that I've found for at least one insect.

ROASTED GRASSHOPPERS
    1/2 onion, chopped (for flavor)
    some oil for frying
    salt (to taste)
    paprika (to taste)
    10-20 grasshoppers

CLEAN the outside of the grasshoppers, then boil them until they turn a reddish color. Remove the wings and legs. Heat your oil and fry the grasshoppers over medium heat until crispy. Remove from heat and drain the oil from grasshoppers. Once they are dry, sprinkle the paprika and salt. Garnish with fresh onion. You can eat them on their own or add them to your other dishes as a nutritious, crunchy topping.

Because of the poisonous pesticides that people put on their plants and flowers, it can be dangerous to eat insects that are caught in the wild. I don't know if that's something you have to contend with or not, but I just wanted to add it as a disclaimer.

Happy crunching!

. . .

FRIDAY, MAY 7TH, 2021 - BH

I'm mourning for youth today, especially that little me who was really struggling with their assigned gender back in the early 90s, and for my lil' cousin who is explore their gender identity.

So far this year, seventeen anti-LGBTQIA2S+ bills have been enacted just here alone. Over two-hundred-fifty bills have been introduced in state legislatures, including at least thirty-five bills that would make it prohibitive for transgender youth when accessing best-practice, age-appropriate, gender-affirming medical care.

But, mommy and daddy can buy their cis-gendered daughter a boob job for her 17th birthday because they give their consent?

Around seventy bills have been introduced that would make it impossible for transgender youth (including college students) from playing in sports according to their gender identity.

Over forty bills would allow people to profess a religious belief as a justifiable reason for not abiding by the law or providing services to people whose gender identity they disapprove of.

At least fifteen bills would prohibit transgender people from accessing restrooms or locker rooms according to their gender identity. This is extremely dangerous. Just going to the bathroom in a public place could get you arrested or worse. Where do I pee if I stop at a rest area on the highway that doesn't have a 'Family' restroom.

This constant attack from the overarching powers is exhausting. By targeting transgender people specifically, these bigots are basically clearing a path for more radicalized transphobes to pull out their AR-15s and murder more innocent lives. They, *the politicians* have to know that. Is that why they do it? Keep us afraid and then they won't have to see us out in public? Is that their goal?

SUNDAY, AUGUST 15TH, 2021 - BH

My mind is still blown. I mean, I can't believe that this is happening. It's all happening so quickly.

Since we last spoke, or whatever it is that we do, so much has happened. I haven't told him, the partner, about you. Yet. I promise to tell him. It's just that so much is happening so quickly. I wasn't going to tell him until you contacted me again. I hadn't quite been convinced that you weren't just a figment of my overactive imagination. I mean, talking to someone who claims to be a descendant of one of my siblings, from the future. "Oh, and by the way, we talk through a mushroom." Yeah. I'm not sure how that is going to go over. I will tell him though, now that I'm 100% convinced that you are real. Okay. 90% convinced.

The strange thing is that just two days after you called me this last time, he, the partner, asked me if I wanted to move. He's been working from home since the pandemic began, and, even though we'd just moved to this new house less than a year ago, we can live almost anywhere now.

"How about north?" He asked.

"You mean like up near the border? Where Gary lives?" I asked excitedly. I was more excited for him than for myself. What was I going to do there in such a small town? "Sure! Let's do it. I'll figure out something to do. Maybe I can finally motivate myself to keep writing."

"Are we sure? I mean we just moved here. We bought patio blocks for christ's sake. And you just put in the new compost." He fumbled around his words, unable to believe that he was actually considering it.

Then, as I inevitably do when I find myself looking for a

new job, I log onto the go-to website in my industry and search for job posts in all the places I dream to live and teach in someday. What was next led to some really cool things happening. I found a posting at a school in the hometown of my great grandma on my dad's dad's side of the family. It's basically a small town in the Pannonian Plain with a population of around 12,000. So, the chances of it being listed on this website was infinitesimal.

"What? Your grandpa's mom? That's so cool." He was truly surprised. "Are you going to apply?"

"No way! That means we would be apart for at least a school year. Do we really want to do that again?" Was he being serious?

"I think you should totally apply." His tone was sincere. "You've been studying with your language tutor for the past year. Now's a good time to go and put your hard work to use." He *was* serious.

"Okay. I'll at least send an email to see if they have any openings and how the hiring process works." Was this really happening?

On Monday, I got an email saying that they needed someone last-minute and if I was available to do a phone interview that same evening. Fast forward. They offered me a job in the capital. I was hoping to be in my grandma's village and try and find my family, but that position was already taken. I can travel there at least. Just to step foot where she and her family have possibly walked. How cool!

So, I accepted the offer. I can't believe I'm going.

Now you can see why my mind's blown. Do you have that expression where-when you are? For me, it means that something impossible or at least improbable has happened to me or I've witnessed it happening. The something is so unthinkable that my brain has trouble processing that it is real.

I mean, I've been trying to go and live there since like 2003 when I first heard that I could possibly get EU citizenship. Now, twenty three years later I'm going there to teach! I'm speechless!

And the most incredulous aspect of this entire affair is that it happened only just a few days after you told me that I needed to take the books to this same city. Writing it makes it seem more unbelievable. Am I certain I didn't dream it? You told me:

"Buy a yellow equipment case. It should be just big enough to hold the three books. Don't worry about the other journals for now. But, be sure to print what you've written so far. Also, I need you to write these instructions on the inside of the front cover of The Dispossessed."

Here are the cryptic instructions:

B and T, go to OT at the next full Hold. Ask for the front cover.

Bring along the book.

Then, you left me with these last words before you disappeared, "You are going to be going away soon. Put everything that I've asked for into the yellow case box and take it with you. When it's time, I'll give you further instructions. So, you'll need to find a place where mushrooms grow. Be sure to walk by that place everyday and look for a mushroom that glows green."

I have no idea what any of this is for. But, I'll do as I'm told.

I've decided not to tell him about you after all. I think it's best that we keep this between you, me, and whoever is going to read this in the future.

TAKVER LOOKS over at Bedap who is sitting up in their palette bed, the cover-less book in their hands.

The next full Hold is tonight, Sib.

Makk's sudden name change hadn't really had an impact on her because she still used the nickname she gave them before they'd become Bedap.

Bedap is staring down at the book, obviously in deep thought. Then, they looks up at Takver.

"The strange thing is, Tak, I was just saying that we should go see Old Tátos, and then older me asked if we'd gone yet. Now, this Trell character is telling B and T to go to OT and take the book."

Bedap bites their lip like they tends to do when they's working out a problem.

I hate the thought of going, Takver is staring down at her feet and shaking her head, *but I can't deny all the obvious signs that are telling us to go see her.*

Now, she's standing up, her arms tight to her side and her fists clenched.

Promise me that you won't just trust her, Sib. Promise!

"What do you mean, Tak?" Bedap is staring at her again. "What's the point of us even going if we can't give them a chance to help us. And in order for them to help us we have to trust them."

She, they *switched you and Palat at birth. It had to be on purpose. I mean, look at you. You're as pink as a clover flower. Me, Gomba, Palat, almost everyone else I know is several shades darker than you. How could that have been a mistake? Old Tátos had to know that you came out of the mother! And, yet, they switched you! I just can't trust her,* them *after learning to resent them. Ever since I remember mother talking about you, I started hating them. You asked me before if I was afraid, of them. Yes. I am. But I hate them more.*

Takver flops down on her palette, tears welling up in her beautiful, dark eyes, fists still clenched. The ring doesn't even shift with the sudden jolt.

"I'm sorry, Tak." Bedap puts down the book, stands up and walks over to her, sitting down to her left. "I can't possibly know how you are feeling. But I've lost a brother, too. And mine can be found. I'm sorry that yours can't."

Silence.

Then, Bedap starts up again. "That's why we need Old Tátos's help. They know things. They hold the key. And the instructions indicate B and T. That means both Bedap and Takver have to go."

Bedap takes Takver by the hand and looks at her from the side. Tears are dripping from her eyes, leaving wet spots on the lap of her beetroot-dyed frock.

"Let's get some rest. I say we leave as soon as Hold is out. We can get up a little before and have a good meal before leaving. How long is the journey from here?"

After a few moments, Takver replies.

We're about a twenty-minute foot from the compound, then we cross the bridge, and their hovel is about an hour's foot from the bridge. But crossing the bridge is no easy task. It is littered with the vehiculars from the Old World and parts of the actual structure are crumbling apart.

Bedap is giving her a blank look, as if they isn't understanding anything that is coming out of her mindspeak.

You've really never been to the bridge? Takver is truly shocked. *Growing up, us kids were always pushing the boundaries of the frigy, the treaty. The bridge was a neutral zone. Since our people had established a permanent settlement when we split from the Átmeneti, we don't do the waterfetching anymore. We learn about it, but ever since the split the newly turned sixteens go to the bridge and hang out. They invite their friends, too, some of whom aren't sixteen or are a bit older. It's a big buli.*

She pauses briefly and then continues.

I never got my chance, sadly. Who was I going to celebrate with after they'd all been taken away?

Silence.

Then, Takver picks up where she'd left off.

When we were younger, some friends and I snuck up to the

bridge to watch the small group of sixteens and their friends partying. In the light of Hold, we watched as they...

THE PATINA of the criss-cross metalwork glitters in the moonlight, several tens of meters above the river's surface. For centuries, the chain-type bridge, with its cantilever truss and suspended middle span, has been a place for the youth to comingle and pass the nighttime hours. Whether Takver's people or the university students and tourists from a handful of centuries before, this late nineteenth-century link between the western hills and the eastern flat plain has called out to the youth. And the youth has always answered.

FROM THE JOURNALS OF TRELL
WEDNESDAY, SEPTEMBER 1ST 2021 - FLAT #27

This is my second week teaching here. My colleagues seem mostly amazing. I can pick up a few words here in there in the teacher's room, but for the most part I'm left in the dark. It's fine though. I love listening to them speak to each other. I picture my great grandparents chatting with their friends at the piac market, selling their cucumbers and beans.

I have a crap ton of students. I don't know if I'll learn all of their names but I'll try. I can definitely tell that my seniors have senioritis; they are so ready to be done. It's going to be hard to keep them engaged, but we'll make it work.

I met a fellow genderqueer person today! They is one of my sophomores. We were talking about the "Don't Say Gay" law that the administration passed this last summer. Of course, it's not just about gay people. It's an attack on LGBTQIA2S+ people in general. The legislation outlaws sharing information with students under the age of 18 that the administration considers to be promoting homosexuality or gender change. Does that mean I, someone who presents as a man because I'm afraid to be genderqueer self here, can't talk about my husband? I mean, my colleague talks about her husband all the time, especially be he used to be a teacher here in this same school. What a bunch of fear-mongering bull crap. I made myself a promise that I would break the law every day in class. So, in class today, we talked about the meaning of the recently popularized slogan "A család az család," which roughly translates to "family is family." It was a good discussion and most of the students, all of whom were under 18, shared their opinions about the law. After class, one of the more vocal students came up to me and told me that they prefer the they pronoun. I told them that I do as well. And, then we had a moment. They are so brave at such a young age. I don't have big enough ovaries to share my true gender identity with my colleagues or students, yet. Maybe I'll get there.

Later that day, in another class, I brought up the topic of pronouns to a group of seniors. One student in particular interrupted my presentation and told me, "We don't use the they pronoun here in this country. It's weird." My heart broke in half for my sophomore student who *does* use the they pronoun.

Fighting the good fight is exhausting. But, I won't ever stop fighting it.

SATURDAY, OCTOBER 2ND, 2021 - FLAT #27

Today, I went and explored the other side of the river. And, for the first time, I walked across *the* bridge. Of course, there are other bridges but somehow this bridge seems extra special. The color reminds me of the Statue of Liberty, sea-green patina. It was dark by the time I walked across it on my way back to my flat. To my surprise there seemed to be a party happening. Someone had a guitar and others chimed in, singing an unknown song.

Instead of suspension cables, this bridge has trusses that are held together by a combination of rivets and steel. Thanks to the mathematical equations that go into creating such static structures with a diagonal web-like appearance, the bridge maintains its position over a small section of this almost 3,000 kilometer long river. Where the webs intersect and form the lowest points near the grated-steel road and walkways, people in groups of two, three, or four sit together drinking their beers and spirits while chatting, guitar strings and singing accompanying the din of the pedestrians and car and bicycle traffic.

It's quite a spectacle.

The way people drink and hang out in the street like that reminds me a bit of the old botellón scene from my university days back in Ghaliza. Good times.

Oh, I went to see the family house, too, like you told me to.

I know you already know this, Bedap, but I'm putting this in here for whoever else might need to know.

Two years after the end of the Second World War, in 1947, my dad's dad's older sister, my grand Auntie, received letters from her older brother and his family who lived on this side of the ocean. The letters had the return address from a house in one of the suburbs of the capital city.

Today, I took three buses and walked past tens of streets named after nut and fruit trees to visit that house. Nobody was home. I rang the gate buzzer twice. I don't even know if it's the same house that my family lived in, maybe I'll never know.

Maybe I'll never know who planted the sour cherry tree out front, the one that towers over the uniquely wrought iron covered walkway with its green, grape-leaf screen that stretches from the gate to the front door. And the gated front yard is rather big for local standards. Maybe it's because the house is set far back on the small plat of land, discordant with the neighboring dwellings whose houses butt up against the street. The roof of the house is special, too. Unlike many of the houses around it, with their rectangular frame and a single, gradual peaked roof that forms a triangle that just covers it enough to keep the rain from dripping down its facade, this house has two angular bell-shaped gables that rest at either end of an elongated, dark clay barn-like crown. Three large, arched windows sit evenly spaced at the parapet. I can't help but picture my grand uncle sitting in his chair reading folktales to his little daughter and son, my first cousins once removed, while the sunlight pours through these generous windows.

I wonder if people here have always built fences and other barriers around their gardens. I've been here for over a month and I've yet to see any living quarters that weren't somehow gated or fenced off. Even in the complex of flats where I live we need a key fob to open the gate. And behind almost every fenced-in garden or yard, there's a dog stealthily waiting for you to get just close enough so they can start barking and scare the crap out of you.

There is no dog at the family house. A dog may be able to help deter burglars and thieves, but kerítés kutyák, literally fence dogs as I like to call them, can't do much to deter bombs dropping from planes.

The letters that have this house as a return address were mailed in January of 1947 but that date doesn't match up with the bombings of the capital, which forced my uncle and his family to seek shelter in a bunker.

Here's a translation of the letters. I can imagine great Uncle Pista, whom I never met by the way, sitting at a cold desk—maybe in one of these gables with the arched windows—first in October and then in January, seeing his breath freeze before his eyes as he writes in beautiful cursive.

Dear Erzsike,

We received your kind letter and before that the money, but

it was exchanged for local currency, and I would have preferred your money. Thank you very much for your kindness, which you have shown to us so many times. The money served us very well, and so did the other thoughtful packages. Unfortunately, we had to get help from others, and we are suffering due to almost worse conditions than immediately after the war. The prices are so high and there is a shortage of food due to this year's great drought. As a result, the rations are so small that there is not enough food for mere subsistence, for example, the most basic food like potatoes. I am not even talking about flour because it is not possible to buy it at all. The only food left is from the black market and it's too expensive.

Now, during my vacation, I am at Juliska's place on the other side of the country to get some potatoes and flour that they had to spare from their own supply which is much cheaper than back in the capital. Unfortunately, producers can't sell because they also have to worry about eating. I had to give up waiting on a train. It's been over two weeks and it still hasn't arrived. Now our biggest problem is that if the train doesn't arrive then all our winter food is lost and it can't be replaced. We also had to work here when we had peace, and we didn't need the help of others, because everyone could get what they needed. But now there is a life-and-death struggle for the daily bite. I also really want one of you to come, but only to visit, because you wouldn't stay here anyway, because, Erzsike, think about how it feels to have to give up all the fat and the most basic food and potatoes now, because there isn't any. I really believe it'd be a bad idea for you to live here because there are only two of you and surely time is running out to have kids. You get old, you don't have a child that you really want and so it's not good to stay here forever for someone who is in such a fortunate position and for us going to you is a complete impossibility. But, my dear Erzsike, come just to visit and you will see what life is like here.

We also received a letter from Father and family. Please pass on our loving greetings to them, but to be honest, the daily worries take up so much time that I am forced to write less often.

Once again we thank you all very much. We send many kisses to Mariska.

Marika and little brother mention aunties Erzsike and Mariska every day when they put on their clothes. Isten kisses your father's loving hand. We all love you.

Pista and family,
Rákosszentmihály 22 Oct, 1947

DEAR ERZSIKE!

I don't even know how to thank you for the kind gifts you got for us. We were excited to open the package and very happy. I wish you could have seen her happy face when Marika held the little dress that you sent. The kids were so excited to get a package that they want to keep opening it every day. Momma is also very happy with the many beautiful things, and I wish my dear Erzsike that Isten will give you a thousand times more than what you have given us, and I can only offer thanks for your kindness.

My dear Erzsike, we received your letter that you wrote last year, but I did not answer it, because the difficulty of the current living conditions and the search for work is so exhausting that I am so tired that even writing a letter is difficult for me, because life is full of a lot of worries. Stress completely binds all the strength of man. We also received a letter from our father before Christmas, I replied in more detail and asked him to hand over our letter to you and Mariska. I hope you've got it since. We also received a package from Mariska, both of which arrived within a week. So that our happy unexpected joy has had a very good effect on our great sorrow. For we still have such a sad, troubling life, which worries us more than anything.

The little three-and-a-half-year-old Pityuka has been diagnosed with hip tuberculosis, and this has necessitated a cast. So the poor little guy is wrapped in plaster from waist to toe, which is completely stiff. He can only lie on his back or on his stomach. He can't even sit up because the whole body is rigid due to the plaster. For the time being, six weeks from now, they will tell us about his fate. We hired an ambulance service that was available to us in this case. Unfortunately, we live in a different world now, and his health issues aren't the worst problem. If Isten is generous he'll restore our little boy's health as soon as possible.

Medically, this disease is very serious and long lasting but we hope that Isten will help him and that there will be no complications that will last for many years. Otherwise, thank Isten we are in Marika's eighth year as a student. We thank Isten that she is healthy. However, she is only able to study at home because the school is closed due to lack of firewood during the winter. We work a lot pretty much day and night in order to repair parts of our house because the war wreaked havoc.

My dear Erzsike, on behalf of all of us, thank you very much for the package and may Isten bless you. We send you a lot of kisses with love.

Pista and family,
Rákosszentmihály 18 Jan. 1947

SEVENTY-SIX YEARS HAVE PASSED since Uncle Pista wrote those letters. Food shortage doesn't seem to be an issue now, not at least for the lucky haves, like me. The never-haves, I'm sure, still struggle to get the food they need.

It makes me think, did Uncle Pista not know how to forage? Re-reading these translated letters, I can understand why you asked me to document so much. I've been reflecting and, now, more than ever before I feel the need to learn how to glean the forests and meadows for my own food. I'm lucky right now that I don't have to go without. But, who knows what will happen in my lifetime? Maybe potatoes will be worth their weight in gold someday. Again.

CHAPTER TWO: OLD TÁTOS

The forest, full of new growth oaks, cherries—and whatever else the birds have crapped out as they have flown overhead for the past two centuries—has taken over the once asphalted street that runs from the bunker and its surrounding ruins to Duna. The old university—once the center of map making and other disciplines related to physical geography—still mostly stands intact despite centuries of decaying facades and overgrowth that covers the entire complex of buildings. There are no clouds in the sky. TeliHold, or the full moon, casts its moonbeams as far as the eye can see, illuminating the night sky as well as the ruins of a once vibrant city divided in two by a river once coursing to the brim with water, with Life. In fact, it is so bright that it looks as if the Old City is alight with electricity. But it can't be. Electricity is extinct, if such a thing is possible. At least it has gone out of use here among the peoples that inhabit this greater region.

As the two get closer to the compound, Takver prepares herself emotionally. It's been several Holds since she'd last visited the ruins. Around the time of Harvest, just before Third Forage, she would take her candles and flowers to the compound, lighting the former as a way to guide the deceased back to the realm of the living. For centuries before the Great Dying, the local people would visit the cemeteries of their relatives who'd passed. It was a time to clean the gravesites, light candles, and place fresh flowers. They had referred to this tradition as Halottak Napja, the Day of the Dead. Although Takver's people didn't consider themselves superstitious—another item of contention between them and the Átmeneti—Takver found that taking part in the anachronistic practice helped comfort her, because more than anything she'd missed her people, her family so much.

What she calls the compound is actually a network of buildings that surrounds the old underground station near the foot of Duna Hegy, or Duna Hill. The once subterranean transit hub was converted into a nighttime marketplace. Takver's people, her entire community, had run the market. Takver's immediate family members had operated the candle stall. They had been very skilled at their art of candle making. And they had traded their candles for food and clothing, mostly. Candles are a comfort if not a necessity amongst people who are nocturnal.

Just across the bridge to the east of the river, the people of the Old World constructed an enormous market hall that became a tourist hub. It's still intact today, but because of the frigy, Takver's people weren't allowed to cross the river, only in the case of an emergency. So, they did what they could and turned an old underground station into a market. Such irony.

The stall to the right of Takver's family's stall traded in centuries-old odds and ends from the various landfills that existed on the outskirts of the Old City. Digging through ancient refuse was a dirty and dangerous job. Yet, much of what the contemporary peoples use for their daily lives has been reused or repurposed from the Old World. Some things were inevitably scavenged from old dwellings as well. Hundreds of years earlier, almost overnight, the human population of Earth drastically reduced in size. Centuries later, most quotidian items found in the typical household still persevered despite the houses themselves having become mostly ruins. The once crowded city was a gold mine of ancient artifacts up for grabs to the willing gleaner.

People came from all up and down the Duna to the great sunken marketplace. Its formation was one of the reasons that the Literalists broke off from the Átmeneti. The latter believed that trade should only be done with other Átmeneti communes. The former disagreed. They wanted the freedom to intermingle and exchange with non-Átmeneti. Eventually, a portion of people from the various Átmeneti communes split off and formed this new community. It had survived for almost half a century before it was decimated. Takver was the only survivor. She thought everyone was dead because her telepathic connection with them was severed abruptly that day she sought refuge in the bunker.

This is the closest I've ever been to this mountain. Bedap sends to Takver who has suddenly stopped and is looking off into the distance. To their right, the moonlight dances its waltz on the Duna.

If there were anything more beautiful... Takver shares a half thought. *For most of my life, I'd come right here to this spot and just stare out into the world.*

Bedap puts an arm around her shoulders, squeezing her a bit. It's an emotional moment for them, too, but for different reasons. Most of their life they had been forbidden from venturing too far from camp. The distant hills and the river at their feet had become an imagined border wall from a very young age. *The Youngun Who Crossed the Old River* was told to every Átmeneti child at bedtime when the morning light began to shine high in the sky.

"What are they gonna do to em, Egg?" Bedap can remember

asking their eggblood after he recounted for the first time—at least it was the first time that little Makk remembered the details of the story. That story had been told morning after morning since they was still inside his womb—how little Hegi got kidnapped after crossing the Old River out of curiosity during waterfetching.

"Well, only Isten knows. Little Hegi never came back." Málna had explained.

When Bedap was still Makk and had fewer Reawakenings to account for and their people had their settlement closer to the old Long Road so that the too-far-away hills could be seen from inside the encampment, the hills were a constant reminder of the isolation they had always felt but hadn't always understood why it hurt.

Now, standing only hundreds of paces from the hills and the bridge, Bedap breathes in deeply. Freedom fills their lungs with the cool night air.

Can we go down? Bedap points to the opening in the ground that leads to the old tunnels. It's still very exciting for them to go into places whose entrance had been forbidden their entire life as a youngun. After spending time in the bunker and exploring ruins with Takver, entering the ruins of the Old World had mostly ceased to frighten them. Still, the thought of going down into that darkness raised the hairs on the back of their neck and arms.

Yes. But first thing's first. She takes three candle sticks from her nettle satchel. She gives one to Bedap and then places one at the foot of a figure of a person with a long coat holding a guitar. It must be made of some sort of metal because it looks like a relic of the Old World and it was still intact.

Takver bends down and lights the candle using her fire starter box. Around the wide plinth, there are several adornments, dried up flowers, and puddles of colorful wax that must have been melted by the scorching sun.

Who is this supposed to be, Tak? Bedap shares, along with a feeling of confusion which Takver senses as a mix of yellow and orange hues as well as an itch at the base of her head where it meets the nape of her neck.

I have no scorching idea. She smiles. *No one really does. Palat and I would mess around and pretend they was our spermblood. Since we never got to meet him, we always just played like the statue was him.*

Silence.

Now that everyone is gone, Takver continues, *I've been coming here and leaving flowers, candles, and other offerings. I did it mostly for Palat. But, eventually, I did it for everyone else, too. Once I gave up hope.*

I think it's freaking awesome. Bedap knocks their knuckles on the statue's long, parted metallic hair, making a deep dull clanking sound.

Bedap bends down and lights their candle from the one at the foot of the statue. Then, they turns around and picks up their pace to catch up to Takver who is already standing at the edge of the pitch black entrance.

How is it that your people and my people are so different? Bedap asks, mostly rhetorically, as the two begin their descent down the cement stairs to the old underground space.

With this being the third Reawakening since the whole market was pillaged, there has been no one to keep up with the maintenance of the area. Beautiful dandelions, crawling ground cover of all sorts, as well as other greenery has taken over the once kempt entrance to the market.

Who knows? Takver responds after a few moments. *I guess they were different enough to split up.*

Yeah. Bedap considers. *But how did it start? We don't, well didn't, talk about it at all. I think the older people in our community preferred we'd just forget about it.*

Well. I think it has to do with the fact that the old Literalists felt a divide, a fault line of sorts that couldn't be mended. I mean... Takver pauses for a moment to collect her thoughts. Meanwhile, as they reach the end of the decline, she holds out her candle as if to extend its light further in front of them.

Oh! Takver darts a few steps toward what looks like an old food court and then suddenly stops. She's sending hues of purple and blue to Bedap unintentionally, but also without much bridle. The nostalgia is overwhelming.

Oh, Sib! Can you smell the lángos? Takver turns and looks at her sibling, her lips stretching from ear to ear. *I used to help Lilla Neni knead the dough every evening before the market opened up.* Now, she's looking off into the distance as if she were remembering something far away. *People would line up all the way around that corner,* she pointed the candle deep into the black ether, deep into the tunnels. *The wild thing was that she only ever accepted different flours and potatoes as payment. I got my free one because I helped out, but I can imagine some kids had to learn how to forage potatoes to get theirs. Oh, how I miss her lángos.*

Bedap is acutely aware that they is hungry. Instantly their body language changes, slumping their shoulders and letting their head drop forward. *You might as well be feeding me to the vadkutya with all this talk about food. You're killing me, Tak. Can we change the topic? I hate to ruin your beautiful memory. But, anything but lángos, Tak.*

Bedap takes their candle and walks to the opposite side of the old station, holding it close to the wall; it's cold to the touch and there is no give. Directly ahead, deep down into the chasm, there are four rows of steel stairs. Once upon a time, the stairs had been mechanical and carried pedestrians from top to bottom or vice versa without the necessity of climbing.

Takver had grown up in those tunnels, playing on those stairs. This had been her back yard. There were so many memories here.

Sib, I need to go down to the very bottom. Bedap started,

suddenly hearing their own voice in their head. *It's a long climb down and an even longer climb back up if you wanna join me.*

Okay. Bedap replies. *But promise that you'll tell me more about your people to help me understand why they decided to split off.*

On the grates of the stairs, each foot step they take sends a tapping echo thirty meters down the tunnel. Once Bedap becomes aware of the acoustics, they starts making crow noises and soon squawks are heard over the taps.

Takver holds the candle up to her face and gives Bedap a glaring scowl.

"Oops." They shrugs and then says even louder, "Sorry!"

Sorry can now be heard bouncing off the sleek surface of the ceiling and walls as the duo slowly makes their descent. Bedap shrugs again and gives Takver a coy smirk. Now, this time in a whisper Bedap inquires to Takver.

"What makes our people so different?"

You really know nothing about my people? Takver mindreplies without looking at her sibling.

"Really. No. The only thing I know is that we're not supposed to go on 'your' side of the river." Bedap uses their one free hand to make air quotes as they emphasizes 'your.' The other hand is still holding the ever-diminutive shrinking candle stick with the ring at the base that catches the dripping wax.

Takver pauses for a moment and then begins to recount the history. *Well, stories have it that long ago there was an ideological division...*

For over a century and a half after the Great Dying, the various groups that built their habitats close to the Old River coexisted peacefully. There were occasional raids, but nothing systematic like had happened to Takver and Bedap's respective communities. As for the Átmeneti, disagreements within communes and between disparate communes were resolved in the traditional way through a peace circle.

Most of the larger, collective disagreements that existed fell into four different categories. In no particular order of importance, there were those that advocated for the cessation of the nomadic way of life, those who wanted to open up trade with non-Átmeneti communities, those who sought to abolish the superstitions—which some saw as the root cause of all of the disagreements, and those who interpreted the books very literally.

For Takver's people, the ones who eventually would decide to split from several different Átmeneti communes, the books were sacred. Nowhere in any of the three books was there a person that wasn't gendered according to a binary. There were men and women and boys and girls. The fact that the Átmeneti disregarded this historical fact was seen as blasphemous.

"These are fictional accounts!" One of the older members yells, "they are allegorical. For Isten's sake, the anarchists lived on a moon in a distant solar system! Are you telling us that that moon was real, too?"

"No, Test." Responds one of the Literalists—that's what the secessionists called themselves. They thought the three books were best interpreted literally—pulling at their dark beard as they tends to do when they gets agitated, "Regardless of the fictional worlds, you can't deny the gender binary and the obvious hierarchy that existed amongst the propertarians who inhabited the moon's moon. There must be a reason that she included those people in her book."

"As a way of juxtaposing the non-hierarchical ways of the anarchists!" Another person adds, heatedly.

"It's just that nowhere, and I emphasize NOWHERE in the books is there a person who isn't either a man or a woman. Lauren disguises herself as a man, but only to make herself seem less vulnerable." The spokesperson continues. "We need to abolish these antiquated ways of naming our children after berries and salad greens! Our children are born either boys or girls based on their genitalia. That's how it should be."

There is muttering rippling around the peace council house like waves in a pond. Several people shout out in agreement and in disagreement. Those who are silent are no doubt sharing their own opinions with their genetic kin.

"Istenem! Next, you're going to tell us that we are born with a gender." Exclaims the same older member.

"Yes! That's exactly what I'm saying."

Gasps ring throughout the tent. A younger storyweaver who had not too long before this momentous reunion returned from waterfetching stands up.

"This is a dangerous path you are taking us down, Test." Delores' face is red with anger and frustration. "Have we learned nothing from the stories passed down to us from the Last Ones? Have we learned nothing at all?! Are you suggesting that we have another Gender Cleansing? Are you going to be the one who cuts off my partner's balls for not conforming to the binary?" She spits on the ground in front of her. "Isten help us!"

"Wait." Bedap interrupts, grabbing Takver by the arm of her tunic frock with their free hand. "Do you believe in this gender binary that your people were so passionate about?"

The siblings finally reach the lowest level of the underground complex. They both note, silently, that their nipples have grown rigid from the decrease in temperature. There's also a slight breeze.

To either side of the intricately tiled mosaic platform, a system of seven or eight connected hover wagons with their doors jammed open rests in a long line that fills each tunnel. Centuries before commuters would form staggered lines along the tunnel corridors awaiting the next host of wagons to take them to their job, a concert, or some other destination.

But now, these wagons have been turned into commercial stalls. Takver and Bedap enter the wagon closest to them on the left. The wagons must have been emptied of their seating because there are no vestiges of benches or individual seats that passengers from before the Great Dying would have fought over to rest their weary bodies after a long day of work. Instead, there were rows and rows of stall after stall. Most of the stalls were still filled with goods meant for trading. But, everything was strewn about of course; anything of use that could be scavenged from a landfill or a dwelling in ruins. Bedap scans their surroundings: a tin watering kanna and other gardening implements, a blue tarpaulin, an entire stall of charred blankets and other wovens. The sudden appearance of the marauders three Reawakenings ago would have caused quite a commotion, not to mention the fires that were set to smoke the unexpecting merchants out of their subterranean emporium.

Takver is standing in the middle of the aisle looking down the long corridor of the train. This is the first time she'd been down at the market since she'd had to escape those many moons ago. She hadn't dared venture deep into the cement ravine alone. But now that Bedap was with her, she thought it more safe. Even to her own surprise, she doesn't shed a tear. Bedap looks over at their sister, holding the candle in her direction.

"Are you okay, Tak?"

After a moment of collecting her thoughts, Takver responds.

Our stall was down this way. I hope what I'm looking for is still here. She pauses before taking off again in the direction of her family's old stall, stepping over the piles of wares strewed about. *And, no, to answer your question. I don't believe in the binary.*

I think a lot of people in my community were fanatics. Fortunately, the mother wasn't one of them.

Bedap has a confused look on their face, but, because of the dark, Takver doesn't see. However, she hears it in their voice.

"You hope *what's* still there?"

Payment.

They reach her family's stall. Makeshift walls of woven plant fiber have been erected, enclosing a rectangular space about the size of a typical sleepingroom for two or three younguns in one of the dwellings back at Bedap's commune. At the back of the stall, a plexiglass window encases the mosaic tunnel wall a few meters away. A scorched signboard that reads <FÁKLYÁK>, torches, dangles from the gray plastic strap handles that commuters of old once clung onto in times of turbulence along their route. There is dried, melted wax everywhere, in many different colors that can't truly be appreciated because of the lack of sufficient light. Takver squats down and places her dwindled gyertya candle under a wooden table, wax stalactites dripping along the edges of its surface. With some flat object she finds on the floor, she pries a panel of sorts up from its secured position, recessed in the floor of the wagon.

She pulls out a round box; it might be a tin box like the kind Christmas cookies used to come in back when Spar was ubiquitous in most neighborhoods, even in the suburbs.

Bedap is kneeling down with candle in hand, watching from behind and imagining a much younger, smaller Takver hiding something precious while the market bustles on just meters away from her.

With her back to her sibling, she opens the lid with a pop. She examines its contents, snaps the lid shut, and puts the tin box in her satchel. As she goes to back out from under the table, something cracks off in the distance back toward where they'd entered the train car. Then, a heavy object thuds to the floor, its contents spilling out, creating even more clanks and clonks.

Almost reflexively, the two hold their candles out in the direction from where the noises came.

"What was that, Tak?" Bedap blurts out, trembling a bit.

Just as Bedap finishes their question, they both see a cat-like tail standing straight into the air walking back toward whence they all came. Bedap grabs Takver's free hand, offering to help pull her up.

I've seen that tail before. Let's go, Sib. We need to follow it. I have the sensation that they's trying to get our attention. Takver is on her feet, and they are both off, quickening their pace as they head back to the opened doors.

"What do you mean you've seen them before?" Bedap is slightly out of breath. The sudden adrenaline rush has left them wanting fuller lungs.

It's gotta be the same cat. I never see cats around, especially at the bunker. And, on the rare occasion I do see them, they are never alone. This cat was watching us when you did the impossible and pulled a disk from the base of a mushroom. I saw them scuttle off just as I was climbing back down into the bunker and closing the hatch. Takver remembers feeling like she and her sibling were being watched and just thinking about it has the hairs on her arms standing upright.

As they turn left out of the wagon, they spot the cat sitting at the entrance to the steps, seemingly waiting for them. Bedap squats as if they's going to kneel down on one knee and reaches out their free hand.

"Here cica." They makes a smooching sound, beckoning the cat. "It's alright little cica, don't be afraid."

Takver cocks her head and shoots a glare out of the corner of her eye at her sibling. *Where have I heard that before?*

Bedap shrugs off her attempt at a playful attack and then scooches closer to the cat.

The creature is spectacular to look at. It isn't too often that cats let humans see them, not to mention let them come close. From what they can see, given the dimness of their surroundings, the contemporary progeny of the old domesticated cat is usually a bit smaller than the one sitting just ahead of them. This one has big, almond-shaped yellow eyes that almost glow from the shadowy light that their candles cast onto it from a few meters away.

"They's beautiful, Tak." Bedap starts to move close. And, as they does, the cat hops up onto the stairs and starts climbing.

The two follow the cat.

When they get to the stairs, Takver looks up into the darkness. Despite not being able to see up to the top, she remembers being amazed at how little she felt all those years descending and ascending these steps. There must be over two-hundred of them to climb to get to the top.

"Oh, wow!" Bedap stares up into the abyss. "We climbed down all those?"

Takver tugs as Bedap's satyor satchel. *Come on! I don't want to lose the cat.*

When they finally get to the top, ten minutes or more must have passed. Bedap is leaning over with their hands on the knees trying to catch their breath.

"Why the scorching Nap did your people choose this place for their piac market?"

My people had a belief that if you're not suffering you're doing something wrong. It's obvious that Takver had thought of this question herself at one time. *That was something that I never quite understood about us. Everything seemed to have to be so painstaking.*

She pauses.

Don't get me wrong. We had a lot of playtime, too. Many of the people are, were very lighthearted. We loved to joke around. Where there was work there was always play. My memories of this place are nothing but good.

One of the unexpected advantages of merging was that Takver was able to say all of that with her thoughts without pausing to catch her breath. She is panting, after all, just as much as Bedap.

Up above in the opening of the concrete crevice that was once one of the many mouths of Metro Line 4, the moonlight casts its beam down on the cat, creating a backlit silhouette with a bright white aura around them, like a furry, long-tailed Mexican Our Lady of Guadalupe. The gray with black dots and stripes tabby is waiting for them, yet again. It's not obvious whether they are panting like Takver and Bedap, having ascended much faster than the pair of siblings. The whiskered murder mittens must be used to climbing. They is a cat after all. And, cats like to be up high, whether perched on a tree branch or atop an old ruin of a house or building. These elusive feline quadrupeds have always been the aloft overwatchers of the Old City, staring down at civilizations from their balconies and windows. At a time of celebrated post-human dominance —why would now be any different?

Once the two make eye contact with the cat, the latter takes off running. Takver and Bedap have to run up the stairs so as to not lose sight of their new acquaintance. As they get to the top of the precipice, they see kitty resting on an old electrical transformer box now reddish brown from rust but once the color of lichen, pale patina.

Again the cat scurries away, beckoning the two to maintain their pursuit.

"Where in the scorching earth is they leading us to?" Bedap asks rhetorically, not expecting an answer.

Knowing that it's just Bedap's way of thinking aloud, Takver ignores them. Instead, she picks up her pace, breaking into a slow jog. Her satyor satchel rattles as the forces cause the contents to clash with the tin container.

Moments later, they are at the mouth of the bridge. Bedap can't believe their eyes. This is the closest they've ever been to this iconic landmark. Its deck, from end to end, is covered with vehiculars of all sizes that have become part of the bridge itself after centuries of being parked in the same spot. The green of the crawling vines blends in with the patina of the steel trusses, having taken over as the new surface of the automobiles and the bridge itself. High above, resting on top of the four latticed towers, the moon backlights the falcon-like turul birds that have watched over the Duna since the suspended nexus was first constructed half a millenia before.

From a few meters away, the cat is staring down at them from the roof of an old, yellow and white hover tram that no longer floats over the maglev strip that lines the Old City on almost every main street.

"Mew!" The tabby meows just before it leaps onto the deck and takes off down the trail that, over the years, has been trampled and made unmistakably into a path.

Besides the rusted and ramshackle vehiculars—aircars, hover trams, and a hover bus flipped onto its side—the trail is littered with all sorts of detritus as well as inorganic material. Bedap steps over a broken guitar that has been stripped of its strings and whose slivers jet out in all directions. Guitar strings make good snares for people that hunt animals for their meat and hides as well as other parts; bones can be turned into useful tools and they make a good broth for those who have a taste for such things.

"Why do your sixteens choose this place to celebrate?" Bedap breaks the silence.

At this point, they are already at the other end of the bridge. The cat is nowhere to be seen.

Quiet, Sib. We really should be mindspeaking. We have no idea who is lurking around here.

Takver sends a hue of red, her typical warning color that she emits telepathically when she gets anxious.

And, I don't know why here. I mean it's a pretty cool place. Takver crouches down, seeing something shiny on the edge of the path. She picks it up, stands up, and holds the coin close to her face to get a better look; its number reads two hundred.

Wow, Sib. Takver turns around and holds her arm outstretched in Bedap's direction. *Look at this! I can't believe it.*

Bedap catches up and meets Takver's hand with their arm outstretched as well. They takes the coin from her hand and examines it up close, squinting a bit to get a clearer focus.

I used to collect these when I'd go out scavenging with my eggblood. The blacksmith in the commune next door would give us a whole pumpkin for a basketful of these old relics. Bedap tosses it up in the air. *Heads or tails?*

Takver looks playfully at Bedap. Then, Bedap interjects before she can choose.

Heads, you tell me what's in the tin box.

And what do I get if it's tails?

Before Bedap can reply, a large explosion goes off, shaking the bridge and causing the two to duck instinctively. The sudden pressure makes them dizzy, their ears ringing to the point of nausea.

After a few moments, the last of the debris rains onto the bridge's entrance, splashing down into the stream below like someone dumping a construction crane's claw full of rocks into a pond. The immediate area is instantly shrouded in a cloud of dust that doesn't quite reach the siblings who are still hunkering down. As the shock wears off, Takver is able to focus her thoughts.

What in the...? Sib, are you okay? We need to get off this bridge now.

She doesn't wait for Bedap to respond and just grabs their hand and starts pulling. Bedap doesn't hesitate and lets her pull them several meters to the other side of the Old River.

We need to hide quickly. Takver says as she is looking all around for some sort of cover.

Look. Bedap points to what looks like a complex of old ruins covered in creeping vines and other foliage. The dew on all the various leaves glitter in the moonlight. *Come on. This way.*

Now, Bedap takes Takver by the hand and leads her to a building that is still half standing on a corner, three-dimensional words dangling off the facade: <B RGE   ING>. A thicket of trees near its entrance creates a privacy barrier from the semi-openness of the old square. Centuries before, this was a very busy area of the city because of the famous piac market where tourists could buy their souvenir bag of paprika. One of the universities was located here as well, thus the square had offered a variety of options for the thirsty students to quench their study-induced drought with a cold beer on tap.

As the two do a preliminary scan of the hideout, Takver interrupts the mindsilence.

Sib, we could've...if we would've... She takes a deep breath and lets her mind relax a bit, her thoughts running like a speeding train. *Just a few more minutes down there and...*

The sheer terror of what has just occurred is overtaking her. Her hands are trembling like a hypoglycemic having an episode from low blood sugar. Bedap grabs her shaking hand and steadies it.

But we're okay, Tak.

Bedap is still in shock, adrenaline still flowing through their body. It hasn't hit them yet. If it hadn't been for the cat getting their attention, they'd probably still be down in the market that is now, undoubtedly, a mere crater filled with chunks of broken cement and other rubble.

If it wasn't for that feral cat... Bedap begins sending their thoughts before the two are startled by the sudden appearance of something or someone in the entrance to the thicket.

Bedap grabs Takver's arm and squeezes it. Both siblings are sending red hues to each other. And as they both scurry to their feet, ready to fight if they have to, the fluffy tabby comes into view.

"Mew. Mew. MEOW!" Their cica savior yowls at them, fluttering their puffed out tail like they's about to spray. But instead, they jumps up into the air about a meter off the ground and karate kicks off the wall of the building and dashes in the direction that the two were planning on heading anyway before they were almost blown to pieces.

The two siblings just look at each other, their mouths slightly agape in awe of the coincidence that they both just witnessed. They have no doubt now who is orchestrating their journey. This realization is both unspoken and unmindspoken, so much so that there is no need to consider the next steps. They both look down, making sure they have their satchels, and take off in the direction in which the tabby went.

AFTER ABOUT FORTY-MINUTES of following the quick-pawed tabby cat through the winding streets of the Old City, the two siblings stop just before the entrance of an old university campus park turned forest. The full moon shines through the sparse leaves of the ash trees, casting their shadows onto the path before them. As they round the corner, the cat disappears into the entrance flanked by crumbling stucco walls that are overgrown with wisteria, its woody twining vines enveloping the parapet and its flowers giving off a perfume so sweet that Bedap is compelled to stop and breath in its aromatic splendor.

Come on, Sib. We're going to lose them again. Takver pulls at Bedap's cloak as she takes the turn around the corner into the barrier free but obviously formerly gated entrance. No sooner had the cat disappeared, than a hooded crow seemingly appeared in its place. Hooded crows look a lot like black crows with the main difference being that the back from their neck down to the base of their tail tends to be silvery gray as well as their lower torso. In the right moonlight, their obsidian feathers shine blue black. The interesting thing is that these corvids are diurnal—active during the day—and this one should be nesting with the rest of its roost high up in some towering trees somewhere.

Takver stops in her tracks causing Bedap to bump into her from behind. The bird is twitching and at the same time staring up at them from the duff covered ground that was once paved with gray bricks like the kind that is used in patios and driveways.

The crow's gray beak opens in a shrieking squawk as the two siblings stand there just staring, jaws dropped in disbelief. With a twist of the body, the corvinus' feathers ruffle in a frenzy of gyrations. Bedap swears they catches a glimpse of fur awkwardly morphing into feathers: azure obsidian wings and bib; raven eyes that reach deep into mind, stealing thoughts. Then, with a vibrato flap of wings the feathered creature takes off into the air, flying into the direction of a small pond off into the distance.

The siblings shake off their ephemeral stupor and are off once again, picking up the pace so as to not lose track of the bird that is now swooping down on the other side of the pond. Takver takes note of the parklike area surrounding the pond and how it looks maintained as if a whole community lived there. But there are no signs of dwellings or other structures to suggest that the park is inhabited.

As they pass the pond on its northwestern edge, Bedap points as the bird makes a sudden descent into the wooded thicket just beyond the water.

"Over there. It looks like another path." Bedap pants, signaling directly ahead in the opening of the dense growth of trees, chestnuts and ashes.

As they enter the path, up ahead there is a gate of sorts like the ones on the fences around the houses from the Old World. In fact, the entire fenced-in area looks like it came from two-hundred years ago: a small, square, yellow stucco-walled house with a clipped gable roof, typical of this region of the world for centuries. And, like the houses of old, this one looks like the roof is about to cave in.

From afar, the siblings can see a figure at the gate. It doesn't move. As they get closer, they can make out a person. They is wearing a patchwork cloak, its hood rests just above the shoulders. The first thing that stands out to Bedap is that this person has pale, pink-ish peach skin like them. If their hair were down it would hang low to the top of the buttocks and ash blonde with strands here and there of grays and whites. They keeps their braided locks up in a bun like Bedap does. In fact, this person could be an older Bedap, if only Bedap had a short, dark brown beard with hints of red in the right light, puffy bags that rest beneath each of the two saggy-lidded, almond-shaped eyes.

"It's about time you two got here!" Old Tátos exclaims, extending their arms and wearing a toothy grin that stretches from pointy ear to pointy ear. "Come in, come in. You two must be exhausted."

Takver scowls, lowers her gaze, turning to her sibling, and whispers, "Did she just imply that she's been expecting us?"

"Oh! No need to keep secrets around here, little one." Old Tátos chuckles. *We're already in your thoughts.* They mindspeak to both of them. Then, switching back to an audible voice, "But don't worry. We won't intrude too much without your permission."

Bedap is quite taken aback. This is only the second person that they has ever shared with.

"I know you have lots of questions, but do come in. We all can rest soon. You two sure wore me out. Could anyone possibly walk any slower than you two?" Old Tátos chuckles, holding the gate open and beckoning the two siblings to enter with an arm stretched out in the direction of the dilapidated hovel. "Come. Come."

"How did you know..." Bedap begins to ask.

"Oh. Don't you worry your mind about that." Old Tátos is still grinning. "Let's just say we know a lot of things."

Old Tátos is looking at Takver who isn't following behind Bedap as they cross the threshold of the gate.

Now, don't you worry either. Those nasty things they say about us are mostly untrue. Old Tátos winks as they enters Takver's mind. *If we betray you in any way, you can keep that little trinket that you brought in the tin box.*

Takver's mouth drops open for a second. She realizes this and quickly straightens up and starts catching up to Bedap. Her eyes are still squinted but most of the cold shoulder that she's giving to Old Tátos has begun to thaw.

As Old Tátos closes the gate, they brush off a patch of silvery gray and blue black feathers from the sleeve of their frock, making an 'oopsy' face and giggling to themselves.

"Oh, silly us, let us get that door for you."

With a snap of their fingers, the door to the ruin of a dwelling opens. Takver and Bedap look at each other in awe. Bedap grabs Takver's cloak, almost pleadingly, as if saying, "if I'm staying you're staying." Then, in the next moment the three of them disappear into the dimly lit ramshackle abode.

Off in the distance, an owl's wings silently flap as it swoops down just above the pond, talons dragging, sending ripples that cause the moonlight to dance its fluid csárdás folk dance across the murky surface.

CHAPTER THREE: PRISON LETTERS

As you sit on your bunk, you squeeze your eyes shut, trying to force your thoughts to any of your kinfolk who might receive them.

Mindsilence.

Thanks to your new position working in the kitchen, at least now you know that Delores and Téjuti are alive; news has it that Delores isn't doing well, and that breaks your heart. She's always been so strong. But with not having Octavia around and all, she's lost her will to live.

Just hang on a little longer. You think, tugging gently at her imperceptible diaphanous rope that you can't feel but you know connects the two of you through some genetic link that you share passed down through mitochondrial DNA.

No one knows anything about Octavia's whereabouts. But, that doesn't stop you from searching for the tug of her invisible string, you think you feel it sometimes, and whether it's psychosomatic is besides the point. You want her to be alive, so to you, in the absence of knowing, she is.

Your new job is how you know all the different people that you've grown to know and recognize over the course of your imprisonment and forced labor. As a dishwasher, you know everyone who passes through the kitchen in your ward, handing you their dirty dishes, and they know and recognize you. You give off an almost addictive charisma and get a smile out of the grumpiest of your fellow inmates. Little pieces of scrap fibrous material—the prisoners with XX chromosomes who the overseers have caged together at a facility in a small valley of the mountain are put to work weaving fiber and grinding dolomite into powder, so naturally they have learned to make ink with the powder and plant-based vellum with the fibers—this writing material can be easily passed under a bowl or around a spoon. When it's your turn to mop the floors, you can move around the dining refectory, picking up the small missive strips that get dropped from someone's hand. Everyone, who can, employs you and others like you to send their correspondence around the greater interconnected web of facilities that makes up the entire mining complex. Not everyone can write, but there is always someone around who can write. You and the others are the equivalent of messenger pigeons in some ways. You don't read the messages—you couldn't if you wanted to—you just get the messages to the right person. And, you do so without getting caught by the shiny faces. That's what you like to disparagingly refer to the sentries as. You don't actually know whether they have faces, but that doesn't matter. They are a threat and, thus, subject to ridicule. Plus, how can anything be that shiny in such dull and dimly lit quarters?

Your efforts to convince your people to open up to others hasn't been as successful as you would have liked by now. You have, however, convinced Bodza that organizing is your best hope for escape.

"It's not easy, Cuz." Bodza whispers to you during your recreation hour in which you're permitted to fraternize with the other prisoners to a certain extent. You're still locked in your cage, the one with the bunk beds, about ten to a cell. Somehow,

Now. Then. To Come.

Bodza ended up in your cell a few days back. You've been playing it safe and not acting too friendly so as to avoid alerting anyone—or thing—who may be surveilling you.

"I know it's not. It's best to do it one-on-one. Who do you work with mostly? Our people or?"

"It changes. Sometimes I'm with people from our own commune and other times I'm with a complete stranger. If they are our people but from a community that I'm not familiar with I can usually tell if they greet with one hand or two. But, with our people, I usually have to initiate an interaction." Bodza shakes their head in frustration.

"Don't give up. We have to convince our people to open up." The person on the top bunk of the bed where you and Bodza are sitting shushes you, so you lower your voice. "We, our people need to realize who the real enemy is. If everyone here would just join together as one team, we could combine all our might and overthrow these machines. I just know we could. Nothing built by people is indestructible."

"And how long is that going to take, Cuz?" Bodza puts their hand on your arm. "I'm not sure how much more of this we can take. I mean, Test, you aren't as young as you used to be. I just worry..."

You interrupt them in mid sentence.

"Now, don't you worry about me, my young cousin." You put your other hand on their hand and squeeze. "I'll be fine. But, you're right. We may need to take more drastic measures."

Silence. You take a moment to gather your thoughts. There is something that you've been wanting to try and it just might work. You start up again.

"We're going to need Tirin if we're going to pull this off."

∼

THE ALARM GOES off as the light comes shining through the wall vents near the ceiling. The usual unintelligible voice announces mealtime. The automated doors of your mass cage begin to open slowly and you and your fellow prisoners move about your beds to eventually line up and make your way to the refectory. Tirin climbs down from the top bunk of your stacked beds. Placing both feet on the ground in a short hop, he looks at you.

"Are you ready for this, Elder?" He whispers as he reaches out a hand, offering to help you up.

"Please, Tirin, call me Test. How many times do I have to ask you?" Your toothy smirk shines through the dimness of the room. "And, yes, more than ever."

The hand he grabs is the one with the T-shaped brand mark. It's been completely healed for a while now, and the white scar tissue contrasts starkly with your brown skin. You've lost track of how long you've been in this mountain, and, as far as you know, there's only been two full moons since this new life. It's no way to live, but it is *your* life now. But, only for now. Change is inevitable. Thank you, Octavia E. Butler, for those paraphrased words of wisdom. Everything and everyone is always changing. Why not do what you can to shape *your* change so that you and your people can go back to something like you had before. It, this new hypothetical life, wouldn't be the same as your life before that fateful night when you lost your freedom, but it could at least look a lot like it.

"I'd be lying if I said I wasn't terrified. But, it's also very exciting." A coy grin forms across his shaggy, bearded face. " I mean, so many things could go wrong. One of us, or all of us for that matter, could get hurt. How much compassion do you think these *things* have?"

You know that last question is rhetorical, so you don't answer him. Instead, you try to set yourself at ease.

"And everyone is on board with the plan?"

"I told those that I could to spread the word. There was definitely some hesitation and push back. But, I think I've convinced quite a few people that we don't have much to lose. And some of the others have reported back saying that they think they've convinced even more of us. And, the younger ones, around my age, are eager to do some kind of collective action. It's been a long time coming. We've been here the longest. Like I told you before, I think our people were the first, or at least the first in this mine in a long, long time."

"And, the kitchen workers have the pots ready?"

"As far as I know."

You take in a deep breath and let out a quiet sigh. "We've been planning this for at least fifteen sleeps or so. It feels like we're forgetting something. Do you think we're rushing things? I mean, this kind of direct action takes time to organize properly."

"We're about to find out, Test." Tirin closes both eyes in a slow blink much like a cat does to show that they's content, letting you know he's finally given in to your request.

You look up ahead in the line and see Bodza who is looking back intermittently watching for Tirin's signal. As you're herded through the corridor, two more cell doors slide open with a metallic clank, and more of your fellow prisoners join the line. You see the two people at the head of their lines glance at Tirin as he nods his head.

Then, before you can realize it's happening, Tirin gives the signal. He starts coughing and then follows the coughs with intermittent moans and groans and more coughs. Instantly, you and the others in line follow suit. It takes some of the more timid prisoners a few moments before they eventually join in. Whether they'd been convinced to join by their peers or psychological herd effect had taken over, it seemed to be working. Within a few seconds, everyone was on their knees while coughing and moans and groans echoed through the corridor.

As planned, the shiny faces began to move around in different directions throughout the corridor leading up to the refectory as if confused and unable to coordinate an appropriate, collective response. The four other shiny faces that stand guard in the refectory come out to the hallway. At this point, some of you are pretending to have passed out while others continue to cough and produce guttural noises.

While the creepy, shiny-faced humanoid machines are distracted, the kitchen workers, six of them, one for each automated sentry, rush out to the corridor with large steaming pots, some filled with boiling hot gruel and others with scalding water. Tirin gives the next sign, a loud whistle, and everyone who's on the floor near the sentries quickly makes way for the offensive strike. Within a matter of seconds, which to you seems like an eternity, everything in slow motion, the mechanical overseers are covered in liquids and semi-liquid solids.

Sparks begin to shoot from their hoods, sending zapping and whirring noises echoing throughout the corridor.

Then, Tirin is on his feet pulling at you and another older person to your left beckoning you both to stand up.

"Let's go! To the gates! Help the weaker ones! We've got to go, now!"

Chaos ensues as those who are more agile are instantly up on their feet, some making their way directly to the main doors while others do what Tirin asked and help the less abled folks. A synergistic euphoria spreads through you, and you think you can see it in some of the faces of your fellow prisoners around you as you're making your way to the exit as fast as your body will let you.

Now, the sirens begin to blast, their screeching causing instant nausea in you and in others that are auricularly sensitive like you.

Over the blaring alarm, from behind, you can hear crunching and smashing as some infuriated youngun stragglers give blow after kick after blow, demolishing their automated captors while letting out years of pent up rage and revenge. An older prisoner, slumped underneath the sentry that is being pummeled, lies on the ground, unmoving. Someone tries to pull them up, but a fellow captive is pulling at them trying to convince them that it's too late for their friend.

You hear them cry to their friend, "Let's go, Test. They is gone, Test. I'm sorry, Test. But, we can still save ourselves. Come on, please!"

Up ahead, there are four strong younguns prying open the steel gate through which the workers who chop at the mountain wall cross night after night. As they heave and pull, their biceps bulge through their tattered mandarin jumpsuits, their brown faces squished up and flush from the exertion.

Then, with a heavy scrape the doors open, letting in the dry suffocating heat and light as you take turns pouring out through its threshold like rats escaping their laboratory prison. Your eyes squint as Nap greets your flesh with an intense sun kiss.

Seemingly at your feet, but really some meters away, the cliff edge makes a sharp drop. As the wind blows, making your one piece ruffle from the friction, you and your people look down to the distant valley below.

A few hundred meters underneath the precipice, atop an opposing pine tree, a hooded crow squawks and points its beak upward to a cluster of bright orange dots high up on the mountain's cliff.

"It's begun." The bird, balancing on a spiny branch, turns its head around, its side eye staring at the two passengers holding on tightly to the gray and black feathers. "It won't be long now."

FROM THE JOURNALS OF TRELL

MISSING JOURNAL ENTRIES

FRIDAY, APRIL 22ND, 2022 - STADIUM CAMP

"I missed you." He whispers in his groggy voice. "I'm so happy you're back."

I smile and kiss him on the lips, then turn from my right side to a supine position. A chilling draft creeps up my arms. I pull the pink and white striped duvet up to my chin, tucking my arms under it.

"Me too, baby. It was too long." I reply through a yawn.

He strokes my beard. The rising sun peeks through the beige, half-opened curtain: blinding, ripe persimmon. I squint, turning onto my left side to face away from the morning. I take his hand and pull it around me, his muscular arms hugging my furry, plumb chest. The worn out mattress boards creak under us as we shift into a proper spooning position; me, little spoon. The wall clock ticks in the background. The whoosh, gurgle, swoosh of a toilet from above us interrupts the ticking. Suddenly, suburban noises echo around the neighborhood: ambulances whirring, semi trucks huffing. Mmmm. His body is warm next to mine. But...wait... Something doesn't feel right. My stomach wrenches. The apartment. The clock. The city noises. They aren't right. He's not supposed to be here...

What the?

The deafening screech of an air horn jerks me out of my cozy slumber. My crusty eyes open wide onto the dimly lit metal rafters of the ceiling far above.

Crap!

"Out of your cots!"

A deep, violent voice bellows in throughout the now labor camp that was once a stadium. I can't make meaning out of what the baritone voice from the loudspeaker is emitting.

"Time to work, lazy jerks!"

I struggle to put on my tangerine jumpsuit, the preferred fruit of the ruling party; a rainbow is stitched into the left breast pocket. A tear trails down my right cheek as I scratch the itch from the implant in the nape of my neck.

Why the heck did I have to wake up? I think to myself as I struggle to put on my slippers.

From up close, the structure is quite impressive. A combination of sand-toned concrete and graphite-tinted steel forms an oval shape reminiscent of a spaceship resting on tens of wedged-shaped, block pillars made of metallic lattice. But there is no vineal foliage growing and climbing up the criss-crossed patterned pylons. Only the droppings of birds and splattered innards of bugs from gusty storms decorate the cold, silvery gray, sterile walls of this postmodern edifice.

From above, a giant, two-toned metal zero has been delicately placed on the outer rim that are the walls of this twenty-first century coliseum, acting as the roof that shelters the spectators from the atmospheric elements. The immense, null digit is the size of a small city block and looks like someone unraveled a slinky and cut it into strips to shape it. The inner part of the zero that encircles the empty center is a similar shade of metal as the outer shell of the base.

Outside of the complex, it's a normal day. You can hear the sounds of car motors humming, horns honking, and air brakes huffing along Stefánia Út. Pedestrians scurry to catch bus 75 while trying to stay dry under their hand-held nylon shelters: blacks, grays, polka dots, stripes, plaids. The beeping of the double doors warns the would-be passengers that they are about to close. It's now or never. Get on or wait for the next one to come along.

About twenty meters away, there's a crowd of damp people with cameras and phones conversing in an unfamiliar tongue excitedly. Posing in front of what used to be an Institute of Earth Science—before the administration shut it down—they try their best to document themselves with this awe-inspiring art nouveau architecture of the late 19th Century. With its cobalt-blue roof tiles, it's like a polished sapphire gem shining beautifully adjacent to a clumsy, dull 3D printout of an extraterrestrial salad spinner. The two structures couldn't be more opposing.

The latter building, the arena, was finished only months before the viral pandemic reached this urban center, killing thousands, and hospitalizing even more. In fact, this grand sports complex is just one of many that lie dispersed around the city, with its mustard streetcars, lángos stands, and sweet smell of chimney cakes. Yet, presently, rare is the occasion for a chance to spectate a football match in one of these monstrosities. The virus made sure of that. By the first of the year, it, and more importantly political manipulation, was responsible for over forty thousand deaths. This number is significant in a country just shy of ten million inhabitants. Such a tragedy. The perfect tragedy, in fact, to devise a plan that would put the stadiums to good use while padding the pockets of politicians and business moguls alike.

From inside, the stench of humanity and suffering is unbearable. It's been what seems to be weeks—months? I've lost count—since anyone has been able to take a proper bath or shower. At times, I can barely stand my own stench. Sores and rashes have begun to plague my skin despite my efforts to use what little resources we have to keep clean; I make sure to ration three capfuls of the dingy, putrid-smelling refilled bottle of water that we are allotted a day so I can clean myself. Soap is non-existent here. I guess we're lucky to get baking soda and a toothbrush.

When they showed up at my flat late that one night, I wasn't given the opportunity to pack a bag. They were to take me to the police station.

"You'll be able to come back home soon after we have assured your safety from the mobs."

I was told, rather lied to. But, I couldn't understand most of it. I just made out 'come back home soon.' I pulled out my phone and opened the translation app and asked that he repeat what he'd said.

<You are in danger from the mobs.> It read.

"What mobs? I haven't seen any in this neighborhood." I spoke into the phone and then held it up so the officer could read it. I did all of this as I hurriedly pulled my pants up over my legs.

<They are coming. We are legally obliged to protect you.>

Another lie.

The second officer wore an expression colder than the hand that squeezed my right bicep and pulled me toward the door. Luckily, I was able to grab my backpack with my diary and pencil case and a few other useful items. I would be needing my spare masks and hand sanitizer, no doubt.

At the station, before they confiscated my phone and other belongings, I was able to get a message out to my better half that I was being taken into custody. Given the time difference, he should have gotten it.

I hope he got it. I hope he knows that at least I tried to contact him. He knew about the recent escalation of tensions ramping up around me. After the re-election of the current government along with the addition of a few extreme right seats to the parliament who came out in support of the passing of the referendum on April 3rd, people are rightfully afraid.

My colleagues, other teachers, are afraid. The referendum

essentially bans the so-called promotion of LGBTQIA2S+ issues in the context of schools—The anti-LGBTQIA2S+ lobby prefers to use LGBTQP in their propaganda, emphasizing the P, for pedophile. Those people make me sick to my stomach grouping child rapists with consensual relationships between adults or between teens. And their tactics probably work on a large swath of the voting population. Sixty-five percent of voters voted in favor of the ban. Since then, and in the months leading up to the referendum, hate crimes against queer and trans people have been on the rise. One political party that translates roughly to The Old Ways, claimed that LGBTQIA2S+ people were to blame for spreading the virus because of 'their promiscuous nature. They must be contained or we'll never get over this pandemic.' That's when they started rounding us up. Of course, the Romani people and houseless folks were also blamed for spreading the virus, regardless of their sexuality or gender identity. After all, 'They don't know what hygiene is' was the claim. They found themselves sleeping alongside us on layers of cardboard with canvas tarps as blankets.

From inside, we are prisoners. But we are put to work everyday, assembling cardboard boxes for the same grocery store that we used to shop at when we were still free. The irony. Another twist: this stadium, a place of supposed leisure and sport, has turned into a place of suffering and unpaid forced labor, slavery basically. We're tired and scared. No, we're terrified. Many of us have been separated from our families. Who is taking care of Laci's two kids? *Where* are his kids? The kids' mother is no longer in the picture and his life partner, Marci, died from the virus a few months back. I feel so awful for him. At least I don't have that level of worry. Stupid silver lining.

We have no idea what is going on on the outside. We have no access to the news. Our phones were taken away from us. Are people as sick out there as they are in here. The virus is still spreading amongst us. Several people have died; guards wrapped their bodies in the blue and yellow tarps and dragged them outside of the main area through two big, black, metal doors that crashed as they slammed shut.

From inside, however, we also have hope. In the depths of despair, we have hope. Despite not being allowed to gather in groups larger than four people, we talk about our hopes. Despite being filthy and hungry, we hold on to that hope. Despite the anger and frustration, we believe our neighbors, our families, and our students will fight for our freedom. We have hope that they won't let the historical patterns repeat themselves. We have hope that good will overcome evil.

From outside, the silver reflection of the moon casts shadows on us inside through that gaping hole that reminds us that we are but two metal doors away from freedom. Shadows stretch across the astroturf into the rows and rows of stadium seating.

From outside, red, white, and green lights illuminate the exterior of the stadium. The colors of the national banner remind those on the outside of their freedom. Blood red. Freedom white. Avarice green. The colors of humanity. The colors of late capitalism. The colors of patriotism. The colors of a lie.

CHAPTER FOUR: THE WAY

There's only darkness as the three make their way across the threshold of the seemingly once humble suburban cottage. Despite not knowing where they are going, Bedap and Takver walk ahead as Old Tátos follows closely behind them. After a few paces, both siblings begin to experience a sudden bout of vertigo, an abrupt spinning in their heads and stomachs, and there's now a damp chill in the air that hadn't been there a split second before. Their nostrils are filled with the aroma of dank earth like someone lifted a rotting log right in front of their noses.

Takver merges with Bedap, *It's so dark. I don't think I can go any further.* Then, she stops in her tracks which causes Bedap to stop as well.

Old Tátos bumps into Bedap who then falls into Takver but doesn't manage to knock her over.

"Oh, dear me!" Old Tátos giggles, acting embarrassed. "I'm just so used to the dark." Then, they woo-hoos, and as their woo-hoo echoes down what seems to Bedap and Takver to be a long corridor, the walls begin to glow, revealing an earthy, root-woven soil-like texture. Bright, fluorescent cold hues—blues,

Now. Then. To Come.

greens, and purples—ostensibly emanate radiant photons from fleshy vein-like tendrils that create a web along the walls and ceiling of the tube-like corridor. These rubbery looking protrusions vary in girth, ranging from the size of one of Takver's fingers to the size of her leg.

Without realizing it, Bedap and Takver simultaneously send hues of purple—signaling good vibes—to each other as the two look at their surroundings, dumbfounded and obviously pleased with what their senses are perceiving.

Bedap moves closer to a blue-glowing vein about the size of their own forearm, examining it with their eyes as well as their nose. It has a leathery surface and its odor is intense, earthy and sweet while at the same time musky. As they takes a deep whiff of its aroma, getting their nose maybe a bit too close, the tendril wiggles and thrashes from side to side as if it is being tickled.

Bedap takes a hop back, almost falling into a wall of mycelia, "Whoa! What the?! These are mushroom roots! Huge mushroom roots!"

After Bedap speaks the words aloud, a wave of pure white light—all the colors of the rainbow beaming all at once—ripples through the subterranean tunnel like the wake of a pebble as it hits the surface of a puddle.

"Oh, don't mind them. They're not used to human visitors." Old Tátos gently pushes past the siblings, swishing their hips flamboyantly from side to side. Stopping in their tracks, they turns around to face them and rests their hand on the earthen wall, causing chunks of dirt to fall along the wall to the ground. "Okay. Let's get right down to it."

The siblings look at each other and then at Old Tátos, then, back at each other. Old Tátos stretches out their arms, hands in front of the siblings' faces and claps three times. "Pay attention, you two. There's lots to be done. And, you'll have a million and a half questions, and we'll have like double the possible answers and it'll just take forever so let's just skip to the facts."

Old Tátos takes a deep breath. "But, first, would you be so kind as to not freak out when we change out of these skins." They sighs dramatically, tilting their head backward. "Being humanoid can be so exhausting. And, we're tired. We need to relax a bit. So, please just do us the favor and just pretend like it's just another normal, everyday, casual, inconspicuous thing. We're just going to change form and that is that, and you can have questions but we're just going to do it."

And, before the two can protest, Old Tátos's body starts to contort, their shoulders jutting upward and their head cocking awkwardly to the side. As their hips jut out forward, their alabaster skin peels, almost melts away, revealing coarse, blonde and light brown hairs. Eight furry legs sprout out of a bulbous body attached to a head with an overgrown mustache that hangs down almost like fangs but bigger like tusks. And, after a closer look, the siblings realize that the back half of the spider's body is covered in tiny replicas of the bigger spider. There must be over two hundred of them, huddling close and holding onto the giant for dear life, like a nest of recently hatched spiderlings sans eggs clinging to their eggblood for protection and transportation.

The wolf spiders shake off the excess skins. All eight times two hundred or more of their eyes staring, as they adjust their bodies so as to be looking in the same direction, all of them at once. As this is happening, the ground around the spiders is absorbing the fallen pieces of skin that were once Old Tátos.

"There." They let out a collective sigh, shaking their body like a wet dog. "That's much better," their many voices echoing in unison, like talking through an auto-tuner.

Takver takes a step forward and puffs out her chest in a moment of unexpected heroics, "Hey! What di... what did you do with Old Tátos? Bring her back. She is the key. Our key!"

"Silly, child." The spiders laugh in sync, sending ripples of echos far off into the distance. "We don't use the she pronoun. We are many. Multiple. Never one. So, if you're going to talk about us, refer to us as they are, will you? Can you do us that favor? I know your people aren't used to asking about pronouns. Instead, you just assume pronouns based on your ideas of a binary gender and what that looks like to you people. So archaic. But, ask little Bedap over here. They'll tell you how it works. Won't you, little one?" The spiders, Old Tátos, look intently at Bedap with all sixteen hundred and more of their eyes fixed on Bedap's, staring expectantly.

"Uh. Sure." Bedap slowly replies, emphasizing the 'sh' in the last word. "They are Old Tátos. They use they plural pronouns. Their eyes and bodies are many just like they are. This tunnel is theirs." The pronoun drills from all those years ago in training rush back to them as if they had been practicing their etiquette lessons just yesternight.

"Almost, my dear child." The spiders correct Bedap. "This isn't *our* tunnel. It belongs to no one and everyone at the same time. We just use it." They pause. "Now, let's get down to business as they used to say back when capitalism was a well oiled machine." The largest spider abruptly turns around and continues walking in the opposite direction, facing away from Takver and Bedap, moving further down the fungus laden shaft, the other miniature carbon-copies shifting to maintain their gaze with Bedap and Takver who aren't far behind them. "Try to keep up." They all cry in unison.

"So, here's the gist of it. You two are in so much danger, and to make it even worse you don't even realize it."

Bedap slows their pace. "Hey. You gotta slow down or we need to stop for a break or something." They grabs at their side as the lactic acid builds up in a muscle causing a cramping sensation. It seems like they've been walking at a fast pace or jogging for over an hour straight now.

Then, Takver, who has been trying to figure something out ever since the spiders took shape, mindyells out in a fatigued cloudy thought, *Why do you make the bigger spider so huge? Isn't it harder to hide when you're so big?*

To the tiny spiders the large spider is a giant, but for Takver and Bedap the highest point of the big spider comes up to the tip of their heads when they are standing up their tallest, not slouching. That's why Takver used the word 'huge.' Compared to the size of an everyday wolf spider, which isn't much taller than the tip of a human thumb, this spider is not a giant, but rather a colossal mammoth. It must be a thousand times the size of any spider that the two siblings are used to seeing around the forests.

The spiders let out a synchronous guffawing laughter. "Silly, child. You two are the ones who are abnormally small." They pause. "Oh, sorry. We forgot to mention that bit of information. You've shrunk to the size of a small garden beetle. No one will be able to find you while you're this small. Well, at least the ones that are looking for you won't."

The spiders slow down, suddenly, and come to a complete halt. "We're here." The many voices speak, all at once.

Looking up through the tunnel opening, the two siblings see an auditorium, but with no seats, just openness and forest detritus that has collected here over the seasons, leaves the size of entire thatched roofs, pieces of bark bigger than large canoes. The cathedral ceiling is the underside of a hollowed out rotten section of a century's old maple tree trunk. The spiders, Takver, and Bedap slowly walk out of the tunnel into the vast wooden cavern, taking in the awe that such a spectacle inspires, hues of purple flowing telepathically like a shared aura amongst the journeyers. Creatures of all sorts can be seen scurrying into hiding spots, some even exiting through a small hole where moonlight penetrates the mostly vacuous stump hollow.

The large spider shifts its body to face the siblings, the little ones changing position as one to match the gaze of the giant, like synchronous swimmers performing a swimming pool ballet, flowing in flawless accord.

"If there's no protest from you lot, we're going to go on a bit of a meditative journey. Like we said before, there's so much that you need to know, and only so much time. As they say, a picture is worth a crap ton of words. So, we're going to collectively mindtravel to a place-time where we can be present with the knowledge we're about to absorb."

The large spider squats down and the hundreds of mini spiders scurry off its back in one big swarm of furry legs. They almost buzz as they zoom around the debris-filled cavern, collecting small twigs and other duff that fits into their claws that protrude from the coda of their tarsuses, or their limbs, covered in pedipalps—the hairs that make their appendages look like they have fur. They collect pieces of woody material that fit in their claws, making them look like eight-legged, furry percussionists.

The tiny arachnids make their way back to where Takver, Bedap, and the giant arachnid are standing, watching as the scene unfolds. Staggered in rows of five or six, they quickly and scrupulously form a circle around the three giants, wooden slivers in claw. And, as effortlessly as is customary of them, each of the hundreds of wee spiders claps their sticks together. Instantly, Bedap and Takver are feeling relaxed. The beat is constant but not too fast at first, then the rhythm of the hundreds of tiny clicks speeds up and then slows back down again, like a small orchestra whose instruments are nothing more than miniature toothpicks.

Thank you both for being with us on this full moon. The voices that are actually thoughts that are emanating from the body of the giant spider no longer sound like they've been run through a voice manipulator. Instead, Bedap mindhears their own voice as they perceives the spiders' thoughts that are being sent to them through sharing, merging, or one of the tens of other names for the communicative practice. Takver, on the other hand, who has never had a voice being nonverbal and all, mindhears the voice of her mother; she's always liked how her mother sounded, her voice melodic and breathy.

We are going to go on a collective journey, so you'll need to be comfortable. Find a position that calls to you. You can stay standing or sit cross-legged. Lie down if that feels good.

A brief pause creates a lull in the telepathic instructions. Only the clicks and taps of the stick orchestra can be heard, but even that feels a bit distant to Takver and Bedap who are drifting presently into a dream-like state. Then, after a moment, the inner voice starts up again.

Once we're in our most comfortable position, feel the ground with whatever part or parts of the body comes or come in contact with it. Now, sense the leathery mycelial filaments as they make their way through the soil to connect with your body, communicating psychochemically with all the other roots that make up the interconnecting mycorrhizal web within the subterranean layers of earth. Picture this happening with your mind's eye.

Suddenly, Takver and Bedap are acutely aware of each other's presence, but they are no longer together underneath the cavernous cathedral of the rotted stump. Instead, they are on the back of a hooded crow, hanging on for dear life as the bird flaps its wings and takes off into the Nap-lit sky.

Their bodies shiver, eyes squishing closed as if the two siblings have to make an effort not to open them.

Somehow, the sky above has fast forwarded through the nighttime hours and rushed into daylight, the clouds unfolding into view as the sunrise casts its rays onto the horizon in double time, like watching a time-lapse image speed through hours as if they were only just fractions of a minute.

All the while this is happening, the three travelers are

resting in different seated positions back under the decaying tree trunk, the tiny marching band percussing a hypnotic rhythm that seems to never cease.

Meanwhile, inside the collective trance, the bird looks back just enough to make eye contact with its right-side eye staring at the passengers while soaring over the tops of the trees that dot the overgrown cityscape below.

"Take a look down at the bridge," the crow squawks through the rustling wind that blows through aerodynamic feathers. "You see. They were expecting you."

From behind, it looks like two colorful moths are resting on the back of a hooded crow. Their clenched grasp on the granite and obsidian plumage leaves their knuckles white as they both peer down, their heads dangling over either side of the majestic, winged airbeast. From the birds' eye view, they watch as a handful of cloaked figures strategically place some sort of hockey puck-sized adhesive devices around the mouth of the opening to the old underground market that Takver grew up in. It looks as though it has been untouched like it has always looked. Except that isn't possible, because Takver and Bedap were both just there only hours before and felt the explosion and saw the implosion and the debris that it left in the air like a dust cloud.

"This has already happened," the bird squawks back, reading the siblings' interconnected mind. "We told you you were in danger. They have orders to keep hunting you down until you're captured. The explosion that will take place later from this perspective, but that already happened in your past, was meant for you two."

"But why us?" Bedap yells through the raucous breeze that makes their cloaks flap as they glide above the canopy and vine-covered ruins. "Why now?"

"Ah, both very good questions. Let's take a look."

Just as the bird squawks this last utterance, everything

around them speeds up, like fast forwarding through the boring bits of a video. And, almost instantly, they are flying over the jagged peaks of a series of once snow capped serrated mountains, like a rough-toothed saw made of dolomite and other carbonate minerals that had first formed over two-hundred and fifty million years before during the Triassic Period when they were once the shallow beds of a warm, tropical sea.

"Look down to your left," the bird cries, straining to be heard over the deafening sound of wind passing over their ears, muffling even the loudest of voices. Then, it swoops down closer to the jagged rocky points of the thousands of layers upon layers of petrified marine debris, a masterpiece that only took its artists a little over two thousand millennia to terraform.

Along a valley corridor shrouded by giant, craggy, peaked mounds that reach high into the sky, there are what seem to be tens of self-propelling airborne transport vehiculars, some statically positioned near various non-organic structures that bespeckle this highland basin. Other smaller aircrafts seem to commute to and fro from the various structures higher up, built into the facade of the mountain bluffs wherever there's a pronounced cliff.

"What is this place?" Takver asks aloud, the first time anyone has ever heard any voice come from her mouth, surprising even herself by the look on her face. Bedap turns to their sister and gives her a wide grin that causes their eyes to squint, wrinkling at the corners, "Wow! You can talk! Is that what the mother sounds like?"

Takver nods, then smiles.

"This is where your people are." The bird crows, side-eyeing the two siblings who simultaneously tighten their grip on its feathers as it descends onto the tippy top of a towering prickly conifer, one of many that floods the periphery of the valley crevice. "Look up and straight ahead."

The siblings look at each other, partly terrified, but mostly relieved. Their people are alive.

"It's begun. It won't be long now." And, just as soon as the bird coos the fateful words, it takes off again, flapping its wings in a raucous swoosh.

"Wait, what's just begun?" Takver shouts.

Suddenly, they are flying over a vine-covered area sparsely dotted with trees, and full of stone monuments in various shapes and sizes that only somewhat pop out from under their green veils of creeping foliage.

"This is where the Old People buried their loved ones who'd passed." Takver remembers the mother explaining to them as children. Exploring ancient cemeteries was a favorite pastime of the mother and her close friends. During days of rest, she and her friends would gather the children and have a picnic in different cemeteries. It was a fun way to practice the alphabet and reading, as well as numbers. Because of the vine carpet that enveloped the granite tombs, much of the carvings have been preserved. The children loved to etch out a name or date by placing a piece of fibrous pulp paper that one could trade for at the market over each letter or number groove, rubbing a stick of colorful wax that creates a lithographic image of the engraving. Tombstone frottage was one of Takver and Palat's favorite hobbies. In fact, until the marauders set fires to her village burning almost everything to the ground, she had a vast collection of headstone frottage from cemeteries all over the western half of Duna.

But this cemetery seems different somehow. It is much less unkempt than the cemeteries that she'd been used to. In fact, this particular graveyard looks like it is well maintained. There's even a house with a fenced garden that stands at the entrance of the cemetery. It must be late summer because the pumpkins in the vegetable garden are the size of her head.

There's a vehicular in the driveway and it has rubber, pneumatic tires.

Off in the distance, wandering around an area that has been overgrown and out-of-use since shortly after the end of a global war the victors of which claimed to be against fascism, there's a middle-aged person carrying a bright yellow case of sorts. They has what can only be described as a crest hairdo, sides shaved closed to the pale, pink skin. They looks like part wanna-be punk rocker and part cardinal, except they isn't cloaked in red or brown feathers, and they lacks an orange beak. Instead, dark, shaggy scruff encircles their mouth, their mustache lighter in color than their failed attempt at a full beard.

Bedap shouts to Takver, "Hey! That looks like your tartó box, Tak!"

"That's Trell." The bird squawks. "You know. Trell from the journals that you've been reading, the ones that led you to us."

The bird looks back again, "Hold on. There's one more place we've got to go."

Chaotic landscapes blur past the travelers as their journey takes them through a kaleidoscope change of scenes. This time, they are flying above what seems to be a small hamlet nestled in the middle of a vast patchwork of a once rich agricultural center known for its flamboyant embroidery and its short lived wealth; the larger region's name could be translated to 'among the mud,' likely from the name sake of a Duna tributary.

From above, it looks like a ghost town. There's not a single person in the tens of streets that form block after block of houses, outlining the cemetery at the heart of the village. The vast majority of the houses are either boarded up or have become dilapidated. There must have been a great exodus here, too, like in other smaller villages whose populations moved to densely peopled urban areas in search of work.

Unannounced, the bird opens its wings so as to catch the air and help it with its descent into the edge of the cemetery. Just

Now. Then. To Come. 303

as it lands, the feathers that Takver and Bedap are holding on to, quickly morph into short, gray hairs. And, before either can comment, they find themselves mounted between the shoulder blades of an all-too-familiar tabby cat.

"There are too many airborne predators in this region, it's safer to stay low to the ground." The cat mews through a soft guttural purr.

"But, aren't we, I thought this was all happening in our heads." Takver's confusion is obvious in her voice.

"Just play along, little one." The cat all but growls back in retort.

It's raining ever-so slightly, dark, ominous clouds hovering over the entire hamlet giving a dreariness to the landscape.

"Ah, yes." The cat purrs, moving into a crouching position behind a vine-veiled tombstone. "There she is."

A young person wearing a celeste rain jacket with a hood covering their short, bleached hair is standing, hovering over a light stone slab, raised tombstone adorned with a phallic, obelisk monument at its head displaying the names of the deceased and the dates of their life spans. The brown arms of the person are hugging a rectangular storage box of sorts, the kind that mail persons often carried, with a lid that was easily removable. It must be made of impermeable material because the intermittent drops of rain roll off the box like water off a duck's back.

"Those are the journals that we're after, little ones. So much depends on you two getting your hands on them." The cat brings up its paw abruptly and starts licking it, then rubbing it over its cocked ear in a combing motion.

"Why are they so important?" Takver interjects.

"Those are the missing journals. Those are the ones that can't be found in your doohickey device that links with your eyeball. If you go through all of them, you'll notice a large chunk of time, about three decades, is unaccounted for. That's about both of your ages combined if I did my maths properly."

"So we need to come to this place to get them? But what do we do with them when we finally get our hands on them?" Bedap reaches back and scratches the top of their bare foot.

"Those journals will have never been written if you don't contact their authors and tell them what to write about. So, first, you need to get those journals, read them, then the rest is history, which includes the future." The cat makes a guttural purring sound that reverberates through the siblings' miniature bodies. "What you call the Last Ones won't stand a chance of surviving their apocalypse if they never get their hands on these journals. So, that's where you two come in."

Suddenly, the cloaked figure crouches into a squat, setting down the box with a muffled thud, temporarily crushing a patch of grass and a single dandelion whose mustard ray florets peek ever-so timidly through the mouth of its green, variegated bud. They begins tugging at the top rose granite slab pedestal that sits on the tomb's equichromatic plinth. Either the person is really strong or the pedestal looks heftier than it is, because it seems to surrender without much hesitation.

"Now," the cat abruptly moves from its crouching position to sit on its haunches, causing Takver and Bedap to unconsciously tighten their grip on their handfuls of soft, tabby fur. "Open your eyes."

The two siblings do what they're told and, suddenly, they are back in the hollowed out stump. As their eyes refocus to their now dim surroundings, the sound of hundreds of clicking sticks comes to a slow halt. And, before they can process everything that's just happened—shrinking to the size of spider, walking through an earthen corridor lined with glowing mycelia, watching as Old Tátos turns into hundreds of baby spiders and one giant one all at the same time, then, journeying to myriad strange places and being told they have work to do or else their ancestors won't survive the end of the world—the giant spider shakes its body as if drying itself off after a swim. And in a split second, the hundreds of tiny spiders that enveloped them in an orchestra of clapping sticks only just a fraction of a moment earlier disappear, seemingly melting into the duff-covered rich, blackened earth, leaving nothing but tiny wooden slivers spread evenly, in perfect rows along the cathedral floor. The spider contorts, its bulbous frame sucking up the eight, hairy appendages, like the ray florets of a daisy retreating back into its protective bud as Nap makes its descent into the horizon. Dropping to the ground, the orbed body vibrates and morphs and shifts, taking its new form.

At this point, nothing surprises the two siblings. They've even stopped looking at each other in awe mouths agape at each new marvel. Instead, they just sit there, legs crossed, watching in something akin to admiration as a new shiny, but course, dimpled shellac shell morphs from the previous furry bulb, reflecting the dull glow that emanates from the various cryptogams, managing to subtly illuminate the vast cavern.

Old Tátos, maintaining the same size as the giant spider, slowly turns their head so they are looking at the two siblings who haven't moved a centimeter, two charcoal antennae feelers wiggling and sniffing about the air in front of them. The imposing, crimson shell is speckled with pöttyös polka dots, black as night, and varying in size. The ginormous ladybird bug clicks its wooly mandibles together and then takes turns lifting up and examining its two forelegs, then the two middle legs, and finally the two hindlegs. It then divides its vermillion elytra, the two haves moving forward toward its head and to either side of its body, revealing two diaphanous wings. They laugh as they flap their veiny wings—about eighty-five flaps in total in that one second—making a loud motor buzzing sound and sending bursts of air that stir up some dust particles like tumbleweeds rolling through a prairie.

"Much better!" There is glee in their voice. "Now, these wings are perfect. Much lighter."

They look at the two siblings staring at them. "How do we look?" If they had eyelids, they would've blinked them coyfully at the two onlookers.

"Nevermind. Follow us." They turn to move in the direction of the opening. Takver hops up off the ground and offers her hand out to Bedap who seems to have gotten tangled up in their cloak. Then, the ladybug stops in its tracks.

"Oh, wait. Silly us. We almost forgot." Then, a boisterous woo-hoo echoes throughout the cave and Old Tátos giggles.

From high up on the decaying ceiling vault, two long-torsoed winged mammoths buzz down, lowering slowly and steadily, propellers flapping, like twin helicopters making a seamless landing, except for these aircrafts have six jointed legs with remnants of pollen dustings covering the them in clumps of yellow powder. More dust tumbleweeds wisp around the floor of the cave in a flurry of swirls.

"Little ones, meet our two helpers. They don't talk much and tend to refrain from individualizing so no need for names, but they did volunteer to make the long journey with us. So, we're grateful for and to them."

As they touch the ground, they elongate their black abdomens in sync, flattening down, inviting Takver and Bedap to climb aboard. Two thick yellow stripes encircle their colossal, hair-covered, ribbed rears, while smooth and rigid, venom-injecting black stingers rest on the ground behind them, one protruding from each of them. Like two large pegasuses would, these enormous creatures tower over the two siblings; they must be at least four or five times the size of Old Tátos, in their ladybird embodiment.

Luckily, neither Takver nor Bedap is afraid of dark-winged mammoth wasps, so neither runs aways. Their hearts, on the other hand, if they could, they'd have jumped out of their chests and high-tailed it out of the cavernous stump.

"Let's go, children. There's no time to waste." The ladybird clicks through its soft labrum that makes up part of its mouth. "We've got journals to fetch!"

Takver chimes in, merging with the ladybug, the wasps, and Bedap simultaneously, *What about our families? We can't just leave them there in those mountains.* Mindspeaking in a group is something that Takver was used to back in her village complex where she had cousins, a parent, and several grandparents with whom to merge. But, it had been what seemed like a century since she'd done so. And, doing so sends reward chemicals racing through her endocrine system, leaving traces of euphoria and making her feel more relaxed.

"Yeah." Bedap backpacks off Takver. "What about our people? Shouldn't we be going to help them? Can't the journals wait?"

"Now, listen, little ones." The ladybug shifts its body and reaches two of its legs toward the smooth faces of the wasps, running its tarsuses from each leg along the top of the wasps' heads as they bow down to receive the customary caresses. "There's nothing *we* can do right now about your people, emphasis on *right now*. But, *soon*, we promise."

The Old Tátos ladybug turns back toward the opening while it continues with its diatribe.

"Look. Here's what is going to happen, has happened, and will happen, all at the same time. I know this is confusing, but just try to focus on our words."

Bedap looks over at Takver, who meets their gaze at the exact same time, and both siblings hike up their cloaks. Takver is closest to her pollinating taxi, and is first to place one foot at a time onto the smooth stinger as she carefully makes her way up onto her winged, daggered, steed. The creature is so large that she looks like a human child climbing on a giant, adult elephant, except for the wasp has a dense coat of fur in ringed patches that alternate between hard, slippery shell-like encasements along its abdomen as well as its thorax. Takver almost slips on the first rung of shell, but she finally makes her way up to the top of the wasp, just behind its head where there's a carpet patch of long, black fur. As she adjusts herself and mimics Old Tátos, petting the smooth head of the massive symphyta, Takver ponders on how the shape of this particular hymenoptera class of insect makes it more ideal than the hooded crow as an aircraft; presently she can easily see around its smaller head, and the setae bristles fit much better in her hands than the oily feathers of the bird did; the latter was like holding onto girthy tree branches that were covered in a fatty liquid.

Bedap follows suit, but isn't as well coordinated as their sibling and manages to slip on the first patch of smooth hard shell of their steed, planting their face right into its fragrant fur. And to their delight, its aroma is of a floral perfume with hints of sweet pollen and something else subtly musky and earthy.

Old Tátos continues, "Besides, the journals are on our way and it'll take us at least a full Hold cycle to get there being this size. And, it'll take much, much longer than that to get to your people. But, don't you worry your little heads. We got it all figured out. Well, it's more like we've got the general layout and we'll have to improvise a bit as we go."

The one downfall to traveling by wasp, is that it's a noisy business. A wasp adorns two pairs of laminate wings, a set of forewings attached to a set of hind wings with small hooks. Clapping and flapping its wings around four-hundred times in a single second, the vibration alone would damage anyone's eardrums.

"Oh! Don't forget to stuff some pollen in your ears. It's gonna be a noisy flight." Old Tátos yells back as they take off into the air through the small hole in the stump.

The two wasps start up, their wings like loud race car motors, zooming just decimeters away from their ears, making it impossible to hear the tail end of what the ladybird was saying. The two siblings need no convincing regarding the make-shift ear plugs; upon hearing pollen, they are pulling gobs of goopy, powdery grains of flower gametophytes—basically bundled up and neatly packaged sperm cells—and stuffing the gooey mush over their ears; it's like trying to frost the inside of a thimble, easier said than done.

Before Takver's pollinating steed ducks through the opening, out of the corner of her eye, she watches as an entire village of diverse crawling creatures comes out from their hiding places so as to see the journeyers off. She quickly bows her head, barely dodging the earthen threshold of the opening.

Bedap and their steed are right behind them. And, as the fresh, abrupt coolness of the open forest smacks Bedap in the face, they takes in two deep lungfuls of the sweet midnight air. They cracks a smile that would split a mountain in half. They can't remember the last time they felt so lightweight, yet so full of life.

EPILOGUE

The light on the Girl Boss brand lipstick applicator is flashing yellow, indicating that its contents is low.
"Avatar."
"Please state your request."
"Send me a lipstick replacement."
"Acknowledged. Order placed. Expected arrival in one sleep cycle."

An alert flashes in the upper right corner of the augmentation lens.

<Urgent message received from Earth Base 15.> It reads.

"Ugh. What is it now? Go ahead."

A uniformed person comes into view, superimposed on the mirror into which the CEO stares as she applies oily crimson onto her full, artificially plump lips, her mouth in the shape of an oblong o, distorting her words.

"There's news from one of the labor camps, Ma'am."

"What kind of news? Be quick. I have places to be."

"There's a small situation?"

"What do you mean by *situation*?"

"Some of the laborers in Mine 8 have escaped."

Silence.

"How many is *some*?"

"About half of them."

"NUMBERS, Corporal!"

"Three fatalities. Twenty-seven escapees. Six decommissioned Automated Surveillance Sentries. Seven injured laborers."

"Scorching scorchers!"

She slams the brown fist holding her lipstick down on the rose marble vanity, cracking the plastic of the applicator.

Silence.

"How did it happen? *Who* is responsible?" She hisses through her clenched teeth. "I want a full report sent to my lens, NOW!"

"Yes, Ma'am."

"Have you located the ones who've escaped?"

"No, Ma'am."

"Why *not*?! It's not like they can go very far with orange jumpsuits on!"

"They left their jumpsuits behind, Ma'am."

"They *wha*...send me the video feed. I want to see all of it."

"That's just it, Ma'am. There's no feed."

A pause.

"The surveillance videos were somehow hacked."

"What do you mean *hacked*?"

"It wasn't a digital hack, Ma'am."

"Corporal, I'm losing my patience."

"Yes, Ma'am. Sorry, Ma'am."

"And how am I supposed to explain this to the shareholders?"

Silence.

"That wasn't a rhetorical question, Corporal! I want answers and I want them, NOW!"

She slams her fists on the marble again, but this time repeatedly.

"End feeeeeed!" She screams.

Picking up the lipstick applicator, she throws it across the sterile room and it smashes up against the porthole window that looks down onto a not-too-distant Earth.

FROM THE DIARIES OF BEDAP

FORTY-THIRD REAWAKENING, FIRST ÚJHOLD (NEW MOON)

I found this journal entry buried deep in a folder that was labeled 2020. I salvaged this particular folder, along with several other gems, from a twenty-second century storage device that belonged to a distant relative of mine. The device—I believed they called them coil or helix drives, essentially data stored in DNA—is really just a strand of hair. Because it was kept airtight, its integrity was maintained. Anyway, I now have confirmation of when the so-called protection shelters (more like labor camps or refugee prisons) began popping up all across that distant land, which at the time was where some of my ancestors were living.

The terrific irony is that this particular journal entry date was written on the day on which it was customary to celebrate the country's independence from their first colonial power. It was a day to celebrate freedom. Little did the inhabitants of that country know that in less than a decade the place that some of them worshiped as patriots would cease to exist at least administratively. But, more on that later. So, on that very day, one of my fourteenth great eggbloods, Infanta, made an entry into her journal from the basement in which she was seeking refuge from the people who were to come and take her freedom away. What awful irony to possibly lose your freedom on the day that your country celebrates its manufactured freedom. What an awful time for my distant relatives. Too many pandemics to juggle all at once. Everything was deadly: a virus attacking millions, systemic racism killing even more, a global police state, private for-profit prisons, fascist leaders. And, I'm afraid history is beginning to repeat itself almost exactly three-hundred Earth years later. Oh, how our human memories can be so short.

[NOTES FROM INFANTA SZARKODI'S diary. Dates are formatted according to the Gregorian Calendar of the time.]

SATURDAY, JULY 18th, 2020

I can't believe any of this is happening! It's all so overwhelming. My hands are shaking so bad, but I have to document what I'm feeling. I'm using my smartphone to record this. I have this app that automatically turns voice into text. I've never really been a good writer, so this will have to do. The past few weeks have been a whirlwind of events. Where do I even start?

Well, for me personally, it happened the Fourth of July. Actually, what happened wasn't an isolated event, I guess. Since a Black guy died at the hands of the police a few states over there have been riots popping up all across the country. I just don't get it. Why would the death of one man cause such an uproar? It wasn't like he was president or anything. Anyway, Black Lives Matter supporters have been causing a raucous throughout almost every major city in the country: looting, rioting, burning down police stations and cars, pulling down and decapitating statues. I can't believe how arrogant they are. I mean, not all police are bad. And how can they say Black Lives Matter?! Don't all lives matter?! Blue lives matter, too! I dated a cop. Yeah, he was a douchebag and he tried beating the crap out of me. But their lives are hard. They sacrifice so much just to protect us.

My mom always had cop friends when we were growing up. She even worked for a local store that was owned by a bunch of cops from the area here in my little town. I always felt that they protected us. Anyway, what has been happening over the last few weeks is beginning to change my mind a little. Although, I still feel like it's just some bad apples. Not all cops are bastards! Well, the ones blindly follow stupid orders are. Luckily, I was able to escape with my baby girl. Here's what happened.

Yesternight, I got a frantic call from my mom telling me to take my baby and leave the apartment *"like now!"* She was on her way over. I guess there was some city ordinance passed in an emergency call with members of city council. They had decided that in order to protect the non-white citizens of our little town from the possible harm from the spreading riots, the council felt that it was in our best interest for everyone who didn't have what they classified as white skin, straight blond and light brown hair, nor blue or green eyes to be under the protection of the city. My baby has blue eyes, but mine are brown and so is my skin. My hair is black. I mean, I'm part Latina. I'm also part white and Black, but most people think I'm just Latina.

Would they really take me away? Would they try to separate me from my blue-eyed, peach-skinned baby?!

My mom heard on the police scanner that city police were starting at all the low-income housing developments in the city and taking the vulnerable people of color to the gymnasiums in the local middle and high schools to be sheltered. She jumped into her vehicular and that's when she called me.

"Infantica! There's no time to argue about this. If you need a reminder, go look in the mirror. You're Latina! Your dad is Black. Anda. Mírate en el espejo, eres a-fro-cu-ba-na. " She pleaded into the phone while she was racing over to my apartment from her house just under a kilometer away. "But, little Alba is clearly white. They won't take her away from me. I'm her mom!" I retorted. I was still in shock from what I was hearing. It didn't make any sense. Besides, I was in the middle of cooking dinner. What do I do just turn off the burners and leave the food out in the pans? It would go bad!

"Por supuesto, mi amor. Deja todo. Oye, I just pulled in. Grab Albita and get out here. I have plenty of baby stuff at the house. Come on! Please!"

I hadn't heard her this ecstatic since I was a preteen. Somehow that worked and the urgency for me to comply with her pleading kicked in. I turned off the burners, grabbed my baby and my purse/diaper bag and was out the door. Mom had her SUV hybrid parked on the side of the street and was standing outside of it, opening the back passenger-side door motioning me to lay on the floor. She looked around nervously to see if any of the neighbors were watching. She didn't trust some of them. Just last week she ripped a confederate flag from a flagpole that the neighbor above me put on his porch. She doesn't mess around.

She grabbed the things out of my arms and threw them in the back seat. Then, she took a hold of my Alba who was still sleeping despite the panicking and loud, chaotic conversation over the phone that was still in progress.

I climbed into the back and lay with my back on the floor. Mom then placed a sleeping-but-slowingly-fussing-a-bit Alba on my stomach, jumped into the driver's seat, and we were off. Less than five minutes later we were pulling into her garage. Thankfully, they live just down the road.

The plan was that I was going to hang out in the basement, while mom and dad "babysat" Alba. If the police were to come to their house, they would explain how "we didn't know where our daughter was, the reason we had her baby was because every Saturday night we watch Alba to give her mom a break, and that should we be concerned for our daughter's safety? Was she in immediate danger? And what could we do to help?" I'd never seen mom and dad in such I'll-kick-your-arse-if-you-mess-with-my-family mode. It was pretty awesome to witness. I'm still scared out of my mind though.

I managed to get some sleep. It helped that I was able to sleep with my Albita. She stayed down here with me yesternight. Nobody came, but if anyone had ended up coming, mom or dad would have run down here and gotten Alba. In that scenario, the secondary plan is for me to hide in the broom closet near the furnace. I've already cleared a path so that I won't accidentally trip over anything and make unnecessarily suspicious noises.

As I sit here and write, I can't help but let it all sink in. The police are probably looking for me, or at least are interested in my whereabouts. I watched the news this morning on cable. I hadn't watched cable in I don't know how long. But, I wish I wouldn't have. It's too scary. The world has gone to crap! The featured story was live on the scene outside the middle school gym. The whole school is behind a perimeter fence that is the same height as the school. The governor deployed the National Guard to set up the so-called protection shelters. The place is heavily guarded, too. And there are places like that all around the state, even the country. Who exactly do they fear will try to hurt us? Them? I got lucky. I don't know how I'll ever thank mom and dad for having my back. I still have my freedom, even though I'm stuck in this basement. But for how long? I can't imagine being anywhere else right now. Like I said the world has gone to crap.

Or maybe the world has always been this way, and I'm just now seeing it. Has the world always been this wild for somebody? I mean, we are living in a pandemic that has killed over 130,000 people to date just in this country alone. People are in the streets protesting the police. People all over the world took to and are still taking to the streets. The police are using brutal force: tear gas, rubber and pepper bullets, flash-bang grenades, not to mention the billy clubs and their fists.

The police and FBI are using social media and cell phone data to track people involved in the more violent protests. Thousands were arrested on June 6th alone, which was the day that the uprisings began. Who are *they* calling violent? From the pictures I've seen on social media, the police are just as bad as some of the more aggressive protesters. Maybe the #policeabolition movement is on to something after all. Maybe the police are out of hand. They might be coming for *me*. What am I going to do? I'm so scared for my Albita, my baby.

MISSING JOURNAL ENTRIES

MONDAY, JANUARY 20th, 2025

Where have the three or so months gone since I last wrote in this old diary? I guess I only write in here when I'm so scared that I don't know what else to do. Praying helps, too. But, writing down everything that's happening to me helps me work it out and think it over.

I look back at the previous entry and I was so naive. Little did I know that worse things were in store for us.

We've been in this camp for a little over two years now, me, Albita, and little Fatima. But we were told this morning that we had to move again. The new president has vowed to cut the funding for these camps and is supposed to sign the emergency order today when she is sworn into office.

We only have two days to pack. The three of us are being relocated to a temporary shelter. In truth, we've been trying to cross the border over to the other side of the wide river to our neighboring country. I have a few friends and family members there now and they said I could probably find work. But, it's just not easy to go anywhere. Plus, who has $10,000 to start the application? I make that in a year and I still have quadruple that in debt for the cost of living in these shelters for the past almost five years.

The worst thing about kicking us out now is that it's January. Even though we haven't had much snow this year, it's still freezing outside. There are record negative temperatures. I mean, I've lived in this state my entire adult life and never has the weather been so extreme as it has these past two or three years.

Last week it was so terribly cold that we lost over fifteen elderly people from our camp to death by freezing or asphyxiation. The generators had gone out and the ramshackle shelters on the outermost part of camp didn't have a safe way to heat, so some went without heat and others built fires and died from the toxic fumes. It's so awful. I knew some of them from the communal kitchen. I'm just heart broken about it. Albita was very close to poor little, old Gladys. I will miss her, too.

I work in the kitchen several days a week. That's how I pay for us to live here. But, this is no life for me and my babies. Sometimes I wish we could just run away from it all. I've heard of people trying to cross the river now since it's been so cold, but we are also shown daily images of people trying to cross and falling through the ice or getting picked off by snipers on the other side. Who knows if any of it is actually true? With the way technology is these days, anything can be made to look real. I don't even know *what* to believe anymore.

I can only hope that the world will be a better place someday for my Albita and her children, and her children's children, and her children's children's children, and her children's children's children's children...

∼

TO BE CONTINUED...

ABOUT THE AUTHOR

Photo by Callie Archbold

Fenn Thornbot is an emerging author of young adult, LGBTQIA2S+, sci-fi, and fantasy who spends most of their time inside their own head imagining new worlds where queer and gender non-conforming people are the protagonists and in which police abolition is a reality. They likes to push the boundaries of standardized grammars and do languaging in a way that creates spaces where they and others like them are not easily erased.

When they isn't writing, they can be caught napping with their twin radical politi-kitties, practicing permaculture, demanding a lot of (too much?) time from their life comrade, observing insects and fungi, or playing around with all sorts of artistic media. Making things, whether weaving stories or working on their watercolor techniques, helps them imagine new possibilities for tackling the larger struggles in the world that, most of the time, forces them into reclusion.

They lives on stolen land that, regrettably, the Anishinaabeg, or 'The People Who Live upon the Earth in the Right Way,' were forced to give up in the so-called 1819 Treaty of Saginaw.

patreon.com/fennthornbot

tiktok.com/fthornbot

Made in the USA
Monee, IL
18 June 2023